It's Up to You, New York

Tess Daly worked as a model for ten years before moving to New York where she began to write for the likes of *Paper* magazine. Tess made her first television presenter appearance on *The Big Breakfast* in 2000. She has gone on to present numerous shows including ten series of *Strictly Come Dancing*. Tess writes a weekly fashion column for the *Mirror* and has her own award-winning Daly Beauty range. Her debut novel *The Camera Never Lies* was published in 2011 following publication of *The Baby Diaries* in 2010, which documents her journey through motherhood. *It's Up to You, New York* is her second novel. Tess is mum to two daughters, Phoebe and Amber.

It's Up to You,
New York

Tess Daly

CORONET

First published in Great Britain in 2013 by Coronet
An imprint of Hodder & Stoughton
An Hachette UK company

First published in paperback in 2013

2

A CIP catalogue record for this title is available from the British Library

ISBN 9781444740585

Typeset in Sabon MT by Hewer Text UK Ltd, Edinburgh

Printed and bound by CPI Group (UK) Ltd, Croydon, CR0 4YY

Hodder & Stoughton policy is to use papers that are natural,
renewable and recyclable products and made from wood grown
in sustainable forests. The logging and manufacturing processes are
expected to conform to the environmental regulations of the
country of origin.

Hodder & Stoughton Ltd
338 Euston Road
London NW1 3BH

www.hodder.co.uk

This book is dedicated to the New York glitterati who made my own bite of the Big Apple that much juicier – to Metz, Rupe, Camils, Liam, C and O xxx

1

'Good morning and thank you for calling the VitaSlim Crispbread careline. This is Holly, how may I help you?'

'Right, my name is Mrs S Bigland. That's B-i-g-l-a-n-d. And I wish to make a complaint.'

Holly Collins groaned inwardly. It wasn't even lunchtime yet and she'd already had one heavy breather and two 'Put me through to your supervisor' calls, which always put her supervisor – a lazy bloke called Alan with grabby hands and cheesy-Wotsits breath – in an even worse mood than he was the rest of the time.

'Hello? Are you still there? I said, I have a complaint.'

'I'm sorry to hear that, Mrs Bigland,' said Holly, getting back to the customer-care script in front of her. 'Here at VitaSlim we take our customers' feedback very seriously. What seems to be the problem?'

'Well, I've been doing your VitaSlim bikini diet for a whole month, eating two crispbreads for breakfast, two for lunch and having a proper tea like it says on the box, but I've not lost a single pound. I want my money back for eight boxes of VitaSlim *and* for the three size-14 bikinis I bought when I started this bloody diet – plus a bit extra to compensate for all the distress this has caused me. I mean, you can't go around telling people they're going to "lose the flab and get bikini fab" when they actually end up putting *on* weight!'

Holly's eyes alighted on the poster near her cubicle. 'Don't forget to SMILE!!!!' it read. 'Our customers might not be able to see it, but they can *HEAR* it!!!!!!'

She took a deep breath and rearranged her features accordingly.

'Can I ask if you've been sticking to our suggestions for recommended toppings on your VitaSlim crispbreads?' she said, as she smiled down the phone.

'Well, that's another thing,' said the woman. 'I couldn't find any smoked mackerel or low-fat cream cheese or any of those fancy things you suggested on the box, so I've had to make some substitutions. Like yesterday lunchtime for instance – where the bloody hell am I going to find hummus? So I swapped that for a KFC topping. It's not easy balancing Hot Wings on a crispbread, I can tell you, but I'm off to Crete at the end of the month and was determined to get into my new bikinis so I stuck with it . . .'

As Mrs Bigland went on, Holly's thoughts drifted

into misery. *How had it come to this?* She had finished university with a good degree in Business Studies, determined to work in marketing, but the closest she could get to her dream career was the VitaSlim customer careline. With the wide-eyed optimism of the just-graduated, Holly had assumed she would quickly make the leap from her cubicle in this windowless room to a junior role in VitaSlim's marketing department, but here she was, nearly two years on, still spending her days dealing with the disgruntled, bored and lonely. Her boyfriend, James, kept telling her that something else would come along, but that was easy for him to say with his mega-successful legal career and executive personal assistant. Holly still scoured the job websites every week in the hope she might find something better, but her optimism was reaching critically low levels.

'Hello? Are you even listening to me?' Mrs Bigland sounded extremely narked off. 'I've had just about enough of this. Put me through to your manager right this minute!'

Bugger. 'Of course, I'm so sorry, just hold on a moment, please.'

Holly pressed a button and dialled.

'Alan, I've got a lady called Mrs Bigland on the line with a complaint about the diet.'

A big sigh. 'Do I have to do *everything*?' In the background Holly could hear the electronic twitter of Angry Birds. 'Well, go on, put her through, then . . .'

'Sorry, Alan.'

Holly transferred the call, then took off her headset and massaged the side of her head where it had been rubbing. This was turning out to be a stinker of a day. She was already in trouble with Alan for speaking to a sweet old man called Mr Palmer, who lived alone and often called the careline just for a chat, and now Mrs Bigland's diet-fuelled fury was sure to push him over the edge.

'It didn't sound like you remembered the three "Cs" of customer care during that last conversation, Miss Collins,' came a crisp Irish voice from the neighbouring cubicle. 'Courtesy, clarity and' – a grinning face suddenly popped up over the partition – 'kiss my arse!'

Holly broke into a smile. The only good thing about this job was Meg O'Hanlon, her colleague and now best friend. Meg was barely five feet tall, but what she lacked in height she made up for in boobs and balls – plus her skyscraper heels and mass of fiery corkscrew curls added a good few extra inches, as well. Although she hated working on the careline as much as Holly, she stuck with it to finance her fledgling rock career as lead singer with the thrash-metal group Babes of Bedlam. Meg had tried to persuade her friend to sing backing vocals, but in her floral tea dresses and flat boots, Holly was decidedly more Boden than Bedlam.

4

'Sounds like you need a break,' said Meg. 'Would a weak, flavourless cappuccino help?'

The pair of them wandered over to the employee lounge: another windowless room containing clusters of plastic chairs, a TV and a coffee machine that produced notoriously bad coffee. While Meg rattled away about her drummer boyfriend, Spunk (by day a primary-school music teacher called Mr Dawson), and his new tattoo, Holly picked absent-mindedly at a box of VitaSlim. Honest to God, it was no wonder nobody could stick to this diet; the box would have had more flavour . . .

'So how are the plans going for the big anniversary celebration tonight?' asked Meg. 'You going out to some swanky restaurant?'

'James isn't sure how late he's got to work, so I'm going to cook a meal at the flat.'

Meg pulled a face.

'Yes, I know that cooking isn't my strong point,' said Holly. 'But even *I* can't screw up spaghetti bolognese.'

'And for pudding?'

Holly grinned, then rummaged in her handbag for the parcel from Asos that had arrived in the post that morning.

'Ta-dah!' She held up a lacy pink and yellow bra and matching thong.

Meg nodded her approval. 'Cute, but slutty,' she said. 'Excellent choice.'

As Holly got up to retrieve their cappuccinos, which had finally finished dripping and spluttering out of the machine, she glanced over at the TV. *Loose Women* had just started and Denise Welch was introducing their first guest: 'If there was an award for the hardest-working woman in television, this lady would be sure to win it – well, she's won pretty much every other award going as it is! And now she's back on our screens with a fabulous new show that's going to be scouring the streets looking for the next Kate Moss or Naomi Campbell. Well, no need to look any further, love, I'm right here!' Denise sucked in her cheekbones and the audience laughed obligingly. 'So let's give a warm welcome to the fabulous Sasha Hart!'

An immaculately groomed brunette in a blazer and leather leggings strode onto the set with the unmistakable confidence of a live-TV veteran. You would have put her in her very early thirties, but she was actually a decade older. In interviews, she put her youthful beauty down to a vegan diet and Bikram yoga, but in reality gruelling daily workouts with a trainer, a subtle brow-lift and regular collagen and vitamin shots had made far more of an impact on her looks. But there was nothing overdone or tarty about her beauty: with her long, honey-brown hair, radiant tan and understated style, she had a real Jennifer Aniston vibe about her.

'Ooh, I love her!' said Holly, as on screen the audience whooped and cheered.

Sasha air-kissed her way along the panel of presenters.

'Hello ladies, it's a pleasure to be here, as always,' she said, taking her seat. 'And Denise, you know I adore you, but I'm afraid you're not quite what we're looking for!'

The audience laughed again.

'So, Sasha, tell us about this new TV show,' said Sherrie Hewson. 'It's called *Street Scout*, right?'

'It is, yes,' said Sasha. 'We have a team of professional model scouts who will be hitting the streets over the next few weeks to look for the UK's next supermodel. The twelve most gorgeous girls we find will be signed up by the world-famous agency Strut Models, and will have to prove themselves in a series of tough weekly challenges, after each of which one of the girls will be told to leave until we're left with our winner.'

'And what will they get?'

'The prize is a two-year contract with Strut and a cover shoot with *Cosmopolitan* magazine,' said Sasha. 'It's an incredible chance for one lucky girl.'

'Now, Sasha,' said Sherrie, 'it's no secret that until last year you were in a relationship with Strut's super-sexy boss, millionaire playboy Maxwell Moore.'

A picture of a square-jawed older man appeared on the screen, his arm draped around Heidi Klum. Denise gave a long, low whistle. 'Ooh, he's gorgeous. Like Brad Pitt, only richer and better-looking!' Cue more laughter. 'But won't it be weird working alongside your ex on the show?'

Sasha's dark eyes narrowed imperceptibly, although her face was still set in a dazzling smile. 'No, not at all! Max and I are *such* great friends. The guy's a genius – and a legend in the world of modelling, of course. Max will be really involved in the show, as he'll be making the decision about which girl will go at the end of each week. Sort of like our answer to Sir Alan Sugar, only *way* sexier! And, of course, he'll be helping mastermind the winner's career. I'm really looking forward to working with him.'

'Well, let's have a quick look at the show,' said Denise.

As the trailer rolled on screen, Meg nudged Holly. 'You should go on that,' she said.

'Absolutely no way,' said Holly. 'Not in a million years.'

The truth was, it wasn't the first time Holly had been told she should be a model. She had the height, the legs and the looks, right down to the sexy little gap between her two front teeth that was currently so in vogue. Although Holly never made much effort with her appearance – apart from regular highlights to turn her thick, long hair from mousy-brown to blonde – even without make-up she was strikingly pretty. But as much as Holly might have liked the idea of being a model, for her the lure of fabulous frocks and first-class flights was far outweighed by the negatives of the job. From a very young age, Holly had known what it was like to worry constantly about money: her dad had left when she was little and had no further contact with the family, leaving her mum, Heather, struggling to make ends meet and constantly having to move around to find work. Then when Holly was fourteen, Heather fell pregnant by her current boyfriend, the latest in a succession of freeloaders taking advantage of her mum's sweet nature. Within a month, the boyfriend had done a runner – and, eight months later, Holly's half-sister, Lola, arrived.

Although they were years apart in age, Holly and Lola couldn't have been closer. Holly adored the smiley little golden-haired girl, becoming her second mum as well as her best playmate, and when Lola was diagnosed with cerebral palsy when she was a toddler, it was Holly who spent hours encouraging her to try and take a few shuffling steps with a walking frame, and cuddling her when she ended up in tears of pain and frustration.

As a consequence, Holly was determined to use her university degree to build a financially secure future for her and her sister – and maybe even earn enough to pay for an operation to help Lola, now a bubbly eight-year-old with a sprinkling of freckles and a seriously cheeky streak, to walk unassisted, although right now the £50,000 it would take seemed ridiculously unattainable. What she wanted more than anything was a solid, steady, reliable career – not one where a tiny wrinkle or a smidgen of cellulite would pack you off to the dole queue. Stability and security were her utmost priorities.

'Besides,' she said to Meg. 'James would hate it. Remember I told you about the fuss he kicked up when his PA wanted to audition for *The X Factor*? He thinks reality shows are "demeaning and manipulative". I really can't see him wanting his girlfriend to appear on one.'

'Well, I'll audition for it, then,' said Meg. 'The catwalk needs more five-foot-two redheads with E-cup bosoms.'

Holly laughed. 'I totally agree. But it doesn't sound like you can audition for the show – I think the idea is that they go out and find you.'

'Well, I'll just have to make sure they find you, then,' said Meg.

Holly shot her a look.

'Oops, sorry, I meant me!' Meg smiled, innocently. 'Find *me*.'

2

Holly poured the last of the bottle of red wine into her glass, not caring that quite a lot of it ended up on the rug, and took a huge gulp. She had planned to have just the one small glass before James arrived, to make sure she was at her most sparkling and fabulous for their big celebration, but it was now 10 p.m., he was two and a half sodding hours late for dinner and Holly was drunk.

James had called several times over the course of the evening, full of apologies for being stuck at work and promises to get over to her flat as quickly as possible, but his loveliness just made things worse. What Holly really wanted to do was yell and rant at him for ruining their special night, but she knew that he was snowed under with an important case, so she couldn't even be justifiably pissed off with him. And the *really* annoying thing was that despite Meg's fears – and despite not having several of the ingredients listed in the recipe (but then who knew that spag bol contained chicken livers?) – Holly had actually made a surprisingly decent sauce. Now, however, it had boiled away to a salty mush, the pasta was cold and the salad, like Holly herself, was wilting.

Draining the last of the wine and getting shakily to her feet, Holly wandered around the room blowing out the candles she'd dotted around the place to give her flat a romantic vibe. As she turned on the light, she caught sight of her reflection in the mirror. She had spent ages getting ready, curling her hair so it fell in sexy waves and slathering herself in cocoa butter, but now the glossy-lipped, lush-haired temptress of a few hours ago had been replaced by someone who looked like they drank Special Brew for breakfast.

Holly was just getting stuck into a bag of Doritos and the *TOWIE* omnibus when her front door intercom sounded.

'Hello . . . ?'

'Darling, it's me. I'm so sorry I'm late.'

It was James.

Despite the disaster that the evening had become, Holly felt a little leap of excitement as she buzzed him into her building. Even after going out for a year she still got butterflies whenever she saw him. They had met at a mutual friend's fancy-dress birthday party, which Holly had gone to as Kim Kardashian, in a brunette wig and bum padding. She'd been waiting at the bar to get a round of Mojitos for her group of mates (who had gone as the rest of the Kardashian clan), when she had noticed a tall, very good-looking guy in a suit standing on his own. She thought he was probably way out of her league, but there was something so intriguing about him, about the way his conservative haircut and clothes contrasted with his broken nose, that in a rare moment of boldness Holly went over to speak to him.

'Let me guess,' she said. 'You've got a Superman T-shirt under there.'

'I'm sorry?' His voice was gorgeously posh and velvety, like a young Colin Firth.

'Clark Kent,' grinned Holly. 'Your costume?'

The man stared at her blankly.

Holly took another look at his outfit: the beautifully tailored suit, classic English brogues and silk tie. 'Ummm . . . James Bond?'

He finally broke into a smile. 'James Wellington, actually. Between you and me, I came straight from work and didn't know this was fancy dress, but I'll definitely take James Bond.'

Holly's friends never did get their Mojitos, as she spent the rest of the evening talking to James. At the end of the night, over the course of which Holly had learnt that he was a solicitor, had broken his nose in a school rugby match and hadn't a clue who the Kardashians were, she was thrilled when James asked for her number, and the very next day called to arrange a date. He took her to dinner at Bocca Di Lupo in Soho, ordering for them both in fluent Italian, then insisting on paying for her taxi home and seeing her off with a gentlemanly kiss on her cheek. Holly was stunned; most blokes seemed to mistakenly assume she'd jump into bed with them after only a Pizza Express Margherita and a large glass of lukewarm house white. By date three – a trip to the National Theatre, followed by dinner at a little tapas bar (during which James also proved himself to be fluent in Spanish) and a riverside stroll – Holly was seriously smitten. Not only was he incredibly charming, intelligent and funny, he was also devastatingly attractive. It would take James a further three dates to invite her back to his Kensington mansion flat 'for coffee', by which time Holly was giddy with lust – and she wasn't disappointed. It proved to be worth the wait, though: the Savile Row suits hid the sort of body that could advertise aftershave. They ended up staying in bed for a whole weekend, by which time Holly was head over heels.

After they'd been dating for a few months, James had taken Holly to meet his parents, whose beautiful Norfolk home looked like something out of *Country Living* magazine. As Mrs Wellington served afternoon tea in what she referred to as the 'blue drawing room', Holly had cringed to imagine what James must have thought of her own family home: a cluttered council semi in Basildon where her mum and Lola were living. Not that he'd been anything other than his usual wonderfully charming, polite self when she had taken him to meet her family, who in turn had been utterly enamored by James. Despite swearing off men, Heather had kept collapsing into coquettish giggles whenever he complimented her, while Lola – who was always shy around new people – had insisted on sitting next to him at lunch. And when the plates had been cleared away Lola had turned to James, her forehead all scrunched up in a thoughtful frown, and asked: 'When you marry my sister, can I be bridesmaid?' Holly had cringed, as they'd only been dating a couple of months at that point, but James had just leaned towards Lola with a wonderfully genuine smile and said, very softly: 'I hope so.'

Later that afternoon, as Holly had watched James joining in Lola's Barbie disco with genuine enthusiasm, she felt such a surge of happiness at seeing her two favourite people getting on so well that she was surprised and embarrassed to find tears springing up. From that moment on, she had no doubt that James was The One.

Just then Holly heard feet running up the stairs and soon after James burst through the door and swept her up into a huge hug.

'I'm so sorry, darling, I honestly left as soon as I could.'

'That's okay, you're here now.' As he held her close, Holly felt a wave of happiness wash away the evening's tensions. 'I think we're going to have to order a takeaway though,' she said, waving in the direction of the congealing plates of food.

'Oh, sweetheart, you went to so much trouble! I really am so sorry, but hopefully I can make it up to you.' He pulled a bottle of Bollinger out of his bag. 'Let's start with a toast.'

James expertly eased out the cork and poured two glasses.

'To us, and the most fabulous year of my life.' He clinked her glass, holding her gaze. 'Here's to many more.' Then he reached into his pocket and presented Holly with a slim box. 'Happy anniversary, Holly.'

She opened the box to find a delicate bracelet of gold links from which dangled a diamond-covered '1'.

'It's a charm bracelet,' he said.

Holly stared at the bracelet, speechless.

'I can always take it back and change it if you don't like it,' said James.

'Oh, no, it's beautiful,' said Holly quickly. 'I love it – I love *you*.'

They kissed and, as Holly shut her eyes, she felt her head spinning – and not just from lust. *God, she really must be drunk* . . .

'Why don't you make yourself comfortable and I'll order the food,' she said quickly. 'Curry okay?' Hopefully a few poppadoms would soak up the booze . . .

As they waited for the takeaway to arrive, James chatted to Holly about the big case he was working on. His client, a wealthy widow named Lady Martina Crosby, was locked in a dispute over her late husband's billions with the eldest son of his first wife. If James could win the case it would not only prove extremely lucrative for his firm, he might even make partner – all but unheard of at the young age of twenty-six. But then James came from a family of scarily impressive high-fliers. His father was a retired High Court judge, his brother ran a hedge fund and his sister was a dentist, plus the entire clan seemed to run marathons and climb mountains in their spare time. Holly didn't know what the Latin was for 'Stiff Upper Lip', but she felt sure that must have been the Wellington family's motto.

The takeaway had arrived and Holly was spooning out curry onto the plates when she heard James's mobile ring. There was a brief, muffled conversation, and then a moment later he came into the kitchen with a sheepish expression on his face. If Holly had been the suspicious type – which she really wasn't – she'd have said he looked distinctly guilty about something.

'Holly, that was Lady Crosby,' said James, rubbing his ear distractedly. 'She's asked if I will go to see her immediately. Apparently she's discovered some new information that will really help our case.'

Holly was stunned. 'But it's eleven o'clock at night! And look, I got lamb rogan josh – your favourite! Can't it wait until morning?'

'I'm so sorry, I know it's a pain, but I really do have to go. Lady Crosby's such a dragon that I can't put her off – and you know how important this case is.'

'James, please. Tell her it's our anniversary. I'm sure Lady Crosby will understand . . .' To Holly's embarrassment, she felt like she was going to cry. She was drunk and emotional and just wanted a cuddle, but James was already shrugging on his coat.

'I'll make it up to you, gorgeous girl, I promise.' He dropped a kiss on her forehead. 'Are we still on for Sunday?'

'Yes, but . . .'

'Great. Can't wait. Love you, Holly.'

3

The opening guitar notes of Babes of Bedlam's 'Twisted Lady' blasted out from somewhere across the other side of the dark room, jolting Holly out of her wine-induced coma. Meg had set the song – her band's signature track – as Holly's mobile's ring-tone as a joke, and now she didn't know how to change it back. As she rolled over, groaning at the sickly throbbing in her head, she felt a weird crunch-ing sensation beneath her. She tried to open her eyes to find out what it was, but her eyelids were crusty and stuck together. *Damn, she'd forgotten to take out her contact lenses last night . . .* Holly eventually winkled out the gummy lenses to discover that rather than being in bed as she'd assumed, she had actually spent the night on the little two-seater sofa in the living room sleeping on a pile of poppadoms, the shattered remains of which were now sticking to her bare legs giving the impression of a particularly unpleasant flaky skin condition. As she stumbled over to the kitchen to get a glass of water, she caught sight of several empty wine bottles sitting among the mess of discarded food and dirty saucepans. No wonder she felt so hideous – she must have cracked open another bottle after James had left. At least it was Saturday, so she could spend the day in bed recovering. But just then the phone started up again.

'Morning! Did I interrupt something sexy?' It was Meg.

'Nope,' croaked Holly. 'James isn't here. Long story . . .'

'Great, that means you're free to come shopping with me,' said Meg. 'It's half nine now . . . could you get to Oxford Street for eleven?'

'Um, probably, but I've got the hangover from hell so I might just . . .'

'Cool, let's meet at that little café on Carnaby Street. See you shortly, doll!'

Meg was already waiting for her with a plate of fried-egg sandwiches, coffee and a jug of juice. She looked her usual sensational self in a tiny red dress and a sort of turban, out of which her curls exploded like a volcano.

'Jaysus, you could have dressed up a bit.' Meg frowned at Holly's outfit of grey leggings, shapeless white T-shirt and her second-best pair of glasses. 'I've never known a gorgeous girl put so much effort into looking shite.'

'You're lucky I'm here at all.' Holly sat down,

recoiling at the smell of the food. 'I feel like death.'

'Get this down you, then.' Meg pushed the plate of sandwiches towards her and stared at her sternly until she forced down a tiny mouthful. Holly's stomach growled gratefully and she realised how hungry she was: she had barely eaten anything last night. By the time the plate was cleared, she was beginning to feel a little less rancid.

After breakfast their first stop was H&M, where Meg did a high-speed smash-and-grab on the rails then headed to the fitting rooms, with Holly in tow. As Meg started working through the pile of clothes, Holly sat in the cubicle corner and told her all about James's swift exit the previous night.

'Are you quite sure this Lady Crosby isn't after more than just James's legal skills?' asked Meg, yanking up a pair of orange PVC hot pants.

'No way!' said Holly. 'James was going on about what an old dragon she was last night. I don't think wrinkly, grey-haired widows are his type.'

Meg was busy checking out her fabulously curvy hot-pant-clad rear view in the cubicle mirror.

'Ooh, I love those on you,' said Holly. 'Very sexy.'

'Not enough arse,' said Meg, ripping them off and moving on to the next item in her pile. 'You never know, perhaps milady is a bit of a GILF.'

'GILF . . . ?'

'You know, like MILF,' said Meg. '*Grandma* I'd Like to Fu—'

'Thank you, Miss O'Hanlon! No, it's *definitely* nothing like that. I just wish he didn't have to work so hard . . .'

'When are you seeing him next?'

'Tomorrow. We're spending the day together.'

'Ooo, you should get these to wear on your date.' Meg held up the discarded hot pants. 'They'd look incredible with your legs, and Mr Wellington would have a heart attack – in a good way, I mean . . .'

But Holly shook her head emphatically. She wished she had just a fraction of her friend's confidence: Meg went out in stuff that Holly wouldn't have even dared to wear in the privacy of her own flat. She was now trying on a black dress that was slashed so low at the front, the bottom of the V reached well below her belly button.

'Blimey, don't you think that's a bit low cut?' said Holly. 'You can almost see your . . . *you know*.'

'My what?' asked Meg, all innocent. Then she gasped in mock horror. 'Sweet Mary, mother of Jesus! Surely you don't mean my *MUFF*?'

She cracked up laughing, while Holly stuck her tongue out at her.

'Don't worry, Miss Prude, I'm not going to get it. Now, if they had it in a leopardskin print, that would be another matter . . .' Meg checked her watch. 'Right, let's get going. Next stop – Topshop.'

As they waited for the traffic lights to change on the crossroads of Oxford Street and Regent Street,

Holly noticed a huge crowd gathered on the pavement outside the store. It was always a particularly busy spot, but today there was clearly something going on. Holly could make out a TV crew and a temporary platform surrounded by posters. A woman was shouting into a loudspeaker to cheers from the crowd.

'Looks like there's a demonstration or something,' said Holly.

'Mmm, yeah, it does,' said Meg.

Holly looked a bit harder. 'I wonder who those people are wearing the bright pink T-shirts?'

'I have absolutely no idea,' said Meg. 'But let's get a bit closer and find out.'

They crossed over the road and although the crowd was now so huge it was spilling off the pavement, they got near enough for Holly to be able to read the words 'STREET SCOUT' emblazoned on the backs of the pink shirts.

Suddenly, it all made sense: the last-minute shopping trip, the hurry to get to Topshop. She turned on Meg. 'You *knew* they were going to be here! You set this whole thing up!'

'Honest to God, I didn't,' said Meg emphatically, her eyes wide. She'd always been a lousy liar. 'Okay, well maybe I *did* have a quick peek at the show's website and perhaps I *might* have noticed that they were going to be here today. But I did it for you – and now we're here, we might as well take a proper look.'

She linked her arm through Holly's and went to push her way through the crowd, which seemed to be largely made up of groups of giggling girls, many of whom were hastily applying lipgloss or streaks of bronzer, but Holly stood firm.

'Uh-uh. No way. I already told you, I'm not interested.'

'Oh, come on, Holly, this could be your big break! Why are you wasting your life on the careline when you could be on the catwalk? Seriously, if I looked like you I'd be milking it for all I could. You're still so young – if modelling doesn't work out, you can always get into marketing and, you never know, you might actually *enjoy* it!'

Holly chewed her lip as she thought over what Meg had said. Perhaps she had a point. Okay, so modelling wasn't the financially secure career she'd hoped for, but until something else came up it would definitely be more fun (and almost certainly better paid) than the VitaSlim job. Perhaps the show was offering a cash prize that would help pay for some better care for Lola? And now that they were here, she might as well just see if she had what it took to be a model. And James? Well, if she *did* get picked, she was sure he'd come round – eventually. All guys wanted to date models, right . . . ?

But just as Holly was thinking about letting Meg lead her into the crowd, a voice suddenly shouted out: 'You've been *Street Scout*-ed!'

4

Holly looked around and saw a girl in a strapless denim playsuit being helped up from the crowd onto the platform. She had a mane of blue-black hair, so long that it grazed the top of her endless, olive-skin legs, and must have been well over six feet tall in her platform sandals.

One of the pink-clad scouts held out a microphone. 'What's your name, babe?'

'Moet Dobson,' she shrieked. 'Like the champagne, cos I'm bubbly and well expensive!'

As the crowd laughed, Moet blew kisses in every direction. Holly heard one of the girls standing near her mutter 'Fake tits!' to her mate.

'Well, congratulations, Moet, you're our first *Street Scout* contestant!

Moet had a body like Barbie and a face like a Bratz doll: even from a distance Holly could make out her chiselled cheekbones and full lips, which were so heavily glossed that her hair kept getting stuck to them.

'She's stunning,' murmured Holly.

'What, that skinny tart?' Meg gave a sceptical snort. 'You're *way* more attractive than her! Come on, Hols, they're bound to get you up there when they see you . . .'

But Holly didn't move. *What on earth had she been thinking?* There was no way she could compete with this glossy, gorgeous creature – next to Moet, she'd look like a cleaning lady. Besides, even if by some miracle the scouts *did* spot her in the crowd, the thought of standing up on that stage and having everyone dissect her appearance was too horrible to even think about. Holly couldn't believe that moments ago she had even been considering it.

She turned to Meg. 'Let's give this a miss.'

'What? But I thought you said —'

'I'm not interested, okay? Please, Meg, let's just go.'

The following morning, James collected Holly from her flat in his battered Golf convertible. He had tickets to a rugby match at Twickenham that afternoon and was taking her for lunch first. He had brought her a spectacular bunch of lilacs – her favourite flowers – to apologise for having abandoned her on Friday night, but Holly wasn't one to hold a grudge. Besides, she was excited about the prospect of spending a whole day together – and what a beautiful day it was turning out to be. It was only April, but as they set off for Twickenham with the roof down on the car the sky was such a vivid blue and the air so warm it felt like summer had arrived already.

'No boring work interruptions today, I promise,' said James, leaning over to kiss her as they stopped at a red light. Holly felt herself melting as James's tongue pushed gently inside her mouth. They were still kissing after the lights changed, prompting a chorus of angry beeps from the cars behind them.

'Oops!' giggled Holly. As they drove on, she rested her hand on his thigh, but James moved it so it was pressed against his crotch.

'See what you do to me, Miss Collins?' he grinned. 'Just wait until I get you home this afternoon . . .'

James had booked an early lunchtime table at The Pig, a pretty gastropub by the river in Richmond, not far from the stadium. They sat outside, soaking up the spring sunshine and watching the ducks and boats go by as they waited for their roast lamb. James was a dedicated rugby fan and hugely excited about the game, which was a decisive Premiership match between his team, Harlequins, and Bath RFC. Despite having joined him at quite a few matches, Holly still didn't really understand the sport (What was the point of the scrum? Did the loose-head prop need a particularly floppy neck?) but she loved the atmosphere at live matches, and the sunshine and promise of sex put her in a brilliant mood.

They arrived at the stadium in good time and found their seats, which were in a fantastic position not far from the edge of the pitch. To James's delight, Harlequins scored within the first ten minutes of the game and were comfortably ahead by the end of the first half.

'What an incredible game!' said James, as the whistle blew for half-time. 'Did you see that last ruck? Absolute poetry . . .'

James was just trying to explain to Holly what a ruck actually was when she glanced up at the large screen at the end of the stadium. A camera was panning around the crowd, picking out supporters. As she watched, a pretty blonde sitting next to a handsome, broad-shouldered bloke in a Harlequins shirt suddenly flashed onto the screen. It took Holly a moment to realise that she was looking at an image of James and herself.

Her hand flew to her mouth in shock. 'Oh God, James, look – it's us!'

They both started laughing and, as the camera lingered on them, James grinned and proudly pulled at the logo on his shirt. It was so surreal to see themselves projected up there. But then the weirdest thing happened. The camera started focusing in on Holly, closer and closer, until her face almost filled the entire screen. She could see the sprinkling of freckles on her nose and – to her humiliation – even the spot she'd tried to squeeze that morning and then plastered with concealer. There were a few whoops and wolf whistles from around the stadium. Holly giggled nervously. Next to her, she sensed James's irritation. 'Is this really necessary?' he muttered.

Still the camera lingered on her face, broadcasting every twitch and blink to the thousands in the stadium, and just as Holly was thinking about going to the toilet to escape the camera's glare (and then immediately worrying that perhaps – *oh God!* – it might even follow her into the loo), a voice suddenly boomed out over the tannoy, leaving her frozen in her seat.

'YOU'VE BEEN *STREET SCOUT*-ED!'

Holly looked around, confused and panicky. What was going on? Where did that voice come from? *Surely they weren't talking about her . . . ?* But, moments later, a woman in one of the now familiar pink T-shirts raced down through the rows of seats with a cameraman hot on her heels.

'Congratulations!' She crouched down next to Holly and thrust a microphone towards her. 'You've been chosen to appear on ITV1's new show *Street Scout*! What's your name?'

'Holly Collins.' Holly cringed as her voice reverberated around the stadium.

'And where are you from, sweetheart?'

'Um, here. I mean London. Hammersmith.'

'Come on, everyone, give it up for Holly from Hammersmith – our next gorgeous *Street Scout* contestant! Wooo!!'

There were cheers and applause and then, to

Holly's intense relief, her face abruptly disappeared from the screen.

'Is someone going to explain to me what the *hell* this is about?' said James.

The girl handed her business card to both Holly and James. 'My name's Buffy. I'm a senior scout with Strut Models. We'd love your girlfriend to be a contestant on our show. She's got a fantastic look and I think has the potential to be a really successful model.' Buffy gave James an appraising look. 'It's a shame we're not doing a men's version of the show, as you'd be perfect. Ever thought about modelling?'

'No, I have not!' spluttered James. 'What a ridiculous suggestion . . .'

Buffy gave Holly a shiny pink folder emblazoned with the *Street Scout* logo.

'Here's a bit of reading material for you,' she said. 'Information about the show, contracts, clearance forms: nothing sinister – just routine.'

'Thanks . . .' said Holly. She was feeling shell-shocked. 'I just need a little time to think about this . . .'

'No problem,' said Buffy. 'You've got my number, so give me a call whenever you like. Great to meet you both, enjoy the rest of the game.' She got up to leave, but then paused and turned back to Holly. 'I really hope you get in touch. I've been a model scout for years and I think you might have something special.' She smiled. 'Till we meet again, Holly Collins.'

Holly watched Buffy go. She noticed people who were sitting nearby looking over at her and smiled nervously at them. One girl gave her a cheery thumbs up. She felt totally disorientated, like someone had just thrown a hand grenade into her life. Then she turned to James, who was looking as dazed as she felt.

'Well,' said Holly eventually. 'That was weird.'

Thankfully, James broke into a grin. 'It certainly was. Not at all what you expect to happen at Twickenham, but then I guess that's my fault for having such a stunning girlfriend.' He kissed her on the cheek. 'Drink?'

Neither of them mentioned what had happened for the rest of the game, which thankfully ended in victory for the Harlequins. As they joined the river of people flowing back to the car park, Holly noticed a bright pink poster: '*Street Scout* is filming here today!' How on earth had she missed it on the way in?

As they sat waiting at a red traffic light near her flat, Holly opened the folder Buffy had given her and started leafing through the pages.

'It sounds like they actually pay you a wage to be on the show,' said Holly. 'And you get to work with the whole team at Strut and build up a portfolio.'

'You're not actually thinking about taking part in this circus?' said James.

'Well, I . . .'

'Darling, this is a reality TV show, not a job offer,' said James. 'And reality shows have their own agenda

31

– which is certainly not to make the poor fools who take part look good. They will manipulate you until you're either a national laughing stock or hate figure.'

'Yes, but Buffy seemed to think I've got potential – and Strut's one of the biggest agencies in the world. Surely if this gives me an opportunity to develop a career in modelling . . .'

'For God's sake, Holly, don't be so naïve! The people don't care about your career; they just want ratings fodder. And what if you don't win? You'll be forever known as that girl who got kicked off a TV show – and how's that going to look on your CV? Honestly, I can't believe you're even considering this. It will ruin your reputation.'

Holly rounded on him, suddenly furious. '*My* reputation? Are you sure you don't mean yours?'

'What the hell are you talking about?'

'Be honest, this isn't even about me, is it? You're just worried about what the firm and your family would think if your girlfriend went on some tacky TV show.'

'Don't be so ridiculous.' James had slowed the car and was now reversing into a parking space outside her flat. He turned off the ignition. 'I'm just trying to stop you from doing something you will undoubtedly regret.'

'I'm quite able to make my own decisions, thank you,' snapped Holly. 'And I can't believe you're not willing to support me in those.'

James sighed. 'Holly, I love you, but you're being overdramatic.'

'Fine.' She got out of the car and slammed the door as hard as she could. 'How's that for drama?' Then she stormed up to the front door of her building, slamming that behind her as well for good measure, and promptly burst into tears.

Later that evening Holly was lying on her sofa comfort-eating mini Magnums. She had eaten all the white ones and was now starting on the mint variety. She hated arguing with James – it was so out of character for her to lose her temper like that – but she couldn't believe how arrogant he'd been. He had called several times since she had stormed off, but Holly let it go to voicemail; she needed time to think. In eight hours her alarm would be buzzing, it would be Monday morning and she would be leaving her flat at 7.45 a.m. for the hour-long journey to the VitaSlim office in Croydon. Alan would probably still be mad at her. She would spend eight hours answering crispbread queries and then come home, watch a bit of telly and go to bed. Exactly the same thing would happen on Tuesday, Wednesday, Thursday, Friday and possibly all the other working days for the rest of her life – unless, of course, she grabbed hold of this wild, crazy opportunity that had been offered to her. Perhaps it would be a huge mistake; but then maybe it would be the best thing that had ever happened to her.

She hadn't called Meg to let her know what had happened yet, but she knew what her friend's advice would be: 'A life lived in fear is a life half lived.'

Holly picked up Buffy's business card and looked at it. 'Buffy Lovekin. Senior Scout. Strut Models.' There was an email address, landline and a mobile number. Holly checked her watch: 10.40 p.m. *Call me anytime*, Buffy had said . . .

Holly picked up her mobile and took a deep breath. *No time like the present*, she thought with a smile – and dialled the number.

5

Holly stood on the cobbled side street that led off Covent Garden's famous piazza and gazed up at the building in front of her. In a former life it had probably been a warehouse, but now it housed an extremely exclusive row of boutiques, sandwiched between two of which was a black door with a discreet metal nameplate bearing just one word: STRUT.

It had been a little over a month since the day of that fateful rugby match and Holly's late-night phone call to Buffy, during which she had somehow found herself agreeing to be a contestant on the new series of *Street Scout*. Holly had surrendered herself to the madness that had then ensued, letting herself be carried along on a wave of excited phone calls and bewildering emails, while still trying to keep her feet planted firmly on the ground – not easy when various TV people kept banging on about her fabulous future career as a supermodel, *Vogue* cover shoots and potential millions. She had met up with the show's producers at their offices a couple of times, but today was to be Holly's first day at Strut – and the first day of filming.

As expected, Meg had greeted the news of Holly's TV break with hysterical excitement, along with a hefty helping of 'I told you so'. Lola was thrilled that her big sister was going to be on TV and kept phoning Holly to ask if she'd met Justin Bieber yet. Her mum had been equally ecstatic: despite her own financial struggles over the years, Heather was still far less pragmatic than Holly and had never understood why her gorgeous, talented daughter stuck with the careline job. 'Haven't I always told you that you should be a model?' she said triumphantly. Even Alan at VitaSlim proved surprisingly accommodating, promising to hold her job open while she appeared on the show – an offer Holly dearly hoped that she wouldn't have to accept. In fact, the only person who didn't seem pleased for Holly was the one person she most desperately wanted to be: James. To his credit, he had accepted her decision to go on the show without question and was trying to be supportive – even whisking her off to a B&B in the Cotswolds on her last weekend as a good-luck gesture for the first day of filming – but Holly knew him well enough to know that he still thought she was being naïve.

'Don't let them talk you into doing anything you're not comfortable with,' he kept saying. Holly just hoped that as the weeks went by she would be able to win him round.

Holly had been told to be at Strut at nine this sunny Monday morning, but it was now twelve minutes past and she was still dithering on the pavement opposite, trying to summon up the courage to go in. The producers had told Holly to dress in her usual style for the day's filming so she was wearing a spotty Oxfam dress and beige suede boots, but after seeing a stunning blonde in a crop top and buttock-skimming shorts stride past her through the black door, she was now fiercely regretting not taking Meg's advice and wearing something 'titty or leggy'.

Holly felt her phone vibrate in her pocket with a text. She glanced at the screen: 'Where are u?! See u soon hopefully. Buffy x'.

Oh God, oh God, oh God . . . she really couldn't put this off any longer. Ignoring the chorus of doubts in her head, Holly crossed over the road and pressed the buzzer.

Behind the first-floor reception desk, the word STRUT was spelt out in three-foot-tall black lettering and was flanked by larger-than-life images of the agency's most famous faces. A harassed-looking girl juggling a clipboard, two BlackBerrys and an iPhone was hovering by the desk.

'Oh, thank God, you must be Holly – hi, I'm Nadja, one of the show's assistant producers – come this way.'

The girl barely took a breath and sped off before

Holly even had a chance to reply. She followed her into a vast, open-plan office with exposed-brick walls and huge arrangements of tropical flowers as spiky and angular as the razor-cheeked girls pouting from the posters around the room. There were several large, circular tables at which people were working, mainly talking on phones that seemed to start ringing again as soon as one call had finished. Holly noticed among them Buffy who, when she saw Holly, waved and gave a relieved thumbs up.

Nadja talked over her shoulder at her as they picked their way through the buzz. 'The contestants have been divided into two groups and each group will have a booker,' she explained, gesturing to the people at the round tables. 'Your booker will become your mum, your confidante, your manager and your best friend. They will get you jobs, advise you on your look and deal with your finances – in short, they'll become the most important person in your life after your boyfriend.' Nadja suddenly stopped and looked round at Holly. 'Unless of course you're a lesbian?'

Holly shook her head.

'Oh, well.' Sounding disappointed, Nadja made a note on her clipboard. 'Right, we're just up here. Take a seat and our director will be with you shortly to introduce the rest of the team.'

She led Holly up a spiral staircase and into a meeting room that was dominated by a huge table that consisted of an expanse of frosted glass balanced on an enormous white rock, around which were twenty white chairs – nineteen of which were occupied by an assortment of beautiful girls, who now all seemed to be staring at her. At the end of the room were three black chairs, which were currently empty. Feeling horribly self-conscious, Holly hurried over to the remaining place, positioned between a stunning Asian girl and Moet, the real-life Bratz doll who she had seen being scouted outside Topshop, whom was now sulkily stabbing at her iPhone with an acrylic-tipped fingernail. Holly was relieved to see a familiar face, even if it wasn't a particularly friendly one.

There were cameras and lights set up around the room and, as Holly looked around, she felt a fresh wave of fear. This was actually happening: she was going to be on TV.

At each place on the table was a grey leather A4 folder with the Strut Models logo and the contestant's name picked out in silver. Holly peeked inside hers; it was empty. Just then, her mobile vibrated with another text and she pulled it out to read it: 'Good luck beautiful, J x'. Thrilled to hear from James, she was just about to compose a reply when the door flew open and a man hurried in, accompanied by Nadja and a couple of the production team she recognised from previous meetings.

'Welcome, welcome, ladies! My name is Nigel Clark – I'm *Street Scout*'s director. It's a pleasure to finally meet you all.' He was tall and good-looking, with a theatrical manner that bordered on camp. 'In a moment we'll film you meeting Strut's main man, Maxwell Moore, but first it gives me great pleasure to introduce you to our leading lady, the fabulous Miz Sasha Hart!'

And suddenly there she was, wearing a clingy orange dress and silver sandals, and looking even slimmer and more stunning than she did on screen. Holly caught a waft of expensive floral scent as Sasha strode past her to the front of the room. It was quite surreal to see her famous features, so instantly famil-iar from countless TV shows, there in the flesh.

'Well, hello, girls,' smiled Sasha. 'How are we all?' A sheepish mumble from the contestants; clearly Holly wasn't the only one who was feeling nervous. 'We're all so excited about *Street Scout* and couldn't have hoped for a more stunning group of contest-ants,' continued Sasha. 'It's going to be a lot of hard work and I'm sure there'll be times when you feel like quitting, but remember you're here to have fun too, okay? I'm really looking forward to working with you and wish you all the best of luck – and if all my years of TV experience have taught me one thing, it's this: if in doubt, just smile!'

'Thank you, darling,' said Nigel, kissing Sasha's cheek as she left the room with a little wave to the contestants. 'Right, girls, now it's down to business. As I said, first of all we're going to film you meeting

Maxwell Moore. As I'm sure you know, Max is something of a legend in the modelling world after single-handedly turning Strut into one of the most successful agencies in the world. We're absolutely thrilled that he's agreed to let us use his agency and expert personnel for the show – and, even more so, that he's agreed to make the final decision each week over who stays and who goes. Remember, this is the man who holds your fate in his hands, so let's get lots of positive energy in the room, okay?'

As Nigel moved into position and the cameramen got ready, many of the girls pulled out compacts and lipgloss to touch up their make-up, leaving Holly wishing once again that she'd made more of an effort with her appearance. The best she could find in her bag was a tin of Vaseline, and she rubbed a bit on her lips and eyelids.

'Okay, all ready?' Nigel looked around the room. 'Right, let's go . . .'

On the director's cue, the door opened and Maxwell Moore strode into the room. He was dressed in a grey, slim-cut suit and open-necked white shirt that highlighted his tan. He wasn't particularly tall, yet even without opening his mouth he exuded power and confidence. Even if someone didn't know who he was (unlikely, as barely a day passed without the zillionaire playboy being splashed over the press – usually with some gorgeous chick on his arm or in one of his many super-cars), they would still assume he was both very important and very, very rich. Perhaps it was his rugged looks, or maybe it was the sandy hair and broad shoulders, but as he made his way to the front of the room, the famous image of Daniel Craig dressed in a pair of tight blue swimming shorts instantly popped into Holly's head. For an older guy – and Holly reckoned he must be nudging fifty – he was undeniably fit.

He sat himself in the middle chair at the end of the table, then a tiny, curvy, dark-haired woman and a skinny black guy with a mohican took the places on either side of him – the two bookers, Holly assumed.

'Good morning, ladies, and the warmest of welcomes to the Strut family.' His voice was caramel-smooth, with a hint of Cockney. 'My scouts have clearly done a terrific job. I'm extremely impressed with the talent here today and I'm very much look-ing forward to getting to know you better. You've certainly brought the raw material, but over the next few months we'll be showing you how to turn that into catwalk gold. In front of you is your port-folio and over the weeks ahead you'll hopefully be filling that with fantastic pictures. You'll be lucky enough to be working alongside the hottest photog-raphers, stylists, designers, models and entertainers who will be sharing their expert knowledge with you. This really is a chance of a lifetime, so try not to screw it up!'

Moet laughed, tossing her hair sexily; Holly

suddenly remembered they were on camera and plastered on a smile.

'Your first task today, ladies, is a simple one: you just have to introduce yourself to me. As you know, first impressions count for a great deal – especially in modelling – so I'm going to call you in one at a time for a brief chat. I'm going to be looking for charisma, confidence and that indefinable special something that separates a catalogue model from a catwalk queen. Assisting me will be your bookers, Rosario and Bear.' He gestured to the pair flanking him. 'As you know, at the end of every week I'll be sending home the girl that I'm least impressed with, but today I'll be getting rid of not one, not two, but eight of you.'

A horrified gasp went up from around the table: nobody had been expecting this kind of cull. Holly remembered James's warnings about how manipulative TV shows could be and suddenly wished she'd listened to him.

But Maxwell chuckled, clearly delighted at the response. 'Sorry to spring that on you, but I'm afraid the TV producers are the ones pulling the strings here! Besides, modelling is a cut-throat world and the sooner you learn that lesson the better. By the end of today, we'll have our twelve finalists. Best of luck, ladies.' He got up to leave, then paused. 'Oh, and please, call me Max.'

* * *

As Nigel signalled the end of the scene, all the girls started talking amongst themselves, but Holly just sat there feeling sick and shell-shocked. *Why the hell had she put herself up for this?* She had vaguely assumed that all she'd need to do was pose for a few photos and maybe walk down a catwalk – she hadn't even thought about the other stuff involved, like actual *talking*.

Well, it was too late to back out now, so she might as well make the best of it. Summoning up the last of her dwindling courage, Holly turned to Moet, who was once again fixated by her iPhone. It would be good to have a buddy amongst the contestants; it might help boost her confidence a bit.

'Hi, I saw you getting scouted outside Topshop,' smiled Holly. 'Pretty crazy, huh?'

But Moet didn't respond. Holly presumed that she hadn't realised she was talking to her, so she tried again.

'It's Moet, isn't it? I was in Oxford Street when you got picked for the show. I'm Holly, by the way.'

Finally, Moet turned to her with a look of total contempt. 'Listen, *babe*. I don't care who you are or what you think. You might as well go home now as you ain't got no hope of winning this show. I mean, seriously, what's with the old-lady dress and them ugly boots? This is a modelling show, not a freak show.'

Moet turned to the pixie-faced girl with a blonde

crop on her other side and Holly heard her mutter 'Loser.' The blonde giggled.

Holly felt her cheeks burning with shame. She looked down at her spotty dress, a dress that she had always loved, and saw herself through Moet's eyes for the first time. A geek in granny clothes. She might be a bitch, but Moet was spot on: Holly didn't belong here.

To her horror, Holly realised she was about to cry. It all felt so overwhelming: all these people, the lights and cameras . . . *I have to get out*, she thought suddenly. *I can't stay here*. Wiping away a tear, she picked up her bag and slipped out of the room. She would send an email to Buffy: explain that she'd had second thoughts. It wasn't like she owed these people anything. She was sure they would understand.

Holly scuttled past the tables of bookers and edged around the reception desk. Nobody had noticed her go, thank God. But just as she started heading down the stairs to the black door and freedom, she heard a voice behind her.

'Hey you! Where d'you think you're going?'

Holly swung round. Sasha Hart was standing at the top of the stairs, her hands planted on her hips – and she didn't look happy.

6

'I'm so sorry,' stammered Holly, frozen to the spot on the stairs. 'I just . . . I . . . I've just got to get some fresh air.'

As she looked at Holly, Sasha's face softened. 'Hey . . . are you crying?'

'No, I'm . . .' But despite Holly's best efforts to hold it together, another tear trickled down her cheek. Her hands flew to her face. 'Oh God, I've made such a mess of everything. I just don't think I'm cut out for television. I'm really sorry . . .'

And with that she started to *really* cry: proper snotty, shoulder-shuddering sobs.

'Shhh, come on, it'll be okay . . .' Sasha came down to where Holly was standing and put her arms around her shoulders. 'Look, why don't you and I have a chat, see if we can sort this out? If you still want to go afterwards then that's fine, but I might be able to help. Does that sound like a good idea?'

Holly glanced shyly up at Sasha, who towered over her in her heels. Her teeth were as even as grand piano keys and twice as white; her hair was as swishy and shiny as a shampoo advert. Everything about her was so glossy and flawless, it was like she'd been airbrushed. Holly imagined what her own appearance must be like, all blotchy and dribbly, and felt even more wretched. Still, she gave a little nod and tried to smile.

'Excellent,' smiled Sasha. 'Come with me – I've got a little bolt-hole where we can get some privacy.'

As they walked through the office, Nadja came bustling up to them, clearly intending to nab Holly, but Sasha waved her off.

'Give us a few minutes,' she said curtly, sending Nadja scuttling away.

Sasha's dressing room was clearly an office that had been annexed for the show's big star. The desk had been set up with a mirror, hairstyling equipment and more make-up than Holly had ever seen in her life: there must have been at least twenty lipglosses alone. On the coffee table there was a stack of paperwork and a couple of bottles of fancy-looking mineral water. Sasha poured them both a glass, then settled herself on the grey leather sofa and patted the place next to her.

'It's Holly, isn't it?'

That took Holly by surprise. 'Yes – how did you know?'

'Homework,' said Sasha, patting the pile of papers. 'It's important for me to get to know you guys. Let me get this right – you were . . . scouted at a rugby match and work on a customer phone line?'

Holly nodded. 'Yes, for VitaSlim.'

'I was in one of their adverts years ago – wearing a yellow swimsuit, if I remember correctly. The director was a control freak and I ended up eating boxes and boxes of the things until he got the perfect take.' Sasha shuddered. 'My mouth was so dry by the end of it I could barely swallow!'

Sasha chatted away, asking about Holly's job, her boyfriend and family, and Holly gradually began to relax. She was so friendly and down to earth it was like talking to a mate. It was only when Sasha's mobile started ringing, and she glanced at the screen and murmured, 'Hmm, Holly Willoughby – she can wait,' that Holly remembered she was having a girlie gossip with the most famous woman in television.

'I have to tell you, Holly,' said Sasha. 'Everyone on *Street Scout* is extremely excited about you.'

'Me? What do you mean?'

'Well, you're very beautiful, of course, and with a bit of guidance you could be a real star, but you're also very natural. I'd say a lot of the girls sitting out there are only here because they want to be famous and date a footballer, but I don't get that impression from you. You're not playing a game. I really think you want to get a career out of this.'

'I do,' agreed Holly, 'but I'm terrified I'll do something stupid on camera.'

'But that's totally normal! Listen, when I was about your age I was offered a chance to host a TV show. I'd never done anything like that before and I was *way* out of my comfort zone so I thought about it for ages, but in the end I did it – and I'm so glad I did, because otherwise I wouldn't be sitting here today.' Sasha took Holly's hands in hers. 'Holly, this show could give you the chance at a life most people can only dream of. Sure, you could probably make it as a model without going on *Street Scout*, but TV will take your career into the stratosphere. It would be a terrible shame to throw such a fantastic opportunity away without even giving it a go.'

'But I can't compete with the other girls,' said Holly. 'They're so much more glamorous and confident.'

Sasha waved her hand dismissively. 'Glamour is just window dressing – and don't confuse arrogance with confidence. Just be yourself and if you're feeling shy, just do what I do and fake it.' Sasha smiled at her. 'We're on your side, Holly, I promise. It's in no one's interest to make you look stupid.'

Holly chewed her lip, thinking over everything that Sasha had said. It made a lot of sense. And if she left now, wouldn't she always be wondering *What if . . . ?*

'Okay,' said Holly, feeling a surge of boldness. 'Let's do this.'

Sasha escorted Holly to a waiting room where the rest of the girls were milling around, getting themselves ready for their TV close-up. To Holly's immense relief, nobody seemed to have noticed her disappearance and, as she made her way to a spot in the corner to compose herself – as far away from Moet and her new blonde friend as possible – the Asian girl who'd been sitting on the other side of her earlier smiled and waved her over.

The pair of them got chatting and Holly discovered that the girl's name was Kinzah: she was a medical student from Manchester and was clearly finding the whole experience just as weird and terrifying as she was. Holly began to feel so much better that her nerves started to give way to excitement – well, just a little.

As the pair talked, the other girls were getting called out one by one for their meeting with Max and the bookers. Some of them returned looked relieved, others shell-shocked. When Moet came back in she looked so triumphant – whooping and high-fiving the pixie-faced blonde – you'd have thought she'd already won the whole show.

Then suddenly it was Holly's turn. Nadja took her up to the meeting room but as Holly hovered outside on jelly legs, waiting to be called in, Sasha came over for a chat – this time with a cameraman in tow.

'So, this is Holly Collins,' smiled Sasha to the camera. 'How are you feeling, hon?'

'Oh, you know, a bit nervous.'

'Max says he's looking for charm and confidence – how do you think you'll do in there?'

In truth Holly was terrified, but she remembered Sasha's advice: *Just fake it*. 'I'm just going to be myself and hopefully that will be enough to get me through,' she smiled.

'Okay, well, it looks like they're ready for you so in you go. Good luck, Holly!'

Plastering on a smile, Holly walked into the meeting room, which was unchanged from when they had been in there earlier except now there was only one white chair facing the panel.

'Hello, Holly,' said Rosario. She had a slight accent – Spanish? – and was very pretty and curvy, with a wild mass of dark hair. 'It's great to finally meet you. Come and sit down.'

Bear was smiling, but Max was looking at the papers on the table in front of him and barely glanced up.

'So, Holly,' said Bear. 'Tell us a little about yourself.'

'Okay, well, my name's Holly Collins and I'm twenty-two years old and from Essex . . .'

'We already know that,' snapped Max. 'We have it written down in front of us, so spare us the biog. Is there nothing else of interest you can share?'

Holly panicked. 'Well, I work on a customer care line.' *Shit, they knew that, too.* 'Um, I like shopping and playing netball in my spare time.'

'Favourite designer?' asked Max.

Holly's mind was horribly blank. 'Topshop?'

'That's not really a designer, is it?' Max gave an

exaggerated sigh. 'How about models – anyone whose career you particularly admire?'

'Um . . . Naomi Campbell.' It was the only model Holly could think of.

Max raised his eyebrows sarcastically. 'How original . . . Look' – he glanced at his papers, clearly having forgotten her name – '*Holly*, do you actually have any interest in fashion and modelling, or did you just come along today to get your face on TV?'

Holly gawped in astonishment. If it was up to her, she wouldn't even be there – it was *his* people who had badgered her into this! But she was far too polite to tell Max to shove his bloody show up his arse (which was what she really felt like), so instead she just plastered on what she hoped was a sincere expression and dug around for something appropriate to say.

'Well . . . I know I've got a lot to learn, but I'd really love to be a model,' she began. 'And I'm hoping that going on this show will be a great opportunity to build a career and the start of a really interesting . . . um . . . journey.'

Max gave a curt heard-it-all-before nod. 'Right, please walk to the door and back.'

Holly did as she was told, trying to forget about the cameras and her churning emotions and channel her inner supermodel, but as she clumped along she feared she looked more Jonathan Ross than Kate Moss.

Max obviously thought as much, because as she

sat back down he leaned over and whispered something to Bear, who nodded and then turned to Holly.

'Thanks very much, Holly, we've seen enough.'

What – was that it? She'd barely been in there a couple of minutes! The other girls had been gone for at least ten.

'Okay, well, thanks for the opportunity to meet you. Bye.'

Well, that couldn't have gone any worse, thought Holly, getting out of there as quickly as she could – and then tripping over a lighting cable by the door.

As she picked herself up, muttering her apologies to the panel, she caught sight of Max's face. To her utter humiliation, he rolled his eyes.

At the end of the long day all the girls were lined up in front of the panel – *like a firing squad*, thought Holly miserably – to learn their fate.

Max was back to his suave, smiling self again. 'Well, ladies, we've had to make a few very tough decisions, but we've reached an agreement on who we want our final twelve contestants to be. Rosario and Bear are going to take turns to call out the names of the girls who will be on their teams. If your name is called, please come out and stand beside your new booker. If it is not, then thank you for your time and all of us at Strut wish you the very best for the future.'

Rosario kicked things off. 'Okay, our first finalist is . . . Jamie!'

The pixie-faced blonde punched the air and trotted across the room. Moet looked pissed off.

'Tabitha,' said Bear.

'Jade.'

'Charlie.'

When Rosario called out Kinzah's name, Holly grinned delightedly at her new friend, who looked stunned to have been chosen. Bear then picked Moet who, unsurprisingly, made the most of the moment, pulling down her top as low as possible to show off a chasm of golden cleavage and blowing kisses at the cameras and Max.

'Chanel.'

'Kirsty.'

'Lauren.'

And so it went on. The girls at the front of the room all chatted and giggled excitedly; the rapidly dwindling bunch at the other end looked increasingly nervous. Soon there was only one space remaining, and Bear was really milking the moment.

'And our last finalist is . . .' – he paused for what seemed like entire minutes – 'Sara!'

7

So that was it. Her dream was in the dumpster before it had even begun. Holly glanced at the other rejects standing around her, all looking as glum as she felt. One of them sniffed and wiped her eyes.

Now that her big chance had been snatched away, Holly suddenly wanted it desperately. Why the hell had Sasha told her everyone on the show was so excited about her when they then ditched her at the first opportunity? She must have *really* screwed up the interview with Max. Perhaps if she'd made herself look more glamorous, been a bit more bubbly . . .

'Guys, we have a problem.' Sasha had suddenly appeared in the room. Rather than stopping filming, however, Nigel signalled for a camera to focus on her.

'What's up?' said Max.

'The *Street Scout* rules clearly state that contestants must never have had a contract with a model agency before, right?'

'That's correct.'

'Well, we've just got an email from Gawk Models.' She waved a piece of paper. 'Apparently Jamie Foster was on their books a couple of years ago.'

Holly glanced over to where Jamie was standing. She looked as if she'd just been slapped.

Max's expression was grave. 'Is this true, Jamie?'

'Well, yes . . . but it was only for a few months, and I had no idea that wasn't allowed!' Holly felt quite sorry for the girl. It was true – she had never heard of that 'rule' before either.

'I'm sorry,' said Max solemnly, 'but we can't make an exception. I'm afraid this means you're disqualified from the show with immediate effect.'

Sasha gathered the dazed girl into a motherly hug, then quickly ushered her out of the room. When she had gone, Max turned to the other girls.

'Well, this means we've got one place still to fill.' He beckoned Bear and Rosario into a huddle for a whispered conversation. As they deliberated, Holly looked around the room, trying to take in what was happening. Nigel seemed completely calm: as if the show's director had not found this shock development in the least bit shocking. Sasha was standing nearby, waiting for Max to finish, but when she saw Holly looking at her she smiled and winked conspiratorially. Holly suddenly remembered what James had said about reality shows being manipulative. But surely this hadn't all been set up . . . ?

At the front of the room, Max and the bookers resumed their places.

'Okay, girls, we've made our decision,' he said. 'It was tough, but we've agreed that our final contestant should be . . . Holly.'

It took a moment for her to realise that she was in.

Holly was still in a state of shock when she arrived home, weighed down with yet more contracts, shooting schedules and information sheets. Rosario, who was to be her booker, had pulled her aside for a brief chat after they had finished filming.

'I'm so happy we're going to be working together, Holly,' she said, reaching up on her toes to kiss her on both cheeks. 'I just love that gap in your teeth. So sexy!'

'Um, thank you . . .'

'You really are beautiful. The complete package.' Rosario smiled at her. 'How much do you weigh, honey?'

'I don't really know . . .'

Rosario was looking her up and down, her head cocked to one side. 'Okay, well, let's knock five pounds off for a start and see how you look. Your thighs are a little on the large side. Here's a diet sheet.' She held out a piece of paper; Holly caught sight of the word 'VitaSlim' and shuddered.

'Do you exercise?'

'Not really . . .'

'You need to start working out regularly. Tone up a bit. Zumba should do the trick.'

'Who?'

'It's a workout class!' Rosario shrieked with laughter. '*Ay, ay, ay!* . . . Zumba is the reason us Brazilian girls have such great butts.' She patted her own curvy behind for emphasis. 'See you on Wednesday, *querida*. Make sure you get some beauty sleep, okay?'

When she had got back to her flat that evening, sleep was all Holly had wanted to do – preferably until 8 a.m. the day after next, which was the next day of filming – but James's firm was having a cocktail party that night and he had invited her along. As tired as she was, Holly had been looking forward to meeting his colleagues and, after an emotional roller coaster of a day, she was desperate to spend some time with him. James had been so busy at work lately they'd hardly seen each other.

James had advised her to wear something 'conservative' so she pulled out a Zara navy shift dress she had bought for job interviews after leaving university (what a waste of sixty quid *that* had been) and tied her hair back in a ponytail. Holly checked her appearance in the mirror. It was certainly conservative; in fact, it was verging on Young Conservative. *Perfect*, thought Holly with a smile, grabbing her bag and running for the door.

The party had been going on for over an hour by the time Holly made her entrance into the grand

St James's club. She handed her coat to a white-gloved door attendant who directed her upstairs to the 'Hanover suite'. When she got there, the room was full and Holly was hovering nervously in the doorway, trying to find James amid the crowd of suits, when she felt a pair of arms wrap around her and a kiss on the nape of her neck. She turned to come face to face with James, who was looking extremely handsome in a dark suit and pale blue tie. She still got the same jolt of delighted disbelief whenever she saw him: *This man is actually mine!*

'Hello, gorgeous.' He smiled. 'You look like a lawyer. An extremely beautiful lawyer.' James kissed her on the lips, far too briefly, but Holly guessed a passionate snog was out of the question in front of his colleagues.

'So how did it go today?' he asked.

'It was fine,' she said brightly. 'My booker's called Rosario and she seems lovely.' Holly thought it best not to mention the bit about her telling her to lose weight.

'Well, you'll have to fill me in later. We should be able to slip away after a couple of drinks, and grab a late bite to eat . . .'

'James, my boy! Tell me, who is this heavenly creature?'

A large man with a mane of silvery-grey hair and cheeks the colour of claret loomed in front of them.

From his broad grin and glazed eyes, Holly guessed that the drink he was holding wasn't his first.

'David, I'd like you to meet my girlfriend, Holly Collins,' said James. 'Holly, this is David Winters, one of our partners.'

'And his *boss*, my dear,' murmured David to Holly. 'So I think I deserve a proper hello.'

Before she knew what was happening, he had planted a sloppy kiss on her lips, then snaked his arm around her and pulled her close to him, his hand resting unsettlingly far down her back.

'She's an absolute peach, James! No wonder you're always so keen to leave the office, eh?'

James laughed obligingly, but Holly noticed an uneasy look in his eye.

'Will you excuse us for a moment, David? I just need to get Holly a drink.'

As he led her off into the mass of people, James whispered, 'Sorry about that,' and gave her hand a reassuring squeeze. That was one of the many things Holly loved about him: how protective of her he was. They were just making their way to the bar when – 'Jimbo! Over here!'

A stocky, sandy-haired young bloke was waving them over. Taking Holly by the hand, James weaved through the crowd to join them.

'Holly, this is Toby Travers, one of my colleagues, and this' – James gestured to a horsey blonde with a chignon and a Chanel bag – 'is his girlfriend, Camilla.'

'*Fiancée* now, darling,' she scolded, thrusting a diamond-bedecked hand in their faces. 'Toby popped the question when we were in St Tropez last weekend and of course I *totally* said "*Oui*"!'

Holly looked at the rock. It was the size of a Cadbury's Mini Egg.

'Wow, what a beautiful ring!'

'Isn't it?' Camilla gazed reverently at her hand. 'Two carats of cushion-cut perfection.'

'Why don't you girls get to know one another while James and I go to the bar for the drinks?' said Toby.

Camilla watched the men head off together. 'I must say, your man is quite the fox,' she said to Holly. 'And it sounds like he's something of a superstar at work, too. Bit of a coup bagging Lady Crosby as a client.'

'Yes, he's certainly working very hard at the moment.'

'Of course, I've met Lady Crosby at a few society events.' Camilla looked around to check nobody was listening, then dropped her voice. 'No class, of course, but then she did used to be an air hostess. And if James can work his magic on this case, she looks set to be richer than that awful Russian man . . .'

An air hostess? Holly wasn't sure why, but she had imagined Lady Crosby to have been something a bit more upper-crust. An opera singer, perhaps. Or something to do with horses . . .

'And, of course, Mummy can't *stand* the woman because Daddy can't keep his bloody eyes off her, but then she is so very *obvious* looking.'

By now Holly had completely lost the thread of the conversation and wasn't even sure if Camilla was still talking about Lady Crosby, so she changed the subject.

'So, Camilla, are you a lawyer?'

'God, no, I'm in fashion PR, but of course I'll stop after the wedding. Can't be carrying on with the career nonsense when I'm Mrs Toby Travers! Do you work, Polly?'

'It's Holly. Well, yes, but I'm just having a bit of a break to appear on—'

'Holly's taking a sabbatical.' James had suddenly appeared with their drinks. 'But she's planning on working in marketing, aren't you, Hols?' He was smiling at her, but he'd made it crystal-clear that the subject of *Street Scout* was considered off-limits tonight.

'Lovely,' said Camilla, dismissively, looking around the room. 'Goodness, is that Bunny Belvedere? She must have doubled in size since I saw her at the polo . . . I must go and say hello. Ciao, darlings.' And she skipped away. 'Bunny, you look fabulous . . .!'

An hour of small talk later, Holly was just wondering how to disentangle herself from a particularly dull conversation with a pair of the firm's wives about the best prep schools in Chelsea when, to her relief, James came over to rescue her.

'Would you mind if I borrowed Holly for a moment?' He took her hand and led her out of the room.

'Where are we going?'

'You'll see,' he grinned.

They hurried along a corridor and up another flight of stairs. The place was intimidatingly grand: all dark wood panelling and oil paintings of stern-looking men with dogs or horses.

'This is actually my father's London club,' said James. 'And if I'm not mistaken . . .' He pushed open a door. 'Yes, this is the Members' private bathroom.'

He closed the door behind them and locked it, turning to Holly with a smile that made her pulse quicken and her stomach turn cartwheels.

'I was looking at you across that room and I couldn't bear to keep my hands off you a moment longer,' muttered James, pushing her against the wall and starting to nuzzle her neck. 'I want you so much, Holly.'

Holding her hands against the wall he kissed her with such intensity she gasped, then he turned her round, unzipped her dress and dropped it from her shoulders so that she was standing in just her underwear and heels. Thank God she had decided to wear the new stuff tonight.

'God, you're so gorgeous . . .' James pulled her bra straps down and suddenly his mouth and hands were moving all over her, sending her into such a wild state of desire that Holly reached for his belt, fumbling with the buckle, and pulled down his trousers and boxers. Then she knelt down on the floor in front of him.

'Oh God . . . ' murmured James, closing his eyes in anticipation.

Brrrrrrrr. In the pocket of his discarded trousers, James's phone started to vibrate.

'Fuck!' he muttered.

'Just leave it,' urged Holly.

'I can't . . . I'm so sorry . . .' He retrieved the phone. 'Hello?' He listened, pulling up his boxers with his free hand. 'Right, of course. I'll be right over. No, that's fine. See you shortly.'

'Don't tell me,' said Holly, still kneeling in front of him. 'Lady bloody Crosby.'

'Holly . . .'

'No, it's okay. Off you go – you don't want to keep her waiting.'

'I'm so sorry, Hols, I feel terrible abandoning you again but this case is *so* important.' James glanced in the mirror, raking his fingers through his hair. 'You do understand that, don't you?'

Holly shrugged petulantly. She knew she was being childish, but she was drunk, tired and aching for him. She felt a sudden rush of anger: James had barely asked about her day and was clearly ashamed of her appearing on *Street Scout*, yet he expected her to put up with his boss letching all over her and to make small talk with a load of over-Botoxed, under-fed, middle-aged women. It all seemed very unfair.

James unlocked the door. 'Call me when you get home, okay?' He went to kiss her, but she turned away. 'I love you, Holly. Please, just try and put yourself in my shoes.'

'How about putting yourself in mine for once?' she said quietly, as she zipped up her dress.

But James had already gone.

8

At 8 a.m. the following Wednesday, Holly found herself at a photographer's studio in Fulham along with the other eleven finalists. The call-time that morning had been 7 a.m., but thankfully there had been breakfast waiting when Holly arrived: pots of coffee, fresh fruit and a few small croissants. Holly had reached for one of the pastries, but then remembered she was meant to be losing weight and swapped it for some pineapple chunks. One of the other girls, an extremely skinny, nervy brunette called Dot, frowned at her choice.

'Pineapple's got a terribly high GI score,' she muttered, her eyes staring and intense. 'Plums are far lower – 24, I think.'

Holly wasn't even entirely sure what a GI score was, so in the end it seemed safer just to stick to coffee – although she had to take it black, as she couldn't find either milk or sugar.

With breakfast and a quick briefing from Nigel out of the way, the girls were all lined up in the studio

– a huge white space with distressed wood flooring – to await instructions from Sasha.

'Good morning, girls,' said Sasha, as Holly's empty tummy rumbled unhappily. 'For today's challenge, you will be working with one of the hottest names in photography. This brilliant young talent has already shot campaigns for the likes of Lanvin and Prada, and has just done his sixth *Vogue* cover. We're especially pleased to have him here today as he actually started his career as a model with Strut, so he knows exactly what to do on both sides of the lens. Please give a fabulous *Street Scout* welcome to Zane.'

A young guy slouched in wearing a tight white vest and a very baggy pair of khaki combats. His body was lean and packed with muscle and – from what Holly could see of it – completely hairless, apart from a buzz of black on his head. Tattoos covered the whole of his right arm and snaked up his neck. Along with the welcoming applause, there was a wolf whistle from Moet's direction.

'Alright, girls?' He was wearing goggle sunglasses and had a cigarette stuck behind each ear. 'Today we're gonna be shooting a calendar, yeah? Each of you is gonna be, like, representin' a month of the year. It's gonna be well sick.'

Holly tried to imagine herself striking a model pose in front of the uber-cool Zane, and cringed with embarrassment.

Sasha went on: 'As this will be your first

professional shoot, this task is to find out how comfortable you are in front of the camera, so just relax, listen to Zane's direction and, above all, enjoy yourselves!'

With the cameras rolling, the stylists handed out costumes to the girls. Kinzah was given a little dress covered with hearts for February; a willowy blonde with a Russian accent named Natalia was the Easter bunny; and Dot was December in a gift-wrapped Christmas present. 'Thank God, it'll cover my fat thighs,' she muttered to Holly, whose own slim legs looked sturdy next to Dot's Twiglet pins.

Holly was chosen to be November, but when the stylist held up a pair of long boots, a neck ruff, a black hat and a pair of tiny hot pants, she was still no clearer about what she was actually supposed to be.

'It's like a sexy Guy Fawkes, yeah?' the stylist explained. 'For Bonfire Night?'

At least she didn't get July, which was a string bikini. That went to Moet who, unsurprisingly, was thrilled.

'Gotta get my money's worth from these babies!' she trilled, jiggling her boobs.

Holly had hoped for a bit of privacy to try on her costume (especially because they had all been told to change into nude thongs to avoid VPL), but she was shown into a room with Rosario and the rest of the girls on her team. At least the cameras had stayed on the other side of the door.

Holly was just wriggling out of her knickers when she heard a shriek.

'Jeeesoos! What the hell is that?'

She swung round to find Rosario staring straight at her. *Down there.*

'What?' muttered Holly.

'Your bush! *Ay, caramba*, I've not seen pubes like that for years. We need to sort that out, pronto.'

'Um, does it matter?'

'Of course it matters! I'm not having my girls look like a Wookie. Christ, Holly, have you not heard of waxing?'

As Holly's cheeks flamed with humiliation, Rosario pulled out her phone and punched a button. 'Eva honey? It's Rosario. We have a code red.' She paused. 'Yes, if you can get down to Click Studios now, that would be great. Okay. Ciao.' Then she turned to Holly. 'You're lucky she's free. Eva is the Brazilian queen. She can get it done while you wait your turn with Zane.'

A short while later, Rosario led Holly through the maze of corridors in the studio, still muttering about her 'crazy booosh', to a little room where a woman with her hair scraped into a severe bun was setting up a fold-up beautician's table.

'Okay, knickers off and hop up on the couch. Knees up, then drop your legs open.'

Cringing with embarrassment, Holly did as she was told, then lay there staring at the ceiling while

Eva got busy with the wax. It actually felt quite nice as the hot wax was applied and Holly was just starting to relax when suddenly – *HOLY SHIIIIT!* It felt as if a layer of her skin had just been ripped off. Holly was just recovering from the shock when it happened again. And again! *Sweet Mary, mother of God.* How much hair did she have down there? And why on earth did women willingly part with money for this torture?

'What style do you want?' snapped Eva.

Style? Holly had no idea there would be options. 'Um, just a bit of a tidy-up?'

Finally, after what felt like hours, it was over. Holly tentatively looked down. She was totally hairless but for what looked like a tiny exclamation mark of hair, as if her bikini area had been as shocked by the ordeal as she was.

She had wriggled back into her bottoms and was trying to find her way back to the studio when she rounded a corner and found herself a few feet from Max and Sasha, deep in conversation. Embarrassed at barging in on what looked like a private moment, she scooted back round the corner before they saw her, but Holly had seen enough to notice that their body language was surprisingly intimate. Curiosity getting the better of her, Holly paused for a moment to listen.

'It really is breathtaking,' Sasha was saying. 'I absolutely love it.'

'I remembered you saying that you liked emeralds.'

'Especially when they're alongside diamonds,' laughed Sasha. 'Seriously, Max, the bracelet is beautiful. And having it couriered over to my home in a vintage Ferrari was quite a gesture!'

'Well, I hope you'll think over my proposal,' said Max. 'I know you've got reservations, but we're a good team.'

'It's certainly very tempting,' said Sasha.

Holly listened with interest. She knew they used to date; perhaps Max was asking her out again – or maybe even to marry him? No, surely then he would have given her a ring . . .

'Holly! What are you doing here?'

To her horror, Sasha and Max had just appeared around the corner. Sasha was smiling, but Max looked pissed off – unsurprising, really, as he was bound to think she had been eavesdropping. Which, of course, she had been.

'Come on, I'll show you the way back to the studio,' said Sasha. But as they turned to leave, Max called them back.

'Actually, I think I need to have a quick word with Holly,' he said. 'There's an office along here we can use. Sash, I'll see you back in the studio.'

9

I'm in trouble now, thought Holly miserably, as Max ushered her into the little office, which was cluttered with photographic equipment and large rolls of paper. She felt like a minnow swimming up to a shark's jaws. On top of the fact that she was bound to get a bollocking, she had felt hugely intimidated by Max since he'd been so utterly dismissive of her in that first interview. At that moment, she would have preferred to have been anywhere else – even back on Evil Eva's waxing couch.

'Take a seat over there,' said Max, gesturing to a chair on the nearside of a desk, then taking a place opposite her. Thankfully, he looked a little less stern than he had a few moments ago and, for the first time Holly noticed how startlingly icy blue his eyes were against his tanned skin. Then, to her surprise, he broke into a smile.

'Buffy was very excited when she first saw you at that rugby match,' he said, leaning back in his chair. 'And when you came to Strut the other day, I could see why. I've been in the modelling business for over twenty-five years and have seen tens of thousands of girls come through our doors, but only a few of them have that special something. I think you could be one of them, Holly.'

Well, that she hadn't been expecting. 'Thank you,' she said in a tiny voice.

'Obviously, you'll have to work on your confidence, and, really, you walk like a bloody bricklayer, but with a bit of work I think you could be the real deal.' Max raked his hands through his hair, his diamond-studded watch catching the light. 'Look, I wanted to tell you that I'm sorry for giving you a hard time in your first interview. The executive producers keep telling me to ham it up and act more like the scary model-agency boss' – for emphasis, Max widened his eyes and made his hands into monster claws – 'so I was just trying to keep them happy and do my bit for the TV cameras. But while I don't know much about television, I'm an expert on modelling – and I've got a great feeling about you, Holly.' Max leaned back and flashed another smile at her. 'Anyway, how are you finding the experience? Pretty weird, I bet, if you're anything like me.'

Holly nodded. 'It's certainly a learning curve.'

'Where did you grow up?'

'Essex. Well, all over really – wherever my mum could get work, but we settled in Basildon when I was a teenager.'

'I've got family in Essex,' nodded Max. 'I was born in the East End, and we East Enders always move to Essex when we've made a bob or two.' He flashed that smile again. God, he must have been a real heartbreaker when he was younger. No wonder Sasha was thinking about getting back together with him.

As Max chatted away, asking about her life and family and seeming genuinely interested in her replies, Holly couldn't help contrasting his attentive behaviour with James, who had only sent her a brief, apologetic text since abandoning her two nights ago. There was something intriguing about Max. Despite his high public profile, he was clearly quite a mysterious character: when she searched his name on Google during some pre-filming research (so she knew a bit more about who she was dealing with), she had found references to 'the secretive billionaire' and 'famously private businessman', and quite how he'd made his immense fortune was not entirely clear. There was Strut, of course, which was a huge success and now had offices in all the major fashion cities of the world, but there was talk of property deals in Moscow, and Saudi business conglomerates, as well. Holly couldn't reconcile this shady-sounding character with the disarmingly charming man sitting in front of her now.

Max glanced at his watch. 'Right, we'd better get you back. And please, if you're thinking about doing a runner again' – Holly cringed; Sasha must have told him she had tried to jump ship on that first day – 'then please come and talk to me first. Okay?'

Holly settled herself on a high stool in front of a brightly lit mirror so the make-up artist and hair-stylist could work their magic before the shoot. This was the part of the day she had been looking forward to the most. Holly's own cosmetics bag contained a dried-up tube of mascara, lipgloss and a blusher that she applied with the doll-sized brush that came with the compact. Even if she had the money to spend on some decent make-up, she wouldn't have had a clue what to do with it, so she was hoping to pick up some tips.

With half an eye on Matteo the hairstylist, her thoughts were mainly occupied with Max. She assumed he must have taken all the girls to one side for a cosy chat, but she'd asked Kinzah and a couple of others, and none of the others had even seen him. It felt a bit weird to be singled out like that, and she was wondering why he had . . .

'Gorgeous hair, babe.' Matteo was swooshing his hands expertly through Holly's thick blonde locks, flipping them this way and that.

'So, what are you thinking, style-wise?' asked Sasha, who had just materialised at his side, a cam-eraman in tow.

'Well, Holly's got fab bone structure, but you can't

see it underneath all this hair. I think she could take quite a drastic cut to really show off her features.'

Sasha nodded approvingly. 'And the colour?'

'Mmmm . . . A bit lighter, I think. Maybe some slices of creamy vanilla and pale ash.'

But Holly wasn't listening: her brain had shut down at the words 'drastic cut'. Her hair had always been her pride and joy; it was one of the things James loved most about her. There was no way she wanted it cut – drastically or otherwise. Besides, she had lost quite enough hair already today.

'Couldn't I just have a trim?' she said, panic bubbling inside her. 'I've been growing my hair for years and would really like to keep it long. If that's okay with you,' she added hopefully.

'Yeah, but I see you with something a bit more gamine.' Matteo was still swooshing and flipping. 'Graduated at the back with razored bangs, yeah?'

Holly turned to Sasha in desperation. She had absolutely no idea what he was talking about.

'Holly, our job is to turn you into the best model you can be,' said Sasha gently. 'If that means losing a few inches off your hair, then you really have to trust us and go with it.'

Holly began to panic. 'I'm sorry, but I really don't want it cut. Please . . . ' *Oh God, she was going to cry again . . .*

As if sensing an impending scene, Rosario suddenly appeared. 'What's the problem?'

'Holly's feeling a bit unsure about getting her hair cut,' said Sasha.

Rosario turned to Holly with her hands on her hips, her dark eyes narrowed. 'Lady, you want to be a model?'

As there was a camera stuck in her face, Holly nodded meekly, although, right then, she wasn't sure she actually did.

'Okay then. Matteo – cut it off.'

As the tears started to fall, Sasha gave Holly's shoulder a comforting squeeze. 'It'll look fabulous, I promise.'

Spinning Holly's stool around so that she was no longer facing the mirror, Matteo gathered her hair into a ponytail and sliced through it – *snip-snip-snip* – then held it up with a flourish for the benefit of the camera. Holly thought about the hours spent on hot-oil treatments and highlights and almost howled. But it was too late to worry about it now and, as Matteo snipped away, Holly gave herself a stern talking-to. *You're being a complete wimp*, she said to herself. *It's only hair. It will grow back.*

When it was finished everyone gathered round Holly, oohing and aahing over her new style. Then Matteo spun her round to face the mirror.

'What do you think?' he said, with a smile.

Her hair was a far brighter blonde than before and was cut to just below her ears, with a long, choppy fringe that covered one eye. Holly looked at the strange girl in the mirror – and promptly burst into tears again.

After the Matteo massacre, posing for the photos was actually a doddle. She had no problem complying with Zane's request to 'Look fierce,' as she was still furious about what had been done to her hair – both on the top and bottom. And when one of Zane's assistants (he had three) beckoned her over to check out some of the shots on the laptop, even Holly had to admit that she looked quite good (apart from that silly bloody ruff around her neck). The make-up artist had done a fantastic job, using a palette of smoky greys on her eyes and soft peach gloss on her lips, and her hair actually looked pretty cool. 'Dude, you look dope,' said Zane, flicking through the images. For the first time, Holly started to believe that perhaps she *could* be a model. And, what's more, it had actually been quite fun.

When all twelve contestants had taken their turn in front of the camera, they were called back to the studio to find out who would be next to leave. Holly glanced around at the other girls' hair and couldn't see any other drastic changes. *How come I'm the only one who's been scalped?* a little voice inside her head began – but Holly instantly shut it up. *Come on, Collins*, she scolded herself. *Stop moaning and enjoy yourself*.

Max was standing at the front of the room between

Rosario and Bear, who took turns to give their assessment of each girl's performance.

'Kinzah, you looked absolutely stunning, congratulations on a terrific performance,' said Rosario, as a huge photo of Kinzah looking like an extremely sexy Sugarplum Fairy flashed up on the screen above their heads. Holly gave her a little thumbs up and she grinned in return.

'Moet, your pictures were amazing,' said Bear. Looking up at the shot of her crouched on all fours, her perfect beach-volleyball bum sticking up in the air, Holly had to agree. 'At times, though, you did look a bit like you were posing for *Playboy*. Remember, this is a fashion shoot, not soft porn.' Moet giggled and pouted.

'Tabitha,' smiled Rosario, turning to a rosy-cheeked brunette. 'Honey, this just wasn't your day, was it?' Tabitha was supposed to have been a sexy witch for October, but with her jolly grin and Mary Poppins air, she looked more like the school hockey captain, brandishing her broomstick like she was about to take a shot at goal. 'Zane did his best, but you really gotta raunch things up a bit.'

'I know!' chuckled Tabitha. 'Totes disaster!'

Next, a picture of Natalia dressed as the Easter bunny appeared over their heads. She was wearing white lingerie with little bunny ears, her long limbs glistening under the lights.

'What can I say?' Bear smiled. 'Natalia, you were

perfection. The best of the lot.' Holly noticed Max staring appreciatively at the photo; she really couldn't blame him. With Natalia's pale skin and white blonde hair, the effect was jaw-dropping.

Then it was Holly's turn. Rosario sighed dramatically. 'Holly, Holly, Holly,' she began. 'Your shoot was good. You looked a little stiff, but you know how to move. But, honey, I got serious concerns about your attitude. You're here to learn how to be a model – and we're here to teach you. That means you need to respect us and *listen to us*, okay?'

Holly nodded meekly. It could have been worse – at least she didn't mention the Wookie . . .

When they had given their comments on all the finalists, Max asked the bookers to choose which of their girls they would be putting in the Danger Zone. Before filming, Nigel had explained that the bookers would each pick the worst-performing girl on their team and then Max would have the final say on who would be booted off the show.

Bear went first. 'It's been a really difficult choice, because they've all been fabulous, but I'm afraid I'm going to pick Dot, just because she seemed a little self-conscious in front of the camera.'

Not for the first time, Holly wished she had Bear as her booker. He was so much nicer than Rosario.

'And Rosario?' asked Max.

She didn't even hesitate. 'Holly,' she said, firmly.

10

Okay, so it wasn't much of a surprise after Hairgate, but still, Holly was gutted. There was no way she wanted to go now: she had only started to relax and enjoy herself in the last hour or so and, besides, if she was sent home then her hair would have been butchered for nothing (although, secretly, she was actually starting to like the new style – and in the heat of the studio it *was* rather nice to feel cool air on her neck). The thought of going back to her VitaSlim cubbyhole now, after discovering that she might actually be able to make a go of modelling – she was still stunned by how good she looked in Zane's photos – was unappealing to say the least. And what was it Max had said to her in their quiet chat – that she had a 'special something'? Surely that would mean he'd want to keep her on the show? Although perhaps the producers had told him to say that to keep her sweet so she didn't try and quit again.

* * *

After Nigel had set up the shot to film the Big Decision, Max beckoned Holly and Dot out of the line to stand in front of the panel. He looked from one to the other with a frown of concentration creasing his brow – Holly could almost hear the heartstring-tugging music they were bound to be playing when the moment was aired on TV. Probably something by Adele or Coldplay.

'The girl who is going to leave us today is . . .' As Max drew out his decision for as long as possible, Holly closed her eyes and tried to steady her breathing. *Please don't let it be me . . . Please don't let it be me . . .*

'Dot,' he finally announced. 'I'm sorry, sweetheart, you're not right for Strut.'

She was still in! Holly was so relieved at getting another chance that as she gave Dot a consolatory hug, she vowed that from then on she would put everything into the show. Or, in reality TV speak, she would give '200 per cent'.

Street Scout was to air in the prime-time viewing slot of 8 p.m. on Saturday. The first episode was scheduled on TV the following weekend, and Meg had asked Holly and James round to watch it at her place. She and Spunk were currently house-sitting Meg's grandmother's sprawling three-storey townhouse in Kennington, as the sixty-seven-year-old had recently run off to southern Spain with a man from her flamenco class. Holly had met Nanna Aileen a couple of times, and could see where Meg got her red hair and love of a drink or dozen.

It was pouring with rain when Holly and James emerged from Kennington tube station that Saturday evening. Neither of them had an umbrella, but James insisted on holding his coat over Holly's head for the short dash to Meg's. *He is such a paradox*, thought Holly, as he pulled her out of the way to avoid a plume of spray sent up by the wheels of a lorry. On one hand so chivalrous and old-fashioned that he was like a Jane Austen hero, but on the other . . . She grinned at the extremely enjoyable memory of the past few hours, which they had spent together in bed and during which the most notably stiff thing about James had definitely *not* been his upper lip. And, in between orgasms, they had finally had a proper talk about *Street Scout*.

It was actually James who had brought the subject up: he had apologised profusely for being dismissive about her taking part in the show, but explained he was just concerned the producers would take advantage of her. 'The most important thing in my life is you,' he had said, propping himself up on his elbow. 'And if this is really what you want to do – and God knows you're more than beautiful enough to make it as a supermodel – then I will support you all the way.'

Holly had stared up at him, his dark hair all

tousled and a sexy fuzz of stubble on his chin, and the problems of the past few weeks were instantly forgiven. As James had bent down to kiss her, she had felt the sort of intense, soul-shaking happiness that only the knowledge that you are loved by the love of your life can bring.

With the rain still hammering down, they dashed up the steps to the shelter of Nanna Aileen's porch. James tapped briskly on the brass lion-shaped knocker.

No answer.

Holly looked at him, puzzled. 'Perhaps they didn't hear?'

He was about to try again when the door swung open and there was Meg.

'Oh, hiiiii! Bloody LOVE the hair, Hols!' Meg kissed them both, then ushered them into the hallway, the walls of which were lined with so many china knick-knacks you had to walk single-file. 'Spunk's just in the living room.'

Meg looked weirdly guilty and Holly was just wondering if perhaps they'd interrupted her and Spunk trying out the new 'sex dungeon' they'd set up in the little room where Nanna Aileen used to have her bridge nights, when she pushed open the living-room door and – 'SURPRISE!'

The place erupted in a carnival of streamers, champagne corks and cheers. To Holly's astonishment, the room was crammed with people: as she gazed around she took in Meg's bandmates, a few VitaSlim colleagues – even some of her friends from Essex.

She turned to James in a daze. 'Did you know about this?'

'Might have,' he smiled. 'Meg and I thought it would be fun to get a few people together to witness your TV triumph.'

Or my TV humiliation, thought Holly, but James obviously read her mind. 'You'll be brilliant,' he whispered.

By the time *Street Scout* started, Holly had drunk enough to ease the embarrassment of watching herself in front of such a huge crowd of people. When they got to the moment when Holly was scouted at the rugby match, everyone hooted with laughter.

'James, will you look at the expression on your face!' screeched Meg. 'That's fucking classic!'

'Christ, I do look furious,' he chuckled.

Then the action switched to show the lingering close-up on Holly's stunned face, and James turned to her on the sofa with a look of awe.

'You really are so beautiful,' he said, softly.

'The camera loves you, babe!' said Meg. And everyone cheered again.

It was a brilliant night. They ate takeaway Chinese food, drank cheap fizzy wine and Holly caught up with old friends and made new ones. James was at his sparkling best, charming everyone, including Spunk, who ended up inviting him to a Black Sabbath gig. And, at 3 a.m., James carried her up to bed in his Kensington flat – but only after they'd had drunken, giggly sex on the sofa, which ended when they fell on the floor in hysterics.

'Will you marry me?' muttered Holly, delirious with exhaustion and happiness, as James tucked her in. Then she promptly fell asleep, so speedily that she wasn't sure whether or not she had really heard James whisper, 'I would love nothing more . . .'

11

As the weeks went by on *Street Scout*, Holly's confidence grew. It was like something inside her had just clicked into place. She had always been quite an anxious person – probably because of the unsettled nature of her upbringing – but now she felt . . . well, brave. Since surviving the Great Scalping, she had started to believe she could achieve anything; Samson might have lost his strength after getting his hair cut, but Holly seemed to have discovered hers.

And it wasn't just her attitude that was slowly being transformed. She picked up make-up tips (and free make-up), and fashion advice from the experts on the show, swapping her floaty dresses and clumpy boots for a sleeker look of cropped tops, rolled-up jeans and heels. If Max had asked about her favourite designer now she could have reeled off dozens of names, from A to Z – or rather from Acne to Zac Posen.

Five weeks had passed since that nerve-jangling moment when she had gone head to head with Dot, but Holly had never been in the Danger Zone again. They were now down to six girls and the buzz about the show in the press was such that the publicist, a hard-nosed, hard-faced blonde named Sara, decreed that the finalists should do their first press interview. And so, during a day off from filming, they were all called into Strut to speak to a journalist from *Hot* magazine, the biggest-selling celebrity weekly.

Sara ushered them into the meeting room for a briefing before the interview.

'Right, ladies, this is just going to be a simple round-the-table Q&A,' she said. 'I'll be sitting in on the interview to check things don't get too personal and we've got copy approval so it should be very straightforward, but if you don't feel happy answering anything, just pass. Any questions?'

Moet stuck her hand up. 'Are we having photos taken?'

'No, they'll use your publicity shots and stills from the show,' said Sara.

Moet, who had clearly dressed up for the occasion in a bra top and hot-pants, scowled, much to the amusement of Natalia. She disliked Moet even more than Holly did.

'Who's doing the interview?' This came from L'Wren, an incredibly statuesque black girl with an afro.

'The magazine's entertainment editor, Joe Taylor,' said Sara. 'Nice bloke and about as trustworthy as journalists get but, still, now is not the time to be airing your dirty laundry, okay?'

Joe Taylor turned out to be tall, young – probably in his mid-twenties – and surprisingly handsome. 'So it's not just the magazine that's Hot,' whispered Chanel, a dancer with a mane of wild curls who was sitting next to Holly. With his messed-up brown hair and easy grin, he had the cheeky-chappy good looks of Robbie Williams in his prime, although it was clear from his clothes (shabby jeans and a check shirt) that he didn't really give a monkey's about his appearance. Holly had the weirdest feeling that she'd met him before, but she couldn't for the life of her think where or when.

'Great to meet you all,' said Joe, after Sara had made the introductions. 'We're all huge fans of the show on *Hot*.'

His seat was next to Holly's and as he set up his Dictaphone and notepad, he smiled at her, almost shyly, and muttered something corny like, 'I must be the most envied man in Britain right now,' but the way he said it was actually very sweet. Holly noted he was wearing a wedding ring and was surprised to feel a tiny flicker of disappointment. *Blimey, get a grip, Collins!*

As Sara had said, the interview was straightforward. Joe asked each of the girls a few silly questions, such as 'What's been the most embarrassing moment of your life?' and 'What's the worst lie you've ever told?' But when it was Holly's turn, he blurted out,

'Have you got a boyfriend?' at which Sara immediately stepped in.

'Too personal,' she snapped. 'Ask something else.'

Joe thought for a moment. 'When were you last naked in front of someone?'

'When I was getting changed in front of this lot,' laughed Holly, and was delighted to see Sara give her an approving nod.

That evening, Holly was checking her Twitter account – set up for her by the *Street Scout* team – and found a Tweet from Joe from earlier that afternoon: 'Just been to meet the *Street Scout* finalists. @HollyStreetScout: WOW. #*majorbabe*'.

The magazine article came out the following Tuesday and, after fielding an overexcited phone call from her mum, who had clearly been down to the newsagent to get a copy as soon as it opened, Holly rang James at work.

'So, have you seen it?'

'Yes, I have.' He sounded uptight, but then he always did at work. 'Hold on a moment, I'm just going to shut my office door.'

Holly waited patiently, excited to hear his opinion. Personally, she was thrilled with how well the article had come out – she hadn't said anything too stupid, and they'd used a very flattering photo of her inside that had also run as a small drop-in on the cover.

'Okay, I'm here,' said James. 'And to be honest,

Holly, I'm really quite angry about this article. I know it's not your fault, but how do you think I feel reading about some bloody journalist drooling over my girlfriend's "cracking figure" and "sexy smile"? And what's all this "Good girl gone bad" crap?'

God, James must be angry. He never swore.

'Oh, you know, since I had my haircut they've wanted to make me out to be this sweet little thing who's discovered her wild side . . .'

'But that's the whole reason I was concerned about you going on this damn show! That they'd manipulate you into some cartoon character.'

'Oh, come on, James; it's just a bit of fun.'

'It might be to you, but I'm now getting stick from my colleagues about my glamour-model girlfriend.'

She started laughing.

'This isn't a game, Holly. It's my career. I'd hate to think what my parents would say if they saw this.'

'Hopefully they'd be proud that I was doing well – as I thought you would be. Whatever happened to wanting to support me?'

James sighed heavily. 'I've got to go. Back in the real world, some of us have jobs to do. We'll talk about this later.'

'There's nothing to talk about. You clearly think I'm a slut.'

'Holly, I—'

'Forget it.' She angrily jabbed at the button to end the call.

12

Holly glared at her phone with a mixture of anger and sadness. She half hoped that James would ring back, as their rare arguments always made her feel horrible, but an hour later the only calls she'd had were from Lola, asking Holly if she could get her Liam from One Direction's autograph, and then one from Sara in the press office confirming her pick-up time for later that afternoon. Along with the other finalists, that night Holly had been invited to the world premiere of a new action-movie blockbuster, *Beyond Hope*. For days she had been looking forward to walking the red carpet and mingling with the celebrity guests, so as she got in the shower – leaving herself a good hour to have a bash at doing a 'smoky eye' – she decided to put the row with James aside so it didn't spoil what was set to be an incredible evening.

The show's stylists had biked over an outfit and accessories for her red-carpet debut and, as Holly unwrapped the tissue-lined boxes, she felt as giddy as a six-year-old on Christmas morning – except with *way* better presents. The first box contained a leopard-skin clutch bag and a jewelled cuff, while in the next was a pair of neon pink strappy sandals with the sort of heel that left twisted ankles and shattered egos in its five-inch wake. *Thank God for the catwalk lessons*, thought Holly, as she managed to make it across the room in them without falling over or looking like a 'bloody baby giraffe' (thanks, Rosario). After a few minutes' practice she was even managing to cross one foot in front of the other so as to get that sexy supermodel hip sway. Then Holly opened the final box and gasped as the light hit the mass of silvery glitter inside, sending flecks of light dancing around the walls of her bedroom. It turned out to be a skater-style mini dress completely covered in sequins: a real showstopper of a frock that screamed, 'Look at me, everyone! LOOK!' and only a month ago would have been the sort of thing Holly would have steered well clear of (along with neon pink sandals and 'fierce' accessories). But now, with her new hair – and new attitude – Holly felt she had found fashion nirvana.

As the stretch limo pulled up at Leicester Square, Holly saw the huge crowds gathered behind barriers outside the cinema and her excitement lurched towards nausea. She'd had no idea there would be so many people there! As if reading her mind, Sara, who had travelled in the ridiculously fancy car (it had a bar! a TV!) with the girls and their bookers, gave them a quick pep talk.

'Now ladies, you're going to follow me along the carpet to the photographers' pen, pose arm-in-arm for a few quick photos, and then we'll head straight into the cinema. As it's your first event we'll keep it easy, so no interviews or autographs today, okay?'

'And don't forget, my angels,' said Bear, who tonight was rocking a pair of gold lurex harem pants, 'SMILE!'

'And for Christ's sake don't trip up,' muttered Rosario, glancing at Holly.

As the girls climbed out of the car one at a time, trying to twist their bodies as Bear had advised so as not to flash their knickers at the waiting paps, they were greeted by a storm of cheers, screams and camera-phone flashes. Her face set in its usual shit-kicking grimace, Sara herded them straight towards the bank of official photographers. As they lined up together for photos, the paps yelled, 'Turn this way, Natalia!' or 'Holly, over here, love!' Struggling to remember to smile and pose correctly while not falling over, Holly found the whole experience terrifying yet utterly exhilarating, like a particularly hair-raising roller-coaster ride. She had been recognised in public before – well, sort of. There had been flickers of recognition at the supermarket checkout and a few double-takes on the tube, although no one had actually approached her. And even if they had,

94

nothing would have prepared her for this craziness, with people screaming her name as if she was actually famous.

As a couple of *TOWIE* girls took their positions in front of the photographers – managing to out-pout even Moet – Sara hurried them past the press pen without stopping.

'No interviews today, guys, sorry,' she snapped to the waiting journalists, sounding anything but. Amongst the mass of outstretched microphones and Dictaphones, Holly noticed Joe Taylor and, when she caught his eye, he smiled and shouted something to her, but his voice was lost in the chaos and Rosario was hot on her heels, so she couldn't stop.

Once in the calm of the foyer, the girls began milling about – trying to buy bags of Revels without Rosario noticing – when Max walked in with Sasha on his arm. They looked incredibly good together: Max in a dark grey, slim-fitting suit with a deep tan, clearly a souvenir from a week on his yacht in Cap d'Antibes (Holly had seen the photos on the *Daily Mail*'s website), and Sasha in a green satin sheath dress that clung to every curve, with her hair in Jessica Rabbit waves and a dazzling bracelet on her wrist. *It's* that *bracelet*, thought Holly, marvelling at the M&M-sized diamonds and emeralds. Even though the *Daily Mail* had reported that Max had been joined by a newly single French actress on his yacht, Holly was now convinced he must be back with Sasha. Surely even gazillionaires don't spend thousands on jewellery for their 'good friends' . . . ?

As they were shown into the auditorium, Holly checked her phone. Still nothing from James. Stifling a pang of disappointment, she turned it off.

The film was something to do with gangsters and corrupt cops in New York, and starred a host of unfeasibly hot young actors, including the latest Brit to make it big in America: Cole Fox. But the plot was flimsier than the lead actress's costume and by half-way through, both had been dispensed with as the movie descended into a confusing mash-up of car chases, gunfights and lap dances – Holly and Kinzah ended up occupying themselves playing 'Dodge the coffee cream' with the smuggled Revels.

After the film had finished, guests were escorted out of the cinema and round the corner to a night-club for the after-party. It had been transformed into the New York dive bar featured in the movie, with waitresses in bikinis and stripper-shoes doling out hot dogs and mini bottles of Cristal. It was loud and crowded and far less glamorous than Holly had imagined; in fact, the only celebrities she spotted were Kerry Katona, some of the *Hollyoaks* cast and a thickset guy in a baseball cap and lots of gold jewellery who might possibly have been someone famous, although it was difficult to tell as Moet currently had her tongue rammed down his throat.

After fighting their way through the D-list celebrity version of a rugby scrum to get some drinks, Holly, Kinzah and Chanel pushed through the crowds to find a quiet corner.

'So, what did you think of the movie?' asked Chanel, pulling a face that suggested a one-star review.

'Terrible,' said Kinzah. 'Full of mindless violence and soulless sex.'

Holly laughed. 'It was pretty crap, wasn't it? But then I guess it's made for teenage boys.'

'Well, I'm very sorry to hear you think that,' said a voice right behind her. 'Because we also made it for beautiful blondes.'

As Kinzah's eyes widened in stunned surprise and Chanel froze in shock, Holly spun round to find herself face to face with Cole Fox.

13

The Cole Fox. Not the life-sized cardboard Cole Fox that they had joked about trying to smuggle out of the cinema foyer earlier. As she looked up at the actor's famous features (he was a few inches taller than her – even in the ridiculous heels), a line from a recent newspaper interview with the actor flashed through Holly's mind: 'There's good-looking – and then there's Cole Fox.' It wasn't an exaggeration. Up close, every bit of him was quite spectacular, but it was those lips that really stole the show. As lush as Angelina Jolie's, yet set against his Action-Man jaw the effect was shockingly sexy.

'Hi. I'm Cole.' *As if they didn't know.*

'I'm Holly,' she managed, after a moment's gawping. 'And this is Kinzah and Chanel.'

'You know, the film wasn't all bad,' stammered Kinzah. 'You were fantastic in it.'

'You were!' agreed Holly. 'And you really nailed that American accent.'

'Totally!' said Chanel.

Cole smiled at them. 'I was meant to be South African.'

Holly cringed. 'Of course you were!' *Bugger*. 'That's what I meant to say! African, American – so easy to mix up!'

But Cole just laughed. 'It's okay. I know the movie's not going to win me any Oscars. But, you know, they made my agent an offer he couldn't refuse. Besides, it means I get to go in the VIP room – if you girls fancy joining me?'

Moments later, they found out where the *real* stars had been hiding. With its soft lighting, vases of orchids and the sexy throb of R&B in the background, it made the main party look about as classy as a hen night in Benidorm. Trying not to stare, Holly scanned the room and immediately clocked Samuel L. Jackson, Channing Tatum, Nicki Minaj *and* an actual real-life Kardashian.

'Come and meet my buddies,' said Cole, leading them to a table where a couple of blokes were swigging from bottles of beer. 'Hey guys – told you I'd find out where the fit girls were hiding! Nick, Harley, this is Chanel, Kinzah and Holly.'

As Holly sat down next to the guy called Harley, Cole ordered champagne, vodka and French fries from a hovering waiter.

'Come on, Harley, budge up,' said Cole. He squeezed onto the banquette next to Holly, then turned to her with his dazzling movie-star grin. 'You ready to have fun, gorgeous?'

Three hours later, they were still there. The girls had to be up for a day of filming next morning, but Cole and his mates (who both worked in movie production) were so entertaining, regaling them with tales of their bonkers Hollywood lifestyle and eyebrow-raising gossip about other stars, that they forgot all about their early start.

It was well past midnight when Holly excused herself to go to the bathroom. She'd had countless vodka and champagne cocktails, but she didn't feel woozy or drunk, she felt euphoric – like she was having more fun than anyone anywhere else in the world. And although Cole was attentive and charming to all three of the girls, asking all about *Street Scout* and their future plans, he had seemed to be paying particular attention to her. It was immensely flattering.

Holly was just coming out of the disabled loo (in her booze-befuddled state she'd taken a wrong turn out of the VIP room and couldn't locate the main toilets) when she heard the muffled sounds of a couple arguing further down the warren of darkened corridors. When she glanced in the direction of the sound she couldn't see anything, so she started back towards the VIP room, but then she heard the tone of the girl's voice turn from anger to fear. Her heart beating a little faster, Holly retraced a few steps so she could hear what was going on, and as she got nearer she heard the sounds of a scuffle, a man's voice muttering 'Bitch,' and then a terrified shriek: 'Get off me! Let me go!'

To her horror, Holly realised she recognised the girl's voice. It was Moet.

14

No one else was around, so Holly dashed down the corridor and rounded the corner, to find the heavyset guy Moet had been snogging earlier holding her arms over her head against the wall with one hand, and trying to get her skirt off with the other, while she wildly flailed her legs trying to kick him.

'What the hell are you doing?' shrieked Holly.

The bloke didn't even look round. 'Fuck off,' he said, panting heavily.

Moet was staring at Holly, her eyes wide with fear. *Please don't leave me*, she mouthed.

'If you don't get away from her, I'll . . .' Holly didn't have any idea how she was going to finish the sentence.

'You'll what?' The bloke turned to look at her, a sadistic smile creeping over his meaty face. 'Listen, babe, you're welcome to wait your turn,' he chuckled, getting back to pawing the terrified Moet.

Holly was really starting to panic now; her heart

was pounding in her chest. 'I said leave her alone!' she yelled as loudly as she could.

The bloke swung round again. 'If you don't shut up, you stupid little bitch, I'm gonna . . .'

But just at that moment he must have released his grip on Moet a little: she managed to wriggle out of his clutches and kicked as hard as she could, right between his legs. It was such an impressive move that even in the midst of her terror, Holly fleetingly wondered if Moet was trained in kung fu.

The bloke collapsed to the floor with a howl of agony, clutching at his groin, leaving Moet and Holly to make their escape through the maze of corridors. Dragging Moet by the hand, Holly found their way to the main body of the club, where she alerted a couple of bouncers who were even beefier than Moet's assailant and clearly very up for a fight.

As they thundered off in hot pursuit, Holly guided Moet to a bar stool and got her some water. Moet's hand was shaking as she reached for the glass.

'Are you okay?' Holly asked, gently. 'Sorry, stupid question.'

Moet managed a smile. 'I'm alright,' she said, putting the glass back on the bar. 'Although the wanker tore my favourite Alaïa skirt.'

Then, to Holly's surprise, Moet suddenly flung her arms around her.

'Thank you so, so much,' she sobbed, her face buried in Holly's shoulder. 'You were amazing. I don't know what I'd have done if you hadn't come along . . . I . . . I'm so sorry I've been such a bitch to you, Holly . . .'

They hugged for a few moments and when Moet had calmed down, Holly took her upstairs to the street and helped her into a taxi, lending her the fare home as she'd lost her bag in the scuffle. As the taxi pulled away, Moet blew a kiss and mouthed a heart-felt *thank you*.

At least one good thing's come out of tonight's ordeal, thought Holly happily, relieved that they'd finally buried the hatchet. As she turned to go back into the club, she heard someone whistle and to her surprise saw Cole leaning against the wall, his arms folded, as if he'd been waiting for her.

'I thought you'd run off without saying goodbye,' he said. 'But I'm very glad to see you haven't.'

'Sorry, a friend of mine got in a bit of trouble,' said Holly, gesturing in the direction of the disap-pearing taxi. 'I was just making sure she got home okay.'

'You're a lovely girl, Holly,' he said. Then added softly: 'Come here, I want to ask you something.'

Holly walked over, her stomach suddenly alive with butterflies.

'So I was wondering,' he said, reaching for her hand and pulling her towards him, 'can I get your phone number? I'd love to see you again. On your own next time, if possible.'

Holly stared into his long-lashed eyes. They were standing so close she could feel the warmth of his breath. She knew exactly what she should have said to him. The correct answer would obviously have been: 'Thanks so much, Cole, that would have been lovely, but I've already got a boyfriend.' She could even hear herself saying it in her head. But perhaps it was because she had drunk an awful lot of vodka, or maybe it was because the man *Cosmopolitan* had dubbed 'Britain's answer to Brad Pitt' had just asked her on a date, that the correct answer stubbornly refused to come out and Holly found herself giving him her phone number instead.

'Thank you,' said Cole, as he put it in his iPhone. 'I'll definitely be in touch.' He paused, then added softly, 'I'm really looking forward to getting to know you better, Holly.'

And then he looked at her in such a way that she had no doubt what was going to happen next and, as he started to lean towards her, his gorgeous movie-star face moving slowly towards hers, she found herself shutting her eyes and waiting for the kiss that in that crazy, surreal moment, she wanted more desperately than almost anything in the world . . .

15

What the hell was she doing? In an instant, the spell was broken. Cole's famous lips had barely brushed hers when Holly pulled away. This was so wrong.

'Okay, well, great to meet you,' she gabbled. 'Bye.'

Without looking back, she started walking away from him, as quickly as the five-inch spikes would allow. She should have told Kinzah and Chanel she was leaving, but she was desperate to get away from Cole before she did something terrible. By some miracle, a black cab with its light on suddenly appeared and she virtually threw herself into the street in an attempt to flag it down. Thankfully, it pulled over.

Perhaps it was the sudden shock of the fresh air, but as she flopped into the back seat she suddenly felt very drunk. As the taxi pulled away, Holly switched on her phone to distract her from the dizzying waves of nausea that were threatening to wash over her. She had a new text from a number she didn't recognise.

'Did my breath smell? Hope we can get together soon. Cole.'

Holly stared at the message, wracked with guilt but at the same time feeling a little flicker of pleasure . . . *Christ, what was wrong with her?* She immediately pressed delete. It was only then that she noticed she had a voicemail, left around eight that evening.

'Holly, darling, it's James. I just wanted to tell you how deeply sorry I am about our argument earlier. I would have called you straight back, but I had to go into a meeting with Lady Crosby and her team and it's only just wrapped up now. I know that what I said to you was completely and unforgivably out of order and I've got no excuse – except for being a stupid, jealous oaf. It was just so obvious from that article that the journalist fancied you . . . But then who can blame him . . . ? Look, I know you're out with the girls tonight but if it's okay with you I'm going to go to your flat now, let myself in with the spare key and wait for you there. I just need to hold you and tell you how sorry I am in person. I love you, Holly. See you soon.'

Listening to the message, Holly felt as bad as if she had actually cheated on James – which, of course, she hadn't. Unless lustful thoughts counted as cheating, in which case she was going straight to hell. Holly held her head in her hands. *Stupid, stupid girl . . .* How could she have risked losing her perfect boyfriend for a quick snog with some movie himbo?

She checked the time: 1.40 a.m. James was bound to be asleep by the time she got home and she would hopefully be able to slip into bed without waking him up, as she was in no fit state for a heart-to-heart. Not only did she need to get some sleep before her early start, but all that booze had finally caught up with her, making her head spin and stomach lurch every time the taxi swerved round a corner (who the hell was driving this cab? Jenson bloody Button?). And she was feeling so guilty about the non-snog with Cole she wouldn't be surprised if James could tell by looking at her as easily as if she'd had 'I AM A HO' tattooed across her forehead.

Twenty minutes later, Holly crept up the stairs to her flat, turned the key in the lock a millimetre at a time, then shut it so softly that the latch barely clicked. She paused to listen, but all was quiet. She tiptoed through the living room, wriggling out of her clothes as she went, then downed a pint of water and two paracetamol, gave her teeth a quick brush (her make-up would have to stay on) and opened the bedroom door ever so gently . . . to find James sitting up in bed surrounded by official-looking papers.

'You're awake,' said Holly in surprise, steadying herself against the door frame to prevent any drunken swaying.

'Just catching up on some work.' He shuffled the documents into a pile and patted the space next to him. 'How was the movie?'

'Oh, pretty rubbish.'

She flopped into bed beside James, who dumped the papers on the floor and then lay down so he was facing her.

'Listen, Hols, I am so, so sorry about earlier.' He stroked her hair off her face. 'I was an idiot.'

'Shhh, it's okay. *Really*. This must be pretty weird for you, too.'

'It is, but what I said to you was unforgivable. Deep down I suppose I worry you'll get famous and run off with some celebrity.' He snorted. 'Ridiculous, I know . . .'

'Ridiculous,' agreed Holly in a small voice, nuzzling her face into his chest so James couldn't see her expression.

'Holly, I'm so proud of you, and I promise that from now on I'll be there for you all the way . . .'

She pulled back to look at him. 'Why do I feel like there's a "but" coming?'

James took a deep breath. 'Darling, you know I work for a very conservative firm that relies on its reputation for utmost discretion to attract an extremely powerful, private clientele. I'm one of the youngest there and I still have an awful lot to prove so please, just don't let yourself be talked into doing anything too . . . shocking, or embarrassing? I'm sure you appreciate that it wouldn't go down at all well to have the girlfriend of one of the firm's junior associates splashed over the tabloids! I desperately want you to do well, Holly, but I need to think of my future career as well – for both our sakes. I hope that makes sense?'

'Of course it does,' said Holly, snuggling closer to him again. He smelt so wonderfully familiar – a mix of spicy aftershave and the musky warmth of his skin – that even the thought of losing him made her feel like crying. 'And I promise to be careful.'

At nine the next morning, feeling knackered and hung-over, Holly arrived at Strut. Today they had a session with another special-guest mentor in preparation for the weekly challenge although, as usual, the details of both had been kept under wraps to retain the element of surprise. Holly's favourite session so far had been their day with the TV presenter Britt Baxter, herself a former model, who had coached them how to speak and move on camera. Holly had imagined she'd be quite intimidating, but she was actually very sweet and humble and had even handed out her personal mobile number in case they needed any help in the future.

The contestants had been told to assemble in the main meeting room, but first they were expected to check in with their bookers. It was meant to be an opportunity to air concerns and receive guidance and encouragement, but Rosario usually used their weekly get-togethers to berate Holly over a) her 'hoooge' thighs and b) her non-attendance at

Zumba. The other week, unable to face another bollocking, Holly had lied and said that she had gone to a class, but it ended badly when Rosario promptly told her to demonstrate the 'body ripple' and 'booty shake'.

Anxious to avoid such an ordeal today – and keen to see if Moet was okay – Holly crept around the edge of the open-plan office and kept her head down, but she had barely made it halfway when Rosario nabbed her. Honest to God, the woman was like a tiny Brazilian Usain Bolt . . .

'*Ay, ay, ay* . . .' Rosario clicked her tongue disapprovingly as Holly stood on the scales. 'You still not losing any weight, honey. You eating a healthy diet?'

Holly thought back to last night's dinner of Revels, chips and cocktails, and the bacon sandwich she'd grabbed from the café near her flat for breakfast. 'Pretty much,' she said.

'Eat less then,' said Rosario. She peered at her face suspiciously. 'You look like shit. Late night?'

Holly nodded miserably.

'Well, get a facial when we've finished filming. It's challenge day tomorrow and I'm not losing another of my girls 'cos she got bags under her eyes the size of bloody Birkins.'

After Rosario had finished with her, Holly made her way up to the meeting room where she found the rest of the girls, including Moet, who was slumped in the corner with a black coffee.

'How are you doing?' Holly whispered. She wasn't sure Moet would want the details of what happened last night broadcast to the other girls.

'I'm fine – honestly.' Moet grinned at her. 'I owe you big time for this, Collins. Seriously, babe, from now on I got your back.'

Holly returned her smile. At one time she wouldn't have believed it possible, but it looked like she and Moet were going to be friends.

Holly was getting a coffee from the machine in the corner of the room when Kinzah skulked in. She was wearing dark glasses and clearly felt as terrible as Holly did.

'What happened to you last night?'

'Oh, you know . . . I went out to get some air then I saw a taxi and thought I should get home. Sorry for not saying goodbye.'

Kinzah looked around to check no one was listening, then asked: 'So – what happened with Cole?'

'What! Nothing!' Kinzah gave her a knowing look. 'Really nothing,' said Holly firmly. 'I love my boyfriend, okay?'

Thankfully at that moment Nadja, the assistant producer, bustled into the room and clapped her hands for attention.

'Okay, listen up, ladies. As you know, today you have your next mentoring session. There's a coach waiting outside to take you to the Raghorn Dance Studio where you'll have a movement workshop with

Martha Raghorn, the legendary contemporary-dance pioneer.'

'Is that like hip hop or sumfink?' Moet piped up.

'Don't be daft,' scoffed Chanel. 'Martha Raghorn is the queen of interpretative dance. We studied the Raghorn Technique at dance college.' She turned to Holly. 'She's rumoured to be a bit *out there*,' she whispered, twirling her finger at the side of her head in the international sign for 'loopy'.

16

The Raghorn Dance Studio was housed in an austere Victorian building in Chiswick, and looked like it had once been a lunatic asylum. In fact, when Holly peeped into one of the rooms to see a group of men in white unitards writhing around on the floor, it seemed possible that it still was. The girls were shown into a large, mirror-lined studio, where the camera crew was already waiting, along with a tiny old lady in a black turban and bright red lipstick, who was swathed in layers of black chiffon and leaning on a stick.

'Good morning, class,' said the woman, in a raspy American voice. 'My name is Martha Raghorn, but you may call me Madame. Today I will introduce you to the basics of the Raghorn Technique, although it would take you a lifetime to master it. I am eighty-four and still have much to learn.'

'It's going to be a long day,' muttered Natalia.

'No talking!' Martha rapped her stick on the floor.

'Our first exercise seeks to translate emotion into movement. I will demonstrate.'

She shut her eyes and took a deep breath, her arms rising and falling in front of her. 'I am finding my centre . . .' She took another deep breath, then suddenly her eyes snapped open. 'I am . . . ANGER!'

Martha leapt around the room in a tiny black blur, swooshing her arms and scissoring her legs as if she was possessed. Holly would never have believed an octogenarian could be quite so bendy. When she had finished, Martha walked along the line of girls and pointed her stick at Moet.

'You – come to the front and try this exercise.'

Moet shuffled sulkily out of the row to join Martha.

'Now, find your centre, feel the muse, then announce to the class what emotion you will be.'

Copying what Martha had done, Moet shut her eyes and took a deep breath. 'I am BOREDOM,' she smirked, folding her arms and slouching on the spot. She had clearly got her bite back.

Martha regarded her coolly. 'Self-consciousness is the enemy of creativity, young lady.'

'Come again?' muttered Moet, winking at Holly.

It *was* a long day. Martha had little patience with her new pupils and the girls struggled to 'feel the muse' without giggling. Apart from Chanel, the only one who seemed to get into it was Charlie, a dreamy, hippyish brunette who never wore make-up, had legs like a thoroughbred racehorse and liked to chant during breaks in filming.

'Be a tree!' barked Martha. 'Now see, I am the goddess of the wind!' She ran between them, waving her arms, trailing chiffon scarves in her wake. 'Wave your branches in worship!'

Holly noticed Charlie swirling around as if in a trance, her eyes closed and a beatific smile on her face.

'Excellent!' Martha paused to watch. 'You are a tender sapling, bending and bowing to the wind! Wonderful, wonderful!'

Holly cringed. It would be bad enough if this was happening in private, but this was going out on prime-time TV. Suddenly Martha appeared in front of her. Her little bird-like face barely reached up to Holly's boobs.

'What kind of tree are you?'

'Um . . . an oak?' said Holly.

'Then stand strong!' Martha smacked her stick against Holly's legs. 'The oak is noble and mighty!'

Then she passed Natalia, who was slumped in the corner checking her iPhone.

'And what are you?' barked Martha.

'A pile of logs,' she smirked.

The day was a disaster.

At the end of the session Sasha appeared to film her piece to camera. She looked her usual immaculately groomed self, while the rest of them were flushed and sweaty.

'Today's session was designed to help get you comfortable and confident with your bodies, ready for the next challenge,' she smiled. 'Hopefully Martha has helped you shed any inhibitions, as tomorrow you will be modelling a selection of designer lingerie in what will be your hottest shoot yet.'

There was a ripple of excitement amongst the girls, but Holly's heart plummeted. After their chat last night, she didn't think James would be particularly happy about her stripping down to her smalls on camera.

'If you've ever seen the shoot that Posh and Becks did for Armani lingerie, you'll know the sort of thing we're looking for,' continued Sasha. 'Classy, but full of raw, sexual emotion.' Sasha paused and gave the girls a knowing smile. 'So I guess you ladies are going to be needing your own personal Becks . . .'

The door opened and the men Holly had seen in the other dance studio earlier filed into the room. They were still in their unitards, the better to show off their perfectly sculpted bodies. *This was bad. Very, very bad.* Holly was pretty sure that James would think simulating sex with a hot-bodied bloke on national TV fell within the embarrassing/shocking category.

'Oh, and I should probably mention just one more thing,' added Sasha. 'The boys are going to be naked.'

Holly shut her eyes and dropped her head. She was totally screwed.

17

As tired as she was, Holly struggled to sleep that night as thoughts whirled around her head like Martha Raghorn's chiffon scarves. It seemed she had a simple choice: refuse to do the steamy, naked-bloke shoot and risk getting ditched from *Street Scout,* or do it and risk getting ditched by James. Put like that, the decision was a simple one: there was no way some TV show was more important than her relationship. But was it really that clear-cut? Perhaps she was just being overcautious and James wouldn't mind at all, in which case she should definitely do the shoot, as Holly was beginning to feel she had a genuine shot at a modelling career. Maybe she should just phone James and ask him what he thought. Holly opened her eyes to look at the clock. 3.27 a.m. *Hmmm, maybe not . . .* Besides, if she *did* ask, and James was horrified by the idea, she would have no choice but to quit the show – and why should she jeopardise her future for the sake of his?

After a sleepless night, Holly was even blearier-eyed

than the previous morning as she emerged from the tube at Old Street and walked through the hipster boutiques and cafés of Shoreditch to the studios where the day's shoot was taking place. She was just waiting for a flat white at a café in which every bloke seemed to have a moustache and skinny jeans when she heard the muffled beep of her phone. Two text messages. The first was from James. 'Looking forward to dinner tonight. Love you x'.

Holly still hadn't decided what to do about the shoot, and his sweet message didn't make things any easier. Hopefully all would become clear when she got to the studio. She checked the second text. 'Hi Holly. I'm off to LA at the weekend – dinner before I go? Cole'.

She felt horribly guilty, but at the same time – and this made her feel even guiltier – she felt flattered. *Cole Fox wanted to take her for dinner.* The thought produced a little flutter of shamefaced excitement, even though she would never in a million years go through with it. Holly's finger hovered over the delete button . . . but didn't press it. She put her phone back in her bag and vowed to deal with it later.

The studio was full of people when she arrived: the production team, make-up artists, stylists and, of course, the male dancers (currently fully clothed, to her relief). Nigel was deep in conversation with Sasha, who was getting her make-up touched up and drinking one of the murky green smoothies she favoured instead of coffee. In the centre of the studio, the photographer's assistants were setting up lights around a black leather couch. Holly recognised them as part of Zane's team and felt a little more relaxed. If she did decide to go through with the photos, she wouldn't feel quite so embarrassed stripping off in front of Zane. It was a case of 'better the devil you know' (especially as she was pretty sure the devil was gay). But then Holly spotted the rails of lingerie and her nerves kicked up a gear. The stuff was clearly hugely expensive but seriously kinky: all straps, lacing and cutout panels, like S&M gear designed by Prada. Hopefully she would be one of the last to be photographed, so she would have a bit of time to decide what to do . . .

'Holly, over here!' Nadja called her over. 'You need to go into make-up right now, you're second on the schedule today.'

Damn. 'Can I please just make a quick phone call?' asked Holly.

Nadja pulled a face. 'Five minutes.'

Holly slipped out of the studio's fire exit and found herself in a stairwell. Climbing up a few steps to get some privacy, she dialled a number.

Come on, come on, pick up . . .

'Why, if it isn't Miss Collins! How are you, darlin'?'

'Meg!' *Thank God.* 'Have you got a minute? I need some advice.'

'Yeah, I'm just on my break. What's up?'

As Holly talked Meg through her dilemma, she heard someone opening the door behind her and glanced round, but they had already disappeared out of sight.

'So what do you think – should I do the shoot?' she asked, after a quick summary.

'I would,' said Meg.

'Of course *you* would. But what about me?'

'Honestly, Hol, I can't believe you're even worrying about this. I'm sure it will be really classy – and surely even lawyers can't be offended by a bit of artistic nakedness? Anyway, whose life is this – yours or his? Just go for it, doll! I promise you James will understand.'

Holly was so tired she was struggling to think straight, but Meg's certainty made her begin to feel that perhaps she was being overcautious.

'Should I phone James to ask what he thinks?'

Meg snorted. 'What? "So, James, how do you feel about me stripping off to do some kinky photos with a hot naked bloke?" Yeah, I'm sure he'll be well up for that . . .'

Good point. 'Okay, thanks, hon,' said Holly. 'I'll call you later.'

As the make-up artist got to work, Holly thought over what Meg had said. *Whose life is this – yours or his?* She was right. James would understand – and if he didn't, she would have to make him.

'Hol?'

She opened her eyes to find Moet standing by her chair.

'I couldn't help but overhear what you were saying on the phone just now,' she whispered. 'And I wanted to tell you, I get why you're worried, babes. I don't have a boyfriend, cos I always seem to end up being attracted to arseholes – as you saw the other night.' Moet grimaced. 'But if I did have a boyfriend, and he was as nice as yours sounds, I wouldn't want to risk him for some stupid TV show.'

'Thanks, but I think I was probably worrying about nothing,' said Holly, more confidently than she felt.

'Yeah, but I heard Nigel talking about the shoot just now and it sounds like it's gonna be proper dirty – bondage ropes and everything!' Moet's Bambi eyes were wide and earnest. 'Just don't let yourself get talked into something you're not happy about, okay, babe?'

Holly thought it over while the make-up artist finished her face. She thought about it some more while the stylist dressed her in a black satin, leather-trimmed bra, matching knickers and black patent Louboutin heels. She was still thinking about it when the make-up artist rubbed her limbs with golden-flecked oil and gave her hair a final mist of hairspray. When she was finally ready, Holly stepped in front of the mirror and gasped. Her eyes were ringed with black, her lips were pale and her bronzed, glistening skin contrasted with the white-blonde of her hair. She knew she looked spectacular – and she knew what she had to do.

'Wowee, mama, you look incredible!' Rosario appeared by her side. 'Zane's ready for you. Let's do this!'

But Holly didn't budge. 'Rosario, I'm afraid I'm not doing the shoot.'

'Yes, you are.'

'No, I'm not.'

Rosario was glaring at her, but suddenly her face softened. 'Is this because of your problem thighs?' she said, gently. 'You don't have to worry, honey, the lighting will be *very* flattering. I'm sure your cellulite won't even show.'

'What . . . ? No!'

'Are you a Catholic?'

'No, I'm just . . . I have a boyfriend,' said Holly. 'I'm not comfortable working with a naked man.'

'Oh come on, the guy will be wearing a G-string! You can't show dick on the TV before 9 p.m.'

'I'm sorry, I'm not doing it.'

Throwing up her hands in frustration, Rosario stormed off, muttering something furious in Portuguese. Holly went back to the changing room, apologising to the bewildered stylist, but before she could start to get changed there was a tap at the door.

'Can I have a word, hon?' Sasha's head appeared.

Reluctantly, Holly nodded and she came in, followed immediately by a cameraman.

'I don't really want to talk on camera . . .' started Holly.

'Don't worry, they won't even use it,' said Sasha. 'Come and sit down with me. Now I hear you're having second thoughts about doing the shoot?'

Holly nodded miserably.

'I'm not here to change your mind,' said Sasha. 'This is totally your choice. That's what you've got to remember, Holly – all this is up to you. You are in control of your own destiny. We can sit around telling you how fabulous you are, how you could make millions as a model, but unless *you* believe it – unless you believe in yourself – it's not going to happen. You've got a chance here that most girls would kill for, but if it's not right for you then you can just walk away now and go back to your old life. It's your decision, Holly.'

By now, Holly had been agonising over this decision for hours and she was so exhausted with going backwards and forwards that she had almost forgotten about what she worrying about in the first place; but amid the confusion, Sasha's mention of her 'old life' hit home. The thought of going back to her desk at VitaSlim suddenly felt like the worst of all her options.

Sasha put her hand on her knee and smiled at her sympathetically. 'What do you think, hon?'

Holly sighed. 'Okay, I'll do it,' she said, finally.

18

Later that afternoon, Holly and the other girls stood in front of Max awaiting his decision. Despite her fears, the shoot had been amazing – even if there were distinct bondage overtones to the styling, just as Moet had warned her. Trey, the dancer Holly had been paired up with, was very sweet and knee-tremblingly gorgeous, but obviously far more interested in Zane than he was in her. As uncertain as she had been about doing the shoot, Holly knew that she looked fantastic and that gave her a kick-ass confidence that shone through in the finished pictures. Holly glanced up at the image projected on the screen above Max's head: her legs wrapped around Trey's waist, her hands in his hair and her head thrown back, eyes blazing and lips slightly open. It was incredibly sexy without being at all sleazy.

Max turned to the bookers. 'Bear, which of your girls are you putting into the Danger Zone today?'

Bear looked between his remaining girls, a tortured expression on his face.

'I'm sorry, but I'm going to have to say Charlie,' he said. Charlie seemed unconcerned, twirling her hair and smiling dreamily. 'You have the most incredible look, my darling, but I'm concerned you lack versatility. You really struggled to do sexy today.'

It was a fair point: in her shot, Charlie looked more like she was playing Twister at a children's birthday tea.

Max nodded. 'And Rosario?'

Holly chewed her thumbnail nervously. Surely she couldn't pick her? Okay, so she had messed around a bit before the shoot, but the pictures looked fantastic . . .

But Rosario looked straight in her direction. 'I choose Holly,' she said. 'I can't work with models who won't listen to me.'

Holly glanced at Max, hoping to see a reassuring smile or a flicker of the connection she felt they'd made during that cosy chat all those weeks ago, but he was back to being that remote, intimidating figure who had so unnerved her at the start of the show.

'The girl who'll be leaving us today is . . .' As Max prolonged the tension, Holly agonised over what an idiot she'd been. If she went home now, not only would she have screwed up her chance at a modelling career, she would still be appearing on TV, oiled up and faking an orgasm, thereby most likely buggering up her relationship too. *Way to go, Hols!*

'Charlie,' said Max finally. 'I'm afraid you're not right for Strut.'

As she gave Charlie a consolatory hug, Holly felt dizzy with relief. Max hadn't finished with her yet, though.

'But, Holly, we all have serious concerns about your attitude,' he said. 'One more slip-up, and you're out.'

On the tube journey home from the studio, Holly planned what she'd say to James when he came over later. She was starting to feel like perhaps she'd been blowing the whole thing out of proportion (it wasn't like she'd been posing in a wet T-shirt for *Nuts* magazine, after all) and after the mess she'd made of things at the shoot, honesty seemed like by far the best policy. All Holly wanted to do that evening was to curl up in James's arms and have a giggle with him about how silly she'd been – because it *was* actually quite funny when you thought about it: especially Rosario thinking she was a Catholic! Yes, she was sure that James would tell her she'd been worrying about nothing . . .

But as Holly sprinted up the escalator from the platform, her phone buzzed with a new voicemail from James. He sounded stressed, explaining that he had a ton of work to do and had to stay late at the office, apologising that he wouldn't be able to come over later, but promising to call first thing in the morning. Holly felt hugely disappointed, yet also weirdly uneasy. It suddenly seemed desperately important that she should see him that night. Her emotions had been so up and down, she just needed him to hold her, to tell her it was all going to be okay and that he still loved her.

As she walked home from the station, Holly tried returning the call on his mobile; it went straight to voicemail. So she called his office, but instead of going through to his direct line, the call diverted to the receptionist.

'Winters, Marlowe and Bates, good evening.'

'Oh, hi, could I please speak to James Wellington?'

'Just one moment.'

Holly waited patiently. She would ask him to come over after he had finished work. It didn't matter if she was asleep – they could have a sleepy cuddle, then chat about the shoot over breakfast.

'I'm sorry, Mr Wellington has left the office for a meeting.'

Holly frowned. 'Do you know where his meeting is? This is his girlfriend, and I need to speak to him quite urgently.'

'Hold please.'

A moment later the receptionist was back. 'His assistant says he's seeing a client at the Ritz Hotel.'

Well, that could only mean one person, thought Holly, as she ended the call. *Lady Crosby*.

Feeling a little dazed, Holly went and sat on a nearby bench. She needed to get her head straight; nothing seemed to make any sense. James had definitely said in his message, 'I've got to stay late *in the office*' – but perhaps it had been a slip of the tongue? He had probably just meant he had to work late. Yes, that must be it . . . Holly tried his phone again, but it was still switched off. She was exhausted, and knew that the sensible course of action would be to go home, get an early night and talk to James in the morning. But as she sat there, anxiety started to bubble up inside her, drowning out reason. *James had lied to her.*

As if on autopilot, Holly found herself getting up from the bench and walking back in the direction of Hammersmith tube station. She caught a Piccadilly Line train to Green Park, staring blankly ahead of her for the entire twenty-minute journey, then walked a couple of blocks to the Ritz Hotel.

Holly had heard somewhere that you couldn't go into the Ritz if you were wearing jeans, but the door-man didn't seem that concerned as she rushed past him into the magnificent chandelier-lit lobby and up to the marble front desk.

'Could you please tell me which room Lady Crosby is in? She's having a meeting with James Wellington of Winters, Marlowe and Bates. I'm his . . . legal secretary.'

Holly caught sight of herself in the huge mirrors behind Reception, still wearing three sets of false eyelashes and tousled bed-hair, and stood up a little straighter.

'Lady Crosby is in the Berkeley Suite,' said the receptionist. 'On the top floor.'

Holly rushed over to the lift and got in just as the doors were closing. There was another person already in the lift, an elderly woman who was dripping in diamonds and had had so many facelifts that the few crows' feet she had left around her eyes stretched vertically upwards. They both got out on the same floor and Holly began to wonder if this was actually Lady Crosby, but she stopped at a different room.

As Holly followed the signs to the Berkeley Suite, it occurred to her for the first time that this was a truly terrible idea. How on earth was James going to react to her barging into an important business meeting? But she had come this far, so she might as well go through with it. (Besides, she was intrigued to see what the famous Lady Crosby was actually like.)

Trying to calm her nerves, Holly knocked on the grand double-doors of the Berkeley Suite. Too late, she noticed that there was a doorbell – but then who ever heard of a doorbell in a hotel? It must be a hell of a room . . . Suddenly, the door swung open to reveal a small, comfortably plump woman with a halo of grey curls and a dimpled smile. Holly relaxed a little – Lady Crosby was nothing like the intimidating figure she had feared. She looked like Cinderella's fairy godmother, but in well-ironed slacks, Pat Butcher earrings and a green cardi.

'I'm so sorry to disturb you, Lady Crosby,' said Holly, 'but I was wondering if I might have a quick word with James Wellington?'

The woman's face creased into chuckles. 'Ooh no, I'm not Lady Crosby, love! I'm her mam.' She sounded like she'd stepped straight off the *Corrie* cobbles. 'Martina's downstairs having dinner.'

As Holly thanked her and turned back along the corridor the way she had come, the uneasy feeling that she had been fighting to keep under control all evening exploded into outright panic. James had told her he was working late at the office, but instead he was having dinner with Lady Crosby. And if that little old lady was Lady Crosby's mum, then Lady Crosby definitely wasn't going to be a little old lady. Whichever way Holly looked at it, it didn't look good.

The restaurant was even more wildly opulent than the rest of the hotel: a riot of gold statues, marble columns, ornate plasterwork and flower displays the size of a small family hatchback. Holly hid herself behind a potted palm by the entrance and peeped through the foliage, trying to locate James amongst the candlelit tables . . .

'Are you dining with us this evening, mademoiselle?'

Holly spun round to find a short, balding man in a black suit looking at her with a questioning smile.

'Oh, yes, hello there!' She extricated herself from behind the palm, breaking off a frond in the process.

'I was just . . . just looking for someone. Some friends.'

'And in what name is the reservation?'

'Um . . .' Holly didn't want to mention either James or Lady Crosby, but she needed to get into that restaurant – and the maître d' looked like the sort of man who operated a *very* strict door policy. 'The name is . . .' Holly's mind went blank. She glanced around, desperately searching for inspiration. *Come on, come on, just think of a name . . .* 'Ritz!' Holly blurted out. 'I mean Ritzman!' she added, quickly. 'Yes, Mr and Mrs Ritzman.' *Oh God.*

The maître d' regarded her doubtfully for a moment, then gave a curt nod. 'Very good, mademoiselle,' he said, and crossed over to his little podium where he started scanning through his reservations list.

'It's okay, I've spotted them!' cried Holly, dashing off into the restaurant before he could stop her.

The room was so dark it was difficult to make out anyone very clearly but, finally, over in the far corner, Holly caught sight of James – although frustratingly an enormously fat Arab gentleman was obscuring his dining companion. Dodging the waiters, Holly scuttled behind a marble pillar just a few metres away from James's table then slowly peeped out – and instantly felt like her world had been turned on its head.

19

Lady Crosby was a goddess. She looked like Kate Middleton, except blonde and way hotter. She had a dazzling smile, a perfect little upturned nose and wide-apart eyes, framed by a mane of honey-gold hair that tumbled over tanned, toned shoulders. No doubt she was sitting on a perfectly pert Pippa Middleton arse, too. She clearly split her time between her hairdresser and her personal trainer – *and her lawyer*, thought Holly, bitterly. James suddenly burst out laughing at something she'd said. He looked so happy and relaxed. To everyone else, they would have looked like a gorgeous young couple enjoying a romantic dinner. *Does James look like that when he's with me?* Holly wondered, choking back a huge sob. *Do I make him light up with happiness like that . . . ?*

She was desperate to rush over and beg James to tell her that there was nothing going on, but the evidence to the contrary was sitting right there in all her size 6, golden-haired, gym-honed glory . . .

'I'm afraid we don't have any reservation in the name of Ritzman.'

The maître d' was standing behind her, looking considerably less welcoming than he had a few moments ago.

Holly froze, like a rabbit in headlights. The people at the table closest to her looked around to see what was going on. Whatever happened, she *had* to avoid a scene.

'Well,' she said, trying to keep her voice down, 'I wasn't sure exactly what name the reservation had been made in, and it turns out it was actually Wellington, not Ritzman.'

'So will you be joining the Wellington party for dinner?'

'Um . . . no . . . You see, they weren't expecting me, but I was passing so I thought I'd just pop by and say hello!' She gave a weak laugh, hoping he didn't see the tears glistening in her eyes. 'They aren't expecting me to be here, so it's going to be a lovely surprise!'

The maître d' eyed her suspiciously, clearly unconvinced, but then miraculously he nodded and left her alone. He obviously wanted to avoid a scene as well.

When he had gone, Holly rested her forehead against the cool marble of the pillar. *Come on, get a grip* . . . She mustn't read too much into this. There was nothing weird about a lawyer having dinner with his client, even if she was stunningly gorgeous and he had lied about it to his girlfriend. It was all perfectly innocent.

But when she looked around the pillar again, she saw Lady Crosby lean over to clink champagne glasses with James – then she put her diamond-bedecked hand over his and smiled at him so suggestively that Holly felt an actual pain in her chest. Just at that moment, there was a sudden lull in conversation at the surrounding tables and she heard – and saw – Lady Crosby say to James quite clearly: 'You've made me happier than any other man has done in my life.'

And then James – *her boyfriend* – broke into a wide smile and said: 'Let's go upstairs and . . .'

'HAPPY BIRTHDAY!' A sudden wild celebration at a neighbouring table drowned out the rest of what James said, but Holly definitely saw him say the word 'bed'. *Let's go upstairs and go to bed.*

Holly was too shocked to cry. Surely James couldn't be having an affair with Lady Crosby? She thought back over all those times he had rushed off in the middle of one of their dates to see his star client, claiming there had been 'important matters to look over'. *Yeah, Lady Crosby's banging body*, Holly thought, bitterly. Suddenly, it all made sense. While she'd been agonising over whether to pose in her knickers, he'd been busy getting into somebody else's. And to think she'd very nearly screwed up her chance on *Street Scout* out of concern for embarrassing James! She would march over there now and *really* embarrass the cheating bastard . . .

And yet . . . This was the honourable, upstanding James Wellington she was talking about, a man to whom 'doing the right thing' came as naturally as wearing Church's brogues. Holly just couldn't imagine him cheating on her; it was so totally out of character. What if this *was* completely innocent – just a straightforward work dinner?

Just then, Holly heard someone come up behind her and she turned to see the maître d' again, this time accompanied by another man. Neither was smiling.

'Mademoiselle, I'm afraid I'm going to have to ask you to leave,' said the maître d' in hushed tones.

Holly glanced back at James and Lady Crosby, and the fight suddenly drained out of her. She felt utterly defeated.

'It's okay, I was just leaving,' she said. 'I don't think I will surprise them after all.'

20

When she woke up the following day, Holly's head thumped like she was suffering from the mother of all hangovers, even though she hadn't touched a drop of alcohol the night before. There hadn't been time for anything like that, what with stalking her boyfriend and his (possible) mistress around the Ritz and scaring a taxi driver by sobbing loudly for the entire journey home. With a groan, she raised her head from the pillow to look at the clock. It was 1.32 – in the afternoon, Holly deduced from the light streaming into her bedroom. She'd been asleep for over twelve hours! Thank God she'd only had a few hours' sleep over the previous couple of nights: she'd been so knackered when she got home from the Ritz that she had collapsed into bed and immediately fallen into blissful oblivion.

Holly got in the shower and adjusted the head to the 'massage' setting – producing jets so lethally powerful they could have dispersed a riot – in an attempt to clear the fug from her head. By the time the water had run cold, she had come up with a plan of action. She would ask James to dinner that evening and they would have a sensible, adult conversation to get to the bottom of what was going on (she decided to leave out the bit about spying on him from behind a potted palm). As Holly towelled her hair dry, she began to feel a little brighter. It was the not-knowing that was so awful, but in a few hours' time the whole mess would be sorted.

But when Holly picked up her phone to call James, she discovered he had already beaten her to it. There were a couple of missed calls and a new voice message.

'Hello darling, I'm so sorry to have missed you last night. It's now . . . nine-thirty in the morning and, would you believe it, I'm just en route to Heathrow. David Winters asked me to join him on a business trip to New York to meet a potential new client. It's all a bit cloak and dagger at the moment, but this guy would be quite a catch for the firm . . . Anyway, give me a call when you get this message, or I'll try you when I get to the hotel. I'm sorry things are so manic right now, but let's meet for dinner as soon as I get back. I should only be gone three or four days. Love you.'

Holly phoned James straight back but it went to voicemail. He was clearly already on the plane. With a howl of frustration, Holly hurled the phone across the room and then burst into tears again.

Over the next few days, Holly spoke to James on several occasions, but each time she chickened out of confronting him about Lady Crosby. As desperate as she was to find out what was going on, it was the sort of conversation that needed to be had face to face, not over a transatlantic phone line. No, it would have to wait until James got back from his business trip – if indeed that was what it was, and not a dirty mini-break with Lady Crosby.

That week's *Street Scout* masterclass was with Frieda Koch, the creative director of the German fashion label Zauber. With her kaftan and wild, greying curls she looked more like a geography teacher, but she was clearly a big deal in the world of fashion as Max stopped by to greet her personally.

Frieda Koch was there to give the finalists guidance on how they should handle themselves at go-sees, the modelling equivalent of an audition, at which fashion editors and brand bosses decide whether a girl is right for the job – with often nothing more than the briefest of glances. To Holly's dismay, it sounded as if models spent a huge amount of time schlepping their portfolio around on public transport to attend these cut-throat cattle calls.

'The go-see is your only chance to impress – so it is vitally important that you make the best possible impact,' said Frieda in precise, accented English. 'Punctuality, politeness and professionalism are vital.'

They had done a bit of role-play and Frieda had said some encouraging things about Holly's look, even offering to give her some 'private tutoring', but her head had been elsewhere. James was on a flight back to London that morning, and they had arranged to meet for dinner at their favourite restaurant at 8 p.m. That night, she would finally get to the bottom of what was going on.

At the end of the afternoon, Sasha briefed the girls on the following day's challenge. 'Tomorrow you will put into practice everything you have learnt today when you are sent on a number of genuine go-sees that could lead to real modelling jobs,' said Sasha. 'We need you here at seven sharp tomorrow morning to pick up your portfolios and find out where your appointments will be. This will be your first taste of what it's really like to be a model, and a real chance to put into practice everything you've learnt. Make sure you remember Frieda's advice, as at the end of the day, Max will be asking one of you to leave – and five will become our final four.'

Holly spent ages deciding what to wear for dinner, in the end choosing an All Saints beaded mini-dress that she had been given by one of the *Street Scout* stylists. It was very short, cut dangerously low at the back and was way too sexy for a casual dinner, but Holly needed to feel fabulous, so she slung on a denim jacket and flat boots to dress it down a bit and rushed out of the door.

On the journey to the restaurant, Holly gave herself a stern talking-to: she must allow James a chance to explain what was happening without jumping to any conclusions; she wouldn't let emotion cloud her judgement. And she would remain calm and reasonable throughout.

She arrived at the restaurant – an Italian place in Bermondsey that did a mean grilled veal chop – and found James already waiting at the table. He stood up as she approached.

'God, I've missed you,' he said, taking her in his arms and holding her close to him. 'You look absolutely beautiful.'

The smell and the feel of him triggered a surge of passion inside her, but her head immediately put the brakes on. *Calm, detached and focused*, Holly reminded herself.

James ordered a bottle of champagne, then told her all about the New York trip – although he was still cagey about who this mysterious new client was – and asked about what was happening with *Street Scout*. Holly answered as vaguely as she could. She didn't want to muddy the waters by getting into a discussion about the lingerie shoot.

When the waiter had poured them a drink, James held up his glass.

'A toast,' he smiled. 'To us.'

Holly suddenly remembered the last toast James

had made – to Lady effing Crosby at the Ritz – and quickly lowered her glass.

'Hey, what's wrong?' he said. 'You've been really quiet. Is something up?'

'James, I know you were at the Ritz the other night.'

'What?'

'With Lady Crosby. You told me you were working late at the office, but I called your office and they said you weren't there.'

'Is that what's worrying you? Oh lord, Hols, I'm so sorry but I wasn't trying to hide anything. I don't remember exactly what I said in the phone message, but I had to go and see Lady Crosby to discuss the latest developments in the case. That was all.'

He reached over to take her hand, but she pulled it away.

'You didn't look like you were discussing developments with her,' she snapped. 'And, by the way, why the hell didn't you tell me that poor old widowed Lady Crosby is such a fucking fox?'

It was out before she could stop herself. So much for staying calm and detached . . .

The smile faded from James's face. 'I beg your pardon?'

'I saw you with her, James. I was there, in the restaurant. I saw the two of you laughing and flirting and drinking champagne. And from where I was standing, you looked more like her lover than her lawyer.'

James flinched – was that a look of guilt? – but quickly recovered his composure. 'What exactly are you suggesting, Holly?'

Suddenly, something inside her snapped. His buttoned-up manner was so infuriating. She felt patronised, like he was talking down to her. *He* was the one who was in the wrong here – why was he making *her* feel like the villain?

'What I'm suggesting, James,' she said, far louder than she meant to, 'is that it looked very much like you're shagging Lady Crosby.'

21

James's face went from shock to confusion to sheer anger. Holly had never seen him look so furious. He opened his mouth to speak but just at that moment, the waiter appeared with their food.

'*Allora, signor*, the dover sole is for you.' He put the fish down in front of James with a flourish, totally oblivious to the daggers that were shooting across the table. 'And the penne alla Norma for you, *signorina*.'

'Thank you, it looks delicious,' said Holly.

'Yes, lovely, thank you,' said James.

The waiter smiled, bowed slightly and then retreated. James leaned across the table towards Holly. 'What on earth are you—'

'Would you like some black pepper?' The waiter had reappeared with an enormous pepper grinder.

'Oh yes, just a little,' said Holly, plastering on a smile.

'No, thank you,' said James, stiffly.

The waiter gave a solicitous little nod and disappeared.

James sighed, then tried again. 'Holly, I don't know what—'

'Parmesan, *signorina*?'

'No, I'm fine, thanks,' said Holly, an edge of desperation creeping into her voice.

'Very good,' smiled the waiter. '*Buon appetito*.'

When they were sure they had been left alone, James turned back to her.

'Holly, I'm struggling to understand how you can even suggest such a thing.' His voice was low and calm, but his eyes were blazing with fury.

'Oh, come on, she was all over you! The pair of you were all giggly and flirty and knocking back the champagne. I don't know much about your job, but I'm pretty sure your business meetings don't usually look like that.'

'No, you're right, they don't,' said James. 'I hadn't had a chance to tell you yet, but it looks like Lord Crosby's son has been persuaded to drop his appeal, which means we'll have won the case. So I had ordered champagne to celebrate.'

'Then why not tell me any of that in your message!'

Holly had shrieked so loudly that the couple at the next table had looked around to see what was going on, so she now dropped her voice and hissed at James: 'And, by the way, I clearly heard you say to her, "Let's go upstairs to bed".'

A look of, what? – confusion? guilt? – flashed through James's eyes.

'I couldn't have said that . . .' he stammered. 'It might have been, "Let's go upstairs and put this thing to bed", talking about the final paperwork . . . You must have got it wrong . . .'

Holly rolled her eyes. James must think she was a complete bloody idiot. She suddenly felt utterly exhausted.

'Look, just be honest with me, please: are you sleeping with her or not?'

'If you have to even ask I have serious concerns about our relationship,' he said, pompously. 'Whatever happened to trust?'

'*Trust*?' scoffed Holly. 'How can I trust you when you deliberately lied to me!'

'I didn't lie, I just . . .' James let out a growl of frustration. 'Oh, this is bloody ridiculous. I've been working all hours to get us a better future and you accuse me of shagging my clients. Why on earth can't you just support me?'

Holly's mouth dropped open in astonishment. 'Me support you? What about *you* supporting *me*?! *Street Scout* has been my big chance to make something out of my life and you've done nothing but criticise and complain since I started this show!'

James gave an impatient sigh. 'For God's sake, Holly, I don't think you can really compare your appearance on some cheap TV reality show with a career that I've dedicated years of my life to establishing.' He shook his head then quickly said: 'I'm sorry, that was uncalled for.'

'No, it's best that you're honest about how you feel. I just wish you'd be as honest about what's going on with Lady Crosby. I see you've managed to dodge the question of whether or not you're sleeping with her. Typical bloody lawyer . . .'

James suddenly grabbed her hand across the table. 'Holly, deep down in your heart, do you really think I'd cheat on you?'

He was staring at her with a desperate intensity, as if trying to convince her that he'd been true. *Then why didn't he just come out and deny sleeping with her?*

'I just don't know,' said Holly, in a small voice.

James instantly let go of her hand, and her gaze. 'Well, if that's truly how you feel then this relationship has no future.' He reached into his pocket and put some money on the table, then stood up to go. 'Holly, if I leave now this is over between us,' he said. 'If you can't trust me, then our relationship is meaningless.'

She looked up at him. The candlelight sharpened the contours of his cheekbones and lit up his eyes, making him look even more handsome. In that moment, despite being infuriated by his patronising, self-righteous attitude, she saw the face of her wonderful James, the man she had always hoped she would end up marrying and spending the rest of her life with.

Surely he wouldn't cheat on her? She wanted to believe it with every shred of her being. But she had been there – she had seen the way Lady Crosby had touched his hand and looked at him. It broke her heart to acknowledge it, but there was no way that relationship was purely business.

There was something else, too. Although James had never once made an issue out of the differences in their backgrounds, she had always struggled to feel good enough for James and his family, and now his comment about *Street Scout* made it blindingly obvious that she had been right to worry. He would have denied it, but it was now crystal-clear that he didn't think she was good enough for him. Of course he'd prefer a beautiful rich widow to some cheap little Essex girl! The only surprise was that their relationship had lasted as long as it had.

'Fine,' said Holly, eventually.

James paused for a moment longer. For a man who kept such a tight control on his emotions, he looked very close to tears. Then he turned and headed out of the door.

Holly sat staring at the empty chair opposite her, too shocked to cry. The whole thing was bizarre. She'd gone from 'in a relationship' to 'single' as easily as changing her status on Facebook.

'Are you alright, *signorina?*' Their waiter had materialised by her side. 'You are far too beautiful to be looking so sad.'

He was looking concerned but also a little frisky. *Bloody Italians . . .*

'I'll just have the bill, thank you,' said Holly, quickly.

She paid using some of the cash James had left her – far more than was necessary to cover the meal – then went into the street and hailed a taxi. During the drive home, she replayed the evening's events in her head over and over, trying to work out if she'd just made a hideous mistake, but she kept coming back to the same, indisputable point: James had never said he hadn't cheated. Why would he refuse to deny it – unless he was guilty?" Holly managed to hold back the tears until she was back in the security of her flat, but then the floodgates burst open.

It seemed pointless trying to get to sleep, so she made herself a duvet nest in front of the TV and watched a particularly gory horror movie, the sort of blood-and-guts fest she usually did her best to avoid, but which seemed appropriate given that she felt like she'd just had her own heart ripped out. At 3 a.m. Holly tried to go to sleep, but the combination of movie-induced jitters and her pain over James made it impossible. She wanted to hate the lousy, cheating bastard, but she just missed him so, so much. After God knew how long, Holly finally fell asleep. Her last thought was of Lady Crosby being dismembered by a chainsaw-wielding, redneck zombie.

* * *

As soon as Holly woke up, she was aware that something terrible had happened, but it took a few seconds for the memory of the previous night to hit her like an avalanche, instantly smothering her in a thick blanket of despair – which quickly turned into anger. *How could James do this to her . . . ?* At least she had managed a bit of sleep, so she wouldn't be too shattered for the *Street Scout* challenge today. Holly's eyes instantly snapped open. *The challenge!* Shit, what time was it? She was supposed to be at Strut at 7 a.m., but it was already worryingly light outside. Oh God, in all the trauma of last night she must have forgotten to set her alarm! She scrabbled around for her phone, but it wasn't on its usual spot on her bedside table. She rushed into the kitchen and checked the clock on the microwave, and her poor bruised heart sank like a stone. It was 7.18.

22

Just then Holly's phone started to ring. She found it under a pile of cushions on the sofa.

'Hello . . . ?'

'WHERE THE FUCK ARE YOU?'

'Oh, hi, Rosario. Sorry, I'm afraid I'm running a bit late. I had a really bad night and I—'

'Get your lazy ass over here RIGHT NOW! You need to pick up your portfolio and be in Mayfair for your first appointment at 9 a.m.'

'Okay, no problem, see you shortly.' But she had already gone.

Fortunately, the girls had been told that they should attend go-sees in minimal make-up so that potential clients could really see what they looked like, so Holly was out of the door in fifteen minutes and at Strut by 8.15. Rosario met her in Reception looking like someone had just suggested to her she should bleach her moustache. For once, Holly was quite relieved to see that she had a cameraman in tow, as it meant that Rosario wouldn't be able to unleash the full four-letter force of her wrath.

'You need to get going NOW,' she hissed, pushing her book into her hands along with a schedule of the day's appointments. 'All the other girls went ages ago. Move it!'

Thankfully, the tube gods were smiling on Holly, as she got to Bond Street with ten minutes to spare before her appointment at the offices of *Perfect Bride* wedding magazine, who were casting for their latest shoot. When she arrived in Reception, Kinzah and Natalia were already there. Although they all had a different schedule of appointments for the day, it looked like some of them overlapped.

'Holly!' Kinzah looked relieved to see her. 'What happened to you this morning?'

'Long story, I'll fill you in later.' She really didn't want to get into the whole James mess now as she was bound to start crying and she was pretty sure that blotchy and snotty wouldn't be the look that *Perfect Bride* was going for.

A girl appeared at the door. 'Holly Collins?'

With a bright smile, Holly stood up. She felt a sudden surge of confidence. Despite the disastrous start to the challenge, she was here on time and still in the running. Her love life might be a total failure, but at least she could make a success out of her modelling career.

She was shown into a meeting room, the walls of

which were lined with framed *Perfect Bride* covers, to find two elegant-looking women sitting at a round table. Without any greeting, one of them held out her hand.

'Your book?'

Holly gave it to her, the woman glanced at the first page and then handed it back.

'Thank you,' she said, gesturing to the door.

What – was that it? Holly was stunned. She had known it might be brief, but she'd been in the room for about twenty seconds! That was more of a no-see than a go-see. Struggling not to feel rejected – she was feeling even more sensitive than usual thanks to her cheating ex-boyfriend – she thanked the women for their time and left.

Holly's next appointment, at an advertising agency in Islington, was slightly better. She was probably in the room for a whole minute this time. But, once again, the casting director, though not explicitly rude, had given the impression that she had wasted everyone's time.

Thankfully – as Holly was beginning to worry she was the modelling equivalent of herpes – it was a case of third time lucky. Kate Shaw was an upcoming young designer who was looking for girls to walk the runway for her next show. The go-see was at her showroom in a converted warehouse just off Old Street. Kate was very friendly, taking the time to look through Holly's portfolio and then getting her to try on one of her dresses, which even Holly had to admit looked great on her.

'Thanks so much for coming to see me,' said Kate, at the end of the meeting. 'I love your look, Holly – we'll definitely be in touch.'

Holly bounced out of the room feeling proud of herself, despite her simmering hurt and anger over James, and cautiously optimistic. She might be single, but she'd just landed her first professional modelling job! She walked passed Moet who was next to see Kate.

'How did it go, babes?'

'Great,' she grinned, as Moet gave her a thumbs up. 'Good luck!'

Back in the reception area, Holly checked her phone and saw she had a bit of time before her next appointment. It would probably be a good idea to check if her make-up needed touching up before she set off.

'Can I just use your toilet?' she asked the smiley girl at the front desk.

'Sure, it's just down that corridor.'

Holly checked herself out in the bathroom's large, well-lit mirror. The lack of sleep was starting to show, so she swirled some peachy blusher on her cheeks, put on another coat of mascara and pepped up her hair with a bit of product. *Much better*.

But when Holly got back to Reception, things suddenly looked a lot less rosy. Her portfolio, which she had left on a chair so it didn't get damp sitting in the bathroom, seemed to have disappeared.

'Have you seen my book?' she asked the receptionist, trying not to panic. 'It's A4-sized, with a pale grey cover.'

The girl looked surprised. 'Your friend said you wanted her to look after it.'

'My friend?'

'Yes – the girl who went in to see Kate after you. Long dark hair. She wasn't in there long – she's just left.'

Holly was confused. Why would Moet take her portfolio? Perhaps she'd assumed Holly had gone and left it there by accident. Holly raced down the stairs and onto the street, but there was no sign of her. Well, at least she wouldn't have got very far.

Holly didn't have Moet's phone number, but she knew Bear would have it, so she texted him and moments later it arrived. She dialled the number, praying Moet wasn't on the tube . . .

'Yeah?' *Thank God.*

'Moet, it's Holly. Have you got my portfolio?'

'Oh, hi, babes! Yeah, I have.'

'Thank goodness! Where are you? I'll come and get it from you.'

'I'm in a taxi on my way to Battersea for my next go-see.'

'Okay, I must only be a minute or so behind you, so if you don't mind asking your driver to pull over,

I'll find a taxi and come to wherever you are. I'll be quick, I promise.'

There was a pause. 'Sorry, babes, no can do,' said Moet. 'You can't expect me to risk being late for my next appointment just because you were dumb enough to leave your portfolio behind.'

Holly felt like the air had been punched out of her. 'But I didn't forget it,' she stammered. 'I was just in the toilet and . . .'

Moet gave a theatrical sigh. 'No, what happened is that I noticed you'd left your book and I very kindly picked it up so that it wouldn't get lost and then it was with me for safe-keeping. I think a "thank you" would be nice in the circumstances, *babes*.'

Holly was struggling to make sense of what was happening. Surely Moet hadn't taken her portfolio on purpose? She certainly wouldn't have put a spot of sabotage past her in the old days, but all that nonsense was behind them now – wasn't it?

'Moet, please, you know I'm going to be in serious trouble if I don't get my portfolio back. I don't even know where my next appointment is.'

'Oh, I can tell you that,' said Moet, breezily. She was obviously looking through Holly's schedule, which she'd tucked inside the portfolio. 'Aw, what a shame, your next appointment is in Soho in half an hour! But I guess you'll have to come to meet me in Battersea first. You'd better get a move on, babes; you ain't got much time. I'll text you the address. Ciao!'

23

Holly stared at her phone in disbelief, hurt and anger bubbling up inside her. How could Moet do this to her after everything that had happened? She had thought they were friends! But then came the sinking realisation that perhaps a leopard – or at least a leopard-print-wearing bitch like Moet – never truly changed its spots . . . Well, she didn't have time to worry about that now. Battersea was south of the river, which meant it was a half-hour's drive away at the very least, and then another half-hour back to Soho. With a surge of panic, Holly realised that there was no way she'd make her appointment on time if she went to meet Moet – but she couldn't go to a go-see without her book. Holly didn't even have any of her contact numbers to warn the clients that she was going to be late, as all the details were on her schedule in her portfolio. She had no choice but to go to Battersea.

By the time Holly eventually arrived at her appointment in Soho – having retrieved her portfolio from an infuriatingly self-righteous Moet ('Let this be a lesson not to leave your portfolio lying around next time, babes') – she was told she was far too late to be seen. She was half an hour late for her next appointment as well, although they agreed to fit her in. Fortunately, it was one of those one-glance-and-you're-out meetings, so Holly managed to get to her final appointment – a casting for a sportswear catalogue – in good time. The casting director was very complimentary, but Holly knew it wouldn't make any difference. She had no doubt that her *Street Scout* days were numbered.

At 6 p.m. all the girls gathered in the large meeting room at Strut. Holly had been the last to arrive and felt utterly wretched as she took her seat opposite Moet, who shot her a triumphant smile. She had thought about telling Rosario what had happened with the portfolio, but Moet was so manipulative and slippery she would have been bound to wriggle her way out of it and cause even more problems for her. And besides, what was the point? After being so late this morning, she knew she was facing the axe. Holly sat staring miserably at her hands. She'd had a shot at building a better future for her – and for Lola – but she'd blown it. Holly just wanted to get this over with and go home so she could go to bed, pull the covers over her head and stay there for the rest of her lonely, jobless life.

At Nigel's signal, Max came in and took his place at the head of the table, with Rosario and Bear flanking him on either side. He was looking his usual suave, handsome self in a pale pink shirt and a pair of jeans. Holly had never seen him wearing a coloured shirt before – he was always in white – and she idly wondered if Sasha had bought it for him as a gift.

'So, today you have had your first taste of what life is really like as a model,' he said. *Yeah, full of back-stabbing and bitchiness*, thought Holly, miserably. 'You all went on six appointments, with varying degrees of success. We now have feedback from the clients you met on your go-sees. Rosario, you have Kinzah, Chanel and Holly left in the competition. Which of your girls did the best today?'

'Kinzah,' said Rosario, immediately. 'Out of six appointments, you were booked by three of the clients, which is incredible. The others were very complimentary about the way you carried yourself, but your look wasn't quite right for them. Overall, a great effort. Well done.'

Kinzah gave a little embarrassed smile; Holly was so pleased for her. She really deserved it.

'Bear, out of Moet and Natalia, who was the best?'

'Without a doubt, it was Natalia. She got booked for four jobs. The clients raved about her. One of them said she was a supermodel in the making.' He turned to Natalia, who was smiling – although her

English was so bad Holly doubted she understood much of what was being said. 'Fabulous work, darling,' added Bear. 'Really amazing.'

Then Max turned to Rosario. 'And who are you putting in the Danger Zone today?'

Her answer came as no surprise. 'Holly – again, I'm afraid. She was over an hour late this morning, even though she was told that punctuality was key, and then she missed one of her appointments because she was late again.'

'Did she get any bookings?' asked Max.

'Yes, she got two,' she admitted. 'And she got some great comments from the clients, who loved her look, but I have serious doubts over her professionalism.'

Max gave a curt nod. 'And Bear? As you only have two girls left, I'm guessing it's Moet.'

Bear nodded sadly. 'She got booked for one job, but she got criticised for wearing too much make-up, and for her attitude. Honey, you gotta be a little more humble and a little less ghetto princess, you know?'

Moet shrugged and tossed her hair, looking very much like she didn't give a shit.

'So now it's decision time,' said Max, gravely. 'Holly, Moet, you've both got the potential to be fantastic models, but I'm afraid one of you is going home.'

He looked back and forth between the two of them, as if weighing up the options. Holly had been there enough times to know the whole pantomime routine, the way Max hammed it up for the cameras, but it didn't make it any easier. Especially because if she left *Street Scout* now, it would really feel like she had absolutely nothing left in her life. She would be going back to VitaSlim and wouldn't even have her relationship with James to soften the blow.

After a few moments, Max nodded, as if he had made his decision.

'The girl who will be leaving us today is . . .'

24

'Holly,' said Max, finally. 'I'm sorry, but you're not right for Strut.'

So that was it. Now it was over, Holly just wanted to get out of the room as quickly as possible, but as all the cameras were focused on her (clearly hoping for tears), she plastered on a brave smile and went through the routine of hugging the other contestants, including Moet, who whispered, 'See ya, loser' while pretending to give her a heartfelt squeeze, and saying goodbye to the bookers. Bear seemed genuinely upset, but Rosario, though putting on a big show of being devastated, had an expression on her face that seemed to say, 'If only you'd done something about those thighs . . .' Then Holly turned to Max to thank him, and found him staring at her with such unexpected intensity that it completely threw her. He quickly recovered and shook her hand, wishing her well for the future, but as Holly left the room she still felt shaken by his expression. He'd all but ignored her over the past few weeks, but in that moment he'd looked like a man with a hell of a lot to say.

When Holly got outside the door she found Sasha waiting with a camera crew.

'Aw, come here, love,' she gushed, gathering her in for a big hug. 'How are you feeling?'

'Well, I can't pretend I'm not disappointed, but after today's challenge I knew that I'd be going home.'

'Yes, what happened today? It sounds like you lost your portfolio, but Moet came to the rescue. Thank goodness she found it!'

Holly smiled through gritted teeth. 'There was a . . . mix-up, yes, and that meant I was late for a couple of appointments. It was just bad luck, really.'

'Well, we're all sorry to see you go, but you did brilliantly to get this far and I'm sure we'll be hearing big things about you in the future.'

'Thanks so much, Sasha. Bye.'

When Holly finally arrived back at her flat, she got straight into bed and stayed there for the next forty-eight hours, emerging only to use the bathroom and eat whatever she could find in the kitchen. By Sunday evening she was down to a tin of chopped tomatoes and a packet of stale Shredded Wheat, so she dragged herself down to her nearest supermarket for a few essentials. On the walk home, she switched on her phone for the first time since Friday night. She had very sweet texts from Kinzah and Chanel and voicemails from her mum, Lola and Meg. Holly had half-hoped she might have heard from James – although why would he be calling her? He was probably busy shooting pheasants with bitch-face Crosby . . . Holly suddenly felt horribly lonely and was desperate to hear a friendly voice. She was longing to speak to Lola, but she didn't want to pour her problems out to her little sister, so she called Meg.

'Well, if it isn't the elusive Miss Collins! I've been trying to get hold of you all weekend. What have you been up to?'

'Oh, nothing much really . . .' Despite trying her hardest not to cry, Holly's voice wobbled with emotion.

'Holly? What's wrong?'

'Nothing really, I just . . . I got chucked out of *Street Scout* on Friday. Oh, and I split up with James because he was shagging his client.'

There was a sharp intake of breath at the other end of the phone. 'I'm coming straight over,' said Meg.

An hour later she arrived at the door.

'I didn't know what you'd feel like so I've got Prosecco, beer, crisps, ice-cream and chocolate. Oh, and I know you don't smoke, but Spunk rolled you a joint, just in case things are really bad.' She dumped the bulging carrier bags in the kitchen. 'How are you doing, hon?'

Holly opened her mouth to speak but instead a choked-up sob came out.

'Oh, come here, darlin'.' Meg put her arms around her, led her to the sofa and rubbed Holly's back as she bawled noisily into her shoulder. After a good cry and a medicinal Wispa, Holly told Meg everything that had happened.

'That cheating bastard!' fumed Meg. 'I always thought he was too good to be true.'

'You don't think I was a little . . . hasty, then? Splitting up with him?'

'Christ, you're joking! Holly, you are utterly gorgeous, funny, smart and an all-round grade-A catch. Even ignoring the fact that James was clearly screwing around, I'd have broken up with him just for being so fucking uptight about you going on *Street Scout*. Honest to God, Hols, you're doing exactly the right thing. Now you've got to move on and forget about him – and the best way to do that, is to shag someone else.'

'Meg! Absolutely no way.' But even as she said it, Cole Fox's face flickered through Holly's mind. She stamped on it immediately. 'What happened to giving myself a bit of time to get over the heartbreak?'

'Bollocks to that,' said Meg, airily. 'I'm telling you, hon, you need to make a fresh start and the only way to do that is with a fresh man.'

After staying up drinking with Meg until the early hours, it was gone 11 by the time Holly finally surfaced on Monday morning. Despite the hangover, she felt a bit more positive about things, thanks to Meg's pep talk. Why waste any more time pining for a bloke who'd treated her so appallingly? Meg was right: for all sorts of reasons, she was way better off without him.

Holly made herself a large coffee and formulated a to-do list for the day:

1. *Clean flat (and chuck out anything vaguely James-related)*
2. *Phone Alan to ask for my VitaSlim job back* <u>ASAP</u>
3. *Do a Davina workout DVD (good for lifting the mood)*

She needed a bit of breakfast first though, so Holly sat herself in front of the TV with a bowl of Shreddies. *This Morning* was on; a dishy Italian chef was demonstrating a lemon drizzle cake. It looked rather good, and Holly decided she'd call Alan after the cookery slot had finished. She was still watching TV two hours later (well, after what she'd been through, surely she deserved a day off?) when her phone started to ring. She didn't recognise the number, and she was in the middle of a really good episode of *Murder, She Wrote*, so she let it go to voicemail, but when it started ringing again straight away, curiosity got the better of her and she picked up.

'Hello?'

'Is this Holly Collins?'

'Yes.'

'Good morning, my name is Flora Ferguson, I'm Maxwell Moore's vice-executive deputy assistant. Do you have a moment?'

Well, she wasn't expecting that. 'Sure.'

'Mr Moore has asked me to arrange a lunch meeting with you. He has an opening tomorrow – would that be convenient?'

Holly was confused. Why did Max want to meet her for lunch? Perhaps he did this with all the ex-contestants. That must be it: an opportunity to give some modelling career guidance, that sort of thing.

'Tomorrow's fine,' she said.

'Great. Mr Moore will see you at Cecconi's at 12.30.'

25

'Can I help you?'

'Um, yes, I'm meeting Max Moore?'

'Just one moment, please.'

As the fiercely chic woman behind the front desk checked through the list of bookings, Holly looked around the restaurant. With its squashy green banquettes, tiled floor and lamp-lit bar, the room itself was understated, even cosy, but she could tell at a glance that the clientele were seriously loaded. There were several groups of businessmen comparing the size of their hedge funds over barely touched bowls of pasta; a table of Middle Eastern kids talking on their iPhones rather than to each other; and ladies-who-lunch galore, all swishy hair, appetizer-sized salads and diamonds. There weren't many couples though, probably because it was lunchtime, for which Holly was grateful. She couldn't stomach seeing people looking all smoochy and romantic at the moment, any more than she could listen to the radio when every song seemed to be about love or losing it.

Holly had guessed the restaurant would be pretty swanky (she couldn't imagine Max in a Harvester) so she had dressed up a bit, teaming skinny jeans with her pink heels from the movie premiere, and a stripy Rag & Bone blazer that she'd picked up from a stylist at a huge discount on a *Street Scout* shoot. Her time on the show had seriously improved her wardrobe – although no doubt she would now have to return to the world of M&S shift dresses. The thought started Holly worrying about money all over again, triggering the usual fears about her future. She immediately pulled out her phone and sent herself an email: 'PHONE ALAN AT VITASLIM RE JOB!!!' Right then, that seemed the most reliable option; she needed to get her confidence back before she even thought about trying modelling away from the safety of *Street Scout*.

Through the restaurant's glass front doors, Holly noticed a very large, very shiny black car with tinted windows pull up outside. She wasn't an expert, but it looked like a Bentley or a Rolls-Royce; the sort of thing that Simon Cowell might travel in. A man in a suit and dark glasses emerged from the driver's seat and briskly went round to open the passenger door. She got a brief glimpse of a beige leather interior and then there was Max in his usual uniform of white shirt and slim trousers, looking like a movie star in a pair of Ray-Bans. He paused to speak to the driver, smiling and clapping him chummily on the back, then walked into the restaurant.

The girl behind the front desk virtually shoved Holly out of the way to greet him, but was beaten to it by a short, mustachioed man in a suit – presumably the manager.

'Mr Moore! So wonderful to see you. How are you today?'

'Fine thanks, Bruno,' said Max, shaking his hand. He looked totally at ease, like he owned the place – which for all Holly knew, he might well have done. Then he turned to her with a smile. 'Holly, great to see you,' he said, like meeting her for lunch was the most normal thing in the world. 'Shall we sit down?'

They followed the manager towards a corner table that was clearly the best in the house, although it took them a while to get there as virtually every diner they passed seem to know Max.

'Max! How was St Tropez, mate?'

'Call me about that Mayfair deal, Max, we'd still love you to be involved!'

'Max, darling, I hope you're still coming to our little soirée on Friday?'

None of them seemed to even notice Holly; she presumed he wasn't usually short of female company.

'Claudio will be straight over with the menus,' said the manager as they sat down. 'Can I get you anything else?'

'A couple of Bellinis and some of those little anchovy crostini would be great. Thanks, Bruno.'

'Right away, Mr Moore.' The manager nodded and was gone, leaving them alone. Holly suddenly felt shy and rather nervous. Max was such a powerful figure and for all his charm, she knew from experience he could be hugely intimidating. Thankfully, however, it soon became apparent that today's Max was the smiley, relaxed version she had last encountered during their cosy chat all those weeks ago. He got her giggling almost immediately by telling a few outrageous anecdotes about some of the people who'd greeted him earlier – 'She's married to a seventy-something sheikh but is currently shagging her sixteen-year-old stepson's best mate' – and shared bits of celebrity gossip so scandalous that they would have given the tabloids a month of front pages. For all his easy-going openness, though, Max revealed frustratingly little about himself, while by the time they finished their main courses (sea bass for Max, lobster spaghetti for Holly), she was still no clearer about the reasons for their lunch.

It was only after the waiter had cleared away their plates that Max finally turned to her and said: 'So I suppose you're wondering why I asked you to meet me.'

'I was rather, yes.'

Max took a sip of red wine and sat back in his chair. 'The thing is, Holly, from the very beginning of *Street Scout* I had you marked down as the show's winner. I wasn't lying to you when I said that I thought you were the real deal. So I was curious: why did it all go wrong?'

'Well, someone told me I wasn't right for Strut and chucked me off the show,' smiled Holly, the wine giving her confidence a boost.

Max chuckled. 'Okay, fair enough. But you appreciate that I had to do that after giving you a warning the previous week. And Rosario had real concerns about your reliability and focus. You clearly wanted to be on the show for the right reasons – what happened?'

Holly sighed. She really didn't want to get into the mess of her personal life, but she didn't want Max to think she had screwed up her chance for no reason. So she told him all about James, how he didn't approve of her going on the show and how their break-up had coincided with her disastrous final challenge.

After listening to her explanation, Max shook his head. 'If I had a pound for every girl who's jeopardised a promising career for some guy . . . I hope you don't mind me saying, but it sounds like you're way better off without him.' He leaned across the table towards her, his face suddenly serious. 'Holly, you don't realise how special you are. Most beautiful girls – and you are extremely beautiful – have this arrogance, a sort of brittleness. You don't at all.

You're sweet and humble and you're also a very wonderful lunch date.' He broke into a grin. 'I really enjoy your company.'

Holly returned his smile, feeling gorgeously intoxicated – not just from the booze, but from the fact that this hugely successful, handsome man seemed so focused on her.

Max was still staring at her, his blue eyes holding her gaze. 'Holly, I wanted to ask you something . . .'

Suddenly, one of Max's phones – he had three, all of them on the table – started to vibrate. Holly glanced down and saw the caller ID: 'Sasha Hart'. But Max clearly hadn't noticed that she'd seen.

'Sorry, it's my assistant calling about my next meeting,' he said quickly, picking up the phone and pushing back his chair. 'I'd better take this. Back in a moment.'

Holly watched him walk outside to take the call. She was puzzled: why would Max lie to her about who was calling him? He was standing by the window, but infuriatingly he had his back to her so she couldn't see the expression on his face as he spoke.

After a minute or so Max ended the call and returned to their table, stopping to talk to the woman at the front desk on the way, but he didn't sit down.

'I'm sorry, Holly, but I need to go and deal with an urgent matter that's come up. I've settled the bill and ordered you a slice of this amazing blood orange tart they do, so why don't you stick around a while and enjoy the rest of the meal? Thanks again for meeting me.'

He leaned over and gave her a double cheek kiss, and she caught a waft of gorgeous musky cologne. And then after saying goodbye to a few of the other diners and shaking hands with the manager, Max was out of the door and straight into his car, leaving Holly no clearer about why he'd really wanted to meet her in the first place.

26

Holly wasn't sure whether to be thrilled or gutted when she phoned Alan to be told he'd be more than happy to welcome her back into the 'VitaSlim family'. She had briefly thought about contacting some model agencies to see if they would be interested in taking her on, but the confidence she had gained over the course of *Street Scout* had all but petered out since leaving the show, and the thought of starting afresh currently seemed far too daunting after the emotional roller coaster of the past few weeks. So it was VitaSlim or the dole queue.

'You're a good little worker, Holly,' Alan had told her when she had called him. 'And I've got to be honest with you, I knew you weren't going to win that TV show. I mean, you've got a nice face and all, but that Moet — well, she's cracking ... Tell you what, any chance you could give me her number?'

Holly imagined what Moet would think about Alan with his comb-over and paunch. A wicked smile crept across her face.

'Of course!' she said, sweetly. 'I'm sure Moet would *love* to meet you. Do make sure you give her a call . . .'

Holly was due to start back at VitaSlim in ten days' time, so decided to make the most of her last few days of freedom. She hung out with Meg, went to stay in Essex for a couple of days with her mum and Lola (who, annoyingly, both kept going on about how lovely James was and asking if Holly was *sure* they wouldn't get back together) and had a night out with Kinzah and Chanel to catch up on the *Street Scout* gossip. Natalia had been the show's latest evictee after failing miserably at the TV commercial challenge (her total lack of English meant she couldn't read a word of the autocue), leaving just the two of them and Moet in the competition. It was great to see the girls, and hearing their stories made Holly wish she were still on the show.

The following morning, still feeling nostalgic, Holly logged on to the Twitter account that had been set up for her by the *Street Scout* team. She hadn't looked at it since leaving the show and Kinzah had mentioned she'd had a load of nice messages. Sure enough, there were Tweets such as: 'Gutted that @HollyStreetScout is out. She was my fave' and 'LUV YOU @HollyStreetScout you shoulda stayed in!! *#BitchfaceMoetToGo*'.

Among the fan messages, there was also one from a user called @ShowbizJoe from a few days ago.

'Holly, could you please follow me so I can DM you? Thanks.' It took her a moment to work out that it was Joe Taylor from *Hot* magazine.

Curious at what he might want, Holly clicked on his profile and pressed 'Follow', and later that afternoon a message popped into her inbox.

'Hi, Holly, any chance of a coffee? I've just got a few quick questions about the show. Nothing too heavy. Hope you're well. Joe'.

It only took a moment for Holly to decide to meet up with him. He'd seemed like a nice guy and, besides, Meg kept banging on at her to 'network' and exploit her new-found TV contacts, and coffee with Joe seemed like the perfect opportunity.

Joe had offered to meet her locally, so the following morning Holly walked the short distance to her nearest Starbucks and found him already sitting at a table in the window. His hair looked a bit longer and messier than when they had last met, but his sunny grin hadn't changed and Holly found herself wondering once again why he looked so familiar. Thankfully, Joe cleared up the mystery soon after she'd sat down.

'You don't remember me from school, do you?' he asked. 'I was a couple of years above you at Oakbrook High.'

Of course, that was it! 'Oh my God, I do!' gasped Holly. 'You used to hang around with Andrew Tyler and Luke Plowden, didn't you? But you've really . . . *changed* since then . . .'

Joe laughed. 'Don't worry, I know what you're thinking. I lost a hell of a lot of weight at uni. Weight Watchers,' he added in a conspiratorial whisper. 'I could still tell you exactly how many points there are in that blueberry muffin you're eating.'

'Please don't,' said Holly. 'I'm a bit paranoid about my weight after my booker on *Street Scout* kept banging on about my huge thighs.'

'Christ, they must have been blind. You're absolutely gorgeous.' Joe suddenly looked a bit awkward. 'You know, I used to have such a crush on you at school.'

'Really? God, I was such a shy little thing I had no idea! I was completely terrified of boys.'

'Looks like you've got over that now,' said Joe. 'I caught a glimpse of you and Cole Fox chatting at the *Beyond Hope* premiere. The pair of you looked pretty close.'

The mention of Cole made Holly feel uncomfortable. She'd already spent far too long imagining what might have happened if she'd taken him up on the offer of dinner. If only she'd discovered James was a cheating bastard a few weeks earlier! She still hadn't deleted Cole's text, but over a month had now passed since he'd sent it – no doubt he'd have forgotten all about her by now.

Changing the subject, Holly asked who Joe was still in touch with from school and they chatted away, reminiscing about growing up in Essex, mutual friends and their terrible school uniform. The conversation was still flowing over an hour later, when Joe glanced at the clock.

'Shit, I need to be back in the office!' he said. 'Listen, I was going to ask if you'd be willing to do an interview about your time on *Street Scout*. Just a fun piece – I'm not digging for dirt, I promise. We're doing an interview with the three finalists, but you were so popular it would be good to get you in the magazine as well.'

Holly pulled a face. 'I'm not sure . . .' She really didn't fancy raking over the mess she'd made of her final few weeks.

'Say you'll think about it, please?'

'Okay,' she smiled. 'I'll think about it.'

They walked out onto the street together and Holly said goodbye and promised to be in touch, but, as she turned to leave, Joe suddenly blurted out: 'Holly, I'm sorry if this is totally inappropriate, but would you like to go out with me for a drink sometime?'

Holly was confused. 'But I thought you were married?' He looked blank. 'Your wedding ring?'

'Oh, that!' Joe grinned. 'I just wear it at work. You wouldn't believe how predatory some female celebrities can be. This very famous forty-something soap actress once asked me for a drink and though she was definite cougar territory, she was very persistent – and extremely sexy, too – so we started to see each other. But after a few weeks she started badgering me about putting all these positive stories about her in the magazine – trying to boost her profile and take five years off her age – and when I refused she dumped me. Turns out the only thing she'd been interested in was the size of my column inches. So the ring's just a deterrent. I'm totally single, honest guv! Anyway – what do you think about that drink?'

'I'll think about it,' said Holly, with a smile. Joe was a nice guy – and God knows her ego could do with a bit of a lift after the trampling it had received from James.

'Make sure you do,' grinned Joe, as he walked away. 'Or I'll have to see what I can do to persuade you . . .'

Later that afternoon, Holly was giving her flat its long overdue clean when the intercom to her front door buzzed.

'Hello?'

'Delivery for Holly Collins,' came a voice.

Holly trotted downstairs to be met by a courier bearing a bouquet of pale yellow roses. There were so many of them the scent was almost dizzying. Wondering who on earth could be sending her such a beautiful bunch of flowers, Holly raced back up to her flat and tore open the attached card.

'Holly. I can't get you out of my head. Please meet me outside Embankment tube station by the river at 8 tonight.'

There was no name beneath the message.

Holly sat staring at the note, as if it might give some clue to the sender's identity. James had often sent her flowers before Lady Crosby appeared on the scene, but it seemed highly unlikely that he would want to meet now – unless, of course, it was to tell her that he'd made a terrible mistake and wanted to try again. She'd heard nothing from him since that awful night they split up and Holly tried to imagine how a potential reunion would play out. She'd like to think she'd tell that lying, cheating bastard to shove the roses up his arse, thorny-end first. The idea gave her a little glimmer of satisfaction.

What about Joe Taylor? He seemed far too laid back to be such a fast mover, but he *had* said he was going to try and 'persuade' her to go out for a drink with him. *And*, it suddenly occurred to Holly, the yellow of the roses was a very similar shade to their old *Oakbrook High school shirts!* Perhaps it was a clue . . .

But then there was Max. He had asked her to lunch, of course, and he was certainly one for grand romantic gestures, but he was dating Sasha – and Holly couldn't imagine a powerful older man like him would be interested in her, anyway. Besides, the note said to meet by Embankment station – and she very much doubted the chauffer-driven Max would have suggested meeting by a station. He probably didn't even know how the tube worked.

Cole Fox? There was an excited flutter in her stomach; it *did* seem like the sort of thing a movie star might do . . . She was pretty sure he was currently in LA (not that she'd been scanning the celebrity gossip websites for a mention of him yesterday afternoon), but maybe he'd just got back to the country and wanted to meet up for that much-delayed dinner . . .

She looked at the note again. 'I can't get you out of my head,' it said. That was a Kylie song. So maybe the person who sent it was . . . *Australian*? Or one of her 'neighbours'? No, no, that was a stupid idea . . . Oh God, what if it was from a deranged stalker who had seen her on *Street Scout* and somehow tracked down her address? Perhaps she should look through the roses to check there wasn't some anthrax powder or something! Holly checked herself, rolling her eyes. *God, get a grip, woman . . .*

Holly arrived at Embankment tube just before eight that evening. Despite a fleeting concern about stalkers, she was too intrigued by the mystery admirer's identity not to go to the rendezvous – and when she had phoned to ask Meg's advice, her friend had threatened to frogmarch her down there herself if she didn't go through with it.

As Holly had no clue who she was meeting or where they would be going, it made choosing an outfit tricky, but it was a particularly warm July so she opted for comfort over glamour, wearing a short lacy sundress and brown leather flip-flops and keeping her make-up minimal. She didn't want this person, whoever he (or – it occurred to her – she?) was, to get the wrong idea.

Just outside the station, Holly positioned herself behind the stairs that led up to the footbridge over the river and scanned the pavement on the opposite side of the road. There were dozens of people sitting on the river-wall enjoying the evening sunshine, but she didn't recognise any of them. She noticed a bloke standing on his own, clearly waiting for someone. *Could that be him . . . ?* But a moment later, a girl ran up and threw her arms around him. After ten minutes and still without any likely candidates for her secret admirer, Holly felt a pang of disappointment. It hadn't even occurred to her that whoever it was might not turn up. Perhaps this was just some elaborate practical joke?

But just then a coach pulled up and a group of tourists started moving away from where they'd been gathered in a large group on the pavement, revealing a door in the river-wall. Holly looked a bit closer; there seemed to be something attached to the door. Something that looked rather like a pale yellow rose.

Holly crossed over the road to take a closer look. Yes, it *was* a rose, identical to the ones in her bouquet. Her heart quickening with excitement, she tried the handle – and the door swung open.

27

Holly gasped in astonishment. In front of her was a trail of lit candle-lanterns leading down a flight of steps and along a wooden jetty, at the end of which was a boat. Actually, to call it a boat was like calling Buckingham Palace a house. It was like the water-going equivalent of a Lamborghini, all sharp angles, blacked-out windows and gleaming white body-work. There were several large outside decks and Holly could make out what looked like a Jacuzzi on the roof. Holly's stomach fluttered with butterflies as she walked down the steps and along the jetty, the light from the lanterns flickering and dancing on the water around her. Even though she was in the middle of London, a hush seemed to have descended on the city – as if, like her, it was holding its breath in anticipation of what might happen. Then, as Holly approached the boat, she saw the vessel's name and any remaining doubts she had over the mystery admirer's identity instantly vanished. Emblazoned across the back in swirly gold lettering it read,

Moore or Less, with the name of its home port – London – in smaller writing beneath.

She sensed movement above her on deck and Holly glanced up and looked straight into the smiling eyes of Max. 'I'm very glad to see you,' he said. 'Would you like to come on board?'

Too stunned at the extravagance of his gesture to speak, Holly just nodded. Max met her at the top of the gangway and took her hand to help her onto the polished wood deck. He looked every inch the gorgeous billionaire yacht owner in a tight navy T-shirt, white linen trousers and bare feet, which were as golden-brown as the rest of him.

'Champagne?'

At Max's signal, a man dressed in black emerged from the shadows carrying a tray with a bottle of Cristal champagne and two frosted flutes. He expertly eased off the cork, poured two glasses and offered one to Holly.

'My chief steward, Nick,' said Max.

As Holly reached for the drink she noticed that her hand was shaking. She was still utterly shell-shocked. Just a few minutes ago, she'd been stuck on a sweaty tube train, her nose pressed into a stranger's armpit; now she appeared to have swapped lives with Mariah Carey.

Max raised his glass to her. He was smiling, but his pale blue eyes had a look of uncertainty, even vulnerability. Holly was surprised; she had never seen him looking anything less than totally in control.

'This is . . . amazing,' she said, shaking her head in wonder at it all.

'Well, I didn't get a chance to finish talking to you the other day,' said Max.

'You could have just phoned,' she said, a smile creeping across her face.

He laughed, suddenly seeming to relax. 'Now, where would be the fun in that? And this way I can guarantee that there'll be no interruptions. I hope you're hungry.'

Holly nodded, although she felt far too full of nerves to fit in any food.

'It's the cook's day off, so it's just a takeaway, I'm afraid,' he said, as he led her up a flight of stairs to the upper deck, where a round table was set for two and laid out with platters of jewel-like sashimi, piles of tempura and tiny dumplings. Another bottle of champagne sat chilling in a bucket of ice nearby.

Holly looked at Max incredulously. 'A *take-away . . . ?*'

'Well, Nobu does deliver,' he shrugged with a smile.

Nick the steward, who had magically appeared from inside the upper cabin, pulled back one of the white leather armchairs from the table for Holly, then laid a napkin on her lap with a flourish.

'Thanks, Nick, that will be all for now,' said Max,

after he had topped up their champagne. 'And you can tell Captain Marco we're ready to go.'

'Go? Where?' Holly suddenly panicked. Christ, what if he was planning on whisking her off to St Tropez or somewhere? She hadn't even brought a spare pair of knickers . . .

'Just a little round trip,' he said. 'Don't worry, Cinderella, we'll get you home well before midnight.'

Once she had started to relax, Holly did indeed feel like a fairy-tale princess – and Max made the perfect Prince Charming. Holly could have talked to him for hours; whatever the subject, he was so knowledgeable and entertaining, without being in the least bit arrogant. And he was incredibly attentive. When Holly shivered slightly during dinner, he immediately called for Nick, who brought her out a cashmere shawl and a hot-water bottle. It was a magical evening. And the food – well, Holly would never be able to think about her Friday-night curry takeaway the same way again. Nevertheless, she couldn't shake a slight uneasiness. Okay, so this was by far the most romantic date she had ever been on – but this wasn't actually a date . . . *was it?* She didn't want to ask Max in case she made an idiot of herself. Plus, of course, there was the question of Sasha: what about *their* relationship?

It was just after 10 p.m. when the boat got back to the jetty. As a pair of deckhands secured the moorings, Holly asked where the bathroom was and Nick was instantly on hand to show her the way. Inside, the boat was fitted out like a boutique hotel, all pale-wood panelling, spotlights, cream carpet and sumptuous leather upholstery. Even the guest bath-room was spectacular, with a huge, honey-coloured marble bath, dozens of fluffy white towels and shelves of brand-new designer toiletries, clearly intended for guests' use. Holly put on a bit of Chanel lipgloss and had a squirt of a Tom Ford perfume. She looked at her face in the mirror; her eyes were wide and sparkling – she was literally glowing.

When she got back outside, Max was leaning on the railings looking out towards the jetty. As she went over to join him, there was a sudden whooshing noise and a firework burst in a shower of silver sparks above them. Holly had barely had time to catch her breath when there was another dazzling explosion, and then another.

She turned to Max in amazement. 'Did you arrange this?'

He grinned. 'Doesn't everyone have fireworks with sushi?'

They watched the fireworks together in silence. She glanced over at him: he was staring up at the sky, looking as delighted as a little kid. Sensing her gaze, he turned to look at her.

'I'm so glad you came tonight, Holly,' he said. 'I meant what I said on that note I sent you – I can't get you out of my head. From the very first moment I laid eyes on you, I haven't been able to stop thinking about you. When we talked that time at the studio . . . I wanted to tell you how I felt, but it didn't seem right, not while you were still on the show. But now . . .' He reached over and took her hand. 'I'd really love to see you again, Holly. As much as possible, in fact.'

Holly was speechless. She had never imagined that such a powerful man would bare his emotions like this. She was in a daze; there was just too much to take in. But then she realised that Max was leaning in to kiss her and she abruptly pulled away.

'What about Sasha?' she blurted out. 'Aren't the two of you dating?'

For a moment he looked taken aback, but he quickly recovered himself. 'Holly, you don't have to worry about that. I promise.'

Max was still gazing at her intently, his eyes boring into hers. So had Holly got the wrong end of the stick about him and Sasha? She looked down at her feet, trying to get her head straight. But then Max put his arms around her waist and pulled her into him. She could feel the warmth of his body and smell that same delicious musky fragrance.

'You're perfect,' he said softly.

She lifted her eyes to his again and, in that moment, intoxicated by his closeness, the champagne and the magic of the evening, her fears just melted away. Maybe this was just what the doctor had ordered to get over the split from James. And this time, when Max started to move his face towards hers, she didn't resist. His lips brushed hers softly and then his hands moved down her back, pressing her even closer to him. As she closed her eyes and surrendered to the kiss, there was an explosion of white stars that had nothing to do with the fireworks in the sky.

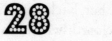

When Holly woke up the following morning in her own bed in her cramped Hammersmith flat, she wondered fleetingly if she had dreamt the whole thing. But then, at the end of the bed, she saw the cashmere shawl Max had insisted she take with her when she went home. She pulled it towards her and pressed her face against it, breathing in the scent of the Tom Ford fragrance that still lingered in its velvety folds. Sinking back on the pillow, Holly closed her eyes and felt a wave of happiness break over her. The events of yesterday had been so completely unexpected that she was still struggling to take in the fact that the mighty Max Moore was actually interested in *her*! But last night she'd had a glimpse of the real man beneath the polished, platinum-plated exterior – and he'd been sensitive, kind and the sort of person she would be very keen to spend more time with. After James had hurt her so badly, Max seemed to be offering just what she needed.

Max had behaved like a complete gentleman after their mind-blowing kiss on the boat. He had escorted her back up to the street, where a car was waiting to drive her home.

'Thank you for a wonderful night,' she had said, settling into the butter-soft leather seat in the back.

'It was my absolute pleasure,' said Max. He leaned in and kissed her briefly on the lips. 'Until next time, beautiful.'

Holly let out a little contented sigh at the memory. Max was an excellent kisser. He might be old enough to be her father – in years, though certainly not in looks or attitude – but he really was knee-tremblingly fanciable . . .

She padded to the kitchen and started making tea and toast for breakfast. The sun was shining through the windows so brightly it made her squint; it looked like another perfect summer day.

Just then her phone started to ring. Holly was surprised to see that the caller was Joe Taylor.

'Hi, Joe.'

'Morning. I hope I didn't wake you.'

'Not at all. What's up?'

'I've just been in a meeting with my editor and she's really keen to get this chat with you for the magazine. Have you had a chance to think about it any further?'

In the excitement of last night Holly had actually forgotten all about the interview – and now things had developed so unexpectedly with Max she really wasn't keen. She wanted to help out Joe, but he was bound to ask about Strut, and her loyalty now unquestionably lay with Max.

'I don't think I can, Joe, sorry.'

'Really? Is there nothing I can do to change your mind?'

'I'm afraid not. But if there's anything else I can help with, just let me know.'

'Fair enough . . . actually, there *might* be something else.'

'Yes?'

'Well, there's been a bit of speculation in showbiz circles that Sasha Hart has got back together with Max Moore. I didn't pay much attention to the rumours, but this morning some paparazzi photos appeared on my desk of Max leaving Sasha's home in the early hours of this morning. I don't suppose you saw anything happen between them while you were on *Street Scout*?'

What the hell . . . ? If what Joe said was true, Max must have gone straight to Sasha's place after they'd said goodbye. She tried to think of a good reason he might be paying a late-night visit to her, but she could come up with none that was innocent.

'Holly, are you still there? Did you notice anything between them on the show?'

'No . . . no, I didn't . . .'

'Oh, well. The offer of a drink still stands, okay?'

'Okay. Thanks, Joe. Bye.'

Holly couldn't believe she'd been so stupid. A few compliments and a flash date and she'd been completely taken in by Max's lies! But actually, he hadn't lied to her about dating Sasha, had he? He just told her not to worry about it – and, in retrospect, if he couldn't deny it then that was pretty much an admission that he was. Well, she was buggered if she was going to cry over another bloke. There was only one thing for it: squats. Holly went straight over and put on her Davina fitness DVD. A bit of physical pain would distract her from the pain in her heart.

A workout and a long, cold shower later, Holly was walking to the shops when her phone rang again. It was Meg.

'Why the fuck haven't you phoned me, Collins? You were supposed to call me first thing this morning to tell me what happened last night!'

Holly sighed. She was still feeling too bruised to talk about it, even to Meg. 'It was Max Moore, from *Street Scout*,' she said. 'He took me on his yacht. It was amazing, but I've just found out he's in a relationship with Sasha Hart. So that's the end of that.'

'Why is that the end? He's obviously into you, so just have some fun. A zillionaire fuck-buddy is not a bad thing to have, Hols. Imagine the presents.'

'Maybe . . . But he just seemed so genuine.'

'Darlin', will you please stop looking for someone

to sweep you off your feet in this grand romance, and just try and enjoy yourself for a while?'

'I don't think I can do that,' said Holly, sadly. 'My emotions keep screwing things up.'

'Well, I might just have some exciting news to take your mind off all that,' said Meg. 'You know VitaSlim have that in-house competition to find an Employee of the Month?'

Holly did – although it nearly always went to someone in Sales or Marketing.

'So guess who won it this month? Me!'

'Meg, that's brilliant! Congratulations.' Holly wasn't sure that a framed certificate really counted as exciting news, but still . . .

'No, no, that's not the good bit,' said Meg. 'To create a bit of an incentive, the powers-that-be are now giving out prizes – and I only bloody won a weekend in New York!'

'Oh my God, that's amazing! Well done!'

'Hang on, that's not the *really* good bit! The really good bit is – you're coming with me!'

'Meg, I . . . but what about Spunk?'

'No, he agrees that I should take you. You've had a really shitty time of late and deserve something nice. Get packing, Miz Collins, we're leaving on Friday!'

They landed at JFK Airport in the late afternoon. VitaSlim had clearly booked the cheapest flights possible, which turned out to be with Uzbek Air's brand-new transatlantic service – although the plane itself seemed to have had quite a few previous owners. The toilet sign was written in Italian, the safety messages were in Chinese and, as they were boarding, Holly could make out 'Uganda Airlines' underneath the new Uzbek Air logo on the side of the plane. Every expense had been spared on the in-flight service, too: dinner was a choice of mutton stew or mutton surprise; Holly and Meg had one of each and they turned out to be exactly the same thing. At least the entertainment system worked, although it only screened one movie on a loop – *Kindergarten Cop* – and that was dubbed in what Holly presumed was Uzbekistani. But none of that mattered in the slightest to Holly and Meg, who both got tipsy on the strangely sweet red wine and spent most of the flight looking through their guide-books, deciding on a to-do list for the weekend. Neither of them had ever been to New York before and, as the plane descended into JFK, their excitement levels remained high amongst the clouds.

Even making their way through the airport was a thrill. Everything about it was just so unmistakably New York: from the gum-chewing cops with guns at their hips and the officer at Customs telling them to 'have a nice day' to the kiosk in the Arrivals hall selling hot dogs and pretzels. And then leaving behind the air conditioning and walking out into the early evening heat, so dense and damp it was like going into a steam room, and getting in line for an iconic yellow New York taxi. But the real buzz came about twenty minutes into the drive, when the Manhattan skyline suddenly appeared on the horizon. Holly actually gasped at the sight. It was at once so familiar to her – there was the Empire State Building! And the Statue of Liberty! – but at the same time completely unknown, like some fantastic fairy-tale city with the promise of magic, adventure and danger hidden amongst its towers and citadels. For the rest of the drive, Holly stared out of the window, drinking in every wonderful detail, and trying not to go flying through the front window every time their lunatic driver slammed on the brakes.

They were staying downtown at a place called the Greenwich Square Hotel, which was brilliantly located near cool spots like the West Village, SoHo, Tribeca and the Meatpacking District, but from the reviews on TripAdvisor sounded more *Gangs of New York* than *Sex and the City*. One reviewer had described it as a 'semi-clean dump'.

But as the cab pulled up outside, Holly couldn't have been happier. The hotel was just off Washington Square (Holly immediately recognised its famous white arch from an episode of *Friends*) and its shabby Art Deco exterior definitely had a sort of olde-worlde charm, even if inside it was infested with bedbugs, as another TripAdvisor review had claimed. While Meg took the bags into the lobby, Holly paid the driver.

'Where's the tip?' he snapped, when she handed over the fare.

'Um, it was fifty-five dollars and I've given you five extra.'

'Whaddabout the rest of it?'

Suddenly, Meg stepped in. 'Listen, mate, you're lucky you got anything,' she said, jabbing her finger at him. 'You drive like a fucking maniac.'

The driver glared at her for a moment then shook his head and muttered, 'Crazy Australian bitch.'

'Crazy IRISH bitch, you idiot!' Meg yelled after him as he sped off.

Holly frowned at her friend.

'What?' Meg glared back. 'Hols, we're in New York! You gotta learn how to talk their language!'

The concierge barely spoke English, the lobby had a very strange smell and their hotel room was tiny, with two narrow single beds, but the air condition-ing worked fine and besides, they didn't intend to spend much time in there, anyway. After dumping their bags and having a quick freshen-up, they grabbed a map and hit the streets. It was too late to go shopping, so they just started walking. They went down Mercer Street through SoHo, then headed along Canal Street to Chinatown and up to Little Italy. With every block, Holly fell ever more deeply in love. Everything about the city was so familiar from TV shows and films – the constant hooting of the cars, fire hydrants at every corner, air vents in the street sending up plumes of steam – that she felt instantly at home. It was like when you see someone famous in the street and fleetingly feel like you've already met them because you're so familiar with their face.

After a while, Meg insisted they stop at an Irish pub, where she persuaded the bemused barman to knock them up a couple of Cosmopolitans, which had been one of the first items on their to-do list. The cocktails were pretty much neat vodka and they hadn't eaten since they'd landed, so by the time they left three drinks later they were feeling distinctly wobbly and starving hungry. It was nearly 11 p.m., but the pavements – *sidewalks*, Holly reminded herself drunkenly – were still radiating heat.

A couple of blocks from their hotel they stumbled across a fast-food place called Sticky's Finger Joint. It served nothing but chicken fingers, but it was clearly pretty good as the queue was out of the door, so they got in line. Meg got talking to a couple of guys who invited them to a thrash-metal gig, but thankfully for once she saw the sense of getting an earlyish night so they could make the most of their day tomorrow. The food turned out to be well worth the wait. They gorged themselves on chicken fingers coated in crushed pretzels and drizzled with salted caramel sauce, with creamy pineapple coleslaw and purple sweet-potato fries dipped in choc-chip BBQ sauce. *Screw you, Rosario,* thought Holly with a smile, as she tucked into their million-calorie late-night feast.

A short while later she fell into bed and lay staring into the darkness, dizzy with the city's sights, smells and sounds. As exhausted as she was, she was filled with happiness and hope. Okay, so she was dreading going back to her old job at VitaSlim and she was still hurting from the way James had treated her; plus, on top of all that, there was the question of Max, who had whisked her off her feet only to drop her on her arse. But here in this cramped hotel room, her problems were thousands of miles away and, as she shut her eyes and snuggled down into the pillow to block out the rattling of the air-conditioning unit, Holly had a sudden sense that something amazing was about to happen to her. New York was that kind of place: it made you feel like you could do anything or be anyone. *If I can make it there, I'll make it anywhere . . .* Holly happily hummed the Sinatra song to herself. And within moments, she was asleep.

29

A combination of excitement and jet lag saw Holly and Meg leaving the hotel by eight the following morning. Despite the early hour, a fug of humidity was already settling over the city like a 15-tog duvet. The girls wandered down Broadway, raring to get started on the shopping, but nothing much was open. It seemed the City That Never Sleeps liked a bit of a lie-in on Saturday mornings.

The girls' guidebook had suggested that the best coffee in town could be found at the gourmet grocer Dean & Deluca, which was conveniently located a short walk from their hotel, so they decided to stop there for breakfast. Spread over several floors of a red-brick building on the corner of Prince and Broadway, it was more like a department store than a supermarket – except with displays of raspberry-cream cookies and artisan sheep's cheese instead of shoes and bags. The girls loaded up with pastries and coffee and sat at the counter in the store's window, watching the city come to life.

'Okay, what's on the list for today?' asked Meg, dunking a praline croissant into a bucket-sized cappuccino.

Holly pulled out their itinerary. 'So we've got Bloomingdale's, Macy's, Barneys, the Empire State Building, the Circle Line boat tour, the Metropolitan Museum of Art, the Museum of Modern Art, the Guggenheim Museum, hot dogs, the Central Park bike tour, Staten Island ferry, a baseball game at the Yankee Stadium, cocktails at the Mercer . . .' Holly paused to pop the last of a blueberry cream-cheese scone into her mouth, looking over the list as she chewed. 'Do you think we might have to lose a couple of things off here?'

Meg gave a decisive nod. 'Strike off anything with "museum" in the name for starters.' She took a sip of pear and ginger smoothie. 'And then anything that involves boats, balls or bikes. Ooh, can I have a bit of that carrot muffin?' Holly tore off a chunk and handed it over. 'God, that is gorgeous . . . So, how does the list look now?'

'Um . . . the Empire State Building, food and shopping.'

'Perfect,' said Meg.

A short cab ride uptown later, Holly and Meg grate-fully swapped the sweaty sidewalk for the turbo-chilled marble lobby of the Empire State Building and joined the queue for the elevator to the outdoors observation deck. Holly had never been that keen on lifts and as they shot skywards, she clenched her eyes shut and struggled to stop thinking about disaster movies involving cables snapping and Bruce Willis dangling in an elevator shaft in a dirty vest. But when they emerged on the eighty-sixth floor, the spectacular views more than compensated for the nail-biting journey to get up there.

A light breeze ruffled their hair as they joined the crowds gathered around the railings. When she was at street level, Holly felt overawed by the sheer size of the place, but up here she could see just how compact Manhattan island actually was, like some mammoth game of Jenga all wrapped up in the silvery-blue ribbon of the Hudson River. They were just trying to locate the city's most famous land-marks when Holly felt a tap on her shoulder.

'Excuse me, ma'am?'

She spun round to find a young couple wearing matching 'I heart NY' T-shirts, green foam Statue of Liberty crowns and huge grins.

'Could you please take a photo of us?' asked the guy in a broad Southern accent, his eyes sparkling. 'I just asked my beautiful girlfriend to marry me – and she said yes!'

'Oh, that's lovely!' said Holly. 'Of course. Just over here?'

The couple stood in front of the railings and kissed while Holly lined up the shot. They were still kissing long after she had taken it. Meg, who was standing nearby watching, rolled her eyes. When they finally came up for air, Holly handed back the camera with a smile.

'Congratulations,' she said.

'I still can't quite believe it!' gushed the girl, admiring her new ring. 'Are you married?'

'No, I'm not,' said Holly. With a pang of unhappiness, she remembered just how recently she had been thinking that she might soon be planning a wedding.

'Oh, never mind,' said the girl, sympathetically. 'I'm sure it will happen for you soon . . .'

As the couple walked off, Meg came over and gave Holly's hand a squeeze.

'You okay?'

Holly nodded. She still got the occasional painful pang of hurt and anger over James, but he'd treated her so terribly that she knew she was far better off without him.

'Let's go and look round the other side,' said Meg. But as they rounded the corner, they nearly knocked over another man going down on bended knee in front of another stunned-looking woman.

'Jeez, what is it with you people?' muttered Meg. 'I blame Tom Hanks . . .'

As Meg hurried her away, Holly remembered how she'd once secretly hoped that James would one day get down on one knee to her – and she wondered if she'd ever love someone that deeply again.

* * *

They went for lunch at a place called Serendipity 3 on the Upper East Side, famed for its foot-long hot dogs and frozen hot chocolate. They ordered both, along with chili nachos, fries and beers, and soon Holly was too distracted by indigestion to worry about heartache.

'Where do you put it all?' she asked in disbelief as Meg ordered a slice of peanut-butter pie 'with extra cream' for dessert.

'Goes straight to my boobs,' she grinned.

It was just a few blocks' walk from the restaurant to Bloomingdale's and by the time they walked through its revolving doors, New York had worked its magic on her again and Holly had forgotten all about her wobble at the top of the Empire State Building. Ever mindful of her cash-flow crisis, Holly had limited herself to a shopping budget of $100 for the weekend, but she hadn't counted on the charming persistence of the city's shop assistants: as they headed off to the changing rooms, Meg armed with a pair of leather leggings, four T-shirts, two dresses and a red satin tuxedo jacket, and Holly with a single vest-top (reduced in the sale), an assistant hurried over.

'I'm sorry, but I saw you looking at this and you just gotta try it on.' She held up a beautiful drapey white dress with a black leather belt that Holly had indeed been admiring earlier. 'It would look so gorgeous on you.'

Holly had originally rejected it for having one too many zeros on the price tag, but the assistant was insistent. And then when she was trying it on (it *did* look gorgeous, Holly had to admit, making the most of her long legs and giving her the illusion of a tiny waist) the assistant reappeared with the most perfect pair of black patent pumps. 'They're almost identical to Louboutin's "Pigalle" heels, but half the price,' she smiled, pressing them into Holly's hands. 'And this would really pull the whole look together,' she added, producing a vintage-style chunky crystal necklace.

It all worked so well together that Holly ended up buying the lot, blowing her budget four times over in a single transaction.

'This is exactly why God invented credit cards,' Meg reassured her as she guiltily handed over the plastic. 'Besides, money spent abroad is like calories consumed standing up – it doesn't count.'

After a quick stop in the make-up department ('You *must* get a red lipstick to go with that dress,' Meg had instructed Holly), they left the store loaded down with its famous brown paper bags and headed to Macy's, and then Saks and the glossy designer emporiums on Fifth Avenue, most of which Holly felt too intimidated to even go inside. She had no such problems downtown at the legendary discount department store, Century 21. It was utter chaos inside, a cross between the world's biggest jumble sale and *Fight Club*, but Holly managed to bag a pair of J Brand jeans for $30 and Meg got a shaggy, white, fake-fur DKNY jacket that looked just like the sort of thing Kate Moss would wear, with a 75 per cent discount.

By the time they arrived back at the hotel late that afternoon – via a souvenir shop to get a New York baseball cap and T-shirt for Lola – Holly was all shopped-out and desperate for a nap, but Meg wouldn't hear of it.

'You can sleep when you're dead,' she said, pushing her in the direction of the shower. 'Right now there are cocktails to drink.'

They had decided to start the evening at the Mercer, an extremely swanky boutique hotel that the guidebook had described as the 'go-to choice for models, actors and rock stars'. The girls had dressed accordingly, Holly in her new dress and Meg in a bright pink number that clashed dramatically with her red hair, but when they got there the only other people in the bar were a few business-men and other tourists.

'I thought we'd see P Diddy or Jay-Z,' muttered Meg as they took a seat. 'Jon Bon Jovi at the very least.'

'Don't worry, it's still early,' said Holly.

But a couple of martinis each later, the closest they'd got to a celebrity sighting was a pixie-ish blonde who looked a bit like one of the Olsen twins.

With its comfy armchairs and soft lighting, Holly loved the place, but Meg had clearly been hoping for a bit more glitz. And when she returned from a trip to the Ladies, the huge smile on her face suggested she'd located it.

'Bumped into Madonna in the toilet did you . . . ?' asked Holly.

'Drink up, Collins, we're in the wrong place,' said Meg, grabbing her bag and fur jacket.

Holly looked at her blankly.

'I got chatting with a woman in the bathroom and apparently there's a secret bar in the hotel's basement called the Submercer, which is where all the beautiful people go, so that's where we're going.'

'Are you sure? I'm actually quite comfortable here . . .'

But Meg was already heading out of the door.

30

The hotel's secret bar turned out to be so secret that it took them a good twenty minutes to find it. Following directions from Meg's toilet buddy, they went out of the main entrance and found a pair of unmarked doors at the side of the hotel. Once inside, they took a juddering freight elevator down a couple of floors then passed along a long, dark hallway stocked with bathroom supplies.

'Are you sure this is the right way?' asked Holly, nervously.

'Yes, definitely,' said Meg – although when they found themselves in what seemed to be a boiler room, even she looked a little uncertain. But then they heard the muffled thump of music and went down another corridor, at the end of which was a heavy door marked with a red letter 'M'. A group of girls who, judging by their clothes, worked in fashion were gathered around the entrance, which was blocked by a heavyset man wearing a black suit and a sneer.

'But my boyfriend's already in theeeere,' one of the girls was saying in a wheedling voice.

'Reservations only,' the guy snapped back.

'I texted the DJ, like, an hour ago and he *totally* said we could come in!' said another.

'And *I* say you can't unless I have your names on my list,' said the doorman. 'Which I don't. So good night.'

As the group of girls pushed past them back down the corridor, tutting and rolling their eyes, Holly turned to Meg. 'Come on, let's just go,' she whispered. 'You heard what the guy said – reservations only.'

But Meg waved her hand dismissively, stuck out her chest and then marched up to the door with a radiant smile.

'Meg O'Hanlon from British rock legends, Babes of Bedlam, and Holly Collins from Strut Models,' she announced loudly.

The doorman looked them briefly up and down – and then, by some miracle, smiled and stepped to one side, without even glancing at his clipboard.

'Have a nice evening, ladies,' he said, pushing the door open for them.

'Thank you,' said Meg, fluttering her lashes at him as she strutted past. 'Works every time,' she muttered to Holly with a wink.

After the trouble they'd had finding the place, Holly had been expecting something pretty spectacular, but with its low ceilings and bare brick walls it looked more like a dungeon than a bar – albeit one with red leather seats and a matching stripper pole. The clientele, however, were obviously loaded, gorgeous or both.

They sat at one of the small, low tables near the bar and ordered a couple of the house cocktails – a potent mix of gin, lemon and mint called a Southside – then settled in for some serious people-watching. Holly had already clocked a famous model with her boyfriend (she'd originally thought the guy must be her dad, perhaps her granddad, but then they'd started licking each other's faces) when Meg suddenly gave a muffled squeal.

'Jesus, you won't believe who's sitting behind you,' she hissed, virtually bouncing off her seat with excitement. 'It's that really famous actor who was in that amazing movie! Oh God, I'm shite with names . . . He was in that film about UFOs a few years back, you know the one . . . Oh Christ, what's he called . . . Don something, maybe . . . ? Anyway, he's sitting a few tables away by the pillar. Quick, take a look.'

As subtly as possible, Holly glanced over her shoulder. She recognised him instantly, of course. It was Frank Isaacs, one of the most acclaimed actors of his generation and, Holly seemed to remember, an Oscar-winner to boot. He was sitting on his own, marking up what looked like a script and flicking nuts into his mouth with his free hand; the epitome of Hollywood cool. He must have been in his late fifties, even though his hair was as thick and dark as ever, but the guy was a bona fide movie legend . . . Holly was so star-struck that it took her a moment to realise that Frank Isaacs had clocked her staring at him – and was now smiling back at her.

She spun back to face Meg. 'Shit, he saw me looking!' she hissed.

Meg sneaked another peak in his direction – and her eyes suddenly widened. 'Oh my God, he's coming this way!'

Sure enough, a moment later Frank Isaacs was standing in front of them. He was tall and skinny, with an intense, intellectual air emphasised by his tweed jacket and the pair of heavy-framed black glasses perched on his long nose. If you hadn't known he was an actor, you'd have probably guessed he was an unusually attractive astrophysicist.

'Care to join me, ladies?' He gestured back towards his table.

'Thank you, that would be delightful,' smiled Meg, and got up to follow him.

'What are you doing?' whispered Holly.

'Oh, come on, live a little,' Meg muttered back. 'Imagine the story we'll have to tell everyone back home!'

It was quite surreal, sitting chatting with *the* Frank Isaacs. Over another round of Southsides – although he was drinking a pot of what looked like green tea – he told them he was in town for a meeting about directing a play on Broadway. He quizzed Meg about Ireland ('one of my favourite places') and even seemed to take an interest in VitaSlim, promising to buy a box next time he was in England. As he had invited them to join him, Holly had assumed Frank might be trying to chat one – or both – of them up, but while he was charming and friendly, he didn't seem in the least bit sleazy. Holly seemed to remember some rumours about his sexuality a few years back; perhaps the guy was lonely and just wanted some company?

The cocktails were strong and the girls hadn't eaten since lunchtime, so when Frank casually suggested they continue chatting in his room and Meg immediately got up and tottered drunkenly after him, Holly followed without complaint. Apart from anything else, she was worried she might not be able to find her way out of the labyrinthine passages if she was left on her own.

Frank was staying in the penthouse suite, which turned out to be about three times the size of Holly's flat. He showed them into the living room, switched on the TV and then disappeared off into one of the other rooms 'to make a call'.

As soon as he'd gone, Meg jumped up from the couch and started opening cupboard doors and drawers.

'What are you doing?' asked Holly.

'There must be a minibar in here somewhere . . .' said Meg. 'Ah, here we go.' She crouched down to get a better look inside. 'What the fuck is all this?'

Holly looked over Meg's shoulder. All the drinks and snacks had been removed and in their place was an array of bottles, tubs and pill bottles with names like 'Nature's Essence', 'Goji-Ginseng Power' and 'Forever Youth Elixir'. It looked like Holland & Barrett had set up a pop-up shop inside.

Just then Frank reappeared.

'You got any booze in here, Frank?' asked Meg.

'I quit in the nineties,' he said. 'The Twelve Steps saved my life. Feel free to get something from room service if you'd like, but I'm telling you, it's a slippery slope . . .'

Meg headed straight towards the phone. 'Mind if I get some chips, too?' she said. 'I'm bloody starving.'

Holly rolled her eyes. Honest to God, she couldn't believe how brazen Meg could be sometimes.

'Chips?' Frank looked like Meg had just suggested sniffing glue. 'Are you serious, guys? Oil? *Oil?*'

'Sorry?'

'I don't do oil,' said Frank, tightly. '*You* shouldn't do oil. Now I'm getting near forty' – Meg stifled a giggle, not very successfully – 'I'm taking my nutrition seriously. I recommend you do the same.'

'No booze, no oil.' Meg shook her head. 'What exactly do you do for fun, Frank?'

He looked at them strangely, as if he was weighing something up, and then smiled. 'Wait there,' he said, disappearing off into the bedroom.

'Jeez, the guy's a total fruitcake,' muttered Meg, throwing herself on the couch and flicking through the TV channels on the remote.

'Shall we just go?' said Holly. She was feeling drunk and on edge. He might seem familiar, but they didn't know Frank and she wasn't at all comfortable being in a stranger's hotel room.

But, just then, the door opened and Frank came back in. To Holly's horror, he was stark naked except for a length of sack-like material wound around his groin.

Meg burst out laughing. 'Jesus, Frank, what's with the loincloth?'

'I am a Tantric master,' he said, solemnly. 'I have been graced with the divine power to bring a woman to a greater understanding of the eternal by physically making love to her.' He placed his hands in the prayer position and bowed his head. 'And tonight, I would like to share this gift with you both.'

The girls were out of the door in an instant and kept running until they got to the street, when they collapsed in breathless hysterics.

The following morning, Holly woke at nine to find the bed next to her empty and a note resting on the pillow.

'Hols. You looked so peaceful that I didn't want to disturb you. I've gone in search of bacon. Mmm, OIL! Give me a call when you're up. Mxxx.'

Wow, she must have been totally comatose to sleep through Meg getting up – although the air conditioning rattled so loudly it had probably drowned out everything else.

As she showered, Holly thought back over their adventure the night before and giggled to herself. Life was certainly never dull with Meg around. They had a day of sightseeing planned, starting with a round trip on the Staten Island ferry, and Holly was desperate to get out into the city again. She couldn't get enough of New York's energy, noise and buzz. *Or, for that matter, its food*, she thought, as her stomach growled loudly enough to be heard even over the thunderous rumble of the air con.

Holly was just rubbing some sunblock into her face when her phone rang. She assumed it would be Meg, chivvying her along, but when she looked at the caller ID she was stunned to see that it was Max. That night on his boat felt like another lifetime. She thought about not answering it, until curiosity got the better of her. But she would *definitely* play it cool.

'Max, hi.'

'Hello, beautiful. How are you?'

'Oh, you know. Fine.'

'I'm so sorry not to have been in touch before now, but I've been extremely busy.'

'Yes, I know,' said Holly. 'With *Sasha*.' Oops. So much for playing it cool.

'Holly? Is something wrong?'

She sighed. 'Max, there's no point denying it. I know you're back with Sasha and I'm just not interested in getting into some weird three-way thing. Sorry.'

'What *are* you talking about?'

'I know about the emerald bracelet you gave her,' said Holly. 'And I know you went to see her after I left the other evening.'

There was a pause. 'Ah, I see. Well, I suppose you could say that I have been . . . *courting* Sasha . . .'

'Then why the hell didn't you tell me the other night?'

'. . . but not in the way that you're thinking. I've been trying to persuade her to become the presenter of the new American version of *Street Scout*, not my girlfriend.'

'What?'

'The US networks loved the show and they wanted to do exactly the same thing at the Strut offices in the States, but although I agreed to reprise my role, Sasha wasn't at all keen. In my opinion she's an integral part of the show and I was reluctant to do it without her, so for the past couple of months I've been trying to persuade her to talk to the US producers about accepting the presenting role on the American show. I couldn't tell you anything before because it was all highly confidential, but she finally agreed to talk to them – and I've just found out that she signed the deal yesterday.'

'So . . . so you're not dating?'

'No, we're most definitely not,' said Max. 'Sasha and I are good friends but we haven't been anything more than that for well over a year. There's only one girl I'm interested in dating – and I'm speaking to her.'

Holly smiled into the phone.

'So, Miss Collins, now we've straightened that out, what are you up to today? Would you like to meet up?'

'I'd really love to, but I'm in New York with a friend for the weekend.'

'I know you are,' said Max. 'I'm downstairs in your hotel lobby.'

31

Holly assumed she must have misunderstood. 'Sorry, Max, where did you say you are?'

'Downstairs,' he said again. 'Standing in the lobby of your hotel. Trying to work out where that strange smell is coming from.'

'But what . . . why . . . how . . . ?'

'I've been in New York for meetings with the network. We're going to be filming *Street Scout US* at Strut's New York office. The team starts pre-production tomorrow.'

'But how did you know *I* was here?' It was all way too confusing; Holly couldn't get her head around any of it.

'Aha, my spies are everywhere,' chuckled Max, mysteriously. 'So, can I come up?'

Holly looked in the mirror. She was naked but for a very small towel wrapped round her middle; her hair was sticking up like a just-hatched chick; and her face was covered in patches of white sunblock. Then she glanced around the room, which looked as if someone had picked up their bags and shaken the contents all over the floor. Clothes and toiletries were strewn over every surface; there was even a bright yellow bra dangling from the light fitting.

'Give me ten minutes and I'll come down,' she said, quickly.

But when she got downstairs, Max wasn't in the lobby; and when she walked outside, briefly blinded by the morning sun bouncing off the sidewalk, there was no sign of him there, either. More confused than ever, Holly began to wonder if she'd somehow got the wrong end of the stick – or, more likely, that Max had got the wrong hotel – but then she noticed a black limo idling at the kerb outside the next building and, as she looked a bit more closely, one of the blacked-out back windows slid down and there he was.

Max's hair was messier than usual and he had a shadow of stubble across his jaw. He was wearing a white T-shirt and tortoiseshell Ray-Ban Wayfarer sunglasses. It suited him, the more casual look; he looked even sexier than in a suit. Holly was taken aback by just how pleased she was to see him – and it was clear that Max felt the same way, as he broke into a huge grin as she walked towards the car.

'Fancy a ride, doll?' he said. 'Hop in.'

The car was ridiculously large. Sitting in the back, she could stretch her legs right out and still not touch the seats in front, while the partition between them and the driver gave her the slightly bizarre feeling that the car was driving itself. As they set off, Max reached down next to him and picked up a brown paper bag. 'Breakfast?'

Holly nodded and he produced cardboard cups of coffee and bagels with smoked salmon and cream cheese. 'They're from Bagel Oasis in Queens – the best in New York,' he said.

'You trekked all the way out to Queens to get bagels?'

'Yes. Well, my driver, Shaun, did,' he said, with an apologetic smile.

The bagels did look delicious – although at that moment she was so hungry she'd have been equally happy with an Egg McMuffin – but then Holly remembered that Meg was waiting for her somewhere in the city. She was sure her friend would understand if she spent some time with Max, as she was always banging on about having adventures and seizing the moment; still, Holly felt terrible about abandoning her – especially as Meg was the only reason she was actually in New York in the first place.

'Can I just make a quick phone call?' she asked Max. 'I was supposed to be meeting up with my friend.'

'Sure. Would you like some privacy?'

'Um, yes please, but . . .' She wasn't quite sure how privacy was possible in a car – even one of this size – but then Max pressed a button in his armrest and a partition slowly slid up between the two of them, sealing her off in her own private little cubicle.

'Give me a tap when you're done,' smiled Max, blowing her a kiss as his face disappeared from view.

As Holly had hoped, Meg was more excited for her than anything. She told Holly – no, *ordered* her – to spend the day with Max, and was adamant that she would be absolutely fine on her own. By coincidence, Meg had stopped for breakfast at a cool little café in the Meatpacking District where the waitress just happened to be Babes of Bedlam's biggest American fan – 'Probably our *only* American fan' – and had invited Meg to hang out with her and some mates in Brooklyn, when she had finished her shift later that morning.

'It's all worked out perfectly,' Meg told Holly, 'because I wanted to go to Brooklyn anyway, to check out this vintage record shop in Williamsburg that Spunk's always banging on about.'

'Well, as long as you're absolutely sure . . .'

'Hon – just go and have some fun. And don't do anything I wouldn't do.'

Holly gave a snort of laughter. 'That leaves the field pretty wide open.'

'Exactly. See you later, darlin'.'

Smiling to herself, Holly knocked on the partition and, as it slid down, Max held out a coffee and a bagel.

'All sorted?' he asked. 'Have I got you all to myself?'

'Yup,' she smiled.

Holly had never imagined a humble bagel could be quite so ambrosial: the dough was so chewy and malty and moreish, and the salmon so buttery and soft, that she managed to polish off three. The cappuccino, which Max had picked up from The Carlyle, the hotel where he was staying, was pretty spectacular as well.

'So,' he asked, as they sped along by the Hudson River. 'What did you two girls have planned for today?'

'Just a bit of sightseeing.'

'Excellent. Let's do that then.'

He pressed another button and the partition between them and the driver opened up.

'Shaun, we're going to Chelsea Piers. Perhaps you could call ahead.'

'Very good, Mr Moore,' said the driver, a huge bald guy in a grey suit and with a strong New York accent.

Holly looked quizzically at Max. 'Chelsea Piers?'

'It's a surprise,' he smiled.

Ten minutes later, they turned into a large open-air car park alongside the docks. *Must be a boat trip*, thought Holly.

'Just nip out and check we're good to go, will you, Shaun?' said Max.

Holly watched as Shaun strode across the parking

lot, marvelling at the size of the guy's huge shoulders; he looked more like a pro wrestler than a chauffeur. Shaun disappeared into a warehouse by the docks, then moments later he re-emerged with a tall, skinny guy in a baseball cap and the pair of them walked back towards the car.

'Good morning, Mr Moore,' he said, as Max and Holly got out. 'She's all ready for you.'

'Thanks, Fred.'

Taking Holly by the hand, Max led her around the other side of the warehouse and there, on a raised circular platform right next to the river, was not a boat, but a sleek, black helicopter.

Holly gasped with delight.

'My new toy,' said Max.

He opened the door, helped her in, then buckled up her seatbelt. 'You'll need this to speak to the pilot,' said Max, handing her a headset.

'Who's the pilot?'

He grinned at her. 'Me.'

32

They lifted off from the ground so quickly that Holly felt like her stomach had been left behind on the tarmac. When they were in the air, the slightest motion was noticeable, far more so than in an aeroplane, which made for a slightly hairy ride – especially as Max's flying technique seemed to be modelled on Tom Cruise's in *Top Gun*. But it was an incredible way to see the city. They flew right around the Statue of Liberty's head, close enough to see the whites of her eyes (if she'd actually had any).

'Why did you learn to fly?' said Holly, trying not to shriek as they made a sharp loop over midtown.

'It's just a hobby,' said Max, with a shrug.

She laughed. 'Most people make do with stamp collecting or golf.'

He beamed at her, his eyes glinting with the same childlike excitement that had so surprised Holly during their evening on the boat. She had imagined such a rich, successful man would be cynical, maybe even spoilt, but Max was the total opposite of that: he seemed to be endlessly delighted by life.

After they had landed, Max leant over to help Holly unbuckle her seatbelt. His face was inches from hers and when their eyes met, Holly felt electricity shooting between them.

'It's so good to see you,' murmured Max. Then he kissed her on the lips, tantalisingly briefly, and Holly's stomach turned somersaults. As shallow as it was to admit it, she fancied him even more now she'd seen him flying a helicopter. It was just so . . . so *manly*.

They walked back towards the car, Max's arm around Holly's shoulders, and, as they approached, Shaun got out to open the door for them. As Holly slid into the cushiony leather seats, she felt a shiver of happiness. *I could get used to this . . .*

'Right, shopping now,' said Max, as they sped off.

'I'm kind of all shopped out after yesterday,' said Holly. She was still feeling guilty about blowing her budget on her new outfit.

Max arched an eyebrow. 'Surely not . . . ? Well, we'll go shopping for me, then.'

When they reached their destination, Holly realised that they were on Fifth Avenue, outside the very stores that yesterday she had been too intimidated by the doormen (and price tags) to venture into.

'Uh, I'm not really dressed for these kinds of shops,' said Holly, looking doubtfully at her cut-off denims, flip-flops and Batman T-shirt. But Max just ignored her and headed straight into Chanel.

There was a barely discernible ruffling of the assistants' immaculate exteriors when they walked into the store. Either they recognised Max personally, or they had some sort of alarm that went off when a high-net-worth individual passed through the doors. Sure enough, they had barely set foot on the white carpet when a dauntingly well-groomed girl appeared at their side.

'Welcome to Chanel, my name is Isabelle. How may I help you today?'

'We're looking for . . .' Max turned to Holly with an enquiring look. 'Handbags?'

'I thought we were shopping for you?'

'We are,' he said. 'I'm buying a gift. For you.'

Holly started to protest, but Max was already following Isabelle up a flight of stairs to the first floor. After fetching them each a glass of champagne, she pulled back a large sliding mirror to reveal a dazzling display of the brand's iconic quilted bags on the shelves in front of them. There were no tags, but Holly knew that the prices started at four figures – and very quickly went up to five.

Max turned to Holly. 'So, what do you think?'

They were all beautiful, but Holly's eye was immediately drawn to a small, oblong leather bag with a chain handle and interlocking 'CC' clasp. It was the sort of thing that would never go out of style.

'Excellent choice, madam,' said the assistant. 'The 2.55 is an eternal classic. And which colour would you prefer?'

Holly looked uncertainly at Max. 'Are you quite sure about this . . . ?'

'It would make me very happy if you would allow me to get it for you,' he said, squeezing her hand in his. 'Okay?'

She gazed at him in wonder, then quickly kissed him on the cheek. 'Okay,' she said, quietly. 'And thank you so, so much.'

Holly turned back to Isabelle. 'I think I'll stick to black, thank you.'

'Of course,' said the assistant. 'I'll just have it wrapped for you.'

After looking in another couple of stores, including Giorgio Armani – where Holly admired a dazzling, full-length evening gown of pale pink silk and ostrich feathers, then had to spend ages talking Max out of buying it for her ('Honestly, I really don't have much opportunity to wear couture evening dresses in Hammersmith') – Shaun drove them to Central Park. Max bought pizza slices and ice-cold Cokes from a vendor and they ate them sitting in the shade of a tree on the bank of the river, watching joggers and skaters zip past. They talked about *Street Scout* – which, to Holly's delight, had eventually been won by Kinzah, who had been such a good friend to her on the show (she'd have loved to have seen Moet's face when that was announced) – and the US series that would be starting filming in the next few weeks. Sasha was lined up to be presenter, Max would take on the role of the show's boss as in the British version, and Zane would also be coming over to take part in the new series. Then they talked a lot about New York. Max told her about when he lived in the city in the nineties in the same apartment block as Madonna, while Holly had him in hysterics recounting her and Meg's encounter with Frank Isaacs the previous night. As they lay on the grass chatting away, the afternoon sun warming their faces, Holly felt as happy and relaxed as she had done in ages. Putting aside all the glitz and glamour of Max's lifestyle, she genuinely loved spending time with him – although she was still at a loss to understand why this incredible man could be interested in her. So, in the end, she just asked him.

'Why wouldn't I be?' said Max in astonishment, rolling over to face her. 'You're beautiful, intelligent, sexy and wonderfully down-to-earth. Right now I feel like the luckiest man alive.' Then he kissed her, softly at first and then with a passion that took Holly's breath away, and she forgot all about what she was worried about in the first place.

That night they went for dinner at a Japanese restaurant called Masa. When Max had asked during the drive back to her hotel if she was free that evening, Holly hadn't hesitated in saying yes: Meg was still busy in Brooklyn and besides, she really didn't want their magical day together to end. Back in her room, Holly changed into her new white dress (thankfully still spotless, despite its adventure the previous night) and accessorised with her fabulous new bag. It was by far the most expensive thing Holly had ever owned and, as she stood on the sidewalk trying to hail a taxi to the restaurant, she couldn't shake the unsettling feeling that she had the price of a small car slung over her shoulder.

Max had told her that Masa was one of his favourite places to eat in the world, so she was expecting something pretty spectacular, but when she arrived she found a small, dark room with just a handful of bare wooden tables. Comfort-wise it was about on a par with a branch of Wagamama – and at least at Wagamama they gave you a menu. Here, there were no such luxuries. But then they took a seat at a counter in front of the chef, whose bald head and monk-like robes perfectly suited the starkness of the room, and Holly watched open-mouthed as he got to work creating food of such astonishing beauty that she wasn't sure whether to eat it or frame it. Diced tuna in caviar, white truffle tempura, lobster with foie gras: it was a banquet fit for an oligarch.

Max was unusually quiet during the drive back to her hotel, staring out of the window as if deep in thought. Holly had a lot on her mind as well. It had been such an amazing day, but she was going back to

London tomorrow – and it sounded like Max was going to be based in New York for the next few months.

'So, here we are,' he said, as they pulled up outside her hotel.

'Max, I've had the most incredible day. I really can't thank you enough.'

'No, thank you, Holly. I'm . . . I'm just so glad I met you.'

He was looking at her quite intently, but made no move to kiss her. The seconds ticked by. Holly suddenly felt a bit awkward.

'Okay, well, bye then.' She reached for the door handle, trying not to feel rejected.

'Holly, wait,' said Max, grabbing her hand. 'I have a proposal to put to you.' He took a deep breath. 'Would you consider staying on in New York with me for a while? A couple of weeks – perhaps a month? I know we've really only just met, but I've fallen for you, Holly, and I'd really like to spend more time with you – a lot more. You could see more of the city while I work, then we could spend time together in the evenings and at weekends. I know this sounds crazy and I completely understand if you'd rather get back to your own life but, please, would you at least think about it?'

33

'*So?* What did you say?'

It was well after midnight and Holly was back in their room at the Greenwich Square Hotel, telling a thoroughly overexcited Meg about her day. Honest to God, her ears were still ringing from the squeal when she showed Meg her new bag.

'I told him I'd have to think about it,' said Holly. 'And that I'd call him in the morning.'

'But you're going to stay, right? I mean, you're not going to miss out on the chance of living the high life in New York with your sexy, new, helicopter-flying, Chanel-buying boyfriend are you?'

'He's not my boyfriend!'

Meg raised her eyebrows sceptically.

'We haven't had that conversation yet,' said Holly. 'It's a little too soon.'

'But *definitely* not too soon to have a wild week or four in New York with him, I hope.'

'I guess not. I do really like him . . . But what about my job? I'm supposed to be back at VitaSlim next week.'

'I'll tell Alan you've broken your leg. And lost your voice. And suffered paralysis of the fingers.'

Holly pulled a face at her.

'Oh, screw the job, Hols!' said Meg. 'You've got the rest of your life to be sensible and boring. Think of this as your year of living dangerously. I know VitaSlim is the prudent option, but if you're not careful it'll be ten years later and you'll still be at the same desk answering the same calls from the same people. Sometimes in life you've just got to close your eyes and take a leap into the unknown – and this is *definitely* one of those times.'

'But I'm down to the last of my savings.' Holly chewed her thumbnail. Just thinking about the state of her finances made her feel jittery. 'What am I going to live on?'

'Well, it doesn't sound like it'll be a problem in New York with Maxwell Moore-money-than-sense. And when you're home, we'll just figure something out. You can stay with Spunk and me while you find a job. A *modelling* job, though, please.'

'I don't know . . .'

'Holly, imagine you were on your deathbed looking back over your life. Would you tell yourself to stick to a job you hate, or take a gamble on some crazy adventure . . . ? You know what I always say: "A life lived in fear . . ." '

'I know, I know, ". . . is a life half lived".'

* * *

'Max, it's Holly.'

'Oh, hi. Just hold on a sec.' She heard him muffle the receiver with his hand. 'Guys, I need to take this call, if you could just give me a moment . . . Thanks.' He was back. 'Sorry about that, I'm just in the middle of a breakfast meeting with the network. I can't wait until all this TV nonsense is finished and I can get back to my day job . . .'

'Sorry, if you're busy I can call back . . .'

'No, don't worry – it's been dragging on for a while now and I'd far rather speak to you, anyway. So have you had a chance to think about my proposal?'

'I have.'

'And?'

'And if the offer still stands, I'd like to take you up on it. I'd love to stay on in New York with you.'

Shortly after Holly had waved Meg off to the airport, Shaun arrived at the hotel to whisk Holly off to Max's hotel, The Carlyle. Waiting in the limo when Holly got in was a woman with a severe brunette bob who introduced herself as 'Mindy, Mr Moore's New York assistant'. During the drive uptown, Mindy told Holly that she would help her settle into the suite and that if she needed anything – 'absolutely *anything*' – during her stay then she should call her immediately, although Holly wasn't really concentrating on what she was saying, as she was too busy staring at Mindy's freakily perfect teeth.

The Carlyle was on the Upper East Side overlooking Central Park on the corner of Moneybags and Sophistication – or rather, Madison and 76th. As Holly followed Mindy's click-clacking Jimmy Choos across the hotel's black and cream marble lobby, gawping at the antique chandeliers and enormous oil paintings as she went, she subtly shifted her handbag so it was positioned in front of her like a shield. It was the only bit of her that looked remotely like it belonged in a place this posh.

Mindy asked the white-gloved elevator operator to press the button for the sixteenth floor: only then did it occur to Holly that she had no idea what the sleeping arrangements would be. Her excitement suddenly lurched towards anxiety. What if Max expected her to share his bed? She fancied him like mad, but she certainly wasn't sure she was ready to sleep with the guy. Christ, she really hadn't thought this through . . .

'All good?' asked Mindy, as they got out of the lift.

'Yes, fine, thank you!' said Holly, trying to ignore the horrible twitchy feeling in the pit of her stomach.

As Mindy pulled out a key card to open the door to 'Mr Moore's suite', and then handed Holly her own copy, her nerves kicked up to full-blown panic. Even the fact that the room (or rather network of rooms) was possibly the most beautiful she had ever seen, let alone *stayed* in, did little to calm Holly's terror that she might be sharing a bed with the nutter out of *Fifty Shades of Grey*.

But then Mindy pushed open a set of white double-doors to reveal a room dominated by a huge, French chateau-style bed and views across Central Park, and said, 'This will be your bedroom. Mr Moore's is on the other side of the suite,' and Holly almost had to stop herself from running over and kissing her.

There was an enormous display of white lilies next to the bed with a note propped against the vase.

'Hey, roomie. I hope Mindy has made sure you have everything you need. I have left you something in the safe: USE IT! For a girl, you're surprisingly bad at shopping and you need the practice. Mindy will give you the relevant codes. Make yourself at home and I'll send the car for you for dinner at 7 p.m. I'm so thrilled you took me up on my crazy offer. It'll be fun, I promise. Max.'

Inside the safe Holly found a black Amex card. *Wow*. As she turned it over in her hands, she couldn't help but think about Lola, and how much difference this card would make to her life. Then it occurred to her that, perhaps, if things worked out with Max, she might be able to talk to him about helping her little sister get her operation . . . It was all so overwhelming she suddenly felt that this must be too good to be true, that there was bound to be some sort of catch, but then she remembered Meg's words – 'Sometimes in life you've just got to close your eyes and take a leap into the unknown' – and ordered herself to stop worrying and just enjoy the ride.

Holly heard someone behind her and looked round to see Mindy hovering in the doorway.

'I've booked you into the hotel's spa in an hour's time for a facial, massage and a mani-pedi. I hope that suits?'

'Yes, that would be lovely. Thank you.'

Mindy smiled and nodded briskly. 'Have a wonderful stay, Holly. Please do call if I can help you with anything.' And with that she was gone.

Left on her own, Holly had a nose around the suite, taking in the kitchen (complete with fully-stocked fridge), two enormous bathrooms, the living room and, of course, Max's bedroom. She stuck her head around the door, but then quickly backed out, feeling guiltily like she was snooping. The suite was decked out with polished wood floors topped with sky-blue rugs, antique gilt mirrors on the walls, pots of orchids on every surface and huge, cushiony armchairs and sofas the shade of palest cream. It looked like the home of a very wealthy art collector (who clearly never drank red wine). But it was the view that really took her breath away. The dazzling green and blue rectangle of Central Park spread out beneath her like a gigantic beach towel laid out over the city. She took a couple of photos on her phone and sent them to Meg. 'Smells better than the Greenwich

Square, even if the view's crap. Wish you were here. Hx'.

By the end of the week, Holly had started to enjoy life as Max's not-quite-official girlfriend. The first evening when she went to meet him at an Italian restaurant she'd felt incredibly nervous. She was going to be living with this guy, but she hardly knew anything about him. Was he close to his parents? Had he ever been married? She didn't even know his favourite food!

'Pie and mash,' Max had laughed. 'I'm very close to my parents, although they live in Spain so I don't see them that often, and I was married once and although it didn't work out we're still friends. Anything else . . . ?'

He was such wonderful company that Holly quickly started to relax and, a couple of glasses of wine later, she couldn't believe she'd ever been worried. After all, they had *plenty* of time to get to know each other!

As it turned out, they didn't actually have all that much. Max left the suite at 6 a.m. for a run with his trainer, then he wasn't back until dinner, but he put Shaun at her disposal and had Mindy check up on her throughout the day to see if she needed anything. Holly didn't mind; she was so in love with New York that she was happy to spend her time ticking off the remaining items on her and Meg's New York sightseeing list and just strolling around the streets, drinking in the atmosphere. Max kept encouraging her to take his Amex card shopping, but although Holly did have a wander around a few shops and bought Lola the sweetest little pink cashmere sweater, the whole thing felt uncomfortably like something out of *Pretty Woman* – which was ironic, considering that she and Max hadn't slept together yet. Their kisses had become increasingly passionate, leaving Holly aching for him and desperate for more, but Max insisted that he wanted to take things slowly – 'Trust me, it'll be worth the wait' – and by night four they had only reached second base. At least when it did happen, Holly knew there would be fireworks: she got the impression Max would know exactly which buttons to press, and the waiting just made her want him even more.

On Friday, Holly set off early to visit the Museum of Natural History. She had persuaded a bemused Shaun that she'd really rather walk, although he insisted he would wait at the museum in case she wanted a ride home. As the Carlyle's top-hatted doorman, Boris, waved her off with a cheery, 'Have a nice day, Miss Collins!' Holly stepped onto the sidewalk and, just at that moment, a taxi pulled up in front of her – and out stepped Sasha Hart.

Holly froze, feeling horribly awkward. As friendly as they had been during the filming of *Street Scout*, Max had told Holly that he and Sasha had first met in New York and lived here together for a while, so Holly wasn't sure how Sasha would feel about her dating Max – especially in the city where it had all begun for them. Well, she was about to find out.

'Sasha! How are you? Congratulations on the new job!' Holly had been planning to go in for a kiss, but there was a distinct frostiness to Sasha's body language that made her pull back.

'Oh, Holly, hi. I heard you were out here. With Max.'

'Yes, it's been a crazy week!'

There was an awkward pause.

'So, what are you up to?' asked Sasha, giving the distinct impression that she really didn't give a shit.

'Just a bit of sightseeing, really. It's my first time in New York, so I'm trying to see as much as possible.'

'No, I mean work-wise.'

'Um, not much right now . . .'

'I see,' said Sasha. 'But I suppose Max is very generous . . .'

'Oh no, it's nothing like that!' The last thing Holly wanted was for Sasha to think she was sponging off him. 'I'm going to try and get back into modelling when I get home.'

'Right . . . well, I'd better get on. Lots to do. Bye.'

As Sasha strode into the hotel, a porter scurrying after her with her luggage, Holly set off down the street prickling with irritation. What the hell was Sasha's problem? She and Max had split up ages ago.

Perhaps all her friendliness on *Street Scout* was just an act for the TV cameras, and she was actually a total bitch.

Later that afternoon Holly was back in the suite writing a postcard to Lola and indulging in her new addiction – room-service lobster club sandwiches – when her phone rang. She had assumed it would be Mindy, who called her with exhausting regularity, but to her surprise it was Joe Taylor. She hoped he wasn't chasing her for an interview again.

'Joe! Great to hear from you. How are you?'

'Well, I was actually calling to see if you're ready to take me up on that drink offer, but I'm guessing from the dial tone that you're abroad.'

'Yes, New York.'

'Lucky you. Are you there with friends?'

'I suppose you could say that.' Holly paused, unsure whether to tell him the truth. He was a journalist, but she liked the guy – and her gut instinct was to trust him. 'Can I tell you something off the record?'

'Ooh, this sounds juicy . . . Yes, of course. I'll keep it to myself – Scout's honour.'

'You won't believe this, but I'm here with Max Moore.'

'What?' Joe sounded stunned – Holly supposed it was a bit weird for him. He probably still assumed Max had rekindled things with Sasha.

'Yes, I was in New York for a weekend with a

friend and to cut a long story short I bumped into Max and now we're . . . spending a bit of time together. Crazy, huh?'

'So . . . so you're going out with him?'

'Yes, I suppose we are. But please don't write anything about it. It's really early days, but he's such a great guy. Oh, and it turns out there was nothing in those rumours about him and Sasha.'

There was silence at the other end of the line.

'Joe? Are you still there?'

'Um, yes, sorry.' He sounded shaken. 'Holly, I know this is none of my business, but I care about you. There's something you should know about Max . . .'

34

Just then Holly heard the click of a key card in the suite door and, to her surprise, Max strode in, at least three hours earlier than he had appeared on previous days. He threw his jacket over the chair by the door, blew her a kiss and wandered into the kitchen.

'Listen, Joe, sorry to interrupt you,' said Holly, quickly, 'but do you mind if I call you back?'

'Um, yeah, no problem. Don't forget, okay?'

'Of course. Bye.'

As she ended the call, Max walked back in swigging from a bottle of Fiji water. He came and sat next to her on the couch, throwing his arm over her shoulders, then leant over to kiss her, his lips lingering on hers frustratingly briefly.

'Hope I didn't disturb anything,' he said, nodding at her phone.

'Oh no, it was just a friend from home.' Max was such a private person, she didn't know how he'd feel about her talking to a journalist: even one she considered a friend. 'You're back early.'

'Well, I thought I could take Cinderella shopping – try and find her something to wear to the ball later.'

Holly felt a prickle of excitement. Ah, yes, tonight's big black-tie dinner. The TV network was hosting a bash at some swanky restaurant to celebrate signing contracts for *Street Scout US*. It would be her and Max's first public outing as a couple (if that was indeed what they were – they still hadn't had *that* conversation) and while Holly was thrilled he wanted her to go with him, she was a bit jittery about the prospect of making small talk with a roomful of TV execs. And then something else occurred to her.

'Will Sasha be coming tonight?'

'Of course,' said Max. 'Plus Zane, and some other key people from the UK team, so there should be a few friendly faces.'

Holly very much doubted that Sasha's face would be friendly after their encounter that morning, but she just smiled and said how much she was looking forward to it and yes, she would love to go shopping with him.

An hour later, Holly found herself sitting in the personal-shopping suite at Barneys department store, a room so luxurious that the walls were covered in *leather*, with a glass of champagne in hand (did rich people ever shop without one?) listening to Max brief a team of black-clad assistants on the sort of dress they were looking for. Holly had been living in

Max's fairy-tale world for a few days now, but she was a long way from taking any of its fabulousness for granted. In fact, Max had taken her to one side a few moments ago and said with a wry smile that while he was delighted she was so grateful, she really didn't have to tell him a hundred times a day.

Holly had never been the greatest shopper, so it was actually rather nice to let someone else do the legwork, but it was weird going out with a bloke who knew more about fashion than she did. James never used to comment much on her outfits, apart from to say she looked beautiful. 'I can't always look beautiful,' she'd said to him once. 'I'm sure that sometimes I only look quite nice, and at other times way below average.'

But – 'No,' James had said, in that very deliberate, serious way he sometimes had. 'You *always* look beautiful.'

It had been a lovely moment, but it was now tainted by the knowledge that he had probably been saying the exact same thing to Bitch-face Crosby . . .

Just then an assistant reappeared with three dresses: a green velvet Gucci number slashed to the waist, a silky Lanvin tunic and a clingy black lace dress by L'Wren Scott. They were stunning, although certainly not the sort of thing Holly would have ever chosen for herself. They were just so . . . *grown-up*.

'Definitely the lace,' said Max. 'What do you think, darling?'

'Yes, definitely,' she said. After all, she didn't have a clue what one should wear to a swanky business dinner – and the most important thing was that Max was proud of her.

The restaurant looked like the sort of place that Wall Street tycoons finalised mega-deals over plates decorated with arty smears, foams and cubes of jellied something-or-other. Everything about the room was big and intimidating: the wine glasses looked like they should have goldfish swimming around in them, there were actual trees in place of flower arrangements, and such loftily high ceilings that Holly half expected to look up and see pigeons flying about.

There were about twenty people at their table, and Holly was relieved to discover she was sitting at the opposite end to Sasha, who seemed just as glacial as she had earlier that day, barely nodding to her in greeting. At least Zane seemed pleased to see her.

'Dude, you look well sick!'

'Thanks, Zane. You look, er, sick, too.' He had swapped his usual GI Joe-style combats for a suit, although he was still wearing his goggle-sized shades. 'How have you been enjoying New York?' she asked.

'Man, I've been havin' an epic keen one, know what I'm sayin'?'

'Um, yeah,' she said. 'Me, too. Epic.'

Zane smiled and nodded. 'All gravy, blud.'

'Yes, er, safe, bro,' muttered Holly.

The conversation revolved around TV production matters and industry gossip, leaving Holly feeling like a bit of a spare part, but then the guy sitting next to her – one of the American producers – found out that she'd been on the UK version of *Street Scout* and suddenly she was the centre of attention. As she chatted away, she caught Max looking over at her with a proud smile on his face; she grinned back and he winked and blew her a kiss. Later in the evening, one of the most beautiful women Holly had ever seen came over to the table to speak to him. Holly couldn't hear what they were saying, but they obviously knew each other: the woman was all over him and Holly felt a horrible stab of jealousy as she stroked Max's face, fluttered her lashes and giggled flirtatiously. But then Holly saw him gesture towards her and, to her astonishment, clearly heard him say the word 'girlfriend', and the woman pouted a bit, kissed his cheek and was gone. Max grinned at Holly and rolled his eyes. God, she fancied him so much.

The food was heavy on style and light on substance, and the waiters kept refilling their glasses – first with champagne, then white wine, red wine and dessert wine – until it occurred to Holly, midway through telling the woman sitting opposite her (the network's vice president of something) a long and pointless anecdote about her GCSE art teacher, that she was completely and utterly pissed. Holly reached up to touch her face but couldn't feel her nose. Yup, she was wasted. She giggled to herself and took another swig of wine.

Then Holly felt a hand on her shoulder and turned to see Zane. 'I'm going for a fag break. Wanna come?'

She didn't smoke, but getting a bit of fresh air seemed like an excellent idea. As they left, she glanced over at Max and even in her drunken state she was jolted by the stern look on his face. He couldn't be jealous – surely it was no secret that Zane was gay?

Outside it was still warmer than in the air-conditioned restaurant.

'So you and Max are an item, yeah?' Zane flicked open his lighter and took a drag on his cigarette.

'I think so,' Holly giggled.

'He's a top mucka, old Max. Been good to me over the years.'

'Yes, I'm very lucky.' Something suddenly occurred to Holly. 'You don't think Sasha still fancies him? She's been a bit funny with me today.'

Zane snorted. 'Nah, man, that was over, like, years ago. Don't worry about Sash – she got her own issues to deal with. Know what I'm sayin'?'

On the drive back to The Carlyle, Holly was still on a boozy high from the evening. Max had his arm around her and she nuzzled into his neck, breathing in the gorgeous, musky smell of him.

'You are so amazing,' she said.

'So are you, my darling.'

Holly looked up at him, then closed her eyes and pressed her lips against his. As they kissed, Max held her face in his hands and then brushed them tantalisingly slowly down her neck and on over her breasts.

'You are so sexy,' whispered Max, as his lips caressed her neck. 'I can't wait to get you undressed.'

'No time like the present,' urged Holly, her head spinning from all the alcohol. She moved her hands up his legs and was thrilled to feel the growing bulge in Max's crotch. Holly giggled to herself. She felt like sticking her head through the sunroof and screaming to the whole of New York: *We're going to have sex! In the back of a limo!*

Suddenly, Holly's phone started to ring in her clutch bag. Having completely surrendered herself to Max's dizzying kisses, she ignored it but, a moment after it had stopped ringing, it started up again.

'You'd better see who that is,' sighed Max, pulling away. 'It might be important.'

It'd better be bloody important, thought Holly irritably, as she rummaged in her bag for her phone, furious at the untimely interruption.

'Hello?' she snapped.

'Holly, it's me.'

Holly's annoyance instantly dissolved as she heard her little sister's voice. She settled back into her seat, mouthing 'Sorry' at Max, who seemed to be as frustrated as she was, but he smiled and shook his head as if to say it wasn't a problem.

'Lola, how are you, darling?'

'I'm okay, I s'pose . . .' But there was a distinct wobble to her voice.

'Lola? What's wrong?'

'Well, some of the girls in my class are being a bit mean to me. About my legs not working properly. I tried to ignore them like you said, but I'm feeling sort of sad about it . . .'

Holly's heart ached horribly. She couldn't bear the thought of anyone being nasty to her sister – especially when she was thousands of miles away from her. Lola had been the victim of school bullies before, but Holly thought the problem had been sorted out.

'Oh, honey, I'm so sorry,' said Holly, her anxiety over Lola instantly sobering her up. 'Why don't you tell me what happened . . .'

As she talked to Lola, Max took out his phone and started checking through his messages. The mad, all-consuming passion that had sparked between them just a few moments ago had completely vanished, as if it had never been there in the first place. When they arrived back at the hotel, Holly was still deep in conversation with Lola, and by the time she had finished talking to her sister – and then straight afterwards to her mum, to discuss what the teachers were doing to help with the situation – Max had gone to bed.

Holly hovered outside his bedroom door for a full minute, agonising over whether she should go in and start up from where they'd left off in the limo, but in the end she went back to her own room. She was too preoccupied with her concerns over Lola to seduce Max – and, besides, her hangover had already started to kick in. Sex would have to wait.

35

The week drifted past on a magic carpet of luxury and laziness. Holly saw all the sights listed in her New York guidebook, got so many mani-pedis she ran out of colours to try, and ate her bodyweight in pastrami on rye. She called Lola at least twice a day and was relieved that she seemed to have recovered from her wobble – thanks to the school taking action against the bullies – and was now back to her usual sunny self.

Max continued to be as wonderful and as frustrating as ever. He had a hugely infectious appetite for fun, whisking Holly off to see *Carmen* at the Metropolitan Opera on Saturday night, then helicoptering her to the Hamptons for lunch the following day. Holly got the impression that she could ask him for anything and he would give it to her – apart from the one thing she wanted most of all, which was him. The kisses were still as knee-tremblingly intense as ever (and there had been some seriously heavy petting in a sand dune at the

Hamptons), but they still hadn't had sex. Despite Max's hints that it would happen soon – and his obvious excitement when things started to get steamy – Holly began to worry that perhaps he'd realised he didn't fancy her after all, and now he didn't know how to get rid of her. With the wound of James's betrayal still raw, Holly even wondered if maybe Max had met someone else – or, as unlikely as it seemed, rekindled his affair with Sasha . . . ? She had so much time on her (now beautifully soft) hands that she fretted about it endlessly. She even spent a few hours online looking up articles about Max's past relationships. She found tabloid interviews with several ex-girlfriends and, although they all moaned about what a workaholic he was, none of them seemed to have any complaints about his performance in the bedroom. Quite the opposite, in fact. There was a Lithuanian supermodel who described him as 'sexual dynamite', some American actress who bragged about him taking her 'to heights of ecstasy she'd never believed possible' and a double-barrelled British socialite who claimed that Max 'had the sexual appetite of Jagger, the sex appeal of Bond and the charm of Casanova'. All of which left Holly feeling like she must be doing something wrong.

'I just don't know if Max fancies me,' she moaned to Meg during one of their almost daily catch-up calls. 'Most blokes can't wait to jump into bed, but this time I'm the one doing all the running.'

Meg's response surprised her: 'For God's sake, stop worrying! Max isn't some spotty teenager with raging hormones – he's an adult. And you've only been there with him for – what, a little over a week? It's not like you're three months down the line and he's still not putting out. As for worrying that he's lost interest in you, I'm sure he'd just ask you to leave if that was the case.'

'No, he'd get Mindy to ask me to leave,' said Holly, sulkily.

'For Christ's sake, Miss Glass-Half-Empty, will you please pull yourself together? I can't believe you're complaining about this! Where are you at the moment?'

'Um, lying by the pool on top of Soho House . . .'

'Right. You want to know where I am? In the VitaSlim canteen eating a round of soggy tuna and sweetcorn sandwiches while that creep from Sales leers at my tits from the opposite table.' Meg suddenly raised her voice. 'Yes, I'm talking about *you,* you perv! Sorry about that, Hols . . .' Meg sighed. 'Look, you were the one who was banging on about wanting a bit of romance. I honestly think it'll be worth the wait. Max has probably got some incredible sex dungeon lined up.' Meg paused. 'Unless, of course . . .'

'Unless what?'

'Well, he is knocking on a bit, isn't he? Maybe he can't get it up.'

'MEG!'

Holly sat in the window of Dean & Deluca, exactly where she and Meg had sat almost two weeks previously, sipping a cappuccino and watching the morning commuters.

One girl in particular caught her eye. She was about her own age, wearing a cool printed smock dress and a pair of snakeskin heels, and she had that glossy, swishy New York hair that could be yours for just forty bucks at blow-dry bars all over the city. She was clutching a folder of papers to her chest and seemed in a rush, checking her watch as she powered through the sidewalk throng. The girl was clearly on her way to work, probably some glamorous job in the media, and Holly struggled to suppress a pang of envy as she watched her. Before now, she had never really understood the saying 'locked in an ivory tower'. She got what it meant, of course, but after experiencing what it was like to worry about whether there would be food on the table when she was growing up, the thought of guaranteed luxury and security seemed rather nice; certainly not something to complain about. She'd take an ivory tower over a tower block any day. But as the days ticked idly by, Holly began to think that perhaps it wasn't such a great thing after all. She missed going to work, having a purpose to her life beyond shopping. In her lowest moments, she even felt a sort of wistful nostalgia for her little cubicle at VitaSlim. Holly had decided to spend the day back in her and Meg's old SoHo stomping ground, so told Shaun and Mindy she wouldn't be needing them: she wanted to walk around and soak up the atmosphere – not see it from behind a blacked-out car window. The area's cobbled streets, quirky cafés and artistic vibe had an almost homely feel compared to the snooty, old-school sophistication of the Upper East Side, and Holly felt far more at home there than she did in the rarefied, orchid-scented surroundings of The Carlyle.

She finished off her coffee, headed out of the store and took a left down Prince Street. Now that rush hour was over, the commuters had given way to tourists and buggy-wielding nannies. Holly wandered in and out of the neighbourhood's boutiques, buying a beautiful book of fairy tales for Lola and spending nearly an hour in the Apple Store, trying out the latest gadgets. Max's black Amex card was still in her wallet, as out of place alongside her Barclays debit card and Nectar card as a Ferrari in a Lidl car park, but as much as Holly would have loved to get an iPad – and Max had been urging her to get one just the other day – she couldn't bring herself to use the card. It just felt . . . weird.

It was nearing midday and the sun was beating down when Holly thought she should probably find herself a bottle of water. She was on a street she was quite familiar with, but when she looked around for a shop she spotted a bar on the corner that she had not noticed before. A small sign over the door read 'Milady's Bar' and a smudged blackboard by the door advertised fried calamari and burgers. With its peeling red-painted exterior and neon beer signs hanging in the latticed windows, it looked like the sort of bar you'd find in some gritty Pittsburgh back-street, not one of the world's trendiest shopping streets. It couldn't have been more different from the gilded palaces she'd been going to with Max, but Holly suddenly felt desperate for a bit of normality – so she walked in.

The bar smelt strongly of fried food and had clearly seen better days. It was largely empty, with just a couple of occupied tables: one with a couple of tour-ists (judging from their rucksacks); and the other with three guys who looked like they worked on a building site. There was a jukebox and a pool table in the corner. Holly sat on a stool by the well-stocked bar.

'I'll have a Coke, please,' she said to the bartender. 'Actually, no, make that a beer.'

There was a baseball game on the TV, the Yankees versus the Red Sox, and Holly watched it as she swigged at the icy bottle of Coors.

'You a Yankees fan?' asked the bartender.

'I'm from England, so I'm not really sure,' said Holly. 'I guess I could be.'

The guy nodded. 'You here on vacation?'

'Yes. Staying with . . . a friend.'

'Well, get your friend to take you to a game. You'd love it.'

'I might just do that.'

She ordered a cheeseburger with onion rings and another beer. A couple of guys started playing pool, and as Holly watched the baseball on TV, punctuated by the slap and click of the balls on the pool table, she felt herself relaxing – *really* relaxing – for the first time in ages. So when her phone rang and she glanced down and saw it was Mindy – no doubt checking up on her – she just let it go to voicemail.

Customers came and went. The burger was fantastic, far better than the Wagyu burger topped with foie gras she'd had with Max at Bistro Moderne a couple of nights ago, and the barman (who turned out to be the Yankees' biggest fan) gave her a running commentary on the game until Holly actually got quite into it.

The bar was getting busy with the lunchtime rush and Holly was on to her third beer and utterly absorbed in the game when someone sat down on the stool next to her.

'I'll take a Coors, thanks,' said the newcomer.

Holly was vaguely aware that the voice was English, but the Yankees had just scored a home run and were on the verge of winning and she was glued to the action. She didn't even really take much notice when the voice then added, 'I didn't have you down as a baseball fan.'

It was only when she felt a tap on her shoulder that she realised the man was talking to her and that his voice was actually familiar, and that was when she turned to look at the new arrival – and very nearly dropped her bottle of beer in shock.

36

His hair had been shaved into a buzz cut since they had last met, but other than that Cole Fox looked exactly the same, right down to that lazy smile that made him seem like he wasn't just undressing you with his eyes, he was doing all sorts of other naughty things, too.

'So we meet again.' He grinned. 'And there you were trying so hard to avoid me.'

'Oh, no, it wasn't like that at all, honest!' Holly was completely flustered by seeing him again. 'Why . . . what are you doing here?'

'Same as you, probably. Beer. Pool. I thought this place was my secret.' The bartender handed him his beer. 'Thanks, buddy . . .' Then Cole raised the bottle to Holly. 'Cheers. Good to see you.'

Holly clinked her bottle with him and muttered 'Cheers' back, but she was still struggling to get her head around the coincidence of bumping into him again. Of all the bars, in all the world . . .

It turned out that Cole was in New York for a

meeting with the director of his new film, an action movie about an American army hero who saves the world from mutant killer crabs (hence the military-style haircut). As they chatted away, Holly clocked a few other changes about him, too. It was clear he'd been hitting the gym: he'd been in great shape before, but now his tight white T-shirt showed off Schwarzenegger-beating biceps. In fact, Cole was looking undeniably fit in all senses of the word, a fact that clearly hadn't escaped the notice of a group of girls sitting at a nearby table, who after giggling and whispering amongst themselves for a few minutes plucked up the courage to come over and ask for a photo and autograph.

Watching Cole work his charm on the group – and seeing the girls steal glances at her, perhaps wondering if she was his girlfriend – Holly was ashamed to admit that she felt a bit smug. *Yeah, check me out, hanging with the movie star . . .*

Once the fans had gone back to their seats, Cole turned to Holly. 'So I've been wondering,' he said. 'Why didn't we have that dinner in London?'

'I'm really sorry, I should have mentioned it when we first met, but I had a boyfriend.'

'Had?'

'Yes. We split up.'

'So no boyfriend now?'

Holly grimaced and gave an awkward shrug. 'I guess I sort of have one.' She really didn't want to get

262

into the nuts and bolts of her strange relationship with Max. 'It's . . . complicated.'

'Well, I've got no plans this afternoon,' said Cole. 'Why don't we have a game of pool and you can uncomplicate it for me?'

Holly had forgotten what great company Cole was. Okay, so he was a chronic name-dropper, talking about going out on his Harley in the Hollywood Hills with 'my mate Ashton' and hanging out with 'Leo DiCaprio, who's just a total dude', but he did it with such charm, as if he knew full well he was being a bit of a show-off, that it was actually quite endearing. Well, that was how it seemed to Holly – after a few beers, she was in that nicely fuzzy haze when everything seems right with the world. Her tongue loosened by the booze, she told Cole the story of how she and Meg had come to New York, did some name-dropping of her own with the Frank Isaacs story (which Cole thought was hysterical) and then got to the bit about meeting up with Max. Cole had been about to take a shot and pot the black, but at the mention of Max's name his eyes flicked to Holly and he lowered his cue.

'Hang on,' he said. 'You're saying that this sort-of boyfriend of yours is *Maxwell Moore*?'

He was staring at Holly like she'd just said she was dating Saddam Hussein.

'Um, yes,' she said, shaken by Cole's reaction. He was usually such a cool character, so why was he now looking so spooked? 'Do you know Max, then?' asked Holly.

'Just by reputation,' he said quickly, although Holly got the distinct impression he was hiding something. 'A friend of a friend worked for him once.'

'It's very early days,' said Holly. 'We're not exactly in a relationship.'

'Well, then,' grinned Cole, having recovered his usual swagger. 'You can hang out with me for a bit longer. Another beer?'

They had played three games (and to her delight, Holly was two games up) when her phone rang. It was Max. She thought about letting it go to voice-mail, but she'd already ignored two calls from Mindy and one from Shaun; Max was probably getting worried.

'I'd better take this,' she told Cole, heading outside for some privacy.

Standing on the street corner, she took a deep breath and then took the call.

'Holly! Where are you? Mindy's been trying to get hold of you. Why haven't you been answering your phone?'

'I'm in SoHo, doing a bit of shopping,' said Holly, hoping she sounded more sober than she felt. 'My phone was in my bag, I must have missed it ringing.'

'Shall I send Shaun over to get you? Mindy's

arranged for you to have a Moroccan body wrap at the hotel's spa at 4 p.m.'

'That's really kind of her, but I'm actually very happy just mooching around SoHo.'

'Holly, I'm not sure that's such a good idea. You're in a strange city – I'd feel much happier if you had someone with you.'

'Max, I am an adult,' she snapped. 'I don't need a bloody babysitter.'

There was silence at the other end of the phone; Holly instantly felt terrible – the last thing she wanted was to appear ungrateful for everything he'd done for her.

'I'm so sorry, Max, I just . . . I was feeling a bit claustrophobic. I need a bit of time by myself.'

'Of course,' he said, eventually. 'I completely understand. Don't forget we have reservations at Per Se tonight at eight. Shaun will pick you up from the hotel at half seven. Oh, and it'll probably be best if you wear the lace tonight; it's quite a dressy place. Bye, beautiful.'

'Bye,' said Holly, with a twinge of irritation. What was she, a sodding show pony? She walked back into the bar, still feeling annoyed.

'Trouble in paradise?' grinned Cole when he saw her face.

Holly sighed and took a swig of her beer. She'd lost count of the number of bottles she'd had, but it was more than enough to make her far less discreet than she would have been usually.

'Oh, it's just that Max can be so bloody posses-sive,' she said. 'He showers me with presents, gives me everything I want, but it's like he wants to keep me locked away like one of his expensive possessions. And I sometimes wonder if the guy even fancies me!'

She moaned on about Max, too drunk to worry about being disloyal. And Cole was such a great listener – reassuring her that she *was* highly desirable – that when he suggested they move on to another bar for some cocktails, she happily went along with him. She wasn't sure if it was the alcohol or Cole's attentiveness, but as they left the bar Holly had a real swagger to her walk. She felt confident, alluring and sexy. *Cole Fox fancied her!* And as for that little voice in her head asking increasingly loudly what the *hell* she thought she was playing at? Holly decided just to ignore it.

'Max, hi, it's Holly. Are you in a meeting?'

'No, it's fine, I can talk. All okay?'

'Yes, all good, thanks. Listen, I've bumped into an old friend of mine and she' – even in her drunken state, Holly winced at the lie – 'has asked me to have dinner with her. Would you mind if I spent the evening with her? I know we're supposed to be going out, but she's only in town for a day or two and I'd love to catch up with her.'

Max was silent for a moment. 'Of course, that's absolutely fine. I've got a little something for you, but I can give it to you another time. Where are the two of you going?'

'Oh, we're just going to find somewhere near her hotel in the West Village. I won't be late. See you later, okay?'

Holly and Cole went for dinner at a tiny Italian restaurant called Luigi's that still had bullet holes in the back wall from a Mafia gunfight during the days of Prohibition. 'Well, that's what they tell people,' Cole whispered to her as they sat down. 'I reckon Luigi just got busy with the power drill . . .' The place was dark, rowdy and served the biggest bowls of spaghetti carbonara Holly had ever seen. Cole was obviously a regular (she noticed his signed photo hanging on the wall over the bar, along with pictures of Donald Trump, some basketball player and Whoopi Goldberg) and the jovial owner kept topping up their wine glasses.

Holly was tucking into a huge slab of tiramisu and was on her second glass of Limoncello – trying to drown her feelings of guilt over Max with yet more booze – when Cole looked at her across the table with a conspiratorial grin.

'Fancy a nightcap at my hotel, sexy? Unless, of course, you think your *boyfriend* would mind . . .'

The candlelight sharpened the angles of his cheekbones and jawline and exaggerated the curve of his lips; the guy was ludicrously good-looking. Holly was feeling giddy – not just from all the booze, but from the high of being showered with attention by a hot movie star. So what if her useless boyfriend had cheated on her with a gold-digging ex-air hostess, and the current one didn't seem to want to go to bed with her? Cole Fox, international pin-up and movie hunk, thought she was sexy! *You're behaving like a spoilt brat*, the little voice in her head scolded. But then Cole leant over the table and kissed her, not on the lips but tantalisingly close to them, and Holly felt a bolt of lightning shoot right down to her groin. Suddenly, nothing else seemed remotely important apart from getting Cole to kiss her again. And again and again . . .

'Yes, please,' she murmured, her voice barely a whisper. 'And, by the way, he's *not* my boyfriend.'

37

As they walked back to Cole's hotel, Holly's emotions lurched drunkenly between excitement and shame. She knew what she was doing was terribly wrong, but she was swept away on a tide of lust for Cole – and Max didn't want her, so did it really matter? *Of course it does*, the little voice snapped back at her. *And besides, Max keeps telling you that he* does *want you . . .* Then Holly started to get the weirdest feeling that they were being followed. She knew it was probably all in her mind, fuelled by guilt over lying to Max, but she kept seeing a black limo with tinted windows that looked suspiciously like the one driven by Shaun. They'd take a turning down a street and, a minute or so later, Holly would look round and there it would be again, lurking ominously a little way behind them, like a panther stalking its prey. But the car was nowhere to be seen by the time they reached the Bowery, where Cole was staying, and Holly dismissed her worries as paranoia – after all, there must be tens of thousands of black stretch limos in New York.

With its moody lighting, Gothic fireplaces, oriental rugs and dark wood panelling, the Bowery looked like an ageing rock star's country mansion. Holly didn't get much of a chance to look round though, as Cole led her straight upstairs to his room.

'Check out the roof terrace while I fix us some drinks,' he said, throwing open the glass doors to reveal a huge balcony with views across the rooftops.

Holly collapsed onto one of the sun loungers, the warm night air caressing her like a blanket; a few moments later, Cole emerged with a bottle of whisky and poured out two huge glassfuls. As Holly struggled to sit up she realised just how drunk she was, but she sipped at the whisky to be polite. She was still feeling unsettled by the walk there and her guilt over Max, which was growing with every moment. Perhaps she should just make her excuses and go . . .

But Cole had other ideas. With a wicked glint in his eye, he reached into his pocket and pulled out a small bag of white powder.

'Now the fun *really* starts,' he grinned.

Apart from the odd puff on a joint Holly had never taken drugs before, but she was pretty sure that the powder was cocaine. Cole chopped out a line and, using a small silver straw, hoovered it up in one long, noisy sniff, then he repeated the process and offered the straw to Holly.

'Cole, I'm not really into that . . .' Her head was spinning and she was starting to feel queasy.

'What? Come on, you'll enjoy it.'

Reluctantly, Holly took the straw from him . . . *No, this was a terrible idea.*

'I'm sorry,' she said, firmly. 'It's just not my thing.'

Cole just shrugged and snorted her line himself, then he jumped up from the lounger, grabbed her hand and led her back into the room. He turned on the stereo and the Foo Fighters blared out at full volume.

'Come here, baby . . .' Cole pulled Holly to him, grabbing her bum with both hands, and kissed her hard on the lips.

It was like someone had suddenly flipped a switch. Moments before, Holly had wanted Cole so badly that nothing else mattered; now, the whole thing seemed like the most awful mistake. *How could she do this to Max?*

'Cole, I'm so sorry . . .' She tried to wriggle out of his grip.

'Shhh,' he said, pinning her to him effortlessly with just one strong arm. 'Enough talking. I want to see that gorgeous body of yours.'

'Please, I've got to go . . .' Holly struggled to pull away, but he was far too strong for her.

'Playing hard to get, eh?' laughed Cole. As he grabbed at her top and tried to pull it over her head, Holly really started to panic.

'I said no!' she said sharply, shoving Cole with all her strength. To her relief, he stumbled slightly and stepped back.

'Jesus, Holly, what the fuck's your problem? You were all over me a minute ago!' Cole's eyes were bulging and his jaw was working from side to side. The square-jawed action hero of earlier had transformed into a sweaty, wild-eyed shambles, the sort of bloke you'd cross the street to avoid.

'I'm sorry,' said Holly, grabbing her bag. 'I have to go.'

She was out of the door before he could say another word.

Oh God. Holly's head throbbed as if a drummer was belting out a solo on her brain. She tried opening her eyes a crack, but instantly shut them against the sunlight flooding the room; she'd obviously forgotten to close the curtains before she got into bed last night. With enormous effort she lifted her head off the pillow to take a sip of water and the room tilted like she was in the middle of the Atlantic. Taking deep breaths to try and keep herself from throwing up, Holly listened for signs of movement in the rest of the suite but all was quiet. Max must have left for work already. He'd been in bed when she got back last night and she'd sent him a rambling, guilty text telling him how sorry she'd been to miss him, but when she checked her phone he hadn't replied. Christ, what if he'd somehow found out about who she'd really been with last night? Holly put her aching head in her hands and tried not to cry.

As the events of the previous day whirled around her head, making her feel even sicker and dizzier, it dawned on Holly that her worries about Max were less to do with the fact they hadn't had sex (because, really, although they were sharing a room they *had* only been together a couple of weeks, so what was the rush?) and more about her nagging fear that he didn't actually fancy her. Holly had never been that secure about her looks and appeal at the best of times, and her self-confidence had taken such a terrible battering after finding out about James screwing Lady Crosby that she'd begun to doubt herself even more. If she wasn't pretty or sexy enough for James, then the idea that Max – a man so worldly, handsome and successful that he had supermodels falling at his feet – could possibly be interested in her seemed ridiculously far-fetched. And it occurred to her that the reason she had nearly jumped into bed with Cole – who in the brutal light of the world's worst hangover seemed infinitely more cocky than charming – was because she got a buzz out of someone like him fancying her. Not that he gave a shit about her; all he'd been after was a quick shag. Holly groaned. She'd risked everything she had with Max – wonderful, generous, gorgeous Max – for nothing more than an ego trip.

Stupid, stupid girl . . . What the hell was wrong with her? She wasn't sure what was making her feel worse: alcohol poisoning, heartache or shame. But then she had no one but herself to blame. She had behaved like a cheap slut and was now paying the price. Holly turned over and began to sob into her pillow. She had made such a hideous mess of everything, lurching from one bloke to another, ready to drop her knickers for a few cheap compliments and the flash of movie-star grin, when all she really wanted was to find someone to love. She thought back to the ecstatic newly engaged couples on top of the Empire State Building and felt further away from finding that than ever.

As much as she wanted to pull the covers over her head and go back to sleep, Holly was desperate to speak to Max to find out if she really had screwed things up with him. First things first: she needed to find some paracetamol so she could actually function. She gingerly climbed out of bed and staggered to the bathroom, taking tiny steps as the smallest movement triggered fresh waves of pain and nausea, but there were no pills in her washbag and none in any of the kitchen cupboards either – although she did find a packet of Oreo cookies and forced herself to eat three. Hopefully they would soak up a bit of the alcohol.

If anything, though, the cookies just made things worse. *If only she could find some bloody painkillers* . . . Perhaps Max would have some in his room? She hesitated outside the door; in many ways, he still felt like a stranger and she didn't want to start poking around his stuff. But this was an emergency; she was sure he'd understand.

Holly searched through all the cabinets in his bathroom. There were no pills, but she did find an unopened box of condoms and even in the hideous fug of her hangover, she felt a little spark of hope. Surely that was a good sign? At least it meant he wasn't impotent . . . She went back into the bedroom and started pulling open the desk drawers. A few pens and stationery in the top one . . . a pile of documents in the second . . . *Shit, there must be some paracetamol in here somewhere!* Then Holly pulled out the bottom drawer and, as she rifled through some papers, she noticed that tucked away at the back was a small, black jewellery box. Did she dare . . .? Her heart thumping, Holly pulled it out and, taking a deep breath, she opened the lid.

38

Inside the box Holly found a charm in the shape of an apple. It was made of a silvery metal (platinum probably, knowing Max) and covered in diamonds – not those tiny little pavé ones, but actual rocks. As Holly held the charm up to admire it, it sent dazzling shards of light dancing around the room. It was stunning. Then a conversation she'd had with Max a few days before popped into her head: 'You should get another charm for that,' he had said, nodding at the bracelet James had given her, which still only had the single lonely '1' hanging from it. At the time she hadn't given it much thought; but now . . . *Oh my God!*

Torn between guilt and excitement, like a kid who's just found her stash of Christmas presents, Holly put the apple charm back in the box and was just about to replace it in the drawer when she noticed a small envelope that had been alongside the box. She untucked the flap, trying her best not to crease the paper, and pulled out the card inside.

'To *my darling*', it read, '*and the city where it all began. All my love, Max*'.

Holly stared at the card. 'The city'? Well, that was easy. New York – the Big Apple. Suddenly, everything fell into place. What was it he'd said when she'd phoned to cancel their dinner date yesterday? 'I've got a little something for you . . .' Holly gave a snort of laughter. Typical Max, referring to thousands of pounds' worth of diamonds as 'a little something'! Last night must have been the night he was planning to sleep with her for the first time – and she'd screwed it up. *Terrific*.

As Holly put everything in Max's room back how she'd found it, she came to a decision. She might have made a hash of things last night, but she was going to do her very best to make it right today.

After calling room service to order a packet of paracetamol and a stack of pancakes, she phoned Mindy and asked her to make her an appointment later that morning for a blow-dry and a Brazilian wax. Mindy seemed thrilled to oblige; she'd clearly been concerned about Holly's grooming regime, which was verging on tramp-like in the face of the Manhattan woman's rigorous approach to beautification. Then Holly plucked up the courage to call Max. She was dreading speaking to him, in case he had somehow found out about her liaison with Cole (what if that *had* been Shaun's limo that had been following them back to the Bowery?), but she was desperate to get their relationship back on track.

Max answered after just one ring.

'Hello there, sleeping beauty.' To her enormous relief, he seemed pleased to hear from her. 'How was your night?'

'It was okay,' said Holly. 'I missed you, though. I was hoping you'd be free to have lunch with me today?'

'It's looking pretty busy, but I can get Mindy to move a few things around. I'm at Strut – why don't you come and meet me here, and we'll nip out for sushi?'

'I'd love to. Oh, and Max?'

'Yes?'

'I can't wait to see you.'

Mindy had booked Holly into a swanky salon on Fifth Avenue, where the stylist persuaded her to go even blonder and styled her grown-out crop into a sexily tousled bob. Barneys was just across the street and on an impulse, Holly popped in there after the salon and bought a gorgeous Marc by Marc Jacobs floral silk top. Back at the suite, she put on a full face of make-up and changed into a pair of J Brand shorts, Acne ankle boots and the new top.

Shaun called to say he was waiting downstairs, and before rushing out of the door Holly took one last look in the mirror: one of those glossily perfect New York girls with gorgeous hair and a Chanel bag smiled back at her.

It was Holly's first visit to Strut's New York office, which was on the fifteenth floor of a futuristic glass and steel skyscraper on Park Avenue. There were only a few weeks to go before the agency's model scouts hit the streets of cities across the States to seek out contestants for the TV show and, from what Max had told her, it was turning out to be a logistical nightmare – hence his long hours at work.

The reception area was similar to the London office – a brilliant white space dominated by the three-foot-high Strut logo – but it was busier and buzzier, with four receptionists behind the desk and a constant stream of couriers and visitors. Holly soaked up the atmosphere, feeling a prickle of excitement at being back in an agency.

'Can I help you?' asked one of the girls behind the desk.

'Yes, I'm here to see Max Moore. Holly Collins.'

'He's in a private meeting at the moment and has asked not to be disturbed, but I'll let his PA know you're here, Miz Collins.'

Holly took a seat on a bright pink sofa and watched people come and go: the wide-eyed wannabes accompanied by their equally nervous mothers, the established models, instantly recognisable from their grey Strut portfolios and bored pouts, and the agents, who seemed even louder and brasher than their British counterparts. As soon as she got back to the UK, Holly lectured herself, she must try and get signed up by an agency. She'd missed being part of this world.

Just then the door to Max's office opened and Holly looked up expectantly, thinking it would be him, but her heart sank as she saw that it was in fact Sasha. She really didn't want her sunny mood clouded by another awkward encounter with the Ice Queen. But Sasha had spotted her, so she couldn't very well hide behind a magazine; besides, they were staying in the same hotel so it might wise to smooth things over as they were bound to bump into each other again.

'Hi, how's it going?' smiled Holly with a little wave. 'Sounds like things are pretty manic with the show!'

Sasha's expression was as frosty as ever. 'Oh, hello, Holly. What are you doing here? I thought you'd be busy shopping.'

Ouch. 'I've come to meet Max for lunch.'

'It must be so nice to be a lady of leisure,' said Sasha. 'Especially when someone else is footing the bill. Now, if you'll excuse me, I'm in a bit of a rush.'

And with that she started to walk away.

Holly stared after her, open-mouthed. *How dare she . . . ?* Then something inside her snapped. 'Just hang on a moment,' she called after her, angrily. 'What the hell is your problem?'

After a moment's hesitation, Sasha turned and walked back towards her.

'Look, Holly, I know this is none of my business,' she said with a long-suffering sigh, as if she was trying to explain something to a small child, 'but do you really think it's such a good idea to give up your career, your whole life, to live off Max?'

Holly felt a surge of rage. *What the hell gave Sasha the right to judge her?*

'You're right,' said Holly, trying to stay calm. 'It is none of your business.'

Sasha looked at her disdainfully. 'You know, when I first met you I thought you were different. I really believed you wanted to be a model and build a career, but now I realise you were just like all those other wannabes – looking for a rich man to sponge off.'

Holly was stunned. 'You're unbelievable, you know that? It's so obvious what's going on here. You don't give a shit about me or my life; you're just jealous that I've got Max and you haven't.' At this Sasha raised her eyebrow patronisingly, making her choke with anger. 'In fact,' Holly went on, 'as far as I can tell, you don't have anyone. I've got plenty of time to build up my career, but who's going to want a relationship with . . . with a lonely, bitter old cow like you?'

Holly instantly regretted saying it. It wasn't what she thought at all – even if it was, she'd usually have been far too polite to say it – but the words were out of her mouth before she could stop herself. Sasha's patronising attitude made her so angry but, she hated to admit it, what she had said had hit a nerve.

She was about to apologise, but Sasha got in first.

'You have no idea what you're getting yourself into, little girl. When things come to an end with Max – and they will come to an end, believe me, a very *abrupt* end – then you'll be left with absolutely nothing. And then we'll see who's lonely and bitter.'

And with that Sasha turned on her heel and stalked through the doors to the lift, leaving Holly staring after her open-mouthed, tears welling up in her eyes.

39

'Hello darling, so sorry to have kept you waiting.' Holly spun round to see Max walking towards her. 'Hey, what's wrong?'

Holly wiped her eyes and plastered on a smile. 'I'm okay; it's nothing. I just had a bit of a run-in with Sasha.' She grimaced. 'I don't think she likes me very much.'

'Well, I think it must be tough for Sasha, seeing me so happy with you. Don't forget we went out for quite a while – and it all started for the two of us in New York, too. I'm sure this must be stirring up some painful memories for her.'

'Yes, I know that . . .' But Holly couldn't get Sasha's words out of her head. *A wannabe looking for a rich man to sponge off.* How dare she? 'I have no idea why the production company wanted her to be the presenter of *Street Scout* over here,' Holly went on. 'I can't imagine she'll go down particularly well in America; in fact, she'll probably lose the show viewers. She's got as much warmth as a great white shark – and considerably less charm.'

She'd meant it as a joke, but to her surprise Max didn't laugh. He looked at her with a thoughtful frown, as if he was taking her seriously. After a second, however, the clouds lifted and he broke into a smile.

'Well, let's forget about all that. How about this lunch?'

Holly was in the hotel's gym by 7.30 the following morning. Her clothes had been feeling a bit tight after weeks of burgers and beer, and if she was serious about getting into modelling when she got home, she definitely needed to lose the love handles. Not only that, but Max had told her that he had arranged for them to have dinner in the suite that evening – 'Just the two of us' – and, with a shiver of excitement, Holly had realised that meant tonight must be The Night. Now that she realised – to her delighted relief – that Max *did* want her after all, she wanted to make sure she looked as good as she could for him. The guy was used to dating super-models, after all. Okay, so she wasn't going to be transformed into a hard-bodied goddess after just one session in the gym – especially as she couldn't work out how to use any of the machines, which looked more like modern art installations (in fact, it occurred to Holly, as she struggled to find the 'on' switch, perhaps they *were* modern art installations) – but it was a start, at least.

When Holly got back to the suite, she jumped straight in the shower and then ran herself a bath in the huge marble tub, tipping in almost a whole bottle of bath foam, before relaxing in the fragrant bubbles and calling Lola direct from the in-bathroom phone for a leisurely catch-up. *At times*, Holly thought happily, as she sipped at a room-service cappuccino, *I really could get used to this ivory-tower stuff* . . .

It was nearly 10 a.m. and her skin had gone all pruney by the time she emerged from the bathroom. As she wandered around her room, planning what to wear for her date with Max and singing along to Lady Gaga on MTV, Holly glanced at her phone and saw she had a missed call. She picked it up to look at the number: it had obviously been an international call as the number hadn't come up, but whoever it was had left a voicemail.

'Holly, hi, this is Joe Taylor. Please could you give me a call as soon as you get this? I need to talk to you about something urgently. Thanks.'

Shit. Holly had completely forgotten that she was meant to be calling Joe back! It was well over a week since he'd phoned; he must think she was so rude. She pulled on a pair of jeans and a sweatshirt and dialled his number.

'Joe, it's Holly. I'm so sorry, I meant to get back to you, but then . . .' It sounded lame to admit she had

285

forgotten – she hadn't exactly been busy. 'Anyway, what did you want to talk to me about?'

'Well, I was actually calling you about something else today. I don't know if you've seen any of the gossip websites, but everyone's gone mad for this story that Sasha Hart has been dropped as the presenter of *Street Scout US* just before filming starts. I hate to ask, but do you have any idea what's been going on?'

'Are you sure that's right, Joe? I bumped into Sasha in the offices of Strut just yesterday . . .'

She tailed off as she thought back to their disastrous encounter. What was it she'd said to Max about Sasha? *She'll probably lose the show viewers.* Surely he hadn't taken her seriously? That would be ridiculous!

'Well, there hasn't been any official comment, but the story's all over the internet,' said Joe.

'I don't know anything, I'm afraid. Let me make a few calls and I'll get back to you.'

'Thanks, Holly, I'd really appreciate it. My editor is threatening me with the sack unless I come up with a front-page exclusive sooner rather than later . . .'

'Okay, bye.'

As soon as she finished the call with Joe, she logged on to the laptop Max left in the suite and went on to one of the gossip sites. Sure enough, there was a big photo of Sasha under the headline: 'Sasha

Hart FIRED from *Street Scout USA*'. With a horrible feeling brewing in the pit of her stomach, Holly scrolled down to read the story.

'Sasha Hart is believed to have been sensationally sacked from *Street Scout US* before the show has even hit TV screens,' it said. 'The brunette star, 40, who is one of Britain's highest-paid presenters, jetted out to New York to begin work on the show just two weeks ago.

'But, according to reports from America, the network has pulled the plug on her $2 million a week contract before filming was due to start.

'Last night, sources said Hart was dropped from the show because she "wasn't right" for American audiences.

'A spokesman for Strut, the model agency at the centre of the show, declined to comment on the story.'

Now starting to panic, Holly tried to get hold of Max but his phone went straight to voicemail, so she called Mindy.

'I'm sorry, Mr Moore is in meetings with the network all day,' she chirped. 'Could I arrange for you to have a facial this afternoon?'

'I don't want a sodding facial!' snapped Holly, and instantly felt awful. 'I'm so sorry, Mindy, I'm just . . . I don't suppose you know anything about Sasha Hart, um, leaving *Street Scout*, do you?'

There was a pause. 'I'm afraid you'll need to discuss that with Mr Moore.'

'Okay. Could you please ask him to call me as soon as he can?'

Holly put the phone down. She felt sick. What if Max had ditched Sasha because of what she'd said about her? Oh God, this was absolutely terrible. Whatever their disagreements, she didn't want to see the poor woman lose her job! *But hang on a moment,* she thought, *surely Max wouldn't be the one who would make important production decisions about the show?* He was just the hired help; it would only be the executive producers or network bosses who had the power to hire and fire. Relief began to flood over Holly: she wasn't to blame for this mess after all! Unless . . . well, the show *was* being filmed at Max's company – and Strut's reputation was on the line if it was a flop – and so if Max didn't want someone on board like, say, the presenter, Holly was pretty sure he would have the clout to get rid of them. Her rays of positivity were engulfed by another huge black cloud.

Suddenly Holly realised that the solution to the mystery might be just a couple of floors away from where she was standing: Sasha was staying at The Carlyle, too – and if anyone knew what was going on, it would be her! If she could just talk to her, find out what was going on – perhaps this was all some crazy rumour that had got out of hand? One way or another, she needed to know.

Holly had no idea what Sasha's room number was,

but she was pretty sure she would find it amongst the mass of *Street Scout* paperwork sitting on Max's desk. She started rifling through the documents: endless pages of shooting schedules, contracts, information sheets and then – *bingo!* the production contact sheet. And the third name down: 'Sasha Hart – The Carlyle Hotel, room 802'.

Praying Sasha would still be there, Holly sped down to the eighth floor, found room 802 and banged on the door.

40

'What do you want?' asked Sasha, wearily. Her face was make-up free, her hair pulled back into a ponytail and she was wearing a grey tracksuit. She looked exhausted, but her skin was glowing and radiant. *Must be all the yoga and mung beans*, thought Holly.

'Sasha, I'm so sorry to bother you, but could I come in for a moment? I really need to talk to you.'

'It's not a good time right now.'

In the room behind Sasha, Holly glimpsed a pile of suitcases and clothes on the bed.

'Please, it'll only take a minute,' she said.

Sighing heavily, Sasha stood aside to let Holly in.

'So – the rumours are true then.' Holly nodded awkwardly towards Sasha's packing. 'I'm so sorry.'

Sasha just shrugged.

'Look, I can talk to Max and I'm sure we'll be able to sort this out,' said Holly. 'You see, I think there might have been a bit of a misunderstanding over something I said to him that might have ended up causing this whole mess.'

Sasha gave a short laugh. 'Oh, Holly, you have absolutely no idea . . .'

'No, I'm serious,' said Holly, earnestly. 'After you and I talked yesterday, I was so angry, I said something stupid to Max in the heat of the moment and I've got a horrible feeling he might have taken me seriously. I feel terrible about it.'

Sasha rolled her eyes. 'You really think Max would fire me because of something *you* said?'

'Well, I'm not sure, which is why I'm here.' Holly bit her lip, trying to work out what to say. She really had no alternative but to come clean. 'Look, after we argued I basically told Max that I thought you'd lose the show viewers. I said you had as much charm as a . . . a great white shark. I'm so sorry.'

To her surprise, Sasha started to laugh. 'Holly, I can assure you this is nothing whatsoever to do with you. Okay?' She started walking back towards the door. 'Now, if you'll excuse me, I need to finish packing and get out of here before the paps start gathering outside – if they're not there already.'

'But what happened? Why are you leaving the show?'

'It's not me you should be asking about this,' said Sasha, opening the door.

'Who then? Max?'

Sasha nodded, then added bitterly, 'Talk to Max – and if he won't help you, try Zane.'

* * *

Holly didn't hear anything from Max all day, apart from a message via Mindy to say that he'd ordered dinner for 9 p.m. and he'd make sure he was back by then. Holly paced the suite, counting down the hours before Max returned, trying to work out what the hell was going on. She went over and over Sasha's parting words: *Talk to Max – and if he won't help you, try Zane*. Well, that had to mean that it had been Max's decision to axe Sasha; for some reason, he must have put pressure on the producers to get rid of her. But what about Zane? What role was he playing in all of this?

As it turned out, dinner arrived before Max did. Two white-coated waiters arrived at the suite each pushing a double-decker trolley piled with silver-domed plates.

'Are you celebrating, madam?' one asked pleasantly, as he nestled a bottle of champagne in an ice bucket.

'I'm not really sure,' said Holly. It felt like she wasn't sure about anything.

'Well, enjoy your evening,' he said, bowing slightly as he left.

The waiters had only just gone when Max appeared. He was smiling, but looked tired.

'What a day . . .' he said, wrapping his arms around Holly and pulling her towards him. 'I'm so looking forward to a quiet evening with you and not having to spend another moment thinking about that bloody TV show. At times like this, I can't imagine why I allowed myself to be persuaded to get involved with this farce. Those idiots at the TV company told me I'd just have to pop in once a week, say my bit to camera and then get back to my real job, but as it is I'm having to deal with their incompetence on a daily basis!' He pulled Holly even closer to him. 'Well, this is it for me. I don't care if the extra exposure is good for Strut – I'm never getting involved with the world of TV again.'

Holly nestled into his chest, enjoying the feeling of her body pressed against his. It sounded as if she'd have to pick her moment carefully to ask about Sasha.

'Anyway, enough about my shitty day,' said Max, dropping a kiss on her forehead. 'Let's eat.'

For their starters, Max had ordered Maryland crab cakes, oysters and Caesar salad.

'Are we expecting company?' asked Holly, raising an eyebrow at the gut-busting volume of food.

Max laughed. 'I guess I have been a little over-enthusiastic. I didn't know what you'd want to eat . . . So what have you been up to today?' he asked.

'Well, I went to the gym this morning . . .'

'Do you want to try a session with Jed, my trainer? He's amazing. Sadistic, but amazing. I could get him to come up to the suite after he's finished with me in the morning?'

'That would be great, thanks . . .'

They ate for a moment in silence.

'So – I saw Sasha today,' said Holly, curiosity getting the better of her.

Max looked up sharply. 'Where?'

'In her hotel room. I went to see her because I read on the internet about her getting sacked, and I wanted to know what happened.'

'And what did she say to you?' Max was looking at her so intently that Holly felt quite uncomfortable.

'Nothing at all. She said I should ask you about it.'

Max nodded slowly, appearing to relax a little. 'It's all such a mess,' he said. 'I can't say too much for legal reasons, but Sasha has had . . . issues for some time.'

'Issues?' Holly vaguely remembered that Zane had told her the same thing.

'Drugs,' stated Max, grimly. 'I thought she'd cleaned up, but it came to light yesterday that she'd started using again. I had no choice but to tell the network, as I couldn't risk letting Strut get caught up in some big scandal, and when they found out they dropped her immediately.'

Holly would have been less surprised if Max had said she was a mass murderer. This was Sasha Hart they were talking about, the well-known vegan activist and yoga freak!

'But I didn't think she even drank?' she said.

'She doesn't, but she's been battling a coke habit

for years. I first found out when we were dating, but I persuaded her to go to rehab and I had thought that was the end of it.' Max sighed. 'It's such a shame, because she could have been a huge star over here.'

Holly was struggling to get her head around this latest bombshell. The idea that the poster girl for clean living was a closet junkie seemed ridiculous. The woman radiated tofu-fuelled smugness.

'So who are they going to have to present the show now?' she asked.

'I'm not sure . . . Though it occurred to me on the way back here that Zane might be a possibility. I was thinking about suggesting it to the production company. What do you think?'

What Holly thought was that it was a terrible idea. The guy mumbled, every other word was 'sick' or 'dope', and he never took off his sunglasses.

'Well, I suppose he's already familiar with the show,' she said, carefully. With Sasha's advice to 'ask Zane' ringing in her head, she then added: 'I don't suppose Zane was involved in Sasha leaving the show, was he?'

Max looked blank. 'Zane? God, no. He's got nothing to do with that side of things, although he does know about her past issues. As far as I know, the two of them have always got on really well. Anyway, let's forget about work – I want to focus on *you*.' He smiled and reached for her hand across the table. 'Now, don't get too excited, but I've got a gift for you. I meant to give it to you the other night. Wait there . . .'

Giving her hand a squeeze, Max got up from the table and disappeared into his room. While she waited for him, Holly – who'd made sure she was wearing the charm bracelet tonight – reminded herself to look surprised when he gave her the apple charm.

As it happened, however, Holly didn't have to pretend to look surprised, because when Max reappeared he was holding a large, flattish package that looked nothing like the small, square jewellery box she had seen. Perhaps Max had put the charm inside another box for an extra surprise? It seemed like the sort of thoughtful thing he might do . . . With a grin of excitement, Holly tore off the wrapping paper.

'Oh, wow, it's an . . . iPad!' Holly was totally confused. *What about the charm?* 'Thank you so much, that's really . . . useful!'

'Well, you were talking about getting one the other day and you're such a rubbish shopper that I knew you wouldn't buy one for yourself,' Max chuckled. 'Oh, and there's something else too . . .' He reached down to pick up something from the floor.

Holly gave a little sigh of relief and subconsciously touched her bracelet. 'Max, you shouldn't have . . .' she smiled.

'Well, we can't have you getting the screen scratched,' he said.

Holly stared at the pink leather iPad cover in his hands; this time, she was too surprised to even try to cover up her confusion.

'If you don't like the colour, I can always change it,' said Max, on seeing her expression.

'No . . . thank you, it's lovely. Just what I wanted.'

For their main course Max had ordered lobster thermidor and rack of lamb, but Holly struggled to eat much of it – and not just because she was already full from the starters. Although she'd have been thrilled to get an iPad in any other circumstances, she couldn't help feeling a teeny bit disappointed. But as Max rattled on about a vintage Mercedes he was thinking of buying, Holly began to see that she was behaving like a spoiled brat. *Jesus, woman, disappointed with an iPad!* Max was obviously going to give her the charm on another occasion instead, so she should stop whinging and just be grateful. And by the time Holly had polished off a large portion of chocolate mousse, she was feeling much happier.

'That was amazing, thanks so much,' she smiled. 'And thank you for the gift, too.'

'My pleasure, gorgeous. Let's sit on the couch . . . Oh, I forgot to mention something to you. You know Cole Fox, don't you?'

His tone was casual, but Holly's head snapped up at the mention of his name.

'Know him . . . ?' she said.

'Yes, didn't you meet him at that movie premiere in London with the rest of the *Street Scout* girls?'

'Oh, yes. Only briefly.' She just hoped she didn't look as guilty as she felt. 'Um, what about him?'

Settling himself on the sofa, Max reached over to get the TV remote and started flicking through the channels. If he *did* know about Holly's night with Cole, he was doing a very good job of hiding it.

'Well,' he said, pausing on CNN to check the news headlines, 'apparently he was found unconscious in his New York hotel room this morning.'

Holly felt like she had been punched in the stomach. *Unconscious?* As pissed off as she had been at Cole for jumping on her, she was instantly worried for him.

'What happened?' she asked, trying to stay calm.

'The press haven't got hold of it yet so I'm not sure about the details, but it sounds like he's in hospital in a pretty bad state,' said Max, as he looked over at her. 'God knows what happened to the guy. Perhaps he got caught up in something he couldn't handle . . . ?' Max's expression was one of mild concern, but there was a flash of something in his eyes that sent shivers racing down Holly's spine. *He knows about me and Cole.* Then, still staring in her direction, Max said: 'Terrible business, isn't it, Holly . . . ?'

41

Holly could barely breathe, let alone speak. But Max was looking at her, waiting for her response. She had to say something.

'That's just awful,' Holly stammered. 'I wonder what happened to him?'

Max shrugged. 'I've no idea, but I'm sure the full story will come out soon enough.' Was there something implied in that comment – a threat, perhaps? – or was she just being paranoid?

Max had started flicking through the channels again. 'Jesus, what a load of crap . . . what do you feel like watching? A movie?'

Holly nodded distractedly. She couldn't focus on anything but the turmoil inside her head. *Has Max found out that I spent the day with Cole? Is that why he's telling me this?* If she was right and he had, then perhaps she should just come clean and explain that nothing actually happened between them. She could tell him they met up for a drink and she lied about it to him because . . . because . . . Oh God, whatever way she looked at it, it didn't look good. But then something far more terrible occurred to her; so hideous it made her want to run out of the hotel and get on the first flight back to London. What if Max *had* found out about her evening with Cole, and then arranged for something to *happen* to him? Something . . . bad? Holly felt faint; there was a humming in her ears. Surely that couldn't be true. Max was a highly respected businessman, not a Mafia thug. But then she remembered those stories she'd found on the internet about him back when she started on *Street Scout*, linking him with shady Russian businessmen and mysterious 'international conglomerates'. A rich, powerful man like Max could easily pay someone to sort out his 'problems' for him. Holly thought about Shaun with his massive shoulders and ham-hock fists, and felt a genuine shiver of fear. What had she got herself caught up in?

They started to watch a movie, but Holly couldn't concentrate. She needed to be on her own – to think.

After a tense few minutes sitting next to Max on the sofa, visions of *Goodfellas*-style revenge beatings spinning through her mind, she said, 'I'm sorry, Max, I think I'm going to have to go to bed.'

'Are you okay?' His face was a picture of concern; he certainly didn't *look* like a murderous psychopath.

'Just a bit of a headache. It's been on and off all day. I'm sure I'll be fine after a good night's sleep.'

'Okay, darling. I'm sorry I've been so busy recently, but we'll have some quality time together at the weekend.'

'Sure,' she said, smiling weakly.

Holly had a restless night. She trawled the internet on her iPad, but she couldn't find any trace of a story about Cole being hospitalised. She thought about calling him on his mobile, to see if he was okay, but she had no idea whether Cole was currently in a fit state to even answer his phone. Oh God, perhaps he was in a coma! Holly imagined him lying in a hospital bed, surrounded by bleeping equipment, his face barely recognisable beneath all the bruises . . . With that thought, she jumped straight out of bed and crossed over to lock her bedroom door. She was probably being ridiculously paranoid, but she had whipped herself up into such a state it felt like the sensible thing to do. It was well past 2 a.m. by the time she finally fell asleep.

By the following morning, Holly had started to calm down. In the brilliant light of another perfect New York summer's day, the whole notion that Max might have somehow found out about her and Cole then had him beaten up in revenge seemed way too far-fetched to be true. This was real life, not *The Sopranos*! As she pounded the treadmill, Holly realised the far more likely explanation was that Max had mentioned Cole to her because he knew they had once met. It was just a piece of showbiz gossip, pure and simple. That was all.

That afternoon, Holly went to the huge Barnes & Noble bookstore on the corner of 82nd and Broadway and spent ages picking out a couple of novels, then walked the couple of blocks to Central Park, stopping off to pick up a turkey and avocado sandwich (which, in typical New York style, was twice as much filling as bread) on the way. It always felt cooler in the park and she found a shady bench near the jogging track circling the reservoir, and settled in for an afternoon's reading. As she ate her sandwich, Holly thought about how, in just a matter of weeks, New York had gone from being a fairy-tale metropolis to somewhere that felt almost like home. But while the city had become normal, her life was getting increasingly weird. Max, Sasha, Cole . . . She had a horrible feeling she had got herself tangled up in something, but she had absolutely no idea what it was – and that worried her. She felt as blind and helpless as if she was in a tiny dinghy approaching an iceberg: she could only see the tip, but she knew that the rest was lurking murkily underwater, ready to send her plummeting down to the depths. Suddenly, Holly was engulfed by a wave of longing for her old life in London. She wanted to be drinking Guinness in some dingy pub with Meg, to be squashed into a tube train on the Central Line, to feel drizzle on her face, to have a lazy Sunday morning pottering around her flat, to watch *Sleeping Beauty* with Lola for the millionth time. Life had seemed so much simpler then. With all the drama in her life now, she seemed to have got stuck in some soap opera – and she was beginning to think she'd quite like to be written out of it.

As she watched the groups of runners and dog-walkers go by, Holly came to a decision. She would talk to Max that evening and tell him that she wanted to go back to London. It wasn't that she wanted to split up with him – if, indeed, they *were* actually going out – but she needed to get her own life back so her sole focus wasn't Max. It wasn't healthy, this weird limbo their relationship was in. Holly felt sure he would understand.

But Max didn't come back that evening. He sent her a message (via Mindy, naturally) to say that he had to take some big Strut clients out for dinner, that he wouldn't invite her because it was bound to be extremely boring, and that he'd see her the next day. And the following morning Max had gone by the time Holly woke up, but he had left her a note.

Darling,
I've arranged for Jed to meet you for a workout at 9 a.m., I hope that's okay. The network is having a reception at lunchtime today to drum up interest among advertisers for the show – a bit of a meet-and-greet thing. I'd love you to come along with me

if you can be bothered? I'll get Shaun to pick you up
at midday. Jeans/heels are fine.

Max

x

Holly groaned. The last thing she felt like was being wheeled out like some trophy girlfriend again, but she felt obliged to go for Max's sake. And perhaps she'd be able to corner him for a quiet word during the afternoon about her plans to go back to London.

The reception was taking place on the roof terrace of the Gramercy Park Hotel. Holly took the elevator up to the sixteenth floor and emerged onto a terrace covered with large pots of exotic trees and shaded by vine-covered trellises. It was like being in one of the greenhouses in Kew Gardens, but with the added bonus of waiters handing round cocktails and beautiful little canapés that were as vibrant as rainforest butterflies.

Holly took a drink and looked around for Max, but when she located him he appeared to be deep in conversation with a group of suits, so she left him to it and wandered over to the edge of the terrace to admire the view. The terrace where Holly was standing was about ninety floors lower than the top of the Empire State Building, but the view was just as intoxicating. From it she could see the city's charming older buildings, the stout red-brick towers with their turrets and the tree-dotted terraces that had been there long before the glass and metal monsters that now dominated the skyline. The view from there was neighbourhood – rather than city-wide – and New York looked even friendlier and more welcoming from that perspective. Holly's gaze fell on a distant clock tower made of pale-coloured stone that seemed to glow against the vivid blue of the sky, then moved down to street-level to admire the green and grey mosaic of Gramercy Park. God, she would never get tired of this city . . .

'Hey, Holly!'

Holly turned to see a man walking towards her through the crowd. *Who was that . . . ?* It took Holly a moment to realise that it was Zane, who looked completely different without his usual bug-eye goggles – and, Holly had to admit, extremely handsome. She could see why he'd been such a successful model.

'Hi Zane, how are you?'

'Safe, babe. What's been happenin'?'

'Oh, you know. Keeping busy. Bad news about Sasha, isn't it?' After what Sasha had said to her, Holly was keen to find out if Zane could shed any light on her departure.

'Tru dat,' he said, solemnly. 'I told you girl had issues.'

As he spoke, Holly noticed something sparkling in his ear. She hadn't taken it in before, but she now clocked that Zane was wearing an earring. A very

dangly, diamondy earring. It looked strangely familiar . . . then she looked a bit closer – and felt herself
turn cold.

The earring was shaped like an apple.

Holly felt a wave of nausea wash over her and she
reached for the edge of the balcony to steady herself.
It must just be a coincidence, she reassured herself.
After all, there were apple-shaped trinkets available
on every street corner in New York! But the nausea
didn't go away. *Ask Zane*, Sasha had said. But ask
him what?

'I . . . I like your earring,' she said, lightly.

He grinned and touched it. 'It's sick, innit? I got it
yesterday. An apple for, like, the Big Apple, yeah? But
it's not an earring, it's one of them charm bracelet
things. I styled it into something a bit more Zane,
you know?'

'It's really lovely.' Holly's voice sounded strange,
even to her: sort of choked. It must be a coincidence.
It must. Holly took a deep breath to steady herself.
'Um, where did you get it?'

'It was a present,' said Zane. And then his eyes
flickered over to where Max was standing.

42

As Holly saw where Zane was looking, apparently confirming her very worst fears, her hand flew to her mouth in horror. So Max had given the charm to Zane – the charm she had assumed was intended for her as a sign of his love. So that meant – what? That Max didn't love her after all? That he loved . . . *Zane*? Holly realised she was shaking, although thankfully Zane was distracted by his phone ringing and didn't notice. The words of the note she had found hidden with the charm flashed through her mind. *To my darling and the city where it all began. All my love, Max.* She'd remembered exactly what he'd written because it had made her feel so happy, reassuring her that Max truly loved her, but now every word pierced her heart like a dagger.

As the chatter of the crowd buzzed around her, Holly tried to piece together what the hell was going on. Things started to fall into place, *click-thud-plop*, like a game of Mouse Trap. The diamond charm had always been meant for Zane, not her. Which meant that Max was in love with Zane, not her. All of which led to the conclusion that Max was – what? Bisexual? *Gay*?

That was ridiculous; there was no way Max could be gay! For one thing he'd gone out with Sasha for years. Holly thought back to all the gushing interviews with his ex-girlfriends who couldn't wait to run to the newspapers to tell the world what a stud he was. For God's sake, the guy was the world's biggest shagger this side of Russell Brand! And if Max was gay, why go to all the trouble and expense of pretending to have fallen for her?

He must be bisexual then, and had obviously just decided that he fancied Zane more than he did her. Holly felt the same sickening stab of betrayal as she had when she'd found out about James and Lady Crosby. Her eyes welled with tears of hurt and humiliation. God, if only she'd trusted her instincts! She had known there was something fishy about the way Max kept on putting off having sex with her. All that time he had been telling her how much he fancied her – all the crap he'd been spouting about how it was going to be 'worth the wait' – and he'd actually been shagging Zane—

'Tilapia roe with avocado foam and a ponzu jelly?'

Holly struggled back to the present to find a waiter standing next to her with a tray of canapés.

'Yeah, sweet,' said Zane, taking one. 'Hols?'

Dragging her attention from the chaos in her head, Holly turned to look at Zane, taking in his tattoos, his waxed arms and that bloody earring, and had to stop herself chucking tilapia roe at his perfectly chiselled face. He had known what was going on, yet he had stood there and watched her trailing around after Max like a lovesick puppy and hadn't said a word. They two of them had probably been having a right laugh about it – when they weren't having wild sex, that is. She felt anger surging up inside her and wanted to scream at Zane that she knew what had been going on, that she'd discovered their sordid little secret . . .

'Hols?' Zane was staring at her. 'You alright, bro?'

Holly's head was spinning and there was a hissing in her ears. Oh Christ, she was going to pass out . . . She had to get the hell out of that place with her dignity intact – and then get the hell out of New York. Without saying a word to Zane, she turned and started pushing through the crowd to get to the lift. Her guts were churning with anger, hurt and confusion, and she was aching from the realisation that she had been betrayed by a man that she'd trusted, perhaps even loved, all over again. How could Max have strung her along like this?

As she waited for the lift, Holly glanced over to where Max was standing and, at that very moment, he looked in her direction and their eyes locked. His face was concerned and questioning – Holly supposed she must have looked a right state, pale as a ghost and in shock. To her relief the lift arrived and she got in and jabbed at the button for the ground floor, but as the doors closed, she took a final look at Max and saw that his expression had changed from anxiety to horrified realisation. *He knows*, thought Holly. *He knows that I know.*

As Holly dashed into the street to hail a cab, she caught sight of Shaun getting out of the waiting limo and walking towards her.

'Taxi!' she screeched, almost jumping into the path of one.

As they pulled away, she glanced out of the back window to see Shaun standing on the kerb, talking into his mobile. She had no doubt who he was talking to.

On the drive uptown, Holly thought back over her time with Max, searching for clues she might have missed, but, apart from the lack of sex, came up with absolutely nothing. He genuinely seemed to have fallen for her. What was it he'd said to her? *I feel like the luckiest man alive.* After the horrific discovery on the terrace, Holly now had no way of knowing what was true and what was bullshit, but surely Max wouldn't have gone to the trouble of having her move into his suite if he felt nothing for her? Why not just make some excuse and pack her off back to London? It just didn't make sense. Then she thought about the way Max had always been so keen to show her off when they were out and about, but had never taken their relationship much beyond first base. Perhaps he'd only wanted her in New York with him as some sort of accessory, like his Patek Philippe watch or Chanel loafers? Something to be dusted off for a special occasion and then put back in the safe. After all, that was how he'd made her feel at times; it was part of the reason she'd ended up in Cole Fox's hotel room. *Cole Fox*. Despite trying to get hold of him, he still hadn't returned any of her messages and she had no idea what had happened to him – or whether Max had had anything to do with it. Gripped by a sudden fear, Holly spun round to look out of the back window to check she wasn't being followed, but thankfully she couldn't see anything that looked like Shaun's hulking monster of a car.

Holly had begun running over and over the events of the past few weeks in her head again when she suddenly remembered the phone call with Joe. What was it he'd said? *There's something you should know about Max* . . . She hadn't given what he'd said much thought at the time, but now . . .

She rummaged in her bag for her phone and dialled his number. Thankfully, he picked up.

'Joe, it's Holly, can you talk?'

'Yes, how are you? Are you still in New York?'

'Yes, but I'm coming back soon. Listen, I need to ask you something. What was it that you were going to tell me about Max the other day?'

'Oh, that.' Joe sounded wary. 'Perhaps you should just forget I said anything. To be honest, I'm beginning to think I might have got it wrong, what with the two of you being together.'

'Joe, please, I need to know.'

He sighed. 'Okay. Well, for the last few years – since I've been in journalism, in fact – it's been strongly rumoured that Max is gay.'

Holly shut her eyes. If only she'd phoned Joe back that day . . . But she'd been so taken in by Max's charm and the gorgeous golden fantasy he'd woven for her, would she even have believed him?

'But why hasn't this been reported anywhere?' she asked, faintly.

'No evidence,' said Joe. 'You can't just go outing people in the press unless you have concrete proof. And now it looks like the rumours aren't true, anyway. I'd assumed all those girls he's been linked with were just with him to keep up the pretence, but now you're dating him, I guess that blows the whole thing out of the water, doesn't it? Some pap photos of the two of you landed on my desk the other day coming out of some fancy New York restaurant, arm in arm. You looked sensational, Holly . . .'

'Mmmm,' said Holly, vaguely. She was reeling from what Joe had just said about Max dating girls just to keep up the pretence that he was straight. As sickened as that made her feel, it made perfect sense. Why else would all those girls boast so publicly about how great he was in bed? Perhaps Max even paid them to talk to the press to keep up his act. But that didn't explain *why* he went to such great lengths to keep his sexuality secret. The guy worked in fashion, for God's sake – being gay was practically part of the job description.

Just then the taxi pulled up outside The Carlyle.

'Sorry, Joe, I'm afraid I'm going to have to go,' she said. 'I'm in a bit of a rush right now but I'll call you when I get back to London, okay?'

'Are you sure you're alright, Holly? You sound a bit out of breath.'

'Yes, fine. Honestly. Thanks so much for your help.'

'Okay, but do call me if you need anything. I care about you, and I'd like to help if you need it.'

Holly raced up to the suite and started throwing things into her suitcase as fast as she could. She thought about Cole again, and wondered what Max was possibly capable of. She had to get out of there before he returned.

Holly ran into the bathroom and with one sweep of her arm cleared all her toiletries sitting on the shelf into her washbag. She pulled out drawers and shook the contents into her suitcase, in too much of a rush to spend time folding things. *Oh God, her bag wouldn't close* . . . In the end, she threw herself on top of it belly first and finally managed to get it zipped all the way around.

After a quick check through her handbag – passport, money, cards – Holly rushed out of the bedroom, her luggage bumping around her legs as she ran. She would worry about getting a flight when she got to the airport. But, just as she was heading across the living room, she heard the soft click of a key card in the door . . .

43

'Where the hell are you going?'

Max had the blazing eyes and heaving chest of someone who'd just run up sixteen flights of stairs. It was the first time Holly had ever seen him looking remotely ruffled, and it scared her. There was an air of desperation about him. He looked like a man with a secret he would do anything to protect.

'Tell me, Holly.' Max's tone was urgent. 'Why did you run out on me just now?'

'Max, I need to go . . .'

'For God's sake, *talk to me*! What's happened?' Holly started for the door, but he quickly side-stepped in front of her to block her way. 'You can't just run out on me without an explanation!'

'I don't owe you anything after what you've done,' she said, her voice edging towards hysteria. 'Now, please, get out of my way!'

'No, Holly, I'm not moving. Not until you talk to me – and then I'll get Shaun to take you wherever you want to go.'

'I'll be getting a taxi. I'm not going anywhere with Shaun.'

'Fine! But, please, just tell me what's wrong?'

They stared at each other for a moment, stuck in stalemate. As much as Holly wanted to get out of there, it looked like she'd have to have this out with him – at least until she could make her escape.

'I know about Zane,' she blurted out. 'I know you're bisexual.'

His face flashed with such anger that Holy immediately feared she'd made a terrible mistake. Christ, she should have left while she had the chance. But then, to her astonishment, his shoulders slumped and he dropped his head into his hands. He looked like a broken man.

'You're wrong,' he said, raising his head to look at her. 'I'm not bisexual.'

Max didn't need to say anything more. 'Then you're gay,' said Holly, quietly.

'Yes,' said Max. 'I am so sorry, Holly.'

Now that the last traces of hope that this had all been some terrible misunderstanding had been destroyed, Holly felt like she'd just had all the life and happiness sucked out of her.

'I don't understand,' she sobbed, half falling into a nearby chair. 'When we kissed you sometimes . . . you had an erection. You seemed to be getting turned on.'

Max looked away. 'I'm sorry, it was just . . . in the

heat of the moment, you know? But I am definitely gay.'

Holly shut her eyes as reality sank in. Everything that Max had told her, everything he had promised her – it had all been lies. A great sob rose up from somewhere deep inside her.

'Holly,' said Max gently, 'I know I've handled this terribly and you must be angry with me . . .'

'You're bloody right I am!'

'But let me just try and explain. I don't expect you to forgive me, but at least you might begin to understand why I did it.'

'I'm not going to sit here and waste another moment with you,' sobbed Holly. 'How could you do this to me? To lead me on, let me think you'd fallen for me, and all the time you and Zane were . . .' Holly could barely get the words out; she was struggling to breathe.

'Please, Holly, just five minutes, that's all I ask,' begged Max. 'It kills me to see you so upset. Please, let me try and make it right.'

Holly stared at him for a moment. The adrenaline that had been pumping through her moments ago had now drained away, leaving her utterly exhausted. She sank back into the chair.

'Go on, then,' she murmured. 'Although I can't imagine why you think I'll believe a single word you say.'

'Thank you so much, Holly – I know you didn't

deserve any of this. The last thing I wanted to do was hurt you, I hope you know that . . .'

Holly wiped away the tears that were dripping steadily down her face. 'Please, save me the bleeding-heart crap, Max. Just give me your little speech so I can get out of here.'

'Okay,' he said. 'Okay. Well, I suppose I've known I was gay for as long as I can remember . . .'

Holly gave an incredulous snort. 'And yet you forgot to mention it to me!'

'Holly, please. Just hear me out . . . As a teenager I assumed it was just a phase I was going through, so I did my best to ignore it. Then, when I was eighteen, I set up my first business – property development it was – and started making a lot of money very quickly. I was young and flash, a proper jack-the-lad, and I had girls throwing themselves at me. None of my mates were gay so I thought that maybe if I acted straight I might' – he shrugged hopelessly – '*become* straight. I know how pathetic that sounds now, but I was young and confused and you've got to remember it was very different then, back in Essex in the seventies. The only gay person I knew of was Larry Grayson off *The Generation Game*. And I was terrified about how my parents would react if they found out . . . So I had this succession of gorgeous girlfriends and just met up with men in secret.'

'I get all that, Max, but what about now? Why

don't you just come out? It isn't the seventies any more, haven't you heard?'

Max raked his hands through his hair. 'It's not that simple. By the time I had come to terms with the fact that I was definitely gay, I had set up Strut and was quite a well-known figure and it felt like it would be such a big deal if I came out that I just kept up the pretence. And now . . . Well, I just don't have the guts to face the hounding I'd get from the press. They'd be raking over my past, hassling my exes, digging up every bit of dirt they could . . . Christ, the thought of it just turns my stomach. And the fact that I lied for so long could ruin my reputation.'

'Max, you're not a politician,' said Holly. 'People would understand.'

'If my reputation was my only concern, then I'd come out. But there's something else . . .' He sighed. 'I have a son, Holly. His name's Arthur and he's thirteen. His mum is a model who I was briefly married to in the nineties. She knew I was gay, but we had an . . . arrangement. It suited us both – for a while – but, unsurprisingly, she wanted more, so we divorced. As I told you before, we're on good terms and I see Arthur whenever I can.' Max smiled. 'He's such a great kid – bright, kind, funny, popular. We have a terrific relationship. But he doesn't know I'm gay.'

Holly pulled a face. 'Why not? He wouldn't mind!'

'Oh, it's not that,' said Max, quickly. 'I'd love nothing more than to be honest with Arthur, but our relationship has been hard enough as it is without dropping this bombshell on him. You see, he resented me for leaving his mum when he was little and it's taken him a very long time to trust me. If he found out I'd been lying to him about something like this . . .' Max shook his head. 'We're in a great place now, but it's taken years for us to build up the trust and love we have today. I can't risk destroying that.'

'But I'm sure he wouldn't want you to be living a lie for the rest of your life.'

'Maybe . . . God, I don't know.' Max sounded so anguished that Holly almost felt sorry for him. 'I go over and over this endlessly, as you can imagine, but it just seems easier to keep things the way they are.'

'Max, I understand all this, I really do. But what I don't get is why you lied to *me* for so long. You knew you'd have to come clean sooner or later, surely.'

'I know, I know, I handled it terribly. I was planning to tell you, but it just never seemed like the right time. And I do love spending time with you . . .'

Holly scoffed sarcastically. 'Oh, well, that's great! Let's hang out together, have sleepovers and chat about which boys we fancy!'

'Holly, I can't tell you how sorry I am for all this . . .'

She angrily held up her hand to cut him off, then rummaged in her pocket for a tissue. 'Tell me what's been going on with Zane,' she sniffed.

Max winced. 'It's early days, but we've been seeing

each other for a while.'

'So, basically, you were just using me to keep up your pretence of being this red-blooded playboy billionaire.'

Max gave a guilty shrug and the iota of sympathy Holly had been feeling for him a moment before evaporated. He didn't care about her – she wondered if he even cared about his son. All he seemed to care about was his sodding reputation.

'You're unbelievable, you know that? You made me think you wanted me, that you had fallen for me, and like an idiot I believed you! I put my life on hold to be here with you, Max . . .' She got up, picked up her bags and headed for the door.

'Holly, stop!' He rushed after her and grabbed her arm.

'Let me go,' she hissed, shaking off his hand. 'I won't tell anyone about you, if that's what you're worried about. But I don't want to be part of this . . . freak show any more.'

'Holly, please, I've not finished – there's something else I need to talk to you about – something import-ant. It might help . . .'

'Forget it, Max. I'm done with this whole mess. Have a nice life.'

Holly slammed the suite door behind her, rushed to the elevator and then ran out into the street and hailed a taxi.

'JFK Airport,' she told the driver. She slumped back on the seat and started to cry.

44

'Good morning and welcome to London Heathrow Airport, where the local time is 8.22 a.m.'

Holly stared miserably out of the plane window at the rain outside. It was so grey it was difficult to work out where the runway ended and the clouds began. In other circumstances she'd be thrilled to be back home, but the drama of the last twenty-four hours and a sleepless night, courtesy of toddler twins sitting in the row in front of her, had plunged her into a mood that was bleaker than the British weather. Every time she thought about what had happened with Max, she felt such a sickening twist of pain that tears welled up in her eyes. At least she'd actually managed to get a last-minute seat on an American Airways flight out of JFK yesterday evening. She'd had visions of having to camp out in the airport for days, living off pretzels and Kool-Aid like some baggage-hall bag lady.

While Holly was waiting for her luggage at the carousel, she plucked up the courage to turn on her phone. There were texts and emails from Max, which she ignored, and twenty-two voicemail messages. With a heavy heart, she listened to the first one. 'Holly, it's Max. You have every right to be furious at me, but you didn't let me finish and I really need to talk to you . . .' *Bloody nerve.* Holly promptly hit delete and moved on to the next. 'Holly, it's me again, please call me back . . .' She deleted that message as well and then switched off her phone. She'd face the other twenty when she'd had some sleep.

At least the gods of the London Underground were smiling on her that morning and the tube sped her swiftly back to Hammersmith. She dumped her bags in the living room and looked around at her flat. So much had happened to her since she was last at home, yet nothing here had changed. Still the same sofa, the same broken-legged table, the same weird pottery cat given to her by her mum. It was a surreal feeling, not helped by the jet lag that was now creeping over her like a fog.

To distract herself from the siren call of her bed, Holly busied herself clearing out the fridge of all the food that had gone off (quite a lot as it happened, but then she'd only expected to be away for three nights), then sorted out her dirty laundry. It felt surprisingly good to be doing something constructive, no matter how menial, after the last few weeks of being treated like a pedigree poodle. Despite her heartbreak, as she pottered around tidying up the house, she felt more like herself than she had in weeks.

After nipping round to the supermarket for some essentials, Holly came back and made herself beans on toast and a mug of tea – the most English breakfast she could think of – and ate it while rifling through her post. Bills, more bills, flyers from pizza restaurants, bills . . . Then something caught her eye. It was a letter, addressed to her, from an estate agent.

Dear Miss Collins
Thank you for signing up to our property alert service. We have recently taken on a property that matches your requirements . . .

Huh? They must have got the wrong person, thought Holly, although the property itself, a three-bedroom cottage in nearby Brook Green, would have *definitely* matched her requirements. If you ignored the usual estate-agent guff – all 'bijou residence' this and 'period cornicing' that – the cottage did look gorgeous, with a sweet little roof terrace and airy, open-plan living area. It was the sort of place Holly would have loved to live, if only she could have afforded the decidedly non-bijou price tab. Trying to ignore a ripple of fear over the state of her bank balance, Holly squashed the letter in the recycling bin and then phoned Meg.

For once, her friend seemed lost for words. 'I don't believe it . . . The fecking bastard . . .'

Holly burst into tears – again. It was a surprise she had any tears left. 'Oh God, Meg, my life's such a mess. I've got no job, I can't afford the next rent payment on my flat and my love life is . . . is . . .'

'. . . like something off the *Jeremy Kyle Show*?' finished Meg.

Despite herself, Holly laughed.

'Right, Miss Collins,' said Meg, briskly. 'I want you to throw some clothes and a toothbrush in a bag and then get your skinny arse over here. You're coming to stay with us at Nanna Aileen's.'

'Meg, I can't possibly . . .'

'I won't have any argument. You need to be with people who love you at the moment. Besides, we've got all this space – we might as well take advantage of it. The top bedroom is yours for as long as you want it.'

'It's so lovely of you to ask, but . . .'

'I'm not *asking*, Collins, I'm telling. See you shortly, okay?'

Holly was lying in a bath reading the papers. It was late on Sunday morning and she was on her own in the house, as Meg and Spunk had gone to Borough Market to buy provisions for the huge roast they were planning to cook that afternoon. She chucked the paper on the floor, then closed her eyes and sank under the bubbles, letting the stresses of the last few days drift away in the soothingly warm water. She'd arrived at Meg's yesterday afternoon and, after a proper therapeutic bawl, they'd had a lovely evening together, slobbing out on the sofa in their pyjamas with a curry and a bottle of wine.

Holly was just getting dressed when she heard a knock at the front door.

'Just a minute!' she shouted. Typical Meg, always forgetting her keys. It was just as well Holly was in.

But when she went downstairs to open the front door, she found a pretty girl with a blonde chignon, blazer and loafers waiting on the doorstep.

'Hello, Holly,' she smiled. She sounded very posh.

'Hello . . .' Holly eyed her warily. How did she know her name? Actually, now she thought about it, the girl *did* seem vaguely familiar . . .

'I'm Flora Ferguson, Mr Moore's vice-executive deputy assistant.' Of course, that was it! She'd seen her around when they'd been filming *Street Scout*. 'He asked me to come round to give you a message as there seems to be something wrong with your phone.'

'There's nothing wrong with my phone, I just don't want to talk to him,' said Holly. 'I'm sorry . . .' She didn't want to be rude; the girl was only doing her job. 'How did you know I was here?'

'Mr Moore gave me the address.'

'Well, I'm afraid you've had a wasted trip. You can

tell Max I'm not interested in whatever he has to say.'
And she shut the door.

Holly leaned against the hallway wall and exhaled noisily. How dare Max hassle her like this? And how on earth did he track her down to Meg's house? Sometimes she wondered if he had his own spy satellites . . .

Just then there was another loud knock at the door, making Holly yelp with surprise.

'Holly?' Flora Ferguson's cut-glass tones called out from the other side of the door. 'Holly, I'm afraid I'm under strict instructions not to move until I give you this message.'

Oh God, she'd have to hear her out now. It had started to rain and she didn't want the poor girl getting wet. It wasn't Flora's fault that Max was such a bastard. With a sigh, Holly opened the door again.

'Okay, what is it?'

Flora beamed at her. 'Mr Moore says he is truly sorry about what happened and that the last thing he wanted to do was hurt you. He says he cares for you very deeply.' Holly cringed, but Flora didn't seem remotely embarrassed. Holly supposed she was well used to tidying up the mess of Max's personal life. 'He hugely regrets his mishandling of the situation,' she went on, 'but thinks he will be able to make it up to you. He has an offer to put to you – a *business* offer – and he would be very grateful if you would meet with him tomorrow to give him the chance to explain it to you in person. He's happy to arrange your travel.'

Holly held up her hand. 'I'm sorry, regardless of whether I would meet with Max or not – and it's most definitely a not – there is no way I'm going back to New York.'

'There'd be no need,' said Flora, quickly. 'Mr Moore flew into London today. The meeting would be at his office in Mayfair.'

Oh. 'And what if I refuse to meet him?'

'He says to tell you that if you don't like the sound of his offer you can walk away and he promises never to contact you again, but that if you aren't prepared to meet with him tomorrow' – and at this point even Flora looked a little awkward – 'he'll send me round here every day to ask again until you do.'

Holly was open-mouthed; Max really did have a bloody nerve.

Flora looked pleadingly at Holly. 'I really would agree to meet him,' she said. 'Mr Moore can be *extremely* persistent.' She said it with the weary air of someone who had stood on many doorsteps in her time.

'Well then, I've got no choice,' said Holly. 'But you can tell Max that the only reason I'm agreeing to this is so *you* don't have to waste your time. And that I consider this to be blackmail.'

But Flora just looked relieved. 'Wonderful! I'll send a cab to get you at eleven tomorrow morning.'

* * *

Holly told Meg about her surprise visitor as they prepared lunch together later that afternoon.

'Well, I still think he's the world's biggest asshole, but you're doing the right thing going to meet him,' said Meg. 'Perhaps he's going to offer you a modelling contract with Strut.'

'Yes, I was thinking the same thing,' said Holly, peeling a huge pile of potatoes. 'I don't think I'd accept, though. I don't want to be a pity signing, even though the offers haven't exactly been rolling in since my exit from *Street Scout*.'

The kitchen was silent for a moment, except for the rhythmic *chop-chop-chop* of Meg's knife on the board. Then all of a sudden: 'Oh my God!' Meg screeched so loudly Holly nearly peeled off the top of her finger. 'I know what it is! Max wants you to be the presenter of *Street Scout US*!'

Holly snorted. 'I can promise you that's not going to happen. I've had no presenting experience and besides, he's lining his *boyfriend* up for that particular job.'

'Hmmm, perhaps you're right . . .' Meg went back to chopping her carrots. 'Well, whatever this mysterious offer turns out to be, make sure you don't say yes or no immediately. This is going to need some serious deliberation, okay?'

45

Well, I'll give Max one thing, thought Holly. *He certainly knows how to make an impact.*

She was standing on the doorstep outside Meg's house, gawping at the 'cab' that had been sent to ferry her to Max's office. It was matt black and shaped like a very thin wedge of cheese, with doors that swooped upwards like an eagle's wings: it looked more like the Batmobile than a taxi.

As she walked towards the car, a couple of blokes were standing on the pavement taking snaps of it on their phones, muttering breathlessly about, 'twin-turbo V8 engines' and 'kinetic energy recovery systems'.

She climbed into the front seat (there wasn't the option of a back seat), next to the sharp-suited driver, who handed her a gift bag 'With Mr Moore's compliments'. As they set off, with such a terrific roar from the engine that she felt it vibrating through her, Holly very pointedly put the bag on the floor. She fully intended to snub it for the rest of the journey, but by the time they reached Lambeth Bridge curiosity had got the better of her.

Inside the bag she found a small box, much like the one that the apple charm had been in – the memory of which made Holly feel angry and upset all over again – and a card with just one line written on it: '*I can't thank you enough for agreeing to meet me. Max.*' Rolling her eyes in anger, Holly opened the box. She had wanted to hate whatever she found inside, but infuriatingly it was breathtakingly beautiful: a very thin gold necklace from which hung a single round diamond the size of a pencil eraser. It was understated, yet stunning. *Damn you, Max Moore*, fumed Holly. She was torn between wanting to put it on immediately and chucking it straight out of the window, but instead she tucked it away in her rucksack (she hadn't brought the Chanel today, on principle) and decided she would just give it back to Max when she saw him. If he thought she could be bought with some flashy bauble, he had another think coming! And besides, even if she *had* wanted to throw it in the Thames, there were so many buttons inside the car she had no idea which of them actually opened the window.

Amid a flurry of stares and pointing from passers-by, the Batmobile drew up outside a terrace of grand Georgian townhouses in Mayfair. Holly had always assumed Max's headquarters were at Strut, but she guessed he must need a base for his other businesses

– and from the look of the place, those businesses were booming. The small crowd that had gathered on the pavement as they pulled up, clearly hoping to see Angelina Jolie or Madonna, dispersed with murmurs of disappointment as Holly emerged from the car in her jeans and hi-top Converse. Meg had strongly advised her to dress down for the meeting ('so you don't look like you're trying to impress the wanker') but as she walked up to the imposing entrance, Holly felt woefully underdressed, like some sixth former who'd pitched up for work experience.

A small brass plate next to the door read 'Moore Enterprises' but before she could even ring the bell, the door swung open and there was Flora Ferguson, looking even smarter than she had yesterday in a wrap dress and long boots.

'Wonderful to see you, Holly.' She smiled. 'Please come this way.'

They walked down a lushly carpeted corridor, past an office in which three girls were tapping away at computers, and into a waiting room that looked like it had been lifted straight out of an *Elle Decor* spread. The walls, floors and lampshades were white, but the artfully mismatched sofas were a riot of purples, greens and yellow.

'Mr Moore will be right with you,' Flora said. 'Can I get you a drink?'

'Coffee, thank you,' said Holly, sinking onto one

of the purple velvet sofas. Where on earth did Max find such comfy seats? It was like sitting on a pile of pillows.

There was a pile of magazines (beautiful arranged, naturally) on the low Perspex coffee table in front of her; Holly spotted the latest issue of *Hot* and started flicking through it. She giggled to see pap photos of Moet, who was clearly making the most out of her fifteen minutes of fame, falling drunkenly out of a nightclub with a couple of wannabe WAGs. Then Holly turned the page and froze.

Smiling up at her was a picture of Cole Fox, as smolderingly handsome as ever, underneath the headline: 'The Fox goes to rehab after "drug overdose".'

She started to read:

Cole Fox has checked himself into rehab after an accidental 'drugs overdose' in a New York hotel room.

Sources claim that the British movie hunk, 34, was rushed to hospital last week after he was found unconscious in his room at the Bowery Hotel following a wild night of partying.

On the night in question, a fellow guest reports seeing the star in the hotel's bar looking 'clearly intoxicated', in the company of a group of five or six scantily dressed women.

'He was kissing and fondling these girls in full

view of everyone,' said the source. 'At midnight they all left the bar together and got in the elevator – I presume to go up to his room.'

Friends have been increasingly concerned by Cole's wild lifestyle, which saw him thrown out of a club in LA last month and cautioned by police for possession of a Class A drug.

A pal told Hot: 'Cole's been out of control for some time. Hopefully this will be the wake-up call he needs.'

In a statement released by his representative, the actor explained his reasons for going to rehab and thanked fans for their support.

'I have voluntarily checked myself into a treatment facility for help in dealing with some personal issues and I look forward to resuming work on my new movie, Claws, in the very near future,' he said.

'I ask for privacy at this challenging time and hope that by seeking professional help for my problems I can emerge a better son, brother and artist. Thank you for all your messages of concern.'

Holly gawped at the page, relief flooding through her. So Cole had ended up in hospital after snorting too much coke, not because Max had paid some heavies to beat him up. She thought back to that night in Cole's hotel room, how out of it he had seemed, and suddenly it all made perfect sense. Well, at least Cole was now getting some help with his problems. And now she knew for sure that he wasn't some violent loony, Holly felt herself warming slightly – *ever so slightly* – towards Max. She wasn't anywhere near to forgiving him for all the lies, but she felt strangely relieved that she hadn't been such a terrible judge of character that she had fallen for a psychopath after all.

'Holly?' She looked up to see Flora waiting at the door. 'Mr Moore is ready for you now.'

Taking a deep breath, Holly followed her up a flight of stairs and down another corridor, at the end of which was a pair of huge double-doors.

Flora knocked and then pushed them open to reveal an office that was so huge it must have once been a ballroom. Like the waiting room it was completely white, but with huge works of modern art and framed photos on the walls – was that Damien Hirst's famous pickled sheep sitting in a tank in the corner? There was a wooden desk, as big as a minibus, on a raised platform in front of the windows, and a huge cinema screen with a row of armchairs arranged in front of it. For a moment she couldn't locate Max, but then she spotted him over in the corner on one of the sofas. He stood up as she came in, smiling broadly and holding out his arms. He looked perfectly confident and at ease, in total control of his golden kingdom: a very different Max from the broken shell of a man she'd left in New York just forty-eight hours ago. Holly very nearly turned around and walked straight out. The guy was unbelievable! Thanks to him, her world was in pieces, but Max was acting like nothing had happened.

In that moment, Holly was as furious with herself for agreeing to meet Max as she was with him, but realised that now that she was there she might as well find out what he had to say, so that she could finally close this disastrous chapter of her life.

'Holly, thank you so much for coming,' he said, as Flora laid out their coffee and then shut the doors behind her. 'Please, sit down. I know you didn't want to see me, but I hope you'll find this meeting will be worth your while.'

Holly scowled. 'I'm only here because I didn't want your assistant to have to trek out to deepest south London every day. And, on that note, how the hell did you track me down?'

Max had the grace to look ashamed. 'Yes, I'm sorry about that. When Flora said there was no reply at your flat, my assistant got in touch with the *Street Scout* team to check your file for details of your emergency contact.'

'You phoned my *mum* to ask where I was?'

'My assistant did,' admitted Max, looking even more sheepish. 'She claimed she was a friend of yours who was trying to track you down, and your mum gave her the address. I'm sorry, Holly, but it was really important I spoke to you.'

Holly was stunned. 'Whatever happened to data protection?'

'Emergency contacts are designed for emergencies,' said Max, simply. 'And this was an emergency. Now, shall we get down to business?'

46

'Before we get started,' said Holly, fishing in her rucksack for the necklace, 'I need to give this back to you.'

She held out the box, but Max shook his head. 'No, that's for you. You deserve it for how terribly I treated you. Please, I want you to have it.'

'Thank you, but I really can't accept it,' she said, firmly, placing it on the table between them. There was no way she was having Max think he could buy her forgiveness. 'Now, what's this proposal you wanted to discuss with me?'

'Well, it's a job offer, of sorts.'

'I'm listening . . .'

'It's to fill a vacancy, really. Left by Sasha.'

Holly calmly put her head to one side as if considering what he was saying, but inside her there was a flurry of butterflies, whipped up by the astonished realisation that Meg might well have been right, and that Max was about to offer her the presenting job on *Street Scout US*.

'Before I give you the details, I'll need you to sign a non-disclosure agreement,' said Max.

'A what?'

'A confidentiality document,' said Max, pushing a sheet of paper across the table. 'It's just to make sure that you keep the matters we discuss to yourself. I do trust you, Holly, but you'll appreciate that in my position I can't be too careful. I never do business without one.'

Holly scanned through the document. Unlike most legal documents she'd seen, it did look pretty straightforward. Basically, it was just asking her to agree that she wouldn't blab about Max's private matters to a third party. *Fair enough*, she thought, and signed at the bottom.

'Thank you,' smiled Max, settling back on the sofa. 'Now, as this concerns Sasha as well, I'll just give you a bit of background on our relationship first. We met a few years back through a mutual contact in the TV industry in New York. Sasha knew that I was gay, but we got on brilliantly and had a lot in common. I thought she was smart, funny and beautiful, and I enjoyed hanging out with her. And as we became friends, I saw an . . . opportunity. So I made her an offer.' Max paused and took a sip of coffee. 'In return for a generous salary, I proposed Sasha would become my girlfriend – in name only, of course. She would live with me, accompany me to events and share everything in my life. Apart from my bed. As far as the rest of the world was concerned, the two of us were in love. I proposed that this arrangement should last for five years, at the end of which we would "split up" and move on with our separate lives. Sasha was single at the time; in fact, I think she was a bit disillusioned with the whole dating game and so, after a great deal of understandable soul-searching, she took me up on my offer.'

Holly nodded. Well, that all made sense – although it occurred to her that if she'd heard this story a few days before, she'd now be completely dumbstruck.

'Unfortuntely, in the end, things didn't work quite how we'd hoped,' Max went on. 'A few years in, Sasha was struggling with the arrangement. She was already in her late thirties and was getting increasingly worried that she was running out of time to get married and have children. So we pulled the plug early, but – as you know – we remained on good terms, and, of course, I put her forward for the job of presenter on *Street Scout*.'

'So when did you discover her drug problem?'

Max stared blankly at her.

'Sasha's coke habit?' said Holly. 'Back in New York, you told me you first found out about her addiction when you were dating.'

'Oh, right, yes . . . well, that came out soon after the start of our arrangement, but she agreed to go to rehab and that was that,' he said, vaguely. 'Anyway, the point is that I'd not met another woman who I enjoyed spending time with as much as Sasha until you came along.' He smiled at her. 'I really do love your company, Holly. And before I screwed everything up, I think you liked mine, too.'

Try as she might, Holly couldn't stop the memory of those wonderful early days with Max in New York from flashing through her mind. It was agonising to admit it now, but there was no doubt she had been falling in love with him. Max had made her feel so special, so alive . . . but all the time he had just been putting on an act. It was still painfully raw for Holly to dwell on it without bursting into tears, so she swiftly changed the subject.

'So, what's this job offer then?'

Max leaned forward, resting his arms on his thighs. 'Holly, I want to make the same offer to you as I did to Sasha. I would love for you to be my girlfriend and share my life with me. In return, I would provide you with a salary of £500,000 a year for the five-year period. You would live with me in my properties in London, New York and St Tropez and have my staff and all my possessions at your disposal. Obviously, you wouldn't be able to have serious relationships with any men during our time together, but you'd still be very young by the time the five years were up.'

Holly gawped at him; she was in a state of shock. She hadn't really heard anything after the part about him wanting to pay her to be his girlfriend. 'But . . .

but what about the job of presenter on *Street Scout US* . . . ?' she managed, eventually.

Max looked bewildered. 'Well, that went to Zane, I thought you knew . . . But on the subject of work, I'd be happy to use my contacts to help you establish a career in whatever field you wished after our arrangement had concluded. During the period of the contract, you'll be travelling around the world with me, so you wouldn't be able to take on any serious work commitments alongside that. But you could perhaps get involved in something on a part-time basis while we're together – maybe some fund-raising or charity projects? I have plenty of contacts in that area.' He looked at her. 'So – what do you think?'

What Holly thought was that Max was completely mad. Being paid a salary to be someone's girlfriend? It was ridiculous. No, it was *obscene*. She wouldn't be able to have a career or a proper relationship for five years. What kind of life would that be? And after everything he had put her through! The whole thing was insane.

But then Holly thought about what Max was offering in return. Five hundred thousand a year for five years was . . . *two and a half million*. It was a life-changing amount of money. She would not only be able to pay for Lola's operation to help her walk, but she could also buy her mum a new house and have plenty left over to take them all on a dream holiday to Disney World. Hell, with money like that, she could probably hire out Disney World for the whole week! The security that Holly had always craved in her life would be guaranteed – for both her and her family. And didn't Max say he'd help her establish a career afterwards? In five years' time she'd only be twenty-seven. Medical students didn't even graduate until that age – and few people got married before thirty . . .

But Holly couldn't get past the fact that if she accepted his offer she would basically be selling herself to him. Her whole life would be a lie. Forget whether she could live with Max if she decided to take him up on his offer – would she be able to live with *herself*?

Max was looking at her expectantly and Holly opened her mouth to say something, but then shut it again quickly. It was all too much to take in. She ended up just giving a shrug of confusion.

'You don't have to give me your answer now,' said Max, kindly. 'Take a couple of days to think it over – I appreciate this must all be a bit much to take in.' He smiled at her. 'But I promise you, Holly, we'd have a lot of fun together.'

47

Holly sat on the top floor of the number 3 bus with her chin in her hand, staring out of the window. Anyone looking at her would assume she was deep in thought; in actual fact, she was *so* deep in thought that she felt as if she were drowning. Max had offered to get his chauffeur to take her back to Meg's, but she had refused. She needed to get completely out of his bizarre world, where helicopters were toys and girlfriends were on a salary, so she could get a bit of perspective on his offer.

As they passed through Lambeth, Holly tried to imagine what life would be like as Max's girlfriend. Probably pretty similar to those few weeks in New York, she supposed: shopping, lunches, parties and holidays. It sounded like no hardship when you put it like that – but she remembered how bored and unful-filled she'd felt after just a couple of weeks. Could she hack it for even a month, let alone five years? *Perhaps for two and a half million quid I could,* came a little voice in her head. Then that same little voice reminded Holly of what life had been like when she was young: the endless cycle of moving towns so her mum could find work, changing schools, never feeling like she fitted in anywhere, being bullied for never having the right clothes. Holly remembered all too well what it felt like to worry constantly about money: that horrible anxiety that she carried around for her childhood like a parrot sitting on her shoulder shrieking doom in her ear. And then, of course, there was Lola. If she took Max up on his offer, her little sister would get the chance to lead a normal life – to walk without that cumbersome wheeled frame. The thought made Holly's heart soar with happiness. For that reason alone, she felt like phoning Max right that minute and telling him she'd accept the offer. Okay, so a career in modelling might possibly work out and make her fortune, but the offers hadn't exactly been rolling in. What if she hadn't been as good as people had led her to believe on the show? She would just end up another washed-up wannabe, struggling to make ends meet. When she thought about it like that, could she really afford to even consider turning Max down?

Then Holly thought about her love life – or rather, if she accepted Max's offer, the total absence of it. *No real boyfriend for five years.* People were celibate for far longer than that, surely it wasn't such a big deal . . . But it wouldn't just be the sex she'd be missing out on, would it? There would be no long, melting kisses that left your stomach doing backflips and your head in the stars. No lazy Sunday mornings in bed, cuddling up and reading the papers. No moments of soul-shaking passion that made you feel more alive than you ever thought possible . . .

Just then Holly's phone started to ring. God, she hoped it wasn't Meg – she still wasn't sure what she was going to tell her about Max's offer. Having signed the confidentiality agreement, she wasn't supposed to breathe a word about it to anyone, which was extremely annoying as she could really do with getting Meg's input on this one. To her relief, however, it wasn't Meg – it was Joe Taylor.

'Hi, Holly, how are you? Back in London?'

'I am,' she said. 'Just got home at the weekend.'

'I thought I'd check in and see how you are. You sounded a little flustered when we spoke the other day.'

'Yes, I had a lot going on, but it's all sorted now. It's very sweet of you to think of me.'

'And how's Max?'

Holly was silent for a moment. 'Max and I . . . are taking a break. Everything got a bit intense and I needed some space.'

'Oh, I'm sorry to hear that, Holly.'

'It's okay. We're still talking . . . Anyway, what are you up to?'

'I'm working from home today and could really do with a distraction. I don't suppose you fancy coming round for a cup of tea, if you're not too busy?'

Actually, that sounded quite nice. Holly could do with a dose of normality after the morning she'd had, and Joe was bound to have lots of funny stories about the celebrities he'd been interviewing. Anything to distract her from agonising over The Decision, which currently seemed completely undecidable.

'That sounds great,' she said. 'Where do you live?'

'In Camberwell – do you know how to get here?'

Holly did; in fact, if she got off at the next bus stop she could hop on a number 36 and be there in less than half an hour.

'Great, I'll see you shortly, then,' said Joe. 'Looking forward to it.'

Joe lived in the top-floor flat of a pretty Victorian cottage that looked like it had been airlifted from the Cotswolds and dumped in the middle of inner-city London. There was a passion flower growing around the door, an apple tree in the front garden and, as Holly waited at the doorstep, an enormous ginger cat started twining itself around her legs.

'I see you've met Keith,' grinned Joe, as he opened the door.

'Great name.' Holly tickled Keith under his chin and he purred like a revving motorbike.

'I named him after Keith Richards, because he stays out all night and likes chasing birds.' Joe stood aside to let her in. 'Come on up.'

It's good to see him again, thought Holly, as she followed him up the stairs. Forget Zane, Joe would have made a perfect TV presenter. Cute, funny and with the same cheeky-chappy charm as Ant and Dec.

'Sit yourself down in here,' he said, clearing a jacket and bag off the sofa in the living room. 'I'll just put the kettle on.'

While she was waiting, Holly glanced around the room. A huge bookcase entirely covered one wall and was crammed full of books, magazines and vinyl LPs, with the overflow stacked in piles on the floor. There was a framed vintage *Star Wars* poster over the sofa and a Led Zeppelin tour poster above the desk, on which Joe's laptop sat open amid a mass of papers and notebooks.

A moment later, Joe reappeared. 'Right, the tea's just coming up.'

'What are you working on?' Holly nodded at his computer.

'I was just in the middle of transcribing an interview I did with the latest X *Factor* reject. Fascinating stuff, as you can imagine . . .'

As they talked, Holly got the impression Joe had become rather disillusioned with the world of celebrity magazines. His editor sounded like a bit of a bitch and he was under increasing pressure to break stories – '. . . and I didn't spend three years studying Chaucer at university to trail Imogen Thomas around Mahiki,' he finished, miserably.

'So why don't you try some other kind of journalism?' asked Holly.

'I'm doing some freelance feature-writing for newspapers on the side, so hopefully that will lead to something . . . Anyway, you don't want to hear about that – it's all very dull,' said Joe. He smiled at her, almost bashfully. 'You're looking great Holly – amazing, in fact.'

'Really?' Holly cringed. 'I'm not sure why – I'm horribly jet-lagged from the flight back from New York.'

Joe nodded. 'So, tell me, what happened with the great Maxwell Moore?'

'Oh, it's all extremely messy.'

'I'm a good listener, if you want to talk about it . . .'

Holly hesitated. She obviously couldn't tell Joe the full story, but he did seem to know a lot about Max (or at least the rumours about him), and it would be useful to get as much background as she could before making her decision. Perhaps Joe could shed a bit more light on Max, and any other skeletons he might have in his already overcrowded closet. But could she really trust him?

'I'm not wearing my journalist hat, if that's what you're worried about,' said Joe, clearly sensing her concern. 'I'd just like to talk to you as a friend. I promise it'll be between you and me.'

'Okay,' said Holly, feeling reassured. 'Well, part of

the problem is that Max moves in a world that is utterly unlike mine, or anyone else's I know.'

'Yup, the guy is absolutely loaded. I heard his private jet has got a leopard-print carpet and matching toilet paper – is that true?'

'I've no idea. Probably, knowing Max.'

'So what went wrong between the two of you?'

'Max can be quite . . . possessive,' she said, carefully. 'His people were always checking up on me, seeing where I was, offering to do things for me. I'm sure that would suit some girls, but I found it quite suffocating. Like I was locked in an ivory tower, you know?'

Joe nodded. 'Was he telling you what to wear, things like that?'

'A bit. Although that was quite nice, as I've never been that into shopping . . .'

Holly chatted away, telling Joe all about her time in New York, laughing about Mindy's determination to get her to a facialist and how Max's concept of a 'TV dinner' was oysters, lobster thermidor and Cristal.

'So, what's he really like?' asked Joe. 'Behind the Italian suits and the perma-tan?'

Holly thought for a moment. 'Max loves life. He's generous. Funny. Extremely private. And very, very complicated.'

'Do you get the impression that he has a lot of secrets?' Joe's question jarred, making Holly hesitate. It seemed like a weird thing for someone to be asking purely out of friendly interest; it was more like the sort of question a journalist would ask in an interview. *Well, he is a journalist,* Holly told herself. *And he's promised this is off the record. So stop being so paranoid.*

'Yes, I think he does,' said Holly, carefully. 'I don't feel I got to know the real Max Moore at all. I don't think anyone knows him – not even Max himself, in a way.'

'So he's definitely hiding something . . .'

'Maybe.' Holly was feeling increasingly uncomfortable at Joe's line of questioning and was keen to change the subject. 'Did you say there might be the possibility of a cup of tea?'

'Oh, yes, of course, sorry.' Joe jumped up. He stood looking at her for a moment. 'It is really good to see you, Holly. I've missed you. Weird, right?'

She smiled and sort of shrugged. Joe really was a sweet guy. As he left the room, Keith appeared at the door and then jumped straight onto the warm spot on the chair where Joe had been sitting. Holly went over to stroke him and he started to purr, kneading the cushion with his huge velvety paws.

'How do you take it?' shouted Joe from the kitchen.

'White, no sugar, thank you!'

Sitting on the arm of the chair, Holly was glancing around the room when something on Joe's desk caught her attention. There was a little red light coming from under some papers. *What was that . . . ?*

'Would you like a biscuit?' came Joe's voice again.

'Yes, please!'

'Okay, I know I've got a packet of Jaffa Cakes in these cupboards somewhere . . . Might be a moment!'

With Joe occupied, Holly crossed over to the desk to investigate where the light was coming from. Half hidden by a notepad, she found a small, silver device, about half the size of an iPhone. It had a screen on the front with a digital display that seemed to be some sort of timer; it looked like it had been on for just over twenty-three minutes, and counting – about as long as she had been in the flat. Holly felt herself go cold as she realised what was in her hand. It was a digital Dictaphone. And it looked very much like Joe had been recording their conversation.

48

Holly was horrified. Surely Joe wouldn't do something like that, not after everything he'd said to her about being friends? But then she remembered the sort of questions he'd been asking, how he'd sounded a lot more like an investigative journalist than a mate . . .

Holly had to get out of the flat. She couldn't face another confrontation, not after the emotional roller coaster of the last few days. Joe was still busy crashing about in the kitchen, so she grabbed the Dictaphone, shoved it into her bag and made a run for it.

'Sorry, got to go, family emergency!' she shouted, thundering down the stairs to the front door before he could stop her. She sprinted all the way to the nearest bus stop and then kept on going to the next one for good measure, just in case Joe decided to try and follow her.

Struggling to catch her breath, Holly plonked herself down on the plastic bench and prayed for a bus to appear. *So it's official*, she thought miserably. She was a bloody diabolical judge of character. First James, then Cole, Max – and now Joe. How could she have been so flipping naïve? Thinking back, Joe had as good as admitted that he was using her to get dirt on Max when he'd mentioned he was going to lose his job unless he got some juicy celebrity exclusives. All that guff he'd spouted about wanting to help her. *Unless* . . . Perhaps he hadn't been recording their conversation after all? Well, there was only one way to find out.

Just then a bus pulled up and Holly climbed on board and found a quiet spot on the top deck where she took out the Dictaphone. Luckily the controls were idiot-proof and Holly quickly worked out how to get back to the beginning of the recording and then pressed play.

Holding it up to her ear, the first thing she heard was Joe's voice asking: 'So how do you feel about your own mentor voting you off the show?'

It was, as Joe had told her, a recording of an interview with one of the *X Factor* contestants. Holly wasn't a particular fan of the show so she wasn't sure exactly who the nervous-sounding girl was answering Joe's questions. Their conversation went on for a few minutes and then just as the girl (whose name was apparently Chloe) was going on about how she'd had 'the most amazing, like, journey on the show' she was suddenly cut off. Holly pulled the Dictaphone away

354

from her ear but it was still running so she carried on listening. After a moment she heard the sound of footsteps and muffled voices, then came Joe, loud and clear, saying: 'Sit yourself down in here . . . I'll just put the kettle on.' And, a moment later, her own voice: 'So what are you working on?'

The bastard. The lousy, lying, stinking bastard.

Just then her phone bleeped with a text; it was from Joe.

'Is everything ok? Hope we can get together again soon.'

Not a chance in hell. Holly jabbed furiously at the delete button. *Not if you were the last man on earth.*

Holly was lying on a tropical beach sunbathing with a shirtless Ryan Gosling. As she looked over at him, Ryan smiled at her and then rolled over so they were face to face. He pulled her towards him and their lips were just about to touch when his phone started to ring. 'Just ignore it and kiss me,' Holly murmured. But then she felt herself being sucked away from Ryan Gosling and the sunshine and white sand and found herself lying in her bed in Hammersmith on a rainy Tuesday morning, her mobile trilling on the bedside table. By the time she was fully awake it had stopped; she didn't recognise the number so decided not to bother calling back. At least it wasn't bloody Joe Taylor. He'd been calling her virtually non-stop since she'd run out on him the other day.

Holly lay on her back staring at the peeling paint on her bedroom ceiling. She would miss her little flat – damp patches and all. With no job to pay the rent, she'd had no choice but to accept Meg's offer and move in with her and Spunk at Nanna Aileen's until she could afford a place of her own. She'd given her landlord notice on the flat and was planning to spend the next couple of days packing everything up.

Holly was hoping that a bit of time on her own might help her decide what to do about Max's offer. It had been a few days since their meeting, and she was still no closer to reaching a decision. She had managed to deflect Meg's questions by telling her that Max had just offered to introduce her to a couple of model agents who might be interested in signing her. Meg had been outraged on her behalf. 'Was that it?' she fumed. 'The stingy git! He could've at least given you a "please-don't-tell-anyone-I'm-gay" bribe of a new car or something.'

Holly's phone started ringing again. It was the same number as a moment ago.

'Hello?'

'Is that Holly Collins?' The voice was female and bubbly.

'Yes . . .'

'Hi there, Holly, my name is Kay Banks. I'm calling from *Wow* magazine. Is now a good time?'

'A good time for what?'

'I just have a few questions about your

relationship with Max Moore. I thought you might want to comment following the story in the *Daily Splash* today.'

Oh no. Holly's heart started to pound in her chest. *Joe must have sold the story.*

'Holly? Can you tell me if you're still seeing Max? Our readers would love to know!'

'I'm sorry, I can't talk now.'

'When would be a good time to phone back?'

'Bye,' she said, ending the call.

Trying to stay calm, Holly threw on some clothes, grabbed her purse and dashed out of the flat. *You utter shit, Joe Taylor.* She'd been clinging to the hope that he wouldn't have been able to write a story without his Dictaphone, but it sounded like he'd managed to cobble something together. And for a bloody national newspaper, too!

Holly ran to the newsagent's at the end of her road, bought a copy of the *Daily Splash*, and was back to her flat within five minutes. When she was safely back behind closed doors, she started flipping through the pages, the knot of dread in her stomach growing by the second, until she found what she was looking for on page eight. Holly's mouth gaped in horror. The headline read: 'Max locked me an ivory tower – and threw away the key', and then just underneath it, next to a blurry picture of her and Max leaving a restaurant in New York, was the line: 'The truth about playboy entrepreneur

Maxwell Moore by his latest girl, *Street Scout* wannabe, Holly Collins.' The byline named someone called Gaz Dobbs, but Holly had no doubt who the real writer was.

She groaned, closing her eyes. This was even worse than she'd feared. Her immediate instinct was to chuck the paper in the bin, but she needed to see how bad it was so she could try to sort out this mess.

His charm and good looks have won him legions of female fans, but in private TV tycoon Maxwell Moore is a control freak, a bully and an egomaniac, his new girlfriend has told pals.

Essex girl Holly Collins, 22, says the super-rich stud is so possessive he won't let her out of his sight without one of his flunkies to keep tabs on her.

The wannabe model moaned: 'Max showers me with expensive gifts, but he insists on choosing what I wear and who I meet. He can be so bloody possessive.'

And the sexy size 8 blonde even claimed that Max, head of model agency Strut, fancied HIMSELF more than he did her.

The couple met when Holly was a contestant on Street Scout, *the modelling TV show on which Max stars alongside his ex-love, foxy brunette presenter Sasha Hart. Sources say that sparks flew between the pair during filming, but they started dating after Holly visited Max in New York last month, where he is currently working on the US version of the hit show.*

But Holly confided to pals that she was struggling to cope with the 50-year-old star's controlling behaviour, such as phoning to check up on her several times a day.

'I feel like one of Max's possessions,' she said. 'It's driving me crazy.'

And so it went on, a hideous mix of outright bullshit, fabrications and semi-truths, for an entire page. By the end of it, Holly was feeling physically sick. She was furious with Joe for betraying her trust and worried what her friends and family would think; she was mad at herself for being so naïvely trusting of a journalist; but, most of all, she was horrified at the thought of what Max's reaction might be. He was bound to assume she had sold a story on him. He would probably withdraw his offer. Grabbing her phone, she hurriedly bashed out an email to him.

Max,
I promise you I didn't sell that story to the *Daily Splash*. I said a few trivial things about our relationship to a trusted friend and he must have gone to the papers, but most of the article is nothing to do with me. I feel terrible – I'm so, so sorry.
Holly

She got a message back from him almost instantly. Holding her breath, she opened it . . .

Don't worry Holly, I'm used to it – and I can definitely cope with press stories like that. Who wouldn't want to be described as a super-rich stud?! It will all have blown over in a few days, I promise you.

Now, have you given my offer any more thought? Take care, Max

She exhaled in a great whoosh of relief. *Thank God*. She sent a reply.

Plenty. I'll get back to you in the next few days, I promise. Thank you for being so understanding. Holly.

Just then Holly's phone started to ring again. Probably another bloody journalist. Well, she couldn't run away from this mess so she might as well try and sort it out.

'Hello?'

'Holly, it's Joe. What happened the other day? Why haven't you been returning my calls?'

The bloody cheek! 'You've got a nerve, calling me after what you did,' she fumed.

'What are you talking about? What did I do?'

'I know you're behind that story in the *Daily Splash* today, so don't even try to deny it. All that crap about wanting to be my friend . . . You *used* me!'

There was a pause. 'Holly, I promise you that story was nothing at all to do with me. In fact, that's the reason I've been trying to get hold of you: to give you a heads-up about who *did* sell the story to the *Splash*.'

'I don't believe you.'

'Why on earth would you think I'd do this to you?'

'Because I know you were recording our conversation when I was at your flat the other day.'

'*What*?'

'I found your Dictaphone.'

'I told you, I'd just been transcribing an interview when you arrived.' Joe's voice was overly patient, like he was trying to explain something to a very small child. 'The interview was on the Dictaphone. Hang on a sec, did you take it? I've been looking for that bloody Dictaphone everywhere! I thought Keith must have hidden it; he's got an annoying tendency to steal my stuff . . .'

'You were recording our conversation, Joe. I checked it.'

'Well, either you're mistaken or I must have accidentally switched it to record rather than turning it off. I swear on my life, Holly, I would never do that to you.'

'Oh, how convenient! You expect me to believe you "accidentally" turned it on? It had to be you,

361

Joe. You're the only person I told those details to about my relationship with Max.'

'Are you quite sure you didn't tell anyone else?'

'Yes,' she snapped.

Joe hesitated for a moment. 'Holly, when I heard that the *Splash* was doing a story on you, I made a few phone calls and persuaded a contact at the paper to tell me who had sold them the story. They said it was Cole Fox.'

'Cole Fox? Don't be so ridiculous.'

But then Holly remembered that drunken conversation she'd had with Cole at the bar in New York. She couldn't remember exactly what she'd said, but she did vaguely remember saying something about Max being a bit possessive . . . Just then, Holly's front-door buzzer sounded. She ignored it.

'Joe, all I know is that I told a showbiz journalist a lot of private information about my relationship with Max, and a few days later it appeared in the paper. That seems pretty incriminating to me.'

'Holly, I—'

'Forget it, Joe. I was so stupid to trust you.' And she angrily ended the call.

But as furious as she was with Joe, their conversation had planted a seed of doubt. What if he was telling the truth after all? Joe would have had no way of knowing that Cole was the only other person – apart from Meg – whom she'd confided in about her relationship with Max; it would have been a pretty big coincidence if he'd just plucked his name out of thin air. But why would a movie star sell a story to a tabloid newspaper? It didn't make any sense.

The front-door buzzer went again: three short blasts and then a long one. Whoever it was clearly wasn't going anywhere.

She crossed over and pressed the intercom button. 'Yes?'

'Holly, my name's Andy Myner, I'm a reporter from the *Sun*. Can I have a quick word?'

'No! I'm sorry, I'm not interested.'

Holly's phone started to ring again and she turned it off without checking who was calling. Panic was bubbling up inside her; she felt like a cornered animal. Just then, the door buzzer sounded again.

'Go away!' she shrieked down the intercom, not even waiting to hear who was outside.

Holly got into bed and yanked the duvet over her head, trying to block out the world. She had no experience of dealing with the press and hadn't the foggiest how to handle the situation. She thought about fleeing to her mum's house in Essex until the fuss blew over, but what if a reporter followed her there? And she couldn't ask Max to help her, as she was still feeling terrible about today's newspaper story. She just needed a bit of advice from someone who'd been in this position before . . . Then suddenly it occurred to her: there *was* someone who might be able to help her sort out this mess – someone who'd had plenty of experience dealing with this kind of thing. She scrolled through the numbers on her phone until she found the one she was looking for, took a deep breath and dialled. A moment later someone answered.

'It's Holly – Holly Collins,' she said. 'No, wait, please don't hang up! I'm so sorry for getting in touch, but I really need your help. Would you mind meeting with me? I don't know who else to turn to.'

She listened for a moment.

'Oh, thank you so much,' she said, relief flooding through her. 'Yes, I'll be there in an hour.'

49

The address Holly had been given over the phone was in Knightsbridge, a stone's throw from Harrods. She turned off the main shopping street and after a few minutes' walk found an archway leading to a cobbled mews of terraced cottages. The houses were quite small and boxy, but from the look of the cars parked along the street, Holly reckoned you wouldn't be able to get one for much less than a few million quid.

Number sixteen was painted pale grey and had a dark grey front door and window boxes, which were filled with an explosion of light pink flowers. It was a seriously nice-looking pad. Holly hovered outside, suddenly unsure about whether she was doing the right thing. She had a feeling she wasn't exactly going to be welcomed with open arms . . . Well, she was here now – and it wasn't like there was anyone else who could help. Plus the drizzly weather of a few moments ago had now turned into pelting rain. So she pressed the bell and waited. A moment later, she heard footsteps approaching the door and it swung open.

Holly gave a nervous smile. 'Thanks so much for agreeing to see me.'

'You'd better come in,' said Sasha, coolly.

It looked like Holly had interrupted her in the middle of a round of sun salutations. Sasha's hair was scraped into a bun on the top of her head, all the better to show off her flawless complexion and high cheekbones, and she was wearing a pair of black yoga pants and a white vest. *There is no way this woman is a cokehead*, thought Holly, as she followed Sasha into a room that was as zen-like and immaculate as its owner.

'Can I get you something to drink?' asked Sasha. 'I've just brewed a pot of fennel tea.'

'No, I'm fine, thank you,' said Holly, perching on the edge of the sofa. She felt incredibly awkward (and not just because she noticed she'd left a trail of wet footprints across the bleached wood floor). 'Sasha, I need to apologise for the way I behaved in New York. Those things I said to you – they were completely out of order. And I really didn't mean any of them. I was just finding the whole situation with Max a little bizarre, and I got the impression you weren't particularly keen on me.'

To Holly's relief, Sasha's frosty expression thawed by a few degrees. 'That's okay, I probably deserved it for being a total bitch.' There was a glimmer of a smile. 'The problem was that I could see you had fallen for Max, but I knew you didn't have a clue what you were getting yourself into – and I had no idea how to warn you that he was actually . . . *is* actually . . .' She tailed off, clearly unsure whether Holly had yet discovered his secret.

'Gay? Don't worry, I got the memo.'

Sasha looked relieved. 'Okay. Well, at least now you know. But I handled the whole thing very badly and I'm truly sorry for that.'

The women smiled at each other and Holly found herself remembering how much she'd liked Sasha when they'd first met.

'Do you mind if we talk about what happened in New York?' asked Holly. She was doubtful about Max's explanation about the drugs and, while there had been plenty of rumours in the press about Sasha's sudden departure from *Street Scout US,* she'd not made any public comment on the stories. 'What was the real reason you got sacked?'

'I wasn't sacked,' said Sasha, folding her legs underneath her in a lotus position. 'I quit.'

Holly hadn't been expecting *that*. 'Why?'

'Funnily enough, I made the decision to leave the show just before you and I bumped into each other in the Strut offices that morning, which is probably another reason I was such a cow to you. I suppose I was trying – in a pretty awful way, admittedly – to warn you off him. I'd literally just had a run-in with Max that convinced me that I should quit.'

'What happened?'

'Well, I'd gone to Strut that morning to speak to Max about the way he was treating you.'

'*Me?*'

'Yes. I'd been on at him for ages to tell you that he was gay as I could see you were falling for him and, of course, I knew what was going on with Zane. It made me so bloody angry to have to stand by and watch while he used you. So that morning in his office, when I brought up the subject again and he started up with the same old rubbish about telling you the truth 'when the time was right', I told him he'd have to find a new presenter.'

Holly was stunned. 'So you quit your job . . . because of me?'

'In a way, but I suppose I just didn't want to be part of Max's circus any more.' Sasha shrugged. 'Despite everything that's happened, I do believe he's a decent guy, but I've seen too many people hurt by his lies over the years. It was the reason I was reluctant to take the presenting job on *Street Scout US* in the first place – I didn't want to play any further part in this fantasy world he's created. But you know how charming he can be, and I let him persuade me to take the job against my better judgement . . . Anyway, I guess I'd just reached the point where I'd had enough of all the bullshit and deceit, so I quit.'

The room fell silent, as Holly thought over what Sasha had told her.

'Max told me about the arrangement he had with you,' said Holly. 'He's made the same offer to me.'

'Have you accepted?'

'No, but I'm thinking about it.'

Sasha grimaced. 'Holly, please, don't do it. I know it sounds like a good deal. I thought so too, which is why I took Max up on it. And I really liked him – I suppose I still do. It's hard not to. He's great company, he has a real lust for life and, of course, he's extremely generous. But his life is a complete pantomime, Holly. And if you agree to be his girlfriend, you'll be sucked into it, too. It will eat away at you, I promise you.'

'Max told me you pulled the plug on their arrangement early . . .'

Sasha nodded. 'I was supposed to stay with Max for five years, but in the end I bailed after three. It was all too much of a sacrifice. I wasted three years following Max around when I could have been finding my future husband and having his babies. And now . . .' Sasha shrugged helplessly. 'Now I've probably left it too late. And all the money in the world can't compensate for that. It's great to be financially secure, but it doesn't guarantee you happiness – believe me. I know you're a lot younger than I am, but if you do this you'll still be sacrificing a huge chunk of your life. And if you're anything like me, you'll end up feeling lonely and ashamed, and will find yourself questioning what the hell you're doing every single day.'

Holly let Sasha's words sink in. Just the other day she'd seen an article about Sasha in one of the weekly celebrity magazines that went on about how she was 'desperate for babies' and worried about being 'left on the shelf'. At the time, Holly hadn't thought much about it, but now – after her own battering in the press – she realised how painful it must have been for her.

'So what are you going to do now?' asked Holly, eventually.

'I've made the decision to quit TV for good,' said Sasha. 'I'm going to set up a yoga studio and lead yoga retreats in Thailand. It's what I've always wanted to do. I've had enough of fame and everything that goes with it.' She smiled at Holly. 'I hope you'll come along to a session when the studio's up and running.'

'I'd like that.'

Sasha smiled at her again. 'You're a gorgeous girl, Holly, and – I know this sounds corny – but you've got a beautiful soul. You've got your whole life in front of you. Please don't throw it all away for Max.'

'I'll certainly give it some serious thought,' said Holly, even more confused about what she should do than before. 'Thanks for being so honest with me.'

They got up and walked towards the front door together.

'Oh, by the way,' said Sasha, 'did you have anything to do with that story in the *Daily Splash* today?'

'God, no,' says Holly, 'I think it was Joe Taylor from *Hot* magazine, although he denies it, of course. He claims the source was Cole Fox.'

To her surprise, Sasha nodded. 'Well, that would certainly make sense.'

'Not to me, it wouldn't,' said Holly. 'Why would Cole need to sell a story? He must have loads of money.'

'Before he was an actor, Cole was a model,' explained Sasha. 'For a while, he was one of Strut's biggest stars. Didn't you know that?'

Holly shook her head. Then she remembered Cole's extreme reaction when Max's name had come up.

Sasha went on: 'I remember Max coming home one evening just after we had started "dating"' – she made quotation marks in the air with her fingers – 'and being so excited about this incredible new guy they'd just signed at the agency. Turns out it was Cole – or Colin, as he was still known then. Anyway, after a few months he landed this huge ad campaign for some major menswear brand. It would have made him the highest-paid male model ever and turned him into an overnight star, but Max told him that there was no way he could take on such a high-profile job unless he straightened out and quit the booze and drugs. I mean, the guy was beautiful, but he was getting his stomach pumped on an almost weekly basis. Cole flatly refused to go to rehab, so Max told the brand's directors about his drug problems and they dropped him at the last minute and went with another model. Since then, Cole has hated Max's guts and has taken every opportunity to stick the knife in.'

Holly was stunned. 'So it wasn't Joe Taylor who sold the story to the *Daily Splash*?'

'I wouldn't have thought so,' said Sasha. 'Joe is one of the good guys.'

50

The rain had slowed to a fine drizzle while Holly had been in Sasha's house, and the sun was now making a valiant attempt to fight its way out from behind the clouds. As Holly picked her way through the puddles and dodged the spray from the traffic thundering along the Brompton Road, she thought over what Sasha had told her. She was still struggling to get her head around the fact that The Fox was the mole. God, he must *really* hate Max to risk flogging a story to a muck-raking rag like the *Daily Splash* just to have a dig at him. Or perhaps Cole had given it to them as part of some sleazy deal? She'd heard that sort of stuff went on in the tabloids and it would certainly make sense: 'I'll give you dirt on Max Moore if you keep schtum about my wild night snorting coke with a bus-load of prostitutes.' And to think she'd nearly ended up in bed with him! What a toerag . . . Holly thought about sending Cole a snarky text, but thought better of it. The guy was clearly a bit unbalanced and, as Max had said, the story would be old news in a few days' time. In the meantime, she had a backlog of messages from concerned friends and family to deal with – she'd just got a panicky text from her mum asking what was going on – and, most importantly, she had to apologise unreservedly to Joe.

Holly tried phoning his mobile on the walk to the tube, but after ringing a few times it went to voicemail. Well, she couldn't blame Joe for screening her call after the way she'd treated him. She was going to leave a message, but then it occurred to her that *Hot*'s office was only a few tube stops away – why not go and say sorry in person? Joe had been a good friend to her over the past few months; she should do her best to try and salvage their relationship. And he was hardly likely to get her thrown off the premises . . . Was he . . .?

Hot magazine's HQ was in an office block on Shaftesbury Avenue, sandwiched between a vintage-comic shop and a lighting showroom. From the rather bland exterior it looked like the sort of place that might be occupied by a firm of accountants, but inside it was a riot of primary colours, neon lights and Little Mix posters – and that was just the reception area.

'Can I help you?' smiled the fake-lashed Cher Lloyd clone sitting behind the front desk.

'I wondered if I could have a word with Joe Taylor?'

'Do you have an appointment?'

'No, but I'm happy to wait if he's busy.'

'Okay, hold on a sec. What's your name?'

'Holly Collins.'

'Yeah, I thought I recognised you! You were on *Street Scout*, right? Love your hair! Right, hold on a sec.'

The receptionist dialled a number, tapping her gold-tipped nails on the desk as she waited for a response. 'Hey, Joe, I've got Holly Collins in Reception for you.'

Holly held her breath waiting for his response.

'Uh-huh,' said the girl. 'Okay, cheers, gorge.' She pressed a button to end the call. 'Joe said to tell you he'll be down in a mo. Take a seat, doll.'

She gestured to a plastic sofa in the shape of an enormous pair of red lips and, struggling to calm her nerves, Holly took a seat. The sofa had clearly not been designed with bum comfort in mind but, thankfully, a few moments later the lift doors slid open and there was Joe. He was wearing a pair of black-framed glasses (either they were a fashion accessory or he usually wore contacts) and a wary scowl in the place of his usual smile.

Joe stood in front of her, his arms tightly folded, exuding hostility from every pore. 'Why are you here, Holly? I thought I was public enemy number one.'

'I wanted to apologise for accusing you of selling that story to the *Daily Splash*,' she gabbled. 'I should have known it wasn't the sort of thing you'd do. But I didn't realise that Cole had a grudge against Max. You must admit, it does seems a little far-fetched: a movie star selling stories to a tabloid . . . But I know I should have trusted you. I really am very sorry.'

He nodded slowly, letting her words sink in. 'So do you have any idea where Cole got all the details in the story?'

'Me, unfortunately.' Holly pulled a 'yes-I-know-I'm-stupid' face. 'I bumped into him when I was in New York and we spent the afternoon getting drunk together. I had a moan to him about Max and then . . .' She tailed off.

'Well, you're a popular girl, aren't you, Holly? First Max, then Cole . . .' The way Joe said 'popular girl' suggested what he actually meant was 'rampant slut'. She winced at the slur, but she could hardly blame him. 'Look, I do understand why you might have thought it was me,' he went on, 'but I did promise you everything was off the record. And it really upset me that you didn't trust me. I thought we were friends.'

'I am so, so sorry,' said Holly. God, it had been a day of grovelling – first to Sasha and now Joe. 'And I'll send your Dictaphone back immediately, I promise.'

He looked at her for a moment – and then he broke into a cautious smile. 'That's okay. And I do appreciate you coming over to apologise. Friends?'

376

'Friends,' said Holly, feeling a great rush of relief.

'Come on, I'll walk you out . . . So what are you going to do now?'

'I'll probably head home. I've got to pack all my stuff up as I'm moving in with a friend for a bit.'

'No, I meant what are you going to do with your life now?'

Holly just smiled and shrugged, but Joe's question hit a nerve. No job, no house, no boyfriend – what the hell *was* she going to do? Well, one thing was for sure. There was no way she could decide what to do about Max's offer on her own. She was going to need a second opinion.

'That is *insane*,' yelped Meg, her eyes like Frisbees. 'I've never heard anything like it in my life! *Two and half million pounds!* Un-fucking-believable . . .'

'Shhh, keep your voice down,' hissed Holly, looking round at the other diners in the restaurant: a curry house in Clapham where they often met. Thankfully, a sizzling tandoori platter had arrived at the next table that very moment and had drowned out the worst of Meg's shrieks.

Meg was still staring at her, shaking her head in astonishment and muttering: 'Two and a half million pounds . . . *two and a half million pounds!*' She'd even put down her onion bhaji, and it took a lot to put Meg off her food. 'So what are you going to do?' she asked.

'I have no idea,' said Holly. 'I'm just going round and round in circles, which is why I wanted to talk to you. Not a word to anyone about this, okay?'

Meg nodded.

'Sasha told me I'd be mad to accept Max's offer, but I don't know . . .' Holly sighed heavily. 'What do you think?'

'Well,' said Meg, putting her hands on the table and lacing her fingers together like she meant business. 'I think you'd be crazy *not* to do it.'

'*What?*'

'Holly, it's only five years. Five years of living like a very pampered, globe-trotting, Louboutin-shod nun, then you and Lola would be set up for life.'

Holly chewed her nail. 'But I'd be missing out on so much . . .'

'Bollocks!' said Meg. 'Holly, this arrangement wouldn't close doors, it would *open* them. Think of the people you'd meet! Max seems to know everyone. And he's already said he'll help you establish a career. Okay, so the no-men thing is a major downer, but you'll still have a gorgeous face and a nice pair of tits when you're twenty-seven – and if you haven't, then you can buy a new pair! And a new face! Besides, it's not like you'll be disappearing off the face of the earth. I presume you can still see friends in between swanning off to St Tropez in your private jet?'

Holly nodded.

'Well then, great! What the hell's stopping you?'

Meg topped up their glasses from a large bottle of Cobra. 'Honey, if you don't accept Max's offer, then I bloody will.'

'I just feel like I'd be living a lie,' said Holly.

Meg waved her hand dismissively. 'Nonsense,' she said, briskly. 'Max is the one living a lie – you'd just be his employee. Think of it as a public-relations job: you'll be employed to help Max present a certain . . . *image* to the public. You're basically going to be the world's highest-paid PR girl.'

'Oh, I don't know . . .'

Meg karate-chopped a stack of poppadoms and then popped a shard in her mouth. 'Holly, you're worrying too much about what will happen if you accept Max's offer. How about thinking what you're going to do if you *don't* accept it? Will you be able to live with yourself knowing the difference this money could have made to Lola's life?'

The two of them discussed what Holly should do over the saag paneer and prawn madras. They debated it a bit more during the mango kulfi. They were still deep into the discussion when the waiter brought them a couple of complimentary glasses of Baileys – and refilled them. But when the hot towels and After Eights arrived, Holly had finally made up her mind what to do about Max's offer.

'Now you're sure about this,' said Meg. 'You're happy with your decision.'

'I think so . . .'

'*Holly*!'

'Yes! Yes, I am sure. As sure as I'll ever be.'

Meg nodded. 'Okay. Then call Max first thing in the morning to tell him before you change your mind.' Then she leaned over the table, reached for Holly's hand and gave it a squeeze. 'I understand your reasons, gorgeous girl. And I'm behind you all the way.'

51

By five the following morning, Holly was wide awake and had abandoned any hopes of getting back to sleep. As she lay in bed watching the chink of light between her curtains turn from grey to white, she agonised over whether she was making the right decision. Why did everything always seem so much more complicated – and catastrophic – in the dark? When she had said goodbye to Meg outside the Spice Boys last night, she had felt fairly happy with her decision, but now she was worried she was about to make the biggest mistake of her life.

At seven Holly's alarm on her BlackBerry started to shrill. When she reached over to turn it off – feeling like a condemned woman – she noticed she had a text. It was from Meg, sent at 6.30, when she would have been getting up for work.

'STOP WORRYING!!' it said. 'You're doing the right thing. Call Max at 8 then call me. Love you, Mx'.

Despite herself, Holly smiled; Meg knew her too well. She wasn't her best mate for nothing.

Spurred on by Meg's message, Holly turned on the radio and got in the shower. Perhaps it was 'Eye of the Tiger' pumping out at full volume, or maybe her 'uplifting' rosemary and mint shower gel actually worked, but as she stood under the jets of hot water, Holly felt a little surge of positivity. She still wasn't entirely sure she was doing the right thing; she wasn't even slightly sure. But a decision had to be made and the one she had reached last night felt marginally more right than the alternative – and that was as good as it was going to get.

Holly towel-dried her hair, made herself a mug of tea and then took her phone and sat on the sofa in her living room, which was now all but empty apart from a stack of cardboard boxes, which she was planning to put into storage. She scrolled through her contacts until she found Max's number, but then hesitated, her thumb hovering reluctantly over the button. Perhaps she should wait until she'd had some toast before she made the call, just to make sure she was on top form . . . ? *No, you can't put this off any longer*, Holly scolded herself. So she took a deep breath, and dialled.

She was half hoping that Max might be busy doing lunges with his personal trainer, but after a couple of rings he picked up.

'Hello, darling, I was just about to phone you.' He sounded his usual smooth, unruffled self – the exact opposite of how she was feeling. 'I hope you're calling to tell me you've come to a decision?'

'I have, yes,' said Holly, hoping Max didn't notice the tremble in her voice.

'And . . . ?' he prompted.

She opened her mouth to speak but the words seemed to stick in her throat, as if her body was trying its best to shut her up.

'Holly?' said Max. 'Are you still there?'

'Sorry,' she gulped. 'Bit of a frog in my throat . . .'

'So, what's your answer?'

Holly felt like she was on *Who Wants to Be a Millionaire*, about to say the words that would either win or lose her a fortune. If only she had the option of Asking the Audience or Phoning a Friend . . . As the seconds ticked by, she closed her eyes and tried to steady her breathing, and then . . . 'Yes,' she eventually managed. 'Yes, I'd like to take you up on your offer.'

It felt like such a momentous occasion that Holly had half expected something would happen – a thunderbolt from heaven striking her down, perhaps – so she was a little surprised to discover that the world just carried on as normal. Max sounded delighted, though.

'That's fantastic! Holly, I am so pleased, I think we're going to make a really good team, you and me. Now, obviously there's going to be quite a lot of paperwork to do before we can make this official . . .'

'How romantic,' she said, with a weak laugh.

'Would you be able to come over to the office this afternoon?'

'That soon?'

'Well, my PR team are itching to set up some press interviews to make our relationship public. They're thinking *Hello!* and *You* magazine for starters. I've got a contract here waiting for you to sign, and then we can get some appointments in the diary with my stylist for you to go shopping for a new wardrobe. Got to have you looking the part! And I thought perhaps we could sort out a party in the next few weeks to mark our official debut as a couple? There are so many people I want to introduce you to . . .'

'Sounds great,' said Holly. *And utterly overwhelming*, she added to herself.

'Okay, I'll get Flora to send a car for you in a couple of hours,' said Max.

'It's fine, I can get the tube.'

'Really?' Max chuckled incredulously. 'Well, enjoy it while you can, my darling, this will be your last trip by public transport for some time – perhaps ever!'

Holly put down the phone in a state of panic. Sign the contract *today*? She had no idea that everything would start happening so quickly! And press interviews? She tried to imagine telling a journalist about how much she loved Max. She was a terrible liar at the best of times; how would she manage when she was faced with a Dictaphone, knowing everything she said was going to be read by thousands?

Come on, Holly, just breathe . . . One step at a

time: she needed to get dressed first. Most of her clothes were packed away into black plastic sacks ready to be transported to Meg's – or straight to Max's now, she supposed. She idly wondered whether millionaires kept all their clothes in one place or shared them out between their various homes. Maybe they bought multiple copies of each item so they had the same wardrobe in every property? Well, she'd find out soon enough when she had her first session with Max's stylist. Holly had visions of swanning around London's top boutiques, being treated like a VIP, with unlimited shopping funds at her disposal. It was like something out of a fairy tale . . . except this time, Cinderella would be on Prince Charming's payroll – and the prince would actually be in love with Buttons. Holly grimaced. *Christ, what a mess.*

Getting back to the task in hand, Holly tried to work out what she should wear to the meeting with Max: there were contracts and lawyers involved, so probably something business-like. She started to rummage through the bag marked 'Dresses' and came across her old navy Zara shift. Holly pulled it out and held it up against herself, looking at her reflection in the mirror. The last time she'd worn it was to the drinks party thrown by James's firm.

James. The thought of him hit her like a punch. She tried not to think about him at all – it was still too painful – but this time it had ambushed her. With a heavy heart, Holly folded the dress up again and stuffed it out of sight at the bottom of the bag, wishing she could do the same with the memory of James.

In the end, Holly decided on a pair of skinny Hudson cords, a loose silk blouse and a pair of high-heeled Burberry Brit ankle boots – another souvenir from her time on *Street Scout* – topped off with a black blazer. If she was going to be Max's PR girl, she might as well look the part.

Holly arrived at Max's office in Mayfair a few minutes after two o'clock. Flora Ferguson greeted her at the door, looking genuinely thrilled to see her.

'Holly!' She stood to the side and ushered her in. 'So lovely to see you again!'

Holly gave her a nervous smile in return. She wondered how much Max's inner circle knew about their 'arrangement'. Surely they must be in on the plan – and, in that case, what on earth must Flora think of her? Well, there was no point in worrying about that now . . .

'Take a seat, I'll let Max know you're here,' said Flora, showing Holly into the waiting room. 'Can I get you a coffee or tea? Maybe a fresh pear, ginger and carrot smoothie? I made it fresh this morning, it's absolutely yummy.'

'That sounds lovely, thank you,' said Holly.

Flora beamed at her again. 'I'll be back in a sec. Just make yourself comfy.'

Little had changed in the room since Holly had

last been there, but there were new displays of roses and lilies dotted around the room, and the latest magazines and newspapers, arranged with OCD precision as before. It occurred to Holly that from now on this would be the sort of life she would be living: one where fresh flowers magically appeared every day and staff would be falling over themselves to juice carrots for her. In theory it all sounded pretty fantastic, but Holly remembered all too well how suffocated she'd felt when she'd been part of Max's world in New York . . . *But it's different now*, she told herself, firmly. *This time it's strictly business.*

Just then Flora arrived with her smoothie and a plate of warm white chocolate and macadamia cookies, swiftly followed by Max himself.

'Holly! Great to see you, darling.' He grasped her shoulders and kissed both her cheeks, then pulled back to look at her with a warm smile. 'I'm so glad you decided to take me up on my crazy offer,' he said. 'Come on, let's go up to my office and get the paperwork out of the way.'

As she walked along beside him, her spike heels sinking into the thick carpet, Holly tried to calm her nerves, which were multiplying with every step. After they got in the lift, Max looked at her with a concerned frown.

'Everything okay?' he said. 'You're very quiet.'

'Just got a lot on my mind,' she smiled.

'I understand this must all be pretty

overwhelming,' nodded Max. 'But I promise, you've got nothing to worry about. This meeting is just to make sure you're perfectly happy with the terms of our arrangement. I want this to work for both of us, okay?'

By now they had reached the imposing double-doors to his office, where Max paused with his hand on the handle. 'I hope you don't mind,' he said, 'but I've asked my lawyer to be present at the meeting. I think it's a good idea – for both of us, really. Then if you have any questions about the contract he can answer them straight away.'

'Okay . . .' she said.

As Max pushed open the doors, it occurred to Holly that perhaps she should have brought her own lawyer along to the meeting as well – if she actually had one, that was. The only lawyer she knew was James, and the idea of phoning him and asking him to come along – 'just to look over my contract with my new gay boyfriend' – made her smile, despite her extreme nerves.

Then Holly glanced around Max's office and spotted the lawyer sitting at the suite of sofas. He stood up and turned to face them as the scene blurred into slow motion. Holly felt the ground disappear beneath her feet as she saw that Max's lawyer was, in fact, James.

52

Holly's hand flew to her mouth, stifling her cry of shock. He was looking incredible. Rather than his usual English gentleman's garb, James was wearing a single-breasted navy suit that looked like it had come straight off the fashion pages of *GQ* magazine. His hair was shorter than she'd seen it before and brushed into a stylish side parting. He even seemed to have grown taller – although that was probably because Max was a bit of a short-arse in comparison. He looked every inch the slick corporate lawyer, with not a trace remaining of the bumbling ex-public schoolboy who had so charmed her back in what felt like another lifetime – before he had trampled all over her heart.

While Holly was frozen to the spot, too stunned to move or speak, James didn't seem in the least bit surprised to see her. He was just looking at her with an expression that might have been either disapproval or regret.

'Holly, this is James Wellington, head of my legal

team,' said Max, utterly oblivious to the drama that was unfolding in his office. 'I wanted my top man to be here in case you had any questions – and James is something of a legal genius, aren't you, mate?'

James gave the briefest of smiles, but he never once took his eyes away from Holly.

'Right then, let's get started,' said Max, gesturing for Holly to take the seat next to him on the sofa, so they were both sitting opposite James. Holly was now just a metre away from him, close enough to be able to see the small scar on his cheek that was a souvenir from his school rugby days. *How many times had she kissed that scar when they'd been lying in bed together . . . ?* As James handed Holly a copy of the contract, his eyes bore into hers. There was so much tension crackling between the two of them that she couldn't believe Max hadn't noticed.

Max was leafing through the pages of the contract, but he seemed distracted and was clearly keen to get the business side of things wrapped up as quickly as possible. 'Let's whizz through the small print, James, okay?' he said, tersely.

In a flat voice, James began to talk Holly through the contract, translating the passages of complex legalese into plain English. He winced slightly at the clause that dealt with Holly not being allowed 'romantic or sexual long-term relationships' for the term of the contract, but only Holly noticed. For her part, she was too stunned to say anything at all, although she had a million questions – and none of them concerned the contract. Her insides were churning with a whirlpool of shame, confusion and anger. If only James hadn't run off with Lady Crosby, then none of this bloody awful mess would have happened in the first place . . .

They had been going through the contract for about a quarter of an hour when one of Max's phones started to vibrate. He reached over to pick it up and glanced at the screen. 'Christ, sorry, guys, I've got to take this. It's the producer of the American show – the shit's hit the fan out there. Back in a bit – just carry on without me.'

They both watched him leave the room, and the moment the door clicked shut, James turned on her with blazing eyes. 'Holly,' he hissed, 'you can't seriously be thinking about accepting this lunatic offer? Max might be my client, but I've never disagreed with anything more in my life!'

'How . . . h-how long have you known about this?' Holly stammered.

'The contract was drawn up by a different team, so I only found out about it yesterday when Max informed me about this meeting,' said James. 'I was going to try and excuse myself, but I decided I would come in the hope that I might have an opportunity to talk you out of this ridiculous farce. Honestly, Holly, I'm still in shock that you're taking Max up on this. What about the morals of the situation?'

'Morals!' Holly felt a surge of anger. 'That's bloody rich coming from someone who was shagging their client behind their girlfriend's back!'

James gave an impatient sigh. 'There was nothing going on with me and Lady Crosby – not then, not now, not ever. I would never have cheated on you, not in a million years.'

'Then why not deny it when I asked outright if you were sleeping with her?'

'For God's sake, Holly, I was hoping to spend the rest of my life with you; I needed to know that you trusted me!' James rubbed his forehead. 'It absolutely killed me when I asked if you thought I was capable of cheating on you, and you said you didn't know. I was devastated that you didn't trust me.'

'Well, what was I supposed to think?' hissed Holly. 'You were always interrupting our dates to rush off and see her ladyship. And you let me think she was some poor old pensioner . . .'

'That's nonsense – you never asked what she was like! And, if you had, I'd have been completely honest with you. I certainly wasn't trying to hide anything. Why would I need to, when I only had eyes for you?' James gave a frustrated sigh. 'Why didn't you just talk to me about your concerns?'

'*Because you were never there!*' shrieked Holly. Their voices had been getting progressively louder and they both now glanced nervously towards the door, but thankfully nobody appeared.

James looked back at Holly, his eyes full of sadness. 'You're right.' He sighed again, shaking his head as if all the fight had gone out of him. 'I hate myself for having neglected you, Holly, and if I'd known what was going to happen, I'd have done things very differently. But I want you to know, the reason I was working so hard on that case was to try and build us a better future. I had . . . plans.'

Holly eyed him suspiciously. 'What sort of plans?'

'I was trying to get a deposit together for a house. For us. I'd even registered our details with a few estate agents in west London. It was going to be a surprise.'

Holly started to scoff, but then she remembered the mysterious estate agent's letter that had arrived at her flat with the details of the sweet little cottage in Brook Green. Her dream home; the place she wouldn't have been able to afford on her own in a million years. She had assumed the property details had been sent to her by mistake, but from what James was telling her, they had very much been meant for her. If things had worked out differently, they might even be living there now.

'I loved you so much,' James went on, leaning across the table towards her. 'Actually, no, it was more than love. We were just . . . *right* together. And I still regret with every fibre of my being the part I played in us breaking up. I was desperate to make things right between us, but I suppose my pride prevented me from trying to make things right – and by the time I'd got over that, I figured you were happier in your new life. You're an amazing girl, Holly. Please, please don't throw your life away for this, you deserve so much more.' His voice was cracking with emotion. 'You deserve the best of everything . . .'

Just then the door opened and Max strode in, making James leap back into his seat as if he'd been electrocuted.

'Sorry about that – bloody Yanks. Now, where were we?'

Nobody answered him. Holly was still struggling to take in what James had just told her. All she could think about was that James apparently hadn't cheated on her after all and had, in fact, been planning on buying them a house. If, of course, he was telling the truth. But as she looked at him across the table, she knew without a shred of doubt that he had never done anything but tell the truth – and if she hadn't worked herself into such a state over Lady Crosby, she might have realised that. Oh God, it was all such a terrible mess . . .

'Holly, have you got any further questions for James?' asked Max.

She shook her head slowly – although she was feeling so confused and dismayed she would probably have struggled to remember her name at that precise moment.

'Great! Then let's make this official.' Max plonked himself down on the sofa and picked up the master contract. 'Holly, you just need to sign here and here,' he said, pointing to places on the page marked with small pink Post-its. He reached in his pocket for a pen and held it out to her with a big grin.

Holly looked at the pen and then at James who, almost imperceptibly, shook his head.

'Come on, sweetheart,' urged Max, oblivious as ever. 'I've got a bottle of Cristal waiting to celebrate our new venture!'

In a daze, Holly reached for the pen.

53

James stood up, so abruptly that he knocked over a glass, sending a torrent of water flowing across the table.

'Oh for God's sake,' snapped Max, grabbing the contracts out of the way before they were drenched.

'I'm terribly sorry – so clumsy of me,' muttered James, leaning over to help.

Holly just sat there, staring dumbly ahead of her as Max cleared away the papers and James dabbed at the table with the monogrammed linen handkerchief he always carried in his pocket, mumbling apologies. She was still reeling from the conversation with James.

'It's okay, no harm done,' said Max, irritably. 'Let's just get this thing signed, shall we?'

But James didn't sit down. For a moment he looked as if he was going to say something to Holly, but instead he turned to Max.

'I'm sorry to do this, Max, but I'm afraid you're going to have to find yourself a new lawyer,' he said.

'My conscience won't allow me to play any part in this charade.'

And with that he strode out of the room without a backward glance.

Max watched him go with a look of surprise that quickly changed to annoyance. 'What the hell's got into the bloke?' he asked, as the office door closed. 'Bloody lawyers, I don't know . . .' Then he shrugged. 'Ah well, plenty more where he came from. Now, where were we?'

He dug around for the contract then presented it to Holly with a smile, having fully recovered his usual, easy-going charm. She reluctantly dragged her eyes away from the door, where she was still gazing in the hope that James might miraculously reappear, to look at Max. And in that moment, it felt like she was finally seeing everything clearly for the first time: Max, his offer, her life . . . *What on earth was she doing?*

As it all sank in, Holly noticed in her hand the pen that she'd taken from Max in a daze, and dropped it as if it had burned her. Then she jumped up.

'Holly?' asked Max. 'What's wrong?'

'I'm sorry,' she said, firmly, feeling more confident and sure of herself than she had done in weeks. 'But you're going to have to find yourself a new girlfriend as well.'

Ignoring Max's calls for her to come back and stop being so silly, Holly ran out of the room and then raced along the corridor to the lift as fast as her heels would allow, but reached the doors just as they slid shut. Swearing under her breath, she looked around and found the door to the stairs, then ran down all four flights, risking a twisted ankle by taking two steps at a time, and emerged panting into the corridor just outside the waiting room.

A little way down the corridor, she saw Flora hurry out of her office. Max had obviously been on the phone to tip her off.

'Holly, wait!' she called, hurrying towards her. 'Max says to tell you that whatever your concerns, he's sure he'll be able to sort them out. Just hold on a moment, please!'

But Holly dashed straight past her, out through the front door and onto the street. The only thing that seemed important at that moment was stopping James and finishing their conversation – the conversation that had changed everything. *He hadn't cheated on her after all.*

54

It had started to pour with rain while she had been in Max's office and as she scanned the street in every direction, trying to locate James through the deluge, all she could see was a forest of umbrellas. Then suddenly she spotted him: standing on the kerb with his arm sticking out to hail a taxi. But as Holly sprinted towards him, a black cab appeared and pulled over to the spot where he stood.

'James!' she yelled. 'Wait!'

But her voice was lost in the rumble of the traffic and rain. *Or perhaps*, she thought with a stab of pain, *he heard but was ignoring me*. She watched helplessly as James jumped into the taxi, slammed the door behind him and sped away into the gloom.

She watched the taxi's back lights until they were lost in the traffic. People hurried past her on the pavement, desperate to get out of the rain, but she just stood there staring into the distance as the rainwater mingled with her tears.

Holly stayed rooted to the spot for a full five minutes after the taxi had disappeared, then turned and started to walk in the opposite direction, her mood as bleak and grey as the weather.

And then – 'Holly?'

She spun round to find, by some miracle, James making his way through the crowds towards her. He was holding a large black umbrella with a polished wood handle and was wearing a mac and an expression of concern.

Holly was stunned. 'You came back,' she managed.

'I did.'

'But – why?'

'To stop you making a huge mistake,' he said, beckoning her under the umbrella. 'Am I too late?'

Holly shook her head. 'I didn't sign the contract. I told Max I'd changed my mind.'

'Well, I'm very glad to hear you've done the right thing,' said James, stiffly. 'I still can't believe you were even considering it.'

Holly looked down at her rain-drenched boots, her cheeks prickling with shame. James clearly had a very low opinion of her – and really, who could blame him? She had basically been selling herself to Max for two and half million pounds . . . Suddenly, it felt vitally important that she explain to James why she had agreed to accept Max's offer in the first place.

'I lost my way after we split up,' she said, pushing

a sodden strand of hair out of her eyes. 'I didn't know what to do about my career and Max just seemed to be offering a way to turn my life around. And with that sort of money I could have paid for Lola's operation. At the time, I suppose I felt like I had no alternative – and, as you probably know, Max can be extremely persuasive . . .'

As Holly tailed off she felt a sharp stab of panic. Turning down Max's decision might have been the right thing for her, but what about her little sister? Had she just taken away Lola's one and only chance at being able to walk properly?

'Holly, you're shivering,' said James, pulling off his mac and draping it over her shoulders. 'Look, I know how important it is that Lola gets this operation, but I'm sure she wouldn't have wanted you to sell yourself to Max to pay for it.'

'It wouldn't have been like that,' said Holly, struggling not to start crying again. 'I had the chance to change her life and I turned it down . . .'

'Holly, there are other ways to pay for the operation,' said James, gently. 'You don't have to try and solve everyone's problems on your own, you know.'

Holly looked up into James's eyes and, in that moment, she remembered how safe and reassured he always used to make her feel: like nothing bad could happen while he was with her. The pair of them stood staring at each other, lost in their own thoughts, as seconds ticked by.

'You know,' said James, eventually, 'I was desperate to get in touch after we broke up.'

'Why didn't you, then?'

'I heard you were in New York with Max and that the two of you were an item, so I figured I had missed my chance.'

'How did you find out?'

'Meg told me.'

Holly gawped at him. *Meg*?

'I got in touch with her to see if you were okay and she told me in no uncertain terms that you were happy with Max – far happier, in fact, than you'd been with me.' James gave a grim chuckle. 'I won't tell you exactly what she said, but suffice to say she made it patently clear that you definitely wouldn't be interested in hearing from me ever again.'

Holly couldn't believe it. 'But she didn't tell me . . .'

'I guess she thought you were better off without me. And perhaps she was right.'

No, she wasn't, Holly wanted to scream. *Everything went wrong after we split up*. Being so close to James was making her realise just how much she'd missed him.

'So,' she said, changing the subject. 'When did you start working for Max?'

'Do you remember when I had to go to New York for meetings with a potential new client for the firm?'

'That was *Max*?'

James nodded. 'I've been working with him for a few weeks now. I wasn't sure whether to take the job after I found out about the two of you, but my firm was very keen and I thought I'd be able to keep my own emotions separate. I knew Max was a bit of a mysterious character, but I had no idea about this arrangement he had with his girlfriends until yesterday. I still can't believe you got mixed up in it.'

'Nor can I,' said Holly, miserably.

They stared at each other again for a moment, and then all of a sudden James reached over and put his hand on her arm.

'Holly, do you believe me that I didn't cheat on you – that I would never have cheated on you?'

'Yes,' she said. And she did – without a single doubt.

James nodded and then finally, miraculously, broke into a grin.

'So – what now?' said Holly, mirroring his smile.

'We need to get you out of the rain. Coffee?'

'That would be lovely, thank you,' she said.

'I know a nice little place nearby,' said James, offering her his arm. 'Miss Collins?'

With a lightness in her heart that she hadn't felt for months, Holly linked arms with James and they started walking along the pavement together. All she wanted to do was talk to him about what had happened since they split up and set things straight. She turned to look at him as they walked and he smiled back at her.

'So, New York, eh?' said James. 'I'd always wanted to take you there. Did you love it?'

'Totally,' grinned Holly.

They strolled along, chatting about the places they'd been in New York, comparing notes on their experiences, when suddenly James stopped and rummaged in his jacket pocket. He pulled out his phone, checked the screen and frowned.

'It's an email from my boss. Max has obviously been in touch and he wants to know what's happened.' He looked at Holly with an apologetic frown. 'I should get back to the office.'

Her heart plummeted to the pavement. 'Of course,' she said reluctantly, extricating her arm from his. 'Maybe we can catch up another time.'

James nodded, but he looked distracted. She recognised the look all too well; he had switched back into work mode.

'Okay, well, take care,' said Holly. 'Bye.'

She turned and walked away, desperate for James not to see her cry. It was ridiculous, but it felt like her final chance at happiness would disappear with him.

Behind her, she heard James making the call to his office. 'Maggie? It's James. Please could you tell Mr Winters that I'm in the middle of a very important meeting and that I'll call him later this afternoon. Yes, I'm afraid I can't come back to the office yet. Okay, thanks.'

Holly turned to look at him, not quite believing what she had just heard.

'Sorry about that,' he said, smiling at her confusion. 'I've turned my phone off now, so no more interruptions. So, shall we go and get that coffee – if you'd still like to?'

Holly gawped at him in astonishment.

'I'd like nothing better,' she said, breaking into a radiant smile.

Acknowledgements

Firstly to you, dear reader, I hope you enjoy the ride as much as I enjoyed writing it – and living pieces of it too!

To my editor, Charlotte Hardman for more hand-holding and calmly overseeing the birth of my second novel while the birth of her own child is imminent! Best of luck with Baby . . . Thanks to the talented team at Hodder for willingly having me back for more, and to my very lovely agent Jess Stone.

Thanks to my girls for letting me lock myself away to work on this, perhaps one day in the not too distant future you might enjoy a few Big Apple adventures of your own.

And last, but perhaps most significantly, it's thanks to YOU New York, for the glamour, the good times and the memories – once it gets in your blood it won't ever go away . . .

Do you wish this wasn't the end?

Join us at www.hodder.co.uk, or follow us on
Twitter @hodderbooks to be a part of our community
of people who love the very best in books and reading.

Whether you want to discover more about a book
or an author, watch trailers and interviews, have the
chance to win early limited editions, or simply browse
our expert readers' selection of the very best books,
we think you'll find what you're looking for.

And if you don't,
that's the place to tell us what's missing.

We love what we do, and we'd love you to be part of it.

www.hodder.co.uk

 @hodderbooks

 HodderBooks

 HodderBooks